PLUNDERING
PICASSO

PLUNDERING PICASSO

A NOVEL

STEVE NEWCOMB

AWARD WINNING AUTHOR

SN BOOKS
ASHEVILLE, NC

A DIFFERENT KIND OF IMMERSIVE TECHNO-THIRLLER

Throughout this novel, you will find QR codes to scan (or tap in eBooks) that lead to supplemental blog posts written by characters within this story.

**And in case you have problems scanning/tapping, you can also find all of them at:
www.plunderingpicasso.com
where they are listed by chapter.**

These posts offer additional background on both real and fictional people and events featured in the book. While entirely optional, they're designed to enrich your understanding of the world behind the narrative.

Feel free to skip them; you won't miss anything in the story.

But if you choose to explore them, you may discover deeper insights into a time in history marked by profound darkness—and the enduring light that rose to meet it.

"The light shines in the darkness, and the darkness has not overcome it."

John 1:15 (ESV)

MY LAUNCH TEAM

Thank you to the members of my launch team.

CynDee Aerts
Sheila Alewine
Kris Bromberger
Mike Burk
Alan Cech
Christy Cech
Jim and Judy Clark
Nancy Collins
Amy Cooper
Ted Erskin
Shirley Florance
Erica Grant
Konnie Hall
Franci Henderson
Gary Hodgson
Terri Kelly
Lisa Lenning
David Lindrum
Wendy McDougald
Hannah McNamee
Nancy Parker
Wayne Pelts

Rhet Peterson
Amanda Powell
Mark Powers
Greg Ramsay
Charles Robertson
Lori Roeleveld
Jeanne Sandow
Dannette Scheiderer
Jack Sedory
Linda Short
Cheryl Stead
Niki Tippets
Fred von Kamecke
Patty von Kamecke
Margot Walker
Warren Watson
Delores Whittaker
Mark Whittaker
Randy Williams
Sherry Williams
Kathy Wright
Mary Young

ACKNOWLEDGEMENTS

I am grateful for…

Salvation by scripture alone, by faith alone, by grace alone, through Christ alone, to the glory of God alone.

My bride from Glide, Charlotte, for her patience, doing many of my chores, cheering me on, and listening to isolated monologues of, "I think I should have AJ do…"

Fred von Kamecke, brother in Christ, friend, fellow writer, author of BUSTED: EXPOSING POPULAR MYTHS ABOUT CHRISTIANITY and WHERE MONSTERS PROWL, for his words of wisdom, "If you are serious about writing, go to a conference."

Lori Stanley Roeleveld, author, speaker, disturber of hobbits, for her part in nudging me toward a writing journey I never expected to take, and caring enough to encourage and connect me with the Christian publishing world.

Bob Hostetler, agent (not mine as it turned out) who pushed me down the road, by showing enough interest from a dinner conversation at Blue Ridge Mountains Christian Writers Conference, 2023, to motivate me to finish the first draft.

Ann Tatlock, editor and mentor, for providing encouraging course corrections and skillful editing until I wrote THE END.

Bonnie Aebi, missionary, for reading and editing my first draft, especially the French and German.

Word Weavers of Maggie Valley and Hendersonville, NC. "You're gonna bring another chapter next month, right?"

Matthew Lee, my son-in-law, for advice on technology.

Gary Hodgson, for his train expertise and California references.

Dr. Mike Sciarra, Senior Pastor, Grace Church, Orange, California for bringing the depths of Romans 8:28 to light. (Chapter23, 45)

BOOK CLUB QUESTIONS
AND
TEACHER LESSON PLANS

Scan or tap the QR code to visit my website to download questions for your book club or lesson plans for class discussions.

CHARACTERS

MODERN SETTING CHARACTERS

ANDREW JAMES MEYER: Known as AJ. Founder and CEO of Meyer Technologies. Married to Grace Meyer.

GRACE MEYER: Art professor at Lines College and amateur water-color artist. Married to AJ Meyer.

LYLE BERNSTEIN: Master of Cultural Restoration at the Albert Becker Art Museum. Grandson of Otto and Emma Bernstein.

FRED: History professor at Lines College.

BRIAN MILLER: Curator of the Albert Becker Art Museum.

THE CLIENT: Anonymous seeker of the Picasso Dozen.

HISTORICAL SETTING CHARACTERS (fictional)

ROBERT MEYER: Grandfather of AJ. Beloved, part-time pastor, and full-time employee of IBM.

OTTO/EMMA BERNSTEIN: The Bernsteins are famous for their glamorous soirées attracting a colorful audience of artists, musicians, authors, and, most importantly, collectors looking for the next lucrative art investment.

FRITZ/CLAIRE HOFFMAN: The Hoffmans commissioned many 1930s artists in Paris, thanks to wealth generated from Fritz's successful munitions company. They partner with the Bernsteins on many artistic projects.

JACQUES PONGE: Leader of a clandestine French intelligence group, the Second Bureau.

HISTORICAL SETTING CHARACTERS (real)

THOMAS WATSON: Thomas Watson is founder and CEO of IBM, International Business Machines. The company forms an international presence, including Berlin during World War Two.

ERNEST HEMINGWAY: Hemingway comes to Paris after reporting on the Spanish Civil War. In 1926, he published The Sun Also Rises, and in 1929, A Farewell To Arms.

PABLO PICASSO: Picasso is a prominent figure in the artistic and political landscape of Paris.

IGOR STRAVINSKY: Igor is a famous Russian composer living in Paris. He is a long-time friend of Pablo Picasso.

HERMANN GÖRING: Göring ranks second only to Adolph Hitler in the Third Reich. His love for collecting art suits him well for his work with the ERR in building Hitler's art collection, by any means possible.

JOSEPHINE BAKER: Josephine is a popular black American entertainer who moves to Paris in her struggle against racism.

BRUNO LOHSE: German art dealer recruited to loot art for the Nazis.

CHAPTER 1

The Box

Home of AJ Meyer, Irvine, California, 2022

THE CARDBOARD BOX BARELY held together. Yellowed strips of tape dangled from the lid over the sides. AJ had plopped it in his home office two weeks ago after visiting his mom and hadn't taken the time to open it. Sipping tonight's first glass of wine prior to dinner, AJ savored the soothing hints of citrus and pear. He closed his eyes and absorbed the calming melodies of Debussy playing from the smart speaker and entered his relaxation zone. After a few phrases, he opened his eyes and put his wineglass on the table. He sat on the floor in the middle of his office, slid the smallish bankers box of his beloved grandfather between his long legs, removed the lid, and tossed it to the side.

That's the moment everything changed.

He couldn't take his eyes off it. His hands tightened on the box. The return section of an envelope on the top of the pile screamed with the shocking red, white, and black Nazi symbol. Debussy's music turned into ringing. He leaned forward and froze, seeing something more disturbing, the name of the recipient.

He ran his fingers through his wavy blond hair. The comfort from the citrus and pear turned into the prickling of barbed wire.

A knock at the door drew his gaze to Grace's hello smile. But her grin wilted as she took in the confusion on his face. She slid next to him, curled up her short legs, and caressed his arm. He stared into her almond eyes, sitting expressionless, like the day they found out he was their fertility problem. In their thirties and no prospect of conceiving children.

"AJ, what's wrong?"

"What's wrong?" He held up the envelope. "This is what's wrong!"

She leaned forward. "Is that a..."

He nodded with raised eyebrows. "Yes, it's a swastika."

She read the recipient's name. "Why is this addressed to your grandy?"

AJ took a deep breath and closed his eyes. In the dark void, the swastika and his grandy's face collided, leaving a jarring impression.

He exhaled and opened his eyes. "Who gets a letter from the Nazis unless..." He couldn't finish. Grace took a sip of his wine. He took a bigger sip. Debussy's melodies gradually replaced the ringing in his ears.

Grace said, "Are you gonna open it? You must be curious."

"Oh, I'm way past curious." He paused. "Here goes."

The return section of the envelope included three initials, IBM, and a New York City address. He examined the seal of the flap. Grandy never opened the letter. AJ's shoulders relaxed with this bit of evidence. The paper appeared decades old, yet in good condition. Still, he opened it with care. He pulled the letter out and paused a moment, mentally preparing himself for what he might encounter. He unfolded it. "Well, at least it's in English."

They both read silently.

March 5, 1938

Mr. Robert Meyer
IBM Corporation
590 Madison Avenue
New York NY

As is our practice, we are sending this tape to your office for secondary archiving. The primary copy is stored in our Berlin archives. The security clearance level of Code Red triggered this event.

The lot number on the tape is 12453.

To ensure security, the encoded key is in a separate communication. The key is the only means to access the tape.

Please secure this in your New York vault using the standard agreed-upon procedure.

In Service to the Reich,

Willy Heidinger
Manager, Deutsche Hollerith Maschinen Gesellschaft
Alexanderplatz Census Complex
Berlin, Germany

AJ sat motionless, rereading the letter several times. Grace shook him. "AJ, breathe! Here, you need this." She handed him the wine. He gulped.

AJ sighed. "Well, Grandy, what was this all about? In service to the Reich? Who were you serving?" He tapped his fingers in a staccato rhythm.

Grace said, "How much do you know about Grandy's work at IBM?"

"I know he worked for them. He always referred to it as a means to support his family while he was a part-time pastor in New York."

Grace peeked inside the box. "Have you checked out this other stuff yet?"

AJ set the letter aside. "I can hardly wait." He picked up a black-and-white photo with zigzag edges and inspected it.

Grace asked, "Do you recognize anyone?"

AJ pointed to one of the men. "I think that's Grandy. Not sure about the others." He turned the picture over and read the inscription on the back. "1937, Paris, Bernsteins. Guess this was from one of his trips helping the French Reformed churches."

Grace took the picture. "What's that in the background? Looks like some kind of art."

"You're the art professor. Can you make anything out?"

Grace rose from the floor and stepped to AJ's desk and rummaged in the side drawer for a magnifying glass. Returning to the photo, she moved the glass back and forth over it. "This is, it's, well, earth shattering."

"More earth shattering than a letter from the Nazis to my grandfather?"

"Maybe." She set the magnifying glass and picture in her lap. "In the 1930s, Pablo Picasso drew a portrait of the Russian composer, Igor Stravinsky, in simple lines. It's famous. I use it to teach drawing technique in my class. The world knows about only one portrait."

"And?"

"There's twelve portraits of Stravinsky in this photograph!"

"So, where are they?"

"An excellent question. If anyone ever finds them…"

"They'd be rich?"

"Are you kidding? There'd be a bidding war at Christie's like you've never seen!"

"What on earth was Grandy doing there?"

Grace studied the other men in the photo. "Hold on! That's Igor Stravinsky in the photo, standing in front of a dozen portraits of himself. That's kind of surreal. And could that possibly be…" She reached for her phone and googled

Pablo Picasso Igor Stravinsky. "Unbelievable! There's Pablo Picasso standing next to Igor. Pablo and Igor were besties, and here they are, with their arms around your grandfather. AJ, did you know any of this? That he ran in such historic social circles?"

AJ stood, crossed the room, and stared at a photo of his grandparents on the wall. "Grandy, what were you up to back then?" Returning to the box on the floor, he picked up another item and turned to Grace. "Ready for more?"

He held the item—an envelope hand addressed in crude cursive to "Robert." The adhesive seal was unbroken. Another relief. AJ slid a knife through the top, then pulled out the contents, a page folded in quarters.

He opened it to full size and faced another puzzling item. Some sort of music filled two lines on a piece of staff paper. The top of the page had a title written in French.

"Do you know enough French to translate this?"

Grace stood next to him and took the music. "Let me see. *Le lot - Hommage à Picasso*. Roughly, it is the lot, or batch, and tribute to Picasso. There's a signature here." She held the magnifying glass over the music. Grabbing her phone, she googled again. "This just gets better and better. That's Igor Stravinsky's signature!"

Two lines of musical notation followed, below the title. "Wonder what all these notes mean." A sequence of twelve notes flowed across the first line, beginning with E flat with each subsequent note one half step above the preceding. The second line had the same twelve notes, but in a jumbled order. Pairs of brackets enclosed the first four notes and the last eight notes.

"What is this?" He pointed to a phrase written above the second line of notes, *rangée 1*. "More French."

"I think that means row one."

"I wonder what any of this music means. And these notes inside brackets. Curious."

"The first bracket is labeled *lot*, and the second is *key*."

"Hold on." AJ picked up the Nazi IBM letter. "This mentions lot and key. How many notes are in the bracket labeled lot?"

"Four."

"Hmm. The lot in the letter has five numbers. One, two, four, five, and three."

"Come on, Mr. Techie CEO. Don't you deal with code numbers at work?"

"Don't do that thing." He smiled, providing a break from the drama.

"What thing?" She smiled back, feigning surprise with her eyes.

He knew she knew what he meant. Appealing to his intelligence. "It could be four numbers. Twelve, four, five, three. Or one, two, four, fifty-three. Hmm. Here's more French at the bottom."

Grace interpreted. "*For my dear friends, Otto and Emma Bernstein.* Their last name is on the back of the photo, right?"

AJ looked. "Yup, Bernsteins. Is this night going from weird to weirder or what?" Another sip of wine helped reduce the swastika shock.

"Time we both had our own glass. Let's take this to the kitchen."

Walking to their millennial-design kitchen, he looked down and tousled her straight bob cut.

They spread the papers out on the island. Grace poured herself a glass of wine and refilled AJ's.

She gave a recap. "So, we have a picture of your grandfather next to Picasso and Stravinsky and, we think, the Bernsteins. There's proof of twelve more portraits by Picasso of Stravinsky. Next, some strange music by Stravinsky dedicated to the Bernsteins. And, of course, the Nazi IBM letter with a code that might also be in the music. Your grandy left you with a bunch of bizarre clues to something."

"And what is that something?" He sniffed. "And what is that amazing aroma?"

"Your favorite. Enchilada casserole!"

"*Muy bueno!*" Closing his eyes, he inhaled, savoring the scent of spices filling the air. The glorious aroma offered a healing balm, helping him recover from the earlier shock.

Grace's unique combination of cheese, beef, onions, tortillas, and sauce topped with sour cream and salsa hit the bullseye of the hunger target. They dug in, relishing every bite, until they scraped the cheese from the bottom of the pan. With empty wine glasses, the earlier crescendo of tension dropped to a comfortable mezzo piano range.

Grace stretched back and fingered her necklace—a jade pendant engraved with a Chinese symbol. Her grandmother believed it would always keep Grace safe, and so far, it had.

AJ thought about the pastor's devotional he'd read this morning from Philippians 4:6. "Do not be anxious about anything…" How could he not be anxious with all this disturbing information from Grandy's past? He was human, after all, prone to worry about things out of his control, like any other human. He needed all his ducks in a row, but Grandy's duck had disrupted the entire line.

He wiped his mouth and leaned back. "Time to regroup and make a plan of attack."

Grace moved behind him, massaged his strong shoulders, nestled her chin on his neck, and smiled. "Or maybe we just sleep on it tonight. Deal with it tomorrow."

"Mmm." He sank into the chair, stretching his thirty-eight-year-old legs. "I guess we could."

Opening Grandy's box felt like a magnitude 7 earthquake, jolting AJ's consistently stable world. Debris lay everywhere. He needed to start digging out, now.

Scan or tap the QR code to see the Nazi letter and sheet music.

CHAPTER 2

THINK

IBM Headquarters, New York, 1937

Robert Meyer stared at the sign across the reception room while he waited for his appointment with Thomas Watson. It displayed a simple message: THINK. Posted throughout the company, it reminded employees to approach tasks with precision. Thomas Watson created the slogan. He also created the world's foremost technology company, International Business Machines, IBM.

Robert Meyer had much to think about. He knew the general responsibilities for this new assignment with IBM. But he didn't know the specific details.

Mr. Watson's secretary apparently had little time to think. Robert glanced in her direction as the phone rang yet again. "IBM, Mr. Watson's office, please hold," she intoned as she pressed the handset to her ear. Calls continued coming, one after another. When all the lines filled, she returned to each caller with calm professionalism. Her desk contained the few items she needed to work efficiently, all precisely placed in company compliance.

A clock hung above the THINK sign. It read 9:55, ten minutes since Robert arrived. He needed this full-time position to provide for his family. His part-time job as pastor of the First Reformed Church of Brooklyn afforded only a part-time salary. IBM made sure he had a stable source of income providing food on the table, a roof over his family, and the means to meet their needs. His church congregation appreciated his sacrifices. A handsome man of thirty-seven—blue-eyed with short blond hair, he had an engaging smile that put his congregation at ease. This gift also proved useful in his work for IBM.

The secretary's intercom buzzed. She pressed the receiver button. "You can send Mr. Meyer in now." She relayed the message with a smile and in he went.

Crossing the office, Robert took in the panoramic view of the forest of skyscrapers visible from the twentieth-floor window. He approached a pair of wingback leather chairs that faced the mahogany desk. Behind the desk sat Mr. Watson, an imposing-looking gentleman who, at fifty-seven, had twenty years on Robert. His gray hair made him appear distinguished and knowledgeable. He stood, matching Robert's six feet, smiled, and stretched out his right hand. "Welcome, Robert. Please, have a seat. Let's get to it." Robert knew of Thomas Watson's direct approach and practice of using time profitably.

He set his leather briefcase beside him on the floor and pulled out a legal notepad sitting next to his Bible. Opening his fountain pen, he prepared to take notes.

"I'm sure you know our business continues to increase in Berlin with the German subsidiary, Dehomag."

IBM used Dehomag as an abbreviation for *Deutsche Hollerith-Maschinen GmbH*, or German Hollerith Machines, Ltd. The company started as a German-owned and operated entity, licensing technology from CTR, IBM's former name. When Germany's post-war inflation ballooned Dehomag's debts, Watson stepped in with the necessary capital and became a majority stockholder. The German entity retained a token ownership for appearance's sake. Hitler's government increasingly relied on IBM equipment, primarily for census processing.

Watson continued. "Dehomag's demand for machines, supplies, and training continues to escalate. I need someone I can count on to keep this operation running smoothly. I hear you are the man for the job."

Robert took the cue to respond. He sat up straight. "I believe I am, Mr. Watson."

Watson smiled. "Good. You will have four areas of responsibility."

Robert began taking notes.

"First, you will coordinate timely delivery of equipment and supplies. Your second task is to ensure they receive appropriate training for using our machines. Third, you will coordinate all development conducted by the Germans."

He flinched at this and made a circle around this item on his pad.

"And the most important thing. There must be strict accounting to separate the German entity from the US company."

Robert rested his pen. "Sir, what do you mean by 'development' by the Germans? Don't we do our own development?"

"Germany has many great engineering minds. We've already learned from some of their specialists how to process more at faster rates."

"I see. Can you elaborate on the accounting issues?" He continued taking notes.

"The corporate accounting director can explain the nuts and bolts. We need to keep German earnings distinguished from American earnings."

He underlined this item twice.

"While you get up to speed, you'll be making frequent trips to Berlin. Will that be a problem?"

Robert couldn't afford to be "a problem." He made a quick, emphatic response. "Of course not, sir."

"Excellent. I like how you think. I'll line up an initial meeting with the directors of accounting, production, and shipping. That should get you up and running."

Watson stood. "Glad to have you handling this."

They shook. Robert forced a smile. "Yes, sir. Thank you, Mr. Watson." Robert collected his things and left the office.

On the way out, he nodded politely toward the secretary. He tried, but failed miserably, to cast her the same friendly smile he had come in with. His face felt as though it was made of stone.

Robert kept abreast of world news, as best as anyone could in 1937. He'd read reports of some of Hitler's actions as leader of the Third Reich. Like many, he had concerns, but he also had a strong faith that his God would protect him, regardless of the circumstances ahead.

CHAPTER 3

Remember

Home of Evelynn Meyer, 2022

Fewer than twenty-four hours had passed since AJ and Grace discovered the earth-shattering items from his grandfather—the picture, the music, and especially the IBM letter from the Nazis. A trifecta of dilemmas. Any one of them, a mystery unto itself, but the combination of the three created a frontal assault and two simultaneous flanking attacks—a difficult battle for AJ to command.

He picked up last night's conversation on the drive to his mother's house. "If Grandy cooperated with the Nazis in some horrendous act, Mom will have some idea about it, right?"

He needed to get a footing on a plan of attack. Maybe Mom knew something to help him take a first step.

"AJ, I don't know. I loved him as much as you did. That will never change."

Her comment threw him for a loop. "What are you saying? I'll find something that could change how I feel toward him?"

"That's not what I'm saying, AJ. We're processing some confusing information. Let's just take one step at a time."

"Instead of three giant leaps, like last night?" AJ chuckled, looking for any way to lighten the situation.

Opening up the box last night opened up a lifetime of Grandy-experiences, flooding AJ's memory. Reminders of his kindness, encouragement, and faithfulness to God.

***

"Take your time, AJ."

"Grandy, I can't do it. I just can't do it. It's too hard."

A young AJ flung the model plane under construction across the room. He'd lost the fight with his awkward fingers. They wouldn't obey him.

"Take a breath, AJ. Here, come sit in my lap."

AJ crawled up. The warmth from Grandy's arms melted the tension, and the rocking relieved his frustration.

Grandy stroked his hair. "It's okay to get frustrated, AJ. It's part of life, even for me. But when it comes, we can ask God to help us. He's always ready to hear us."

"But Grandy, why didn't He help me right now?"

"He did."

"He did?"

"Sure. Don't you feel better after you climbed into my lap?"

"Yeah."

"God used me to comfort you. He did help you."

Grandy kissed the top of AJ's head and sang the refrain of "Trust and Obey."

"It's simple, AJ. Trust and obey."

***

Simple but not easy.

AJ pulled into his mom's driveway.

They walked to the front door. Evelynn greeted them in her well-aged, stained apron.

"Mom, it's about time for a new apron, don't you think?"

13

"Too many memories." She started pointing. "Part of your tenth birthday cake made this brown stain. This blue one, well, I'd rather not talk about how that happened. Come on in."

They gathered in the living room, around Evelynn's mid-century coffee table set with her mother's flowered teapot and matching cups. Fresh scones, straight out of the oven, filled a doily-covered plate.

"Tea, anyone?" Evelynn asked.

"No thanks," AJ said. He was on a mission, ready to get to the point.

Grace smiled. "I'd love some, Evelynn." She sniffed the air. "Those scones smell amazing." She reached and placed one on her plate.

Evelynn poured a cup of tea for Grace and handed her the steaming cup. "Dear, I've always wanted to ask you about your necklace. Seems you're always wearing it."

Grace sipped her cup. "It's very special to me." She smiled. "It belonged to my grandmother. My mother brought it from China when my parents immigrated."

"It's so lovely. What does the symbol mean?"

"It's the Chinese symbol for grace."

"'For by grace you have been saved through faith.' What a beautiful reminder."

Evelynn sat back, enjoyed more of her tea, and nibbled on her cranberry scone. Dabbing her mouth with a napkin, she turned to AJ. "Now dear, what do you want to know about Grandy? You sounded so serious on the phone."

"Mom, how much do you know about Grandy's work for IBM?"

"Honey, that all happened before I met your father."

"But do you remember anything from Dad and Grandy talking about his World War Two days?"

"Mostly, he talked about helping the French churches form their Reformed Association."

"So, he mentioned trips to France?"

"Some. He had a few stories he'd share." She laughed. "Not sure if they were exaggerations or not. Things like meeting Ernest Hemingway in Paris."

Grace leaned in. "Really?" She nibbled on her scone.

"Oh, yes. Even talked about meeting that artist. Let me think now. Who was it?" She took a sip and looked up for the answer.

"Picasso?" Grace glanced at AJ.

"Why, yes." She pointed with her cup toward Grace. "That's it. Not my cup of tea. Oh, ha." She chuckled at her pun. "I guess his trips to Europe added a little adventure to his church work."

"Was that in the late thirties?" AJ asked.

"I'd say so. Certainly before the Nazis occupied France. He never talked about that."

"Do you think Dad knew much about Grandy's job?"

"Well, if he did, doesn't make much difference now, does it?" She took a bite of her scone and nonchalantly mumbled between chews. "What's this all about, anyway?"

"I finally went through Grandy's box of things you gave me. Did you ever look at any of them before you gave it to me?"

"No. Honestly, I've just wanted to leave the past alone. Isn't that what Paul tells us to do? 'Forgetting what lies behind and straining forward to what lies ahead.'"

AJ pulled out the photo from his shirt pocket. "I found this in the box. Do you recognize any of these people?"

She took the photo from AJ. A smile filled her face. "So handsome, your grandy. Always had such a warm smile."

"What about the other people? Do you recognize any of them?"

"No. Judging by how young Grandy looks, I'm sure this was before I even met your father."

"On the back, it references the Bernsteins and Paris 1937. Does that name ring a bell?"

"Bernsteins. No. And 1937 is definitely before I met your father. But Grandy might have visited Paris then." She took another sip of tea. "I barely remember this, but he talked about a few people he knew in the Paris church. One was an American. I remember him saying how surprised he was to meet another American there."

"Was there ever anything odd you remember from his trips?"

Evelynn took a breath. "Wait a minute. You know, he did talk about worrying about a Jewish family in Paris. Maybe that's them. The Bernsteins. Wonder what happened to them?"

AJ glanced at Grace.

Evelynn looked at the picture again. "Maybe Grandy helped the Bernsteins."

"Maybe," AJ agreed.

Evelynn took the last bite of her scone. "Well, it's an interesting picture, isn't it? Loved his smile. Hope you find what you're looking for, dear." She took a last sip of tea and set her cup on the table.

"Mom, if you remember anything else, will you tell me?"

"Of course, dear. I'll let you know if something more works its way through my memory banks." She tapped on her forehead. "Isn't that what you have in your computers?"

They smiled at his mom's attempt to relate to AJ's tech work.

"Right, Mom. Thanks for everything."

"Don't forget dinner this week."

"Of course. Know what you're fixing yet?"

"Nope. Gotta start hunting on recipes.com. I'm sure I'll find something new and fun." She rose from her chair. AJ and Grace stood and followed her to the door.

Grace smiled at Evelynn. "Thanks for the tea and scones." She leaned in and gave Evelynn a kiss on the cheek.

"All right, you two. Have a good night. Time for a little reading before bed."

"What's in progress now?" AJ asked.

"Steven King's latest."

"Mom?"

"Just kidding. I'm reading through the book of John. Dad's favorite Gospel. 'In the beginning was the Word.'"

"Love you, Mom." He bent down and gave her a kiss, a hug, and a smile.

"Me too. Good night." They left, and she closed the door behind them.

Heading to the car, AJ started. "So maybe the people in the photo are the Bernsteins. What do you think?"

They walked across the wet pavement, got in the car, and headed home.

"If it is the Bernsteins, so what?" Grace asked.

The wipers swished back and forth.

Good question. Who were these Bernsteins? The name seemed Jewish. Were they victims of the Nazis?

"You don't know of any Paris art patrons named Bernstein in that time frame, do you?" AJ asked.

"That's an excellent question. I've got some free time at work tomorrow and I think I know where to start. What about the IBM question?"

"Hmm, not sure I can get to that tomorrow. I've got a busy schedule."

"Like that's ever stopped you before," Grace joked.

Right as usual. Nothing would stop him from getting to the bottom of Grandy's IBM career.

CHAPTER 4

Ars Longa, Vita Brevis

Pablo Picasso's Studio, Paris, 1937

PICASSO STOOD BEFORE HIS rough, wood art easel, tapping his pencil on the paper, about to draw the first line for his portrait of Igor. He favored the light streaming through the wall of windows at this time of day, when the sun stood straight above the Eiffel Tower, especially since it permitted him to linger in bed before a new act of creation. This week's shirt hung halfheartedly on a flimsy, wooden folding chair and a half-empty glass of wine stood at the ready on his paint-stained worktable. Canvases of various sizes and states of progress cluttered his studio, leaning in layers against each other. To visitors, his chaotic loft oozed distraction, but for him, each jar of soaking brushes and each paint smear on the wall emanated energy for the particular work at hand.

But even the right tools demanded motivation and inspiration. Did God wait for inspiration before his first act of creation? Did it flow with complete forethought? Oh, Picasso had experienced those times, but this may not be one of them.

Igor Stravinsky, the famous Russian composer, sat in the wooden armchair, enjoying the warmth of the sun and time with his friend. Their camaraderie sprouted like a vine of chardonnay, several years ago in Italy, pressed into fine champagne by countless nights of careless carousing. So wild that their mornings after often found them waking up on splintered benches and looking through bars. Their friendship had deepened now in Paris, in part, thanks to Otto and Emma Bernstein, perhaps the greatest art supporters in 1930s Paris. Their home, a splendid salon, hosted the crème de la crème of artists, authors, musicians and philosophers, fostering creative connections for both Igor and Pablo.

Pablo's pencil made its first attack on the paper.

"Always a moment. The first line, first note, first word," Igor said. "The artist faces a blank page awaiting the first stroke. At least I am greeted with five lines inviting me and my first note. The first note, the first line, the next note, the next line and then sometimes a flurry, more times a drought."

"*Muy cierto*. Very true, *mi amigo*. Does the mind know what is to come, or does the journey lead the mind, which then leads the journey again? Will the end of the journey lead to something profound or to fuel for the fire?" Pablo said.

"And how long before we have more on the fire heap than on the easel?" Igor said.

"I begin with an idea, and poof, it becomes something else." Pablo laughed, with Igor joining in.

Pablo continued the journey of this portrait and seemed to experience not a flurry, but perhaps a gentle rain. He smiled, enjoying the exchange of thoughts on the miracle of creation.

Igor gestured out the window. "Often I discover a kernel, a small germ of inspiration, perhaps while out and about. The canvas of nature is often a stimulant for that first kernel."

"I was inspired to complete a series of works, because I had a *superavit*, mmm, a surplus, of blue paint. And, *voila*, my patrons decide I had a blue period," Pablo said with a chuckle and a wave of his pencil. "But colors, like seasons, follow the changes of the emotions."

"Ah, *emotsiya*, emotion. Passion, that drives us to our mistress. What force is more potent than love?" Igor said.

"Ah, *la amante*. The mistress. For me, the art, for you, the music."

"Certainly, the main mistress. But, ah," he sighed again, "not the only mistress."

"And if not for *those* mistresses, we would not both be here, now, in Paris."

Both had mistresses in Paris, the custom, for so many creatives. But perhaps Paris displaced all those mistresses, the lady to be prized not just by artists but also by the politicians.

"Did you find it curious Madame Bernstein insisted on so many drawings of me? I am the first to admit I am not the handsome model many would pursue," Igor said.

"On that, we can agree." They both laughed. "Perhaps she is *supersticiosa*, superstitious. Attracted to twelve," Pablo said.

"Or she chooses to display one a month through the year."

"Perhaps it relates to her Jewish faith. The twelve tribes of Israel?"

"It is a significant number for you, with the twelve tones in music to work from," Pablo said. His lines continued to expand on the paper on the easel. Could that be a face appearing now on the paper?

"Sometimes they are twelve friends. Sometimes they feel like twelve demons, snarling and hissing at me in a battle to conquer the next hill, the next phrase, the next movement."

"Yes, the demons. Sometimes, they conquer the muses in this battle. But for this drawing, we will celebrate a victory."

He took the paper from the easel and turned it for his friend to see.

Igor leaned forward in his chair and squinted. "The lines do not lie. So, there it is."

Pablo's completed lines brought a whimsical image of Igor into focus. But other lines crept across Europe, lines separating a civilized world from that of a madman.

CHAPTER 5

A Date With A Canvas

Irvine, California, 2022

THE RECENT GRANDY REVELATIONS continued to swirl in AJ's head. A series of next steps filled his mental project list while he pondered the big picture. Grace's project list for this Saturday included a plan to connect with nature and each other.

Driving through the beautiful South Coast hills, they passed field after field carpeted with native golden poppies. The sun from the southeast sky streaming through the opened panoramic sunroof of AJ's Colorado Red Jeep Renegade warmed, the two of them. Such a magnificent contrast between the poppy-gold and pure sky-blue.

An artist at heart, Grace Meyer's soul found refreshment from the rich hues of nature. A fit, petite, thirty-five-year-old, five-foot-four Asian beauty, Grace enjoyed life to the fullest with her professorship at Lines College, a sideline as a beginning watercolor artist, and wife to the best husband in the world.

She lived a life of gratitude, blessed with a husband who understood and shared this love for visual bliss. So much so that he had embraced their plans to honeymoon in Paris, the city of love, but also a world art capital.

"Remember our amazing art date along the Seine, where you smeared your very first dab of oil?" she said.

"Who knew such artistic genius would soon emerge?" he said. They both laughed.

His technique had matured beyond simple smears. And today the two of them would attempt painting simultaneous portraits of each other.

Continuing their drive, they passed the church where they first met, South Coast Reformed Church, founded by AJ's great uncle. Reaching their destination, AJ pulled onto an unpaved road and parked on the crest of the hill. Setting up their easels, they inhaled the invigorating salt air drifting in from the crashing waves of the Pacific Ocean in the distance.

Grace surveyed the surroundings. "'How lovely is your dwelling place, oh Lord.'"

She and AJ spent the next two hours posing for each other, dabbing their canvases, and reminiscing about their honeymoon in Paris.

"Can I see your masterpiece yet?" Grace asked. They had agreed to respect each other's process and wait for permission to take in the work in progress.

AJ rubbed his forehead. "Not yet. My technique is rather slow today."

"Something distracting you?" she said.

"Oh, just Nazis, IBM, and mysterious Parisians, is all," he said, waving his brush in the air.

AJ's life consisted of a series of predictable results he controlled with calculated planning and preparation. His business moved from one successful milestone to the next. His personal life, much the same. Until the day the medical tests confirmed the sad truth of his infertility. There must be something he could do, some procedure to fix it. If so, he hadn't found it yet. It remained an unsolved mystery of "all things work together for good," a wrestling match with shame in one corner of the ring and faith in the other.

Now, he faced another wrestling match with a new set of circumstances out of his control regarding Grandy.

"Can you narrow it down a little?" Grace said.

"In a word—truth. Everything I thought I knew about Grandy might not be true."

"I can understand why you feel that way. After everything we found."

AJ added a few more strokes to his canvas. "I keep wondering about missing pieces, other evidence that could clear his name."

"Perhaps you're making conclusions that aren't true. I'm sure a lot of American companies conducted business with the Nazis before the world knew of their atrocities."

All they knew so far, they had discovered in one letter addressed to Robert. Quite cryptic with nothing concrete to suggest he acted in any way that contributed to the Nazi's evil.

"But you have to admit there are a lot of unanswered questions," he said.

"I agree. But I know how good you are at solving puzzles. You've proved that at work over and over. All those system bugs you've squished to spare your customers from any harm."

"But this is different. It's not like I can just log in and look at code or hardware schematics."

"I'm sure you'll find the right place to log in and find the answers." She glanced at him and added a few dabs of paint to her canvas. "You always do."

A breeze rustled the surrounding grasses.

"So, earth to AJ. Can I see now?"

"Why don't we just dive into that picnic basket first? Then we'll look."

They set their brushes aside and wiped the smudges of oil from their hands. AJ set up the table and chairs. Grace spread out the traditional red-and-white checkered tablecloth. Taking the bottle of white wine out of the ice bag, AJ felt the cool condensation on the bottle and smiled. He poured them each a glassful. Grace made a delightful spread of salami, cheese, grapes, and bread, a custom they appropriated on their Paris honeymoon. The one thing missing, a vase of flowers.

But the view of the blue sky and swaying grass under the tall, menthol-scented eucalyptus trees more than made up for it.

AJ held up his glass. "A toast. To the most beautiful wife on a most beautiful day."

"Just like Paris," Grace said.

"Yes. Just like Paris." They clinked their glasses and took a first sip. "And thank you, Lord, for the beauty of the day and the blessing of this food. Amen."

"Amen," Grace said.

AJ took the first bite of his sandwich. The combination of the smoky Gruyère cheese with the turkey salami on the sourdough bread made impact with his taste buds. "This is amazing."

"Mm, hmm," Grace agreed, mid-bite.

After sandwiches and grapes came the dusted chocolate truffles.

"Hard to keep your fingers clean eating these," AJ said, licking the cocoa powder off his fingers.

"Mm, hmm." Grace smiled as she savored her mouth full of dessert.

They returned to their easels for another hour of work.

"Okay. It's time. You ready to reveal?" she asked.

"As ready as I'll ever be."

"On the count of three. One, two, three," Grace shouted.

They each turned their easels toward one another. They each broke into laughter and huge smiles. They embraced and kissed. Then they packed it in and made their trip home, singing along with Chicago's greatest hits.

But even with the upbeat refrains of the classic brass and vocals filling the air, AJ's thoughts drifted back to Grandy and his mysterious past, a past he wasn't ready to explore yet.

CHAPTER 6

The ERR

ERR Offices, Berlin, Germany, 1937

ALFRED ROSENBERG GREETED EACH member arriving for the initial meeting of the ERR, *Einsatzstab Reichsleiter Rosenberg*, or Reichsleiter Rosenberg Taskforce. Adolf Hitler personally appointed him to head the ERR, and he had now completed filling the committee with other high-ranking Nazis.

Rosenberg had walked in sync with Hitler for fourteen years, since the Beer Hall Putsch, the spark that ignited Hitler's faltering ascent to power. Two thousand Nazi party members marched through the city center and surrounded the *Bürgerbräukeller*, Munich's largest beer hall. Inside, Hitler stood on a stage, flanked by Rosenberg and his comrade, Hermann Göring. Hitler fired a shot into the ceiling, jumped on a chair, and yelled, "The national revolution has broken out!" The revolution never got off the ground and Hitler ended up in jail two days later.

The sensationalistic publicity covering the failed coup attempt allured a disgruntled Germany, ripe for promises of a new nationalist government. Rosenberg's faithful commitment to the Führer propelled him up the success ladder, landing him the current position of *Reichsleiter,* Reich Leader, second only to Hitler.

His rank entitled him to this prestigious suite in the Reich Chancellery, the official center of government for all the Third Reich. A red carpet filled the center of the reception room. The walls testified to Rosenberg's political successes, with framed medals, commendations, and photographs of Rosenberg next to various other Reich Leaders. Behind the desk, a pair of Ionic columns supported bronze busts of the Nazi party eagle, flanking the portrait of Hitler. Doors led to both his private office and a conference room, the location for today's meeting.

Dark oak paneling, adorned with finely crafted inlays, surrounded the room, and reached twenty-four feet high. The conference table made a massive statement of strength. A dozen mahogany tufted chairs encircled the table and rays from the east-facing wall of windows provided natural lighting for the entire room.

Rosenberg's movie-star good looks in a well turned-out uniform and his magnetic personality demanded the attention of his audience. Two long red banners, emblazoned with the authorized Nazi swastika, hung on the wall behind his head seat at the table, an impressive setting for his opening remarks.

In perfect posture, he stood and eyed each member of his committee sitting around the table. "Gentlemen of the Reich, welcome. Today, we embark on a mission of great interest and importance to the Führer. I'm sure you are all aware of his mandate to create the ultimate art collection for all the world to envy. Your membership on this committee to accomplish that goal is a great honor. Please open your plans."

Leather-bound folders emblazoned with the swastika sat in front of each attendee, placed perpendicular to the edge of the table. Other items sat on the table for the appetites of the members—pitchers of water, cut crystal drinking glasses, suitable for water and eventually hard liquor, and ashtrays for the smokers of cigarettes or cigars, already streaming wisps of smoke through the golden rays shining from the windows.

"On page one, you will see our mission: Plan and execute the appropriation of art masterpieces from museums and private collections throughout Europe for the purpose of filling the *Führermuseum*. I named this project *Sonderauftrag Linz*, Special Mission Linz."

Rosenberg smiled and gestured to Roderick Fick. "Herr Fick, please show us your design."

Roderick Fick, one of Hitler's chief architects, had designed the future Führermuseum, or Führer's Museum, for the Linz location.

Fick stood and addressed Rosenberg. "Thank you, Herr Rosenberg." He gestured toward his left. "Gentlemen, join me at the table."

He led the members to a round table next to the windows, covered with a gray cloth. He pulled off the cloth and exposed a three-dimensional model of the entire complex.

With a dignified smile, he said, "And this, gentlemen, will be the finest cultural center in all of Europe."

Rosenberg began clapping, cueing the other members to join him in a round of acknowledgement.

"The location for the center is Linz, Austria, the Führer's hometown. The model you see before you is based on sketches by the Führer himself."

Fisk directed attention to each section of the model, pointing with a large, red rod.

"Here you see a theater next to a library and a cinema. Along this boulevard is the Führermuseum. Once again, our Führer has shown great vision and leadership to dominate the world in all aspects of society."

Rosenberg smirked and waved his cigar in the air. "Not bad for a wanna-be artist."

The members joined Rosenberg in a chuckle. Hitler's earlier pursuit of an art career ended with dismal results. However, the entire world now recognized one of his creations, the swastika.

Fick continued. "As you see, the art museum contains plenty of room to display tens of thousands of artistic works. Only the world's best will make the grade."

"Acquiring the world's best is the mission of this committee, *mein Kamerad*!" Rosenberg said. "Thank you, Herr Fick."

Hermann Göring pointed to the model. "Perhaps there won't be enough room. There is so much to pursue. In Italy alone, we saw an overwhelming abundance of the world's greatest artists."

Göring's ascent in the Third Reich mirrored Rosenberg's, advancing to his current position to oversee all sectors of the economy supporting military rearmament. He loved art as much as he loved his plump, one-of-a-kind uniform.

Hitler's and Göring's earlier visits to Rome, Florence, and Naples enlightened them to the immense riches of Italian museums. Göring had taken notes on these trips to record the pieces he planned to acquire for Hitler and the pieces he wanted for his own private collection.

"France also is full of bountiful collections," Bruno Lohse said.

Lohse, a trim forty-year-old, worked as an art dealer in Berlin and recently joined the Nazi party. His artistic expertise and French connections had impressed Göring, who recommended him for a position in the ERR. He loved art more than duty to the Fatherland.

"That is true, Herr Lohse," Rosenberg said. "But now, time for a break, I think, Kameraden. Please, help yourself to more refreshment before we reconvene."

The members gathered at a side table, prepared with a full complement of libations.

Lohse picked up the cognac, read the label, and raised his eyebrows. He filled his glass and turned to Fick standing next to him. "Impressive choice of French cognac by our host."

Fick selected a different bottle. "He knows his bourbon, too."

The longer the members mingled and refilled their glasses, the grander the boasts of their accomplishments grew.

Rosenberg interrupted and called them back to the table. "Kameraden, today I want to focus on France."

Lohse interrupted. "Is this premature? Germany has no political foothold in France."

"Lohse, surely you've seen how extensively Germany is rearming herself. We successfully threw off the shackles of the Treaty of Versailles. The Führer has great plans for expanding the Third Reich. We are here to do the same in the cultural world."

Germany boldly violated the treaty by moving thousands of troops into the Rhineland and testing new aircraft and weapons in the Spanish Civil War. Hitler publicly preached of long-term peaceful goals, but his inner circle had developed plans to rearm Germany to an extent the world had never seen before.

"It's time to set up an underground network in France's art community and I've decided to focus first on Paris," Rosenberg continued. "We already know of many museums and aristocrats with large personal collections of interest for the Führer."

"What kind of volume are you planning for?" another committee member asked.

"I think we can safely say thousands of items."

"In France alone?" the member asked.

"France?" Rosenberg laughed. "In Paris alone."

Lohse said, "What is your plan for cataloging and transporting so many pieces?"

"A transport plan is in the works and will be completed by the time we infiltrate and locate what we want. As for an inventory plan, I am working with the Dehomag computer center. Thanks to IBM in America, our engineers adapted the computer system IBM designed for census taking. We will use it to inventory and track the movement of the art we acquire. Tracking and moving art is no different than tracking and moving people, is it?"

All of Germany knew about the census. But Hitler and his cronies planned a much darker purpose for the census, one not only counting people, but one asking for religion and race-specific information.

"Herr Lohse will head our first phase," Rosenberg said.

Lohse's face lit up. "Of course."

"Your assignment, infiltrate the art society of Paris. Your experience as an art dealer should make this an easy task."

A true art aficionado couldn't hope for a more attractive assignment than this one.

"I expect you already know some contacts to approach first. You are entitled to a healthy allowance. It is important you have suitable lodging that supports your cover. This packet contains more details of the plan and when and how to report back," Rosenberg said, handing Lohse his assignment packet.

"We will adjourn for now and meet again when Lohse completes phase one. Of course, more phases with different targets will follow. I will contact you when I am ready to initiate those phases. For today, that is all."

Rosenberg stood and extended his arm. "*Heil Hitler!*"

"Heil Hitler!" the committee responded, standing and returning the salute.

The members departed, leaving Rosenberg alone, sitting back in his chair, and holding his glass with the last swallow of whiskey. He raised it and smiled, proud of himself, his station in the Reich, and his value to the Führer.

To the Führer. To his future. To my future. To art.

Scan or tap the QR code to read the blogpost about the Linz Project.

CHAPTER 7

Those Six

Albert Becker Art Museum, Irvine, California, 2022

LYLE BERNSTEIN SAT IN his office, sipping the bottom of his first cup of the day, grabbed on his way to work. He didn't need the caffeine buzz, still sky high from the recent art acquisition to the Albert Becker Art Museum. Six historic pieces, sitting on his workbench, waiting for his first steps of restoration.

Lyle held the title of Master of Cultural Restoration with an advanced degree from the UCLA/Getty Conservation school. Brian Miller, curator of the museum, recruited Lyle personally eight years ago. At five-foot-ten, and 175 pounds, he was no prize fighter, but had a decent build for a man of fifty-four, mastering karate well enough to fend off any attacker.

So many questions. Who had them until now? Where had they been before that? Why had it taken so long to find them? Where were the other six?

The thrust of the door opening and the entrance of Diego Martinez, Lyle's intern, shook him back to the present.

"Hey, boss. Pretty intense face you have going there. What's up?" Diego sauntered to his chaotic cubicle, dropped his backpack next to the trash can overflowing with In-N-Out wrappers, sat, and swiveled to face Lyle.

"Still taking in these new Picasso drawings," Lyle replied.

"Taking in" was a gross understatement. Lyle's connection to these Picasso drawings extended back in a family quest spanning eighty years. The quest began with his grandparents, Otto and Emma Bernstein, mingling among the elite cultural circles of 1930s Paris, a world that celebrated art, literature, and music. The Picasso drawings entered the world at one of the Bernstein's famous soirées.

"Do you recognize any of the portraits that came in yesterday?" Lyle asked.

Lyle hired Diego from twenty applicants for the job. He stood heads above the rest with his thorough understanding of the major art historical periods and the significant artists from each. Lyle also appreciated the guts it took for Diego to liberate himself from a neighborhood valuing turf wars over artistic pursuits.

"I think I've seen one like them in a book. But you're probably gonna laugh when I tell you what book," Diego said.

A Gen Z-er, some of Diego's experiences seemed foreign to Lyle. To kick back, Diego enjoyed online gaming, favoring Minecraft. And boy, did he and his girlfriend sizzle at their favorite salsa dance clubs.

Lyle smiled, needing a little humor. "Go ahead."

Diego wheeled his chair closer to Lyle. "I had a book when I was a kid that taught you how to draw." He smacked the wad of gum in his mouth. "I'm pretty sure there's a drawing a lot like these in that book."

Art teachers have used the picture Diego remembered for years to teach upside-down drawing. This technique focuses on drawing the lines of an upside-down drawing, instead of a preconceived image, such as a hand or an ear. Thousands of aspiring artists have laid their eyes on this drawing and mastered their own reproduction, introducing them to the famous portrait of Igor Stravinsky by Pablo Picasso.

Diego stood and reached for one of the drawings.

Lyle whacked his hand. "Not without gloves, buddy."

Diego wiped the swat off his hand. "Of course, mine didn't look like any of these."

"Well, if it helps, no one else drew quite like Picasso."

Lyle had listened to his grandparents' stories, over and over, how they loved Picasso's unique style, how the simple line drawings captured the essence of Igor Stravinsky. The patrons who paid Picasso's commission, Fritz and Claire Hoffman, partnered with his grandparents on several art endeavors. A dispute about ownership erupted between the two couples and continued, stronger than ever, in this generation. Almost pointless with the drawings sight-unseen for eighty years. Until now.

Diego scooted back to his desk. "Anyway, I wanted to remind you I need to leave early today for that special symposium at school. It's at two, so I'll leave after lunch."

"Thanks for reminding me. I'll see you tomorrow morning then?" Lyle asked, continuing to examine the drawings.

"Yup, you will." Diego stood and headed for the door. "Need some caffeine. Be right back."

Lyle had started searching for the Picasso drawings after his parents told him about them. Oddly, they had expressed little interest in the valuable art.

How could they not have known of their immense importance in the art world? A complete set of twelve drawings by Picasso, lost and unaccounted for, worth a fortune.

Six of them had fallen in his lap, by no effort of his own. And now he had the opportunity he'd hoped for. Over the years of restoring art, his views on art ownership had drastically changed. His grandparents had learned how to profit from the hard work of artists, such as Picasso. With his changed views, he had come to despise this. Yes, they helped promote new artists and put money into their pockets. Too many bad actors came along, seeking personal gain, perverting the purity of art, bastardizing it, reducing it to cold cash, devoid of a soul. These Picasso pieces deserved a soul resurrection and the best place for that to happen: back with the Picasso family.

Was this the chance of a lifetime? An opportunity to finally return them to the Picasso estate?

Lyle walked past the workbench and entered his private office. He walked behind his desk and unlocked and opened the side drawer. Sorting through a few papers, he pulled out the wrinkled, black-and-white photo and grabbed his magnifying glass. He walked back to the workbench with the six Picassos and began comparing them with the photo. Moving the magnifying glass across the photo, he examined the twelve Picasso drawings. His grandparents stood in the foreground, making the photo evidence of provenance, regardless of who had paid for them. The two Bernsteins blocked the view of some of the portraits, making it difficult, along with the photo's graininess, to see which of the twelve portraits sat in his office and which were missing.

He set the photo and magnifying glass down. On a whim, he looked at the back of one of the drawings, something that hadn't even crossed his mind. Turning it over, he saw something shocking. He froze. He turned over another and then another until he saw the backsides of all six. His discovery could change everything about the Picasso Dozen and Igor Stravinsky.

CHAPTER 8

A Joyous Soirée

Paris, 1937

BRUNO LOHSE STEPPED OUT for some fresh Paris air. He'd finished unpacking his boxes and needed a break from the drudgery of setting up his apartment. He walked out into full daylight and welcomed the sun's warm embrace. The noise of life's parade filled the air—laughter of young couples walking arm in arm, squeals coming from nanny-pushed strollers, and music drifting from the cafe down the block. Paris touched his soul in a way Berlin never would. His stern-faced German countrymen excelled in rigidity and bland, routine precision at work and home. Always coloring inside the lines. But the French, ah, the French, and their *Liberté, Egalité, Fraternité*—Liberty, Equality, Fraternity. Their lives radiated passion in their camaraderie, finding joy in a single rose, artfully presented in a hand-crafted vase on a cafe table. Their coloring pages had no lines.

Bruno learned that casually sipping coffee at a Paris street cafe lent itself to making new acquaintances. He used this tactic in phase one of his first ERR mission: secure an invitation to the upcoming soirée hosted by Otto and Emma

Bernstein. Monitoring their home, he'd seen the frequent comings and goings of an attractive, well-dressed woman. He'd determined she must be a good friend, or at least, an acquaintance, of the Bernsteins. He began tailing her to discover whether she might be the key to unlock the Bernsteins' door.

He followed the woman to a popular street cafe and waited from a distance until she settled in with a cup of coffee. She cradled the cup of steaming coffee in both hands, closed her eyes, and took a whiff. She exhaled and a smile spread across her face.

A true coffee connoisseur. Just my type.

She lit a cigarette and started thumbing through pages of the *New York Times*, taking an occasional puff. Lohse moved in and strategically seated himself at the next table. He took a cue from her smoking, pulled out a cigarette, and feigned the need for a light.

Lohse approached the woman with a smile. "*Pardon, madame. Puis-je avoir du feu, s'il vous plaît?*"

She looked up from her paper. "I'm sorry. I'm an American. That is, I'm not sorry I'm American. I mean, do you speak English?"

"Of course, Mrs...?"

"Oh, just call me Dottie. Much friendlier, don't you think? Things can get so stuffy in Paris sometimes."

"Yes, Dottie. Can you please light my cigarette?"

He not only received a light for his cigarette, he walked through an open door into an extended conversation that flowed so naturally that he charmed his way into a blossoming friendship with Dottie. He nurtured the contrived friendship with more coffee dates, meals out, and visits to the Louvre, hitting the jackpot on one of their strolls along the Seine—an invitation from Dottie to join her at the Bernsteins' soirée.

***

Paris art society rated Emma and Otto Bernstein's soirées the crème de la crème, favored over the Peggy Guggenheims and the Gertrude Steins. Emma's famous gatherings captivated a kaleidoscope of colorful attendees who appreciated a vast spectrum of creativity and discourse.

Emma had outdone herself planning tonight's soirée. Merely receiving the coveted invitations had created an excited buzz among the recipients, waiting for the highlight of the season—a gala premier of a set of twelve portraits of Igor Stravinsky by the famous Pablo Picasso.

The art showcased in Emma's early soirées came from the collection handed to Otto. His father started building an art collection working in his antique shop in the late 1800s. Father and son toured together, combing the great art galleries of Paris, London, Berlin, and even New York. Upon receiving the torch from his father, Otto followed in his footsteps, protecting his inherited collection and promoting his generation's up-and-coming artists. Tonight's gala fulfilled his mission, promoting the twelve drawings by Pablo Picasso, or, as they'd been nicknamed, the Picasso Dozen.

Otto, Emma, tuxedos, and formal occasions did not mix well. He had tried on two tuxes for their wedding before the verdict came in.

"Oh, dear, dear, dear, dear. Not in my wedding!"

Emma thrived on color. She couldn't possibly present him in only two on her wedding day. She needed a rainbow, not a photo negative.

He received her seal of approval for tonight's choice: a navy, double-breasted jacket, white linen trousers, and an unbuttoned yellow shirt with a fluffed floral ascot—custom tailored for his slender five-foot-eight-inch frame. Ever the dutiful spouse, he took up his position on the front steps to welcome Emma's guests.

"So now she has an even twelve, right, Otto?" the first guest said.

Otto smiled and shook hands with the guest. "You know Emma. Big thinker. Sky's the limit. Come on in."

Tonight's guests entered through two fifteen-feet high front doors into a foyer with Italian marble floors. Finding themselves immediately in the presence of the twelve portraits, guests caught their breath, involuntarily gasping with "oos" and "ahs."

Everything in the foyer had Emma's artistic touch. Duplicate floral arrangement of gladiolas in Chinese ceramic vases atop Grecian columns surrounded the Picassos. Maroon velvet drapes, held by gold, braided cords, formed a regal background behind the flowers. Jasmine-scented incense flavored the air and a path of candles beckoned visitors to the main salon.

Emma had insisted on a set of twelve drawings of her friend, the great Igor Stravinsky. Undoubtedly, the Russian's giant splash in the Paris musical pond had dazzled her with his avant-garde music for the 1913 ballet, *The Rite of Spring*. The ballet's premier disintegrated into a spectacular kerfuffle between two impassioned factions in the audience—the guardians of the traditionally tame music by the Mozarts and Beethovens, clashing with the advocates for the latest boundary-busting musical styles. The agitated commotion escalated and the verbal war of opinions crescendoed to such a climax, it drowned out the orchestra. This forced the choreographer to spontaneously shout commands from backstage to keep his dancers on track.

The portraits arrived two weeks ago, with Pablo acting as a delivery man. She immediately opened the packages to check the back of the portraits. He saw the twinkle in her eyes.

Pablo smiled. "Ah, yes, senora, he had time to complete the back side. He said you'd be expecting it. Now it is *fini*, mmm, complete!"

Emma's love for art had arrived early in her life, frolicking in a gallery of nature on her parents' estate, with the brilliant tulip beds and striped mowed lawns edged by the forests and meadows manicured by God Himself. How could anyone not believe in a creator seeing the abundance of beauty in His creation? Emma's favorite passage, Psalm 84, encapsulated this essence. The first verse opened with a glorious proclamation, "How lovely is your dwelling place, O LORD of hosts!" For her, the psalm described the glories of nature's temple where worshippers could exalt with joy in the simple beauty of sparrows finding a home for their nest. Here in Paris, she had built her nest, her lovely dwelling place, her temple of beauty.

At Emma's request, Igor had composed a new piece of music for piano, inspired by the twelve verses of Psalm 84. What a master, her Igor. Each section moved flawlessly from one to the next and in a far more traditional style than his ballet. After much practice, Emma's hands were ready to premier all twelve sections of the composition. A special surprise for tonight's guests.

The walk from the foyer to the main salon presented a feast for the senses. American jazz drifted through the air from a piano. Some of Emma's favorite pieces adorned the hallway. Brilliant colors in a painting by Chagall celebrated the love of his life. Dreamlike images mingled with unrelated objects of melting clocks, ants, and a distant seashore in a new work by Salvador Dali. Candles in a variety of hues flickered from their perches of differing heights around the art.

The hallway led to the grand salon, designed by Emma herself, an expression of the joy she experienced from the natural beauty at her parents' estate. The rug, with its bright green wavy lines, the pair of Daffodil Tiffany lamps placed on side tables, and potted palm trees placed at various heights around the perimeter. Overhead, tangled branches dangled from the ceiling, entwined with ivy vines mimicking a forest canopy.

The dozen guests enjoyed champagne, aged bourbon, and whisky served from the art déco bar with its shimmering silver frame, black highlights, and glass top. Clusters of chairs in various groupings around the room invited intimate conversations.

In one of these clusters, Dottie, Emma's vivacious friend from the States, chatted with fellow American Robert Meyer.

"Robert, I can't tell you how happy I was meeting you at church. Hearing your English from across the room drew me like a magnet."

Finding native English speakers in Paris didn't happen often, and Dottie appreciated she'd found one at church.

"Are you in Paris much longer?" she said.

Robert came to Europe to conduct business in Berlin for IBM and had made this side trip to France on church business.

"I have a few days of meetings with The Reformed Church before I head back to America."

"Ah, America. I do miss it."

Dottie turned to her right. "How about you, Ernest? Do you miss being in America?"

Dottie and Ernest Hemingway worked together on the reporter staff at the *Kansas City Star*. Ernest's destiny thrust him into the exotic worlds of warrior, war correspondent, and now, famous author of *The Sun Also Rises*. Dottie followed a lackluster path leading to a stalled career in the slow-rising ranks of reporters at the *Star*. Meeting and marrying a Kansas millionaire, she now enjoyed the luxuries of world travel, with and without her husband.

"Not all that much, to be truthful," Hemingway responded.

"Robert and Ernest, may I introduce you to Bruno Lohse?" Dottie gestured toward Bruno. "He's a newcomer to Paris, on business from Germany."

Hemingway sat cross-legged opposite Lohse, puffing his cigar. "Where you staying in Paris, Bruno?"

"Not far from here, a small flat close to a few cafes."

Ernest tilted back his head and blew some smoke. "And what's your deal, Mr. Lohse? Art, poetry, music, love?"

"I suppose all of those. But along with many others in this city, the art compels me most."

The pianist sent a new song through the salon.

Dottie put a hand on Ernest's knee, a friendly gesture between two old friends. "He's quite the art dealer in Berlin. Isn't that right, Bruno?"

"Yes, that is true. And it is my joy to stay here in Paris and find pieces for my clients in Berlin."

Ernest gestured to the foyer. "What's your take on those Picasso drawings in the front room?"

Bruno perked up, speaking with more enthusiasm. "Oh, yes, very interesting. Simple but compelling. I've looked forward to seeing his work since I first learned about him." He paused and stroked his chin. Shaking his index finger, he continued. "Interesting how Mr. Picasso captured the change of seasons over twelve months, a year. So much can change in a single year." He leaned forward with a sly smile. "Don't you agree?"

The pianist interrupted the conversation with some ta, ta, da chords, grabbing the crowd's attention, and transitioned into Ravel's *Menuet antique*. Emma entered the salon with bridesmaid steps, beaming with her trademark *joie de vivre*, joy of life. She pulled red and white rose petals from a basket woven from twigs, and with large, graceful arm gestures, she tossed them to her guests. Applause ebbed and flowed with each toss.

She'd crafted the crown she wore from eucalyptus leaves, punctuated with gardenias, and decorated with a trail of ribbons flowing down behind her. A scarf she'd selected from her favorite designer covered her shoulders—really a piece of art, with sharp geometric designs in red, blue, and yellow outlined in black. An emerald-green belt wrapped around the simple, canary-yellow sack-like dress on her slightly plump five-foot-five frame. She believed in color and more color, and tonight, she put on a full, brilliant display.

"Welcome, my darlings. Welcome! How good of you to come to this special evening. I hope you've enjoyed yourselves so far at this modest little gathering."

Everyone laughed. Nothing appeared modest about this "modest little" gathering. The flow of champagne and booze. The abundance of caviar and other Parisian delicacies. Nothing. Modest.

"Now, I have a little surprise for you all tonight."

Oohs rippled through the crowd.

"Of course, you've seen Pablo's twelve drawings of his dear friend Igor." She gestured to the side of the room, where Pablo and Igor acknowledged her with a smile and a wave.

"Igor, what can I say about your fabulous ballet? You truly broke new ground with that one. Can't we all agree?" She raised her arms out, pleading for response, and sparked a round of applause.

"Not only do we have twelve wonderful drawing by Pablo, but Igor composed a little piano piece for me." She put her hand on her chest.

More applause. She flashed an impish grin and curtsied.

"Tonight, with great pleasure and much humility, I will perform this new composition for its world premiere."

Her piano lessons with the French composer Maurice Ravel were paying off. Not on par with concert pianists, she nevertheless held the reputation of a competent performer of many classical compositions.

Settling herself at the piano, she adjusted the bench. She held her hands above the keys, closed her eyes, and took a slow breath in and out. In that brief moment, she envisioned the beauty of the forests and meadows of her childhood home. She opened her eyes, slowly lifted her hands, and made gentle contact with the keys. The flow of music began.

Igor perfectly captured the visual essence of the divine beauty of nature in his musical interpretation. The guests listened, transfixed, to the music following an ebb and flow of gorgeous textures and satisfying harmonies. Igor listened with closed eyes, his right hand involuntarily conducting.

Emma played the final note and froze her hands on the keys. Time stood still for the entire audience, experiencing a sacred moment together.

"Hoorays" spontaneously exploded and applause erupted from an audience of true connoisseurs. Emma motioned for Igor to join her, took his hand, and together they acknowledged the continuing applause with a bow. A triumph for the two of them.

"Isn't she amazing? I just love her!" Dottie said, continuing to clap.

"A most enjoyable performance," Bruno said.

Fritz and Claire Hoffman sat along the outer edge of the adoring crowd. Their friends knew they partnered with the Bernsteins for investing, promoting, and selling art. But few of them knew their involvement with the Picasso Dozen. While Emma had envisioned the twelve drawings, it was the Hoffmans who paid Picasso's commission for his labors. Their support of Pablo reached back several years, and they planned, with the Bernsteins, to support his future work. For now, the drawings hung in the home of the Bernsteins, a fitting place to display them, with the constant parade of potential buyers streaming through their salon. But if the drawings remained in the Bernsteins' home for very long, could the confusion of ownership grow into a horrible, contentious misunderstanding between the couples?

Drinks, food, music, and dancing continued to fuel the evening into the early morning. With the guests finally leaving, the photographer Emma hired began snapping the pictures she would send to them for a memento of the evening. The photographer positioned himself in the front doorway, making sure the Picasso Dozen appeared in the background.

Pose. Smile. Flash. Kiss, kiss. "Goodbye, darling."

Lohse returned to his flat and, smugly satisfied with the intel he'd obtained, organized a report to send back to Berlin. Although he'd been on a mission, he'd enjoyed experiencing an evening with other people like him. People who loved art and loved owning art. People who appreciated the value of owning art. He now faced the dilemma of how much of the art he'd seen tonight would end up in his report to Berlin and how much would end up in his private journal. Could he find a way to benefit personally and still comply with his orders from the ERR? Surely he could make this work to his advantage. Right?

CHAPTER 9

The Faculty

Lines College, Irvine, California, 2022

FRED LEANED AGAINST THE wall in the faculty lounge at Lines College, sipping his bottle of Evian water. His throat screamed for water after a history lecture. He stared out the windows. Another ninety minutes piled on top of his twenty years at Lines College.

Lines College opened thirty years before he joined the faculty. The campus stretched across one hundred acres purchased from the Brightman Corporation owned by the Brightman family. They belonged to a group of Orange County pioneers who received land grants from the original landowner—the King of Spain. The family's mega-corporation managed the land with a firm hand to control the density of development. Thanks to this regulation, students and faculty enjoyed unobstructed views of the sprawling hills, wooded with eucalyptus trees and the last remaining orange groves in the area.

Fred moved from the windows to the sitting area and joined Grace Meyer. She sprawled in an overstuffed armchair, munching on a protein bar, with her feet propped up on the coffee table. Grace had a third of Fred's tenure, yet seemed at home with everyone at Lines. The college promoted a unique course of study focusing on the relationship between art, history, music, and architecture. The intersectionality of these areas of study fostered a happy fellowship among the faculty and administration.

Fred, in his creased khakis and dark blue polo, landed in an armchair across from Grace and next to Burt Mackley from the music department. The three friends enjoyed clustering together to catch up on life events, even though they lived lives entrenched in different decades—perky thirties for Grace, Burt in his quirky forties, and Fred, the senior, in his fifties, seasoned with salt-and-pepper hair.

Fred took another sip of water. "Did either of you get out to enjoy the glorious weather last weekend?"

Grace smiled. "Oh yeah. AJ and I had a wonderful day out. We drove over to the bluffs above Salt Creek for a delightful day of painting and picnicking. He's such a good sport about trying new artistic techniques. We painted with oil this time."

Fred turned to Grace. "Did you paint the poppies? They're crazy beautiful this year."

"No, and don't laugh. We painted portraits of each other."

"How'd they come out?"

"Well, we enjoyed a fun time together. Burt, what about you?"

Burt looked up from his journal. "Just a little catch-up reading. By the way, have you heard about those new Picasso drawings at the Becker Museum?"

Grace raised her eyebrows. "Did you say Picasso drawings?"

"Six of them. Something about portraits of Igor Stravinsky."

Grace leaned in and cocked her head. "Are you sure? Six, all of Stravinsky?"

"Yeah. I have a friend there who's restoring them for the exhibit. They haven't made a public announcement yet. Guess I scooped you."

Grace froze, staring out into space. She opened her mouth, but nothing came out.

"Grace, are you okay?" Burt said.

Grace's eyes widened. "Do you know what a big deal this is?"

"What? That Pablo Picasso was obsessed with drawing Stravinsky?" Burt said.

She slid to the edge of her seat and leaned forward. "Not my point. The world knows about one portrait of Stravinsky. Finding six more would send the art world into a frenzy. It's always a big deal finding lost art by an iconic artist like Picasso." She slouched back in her chair. "I can't imagine what they're worth."

Fred listened, but didn't join in.

Burt removed his wire-frame glasses. "But Stravinsky? Not a very attractive fellow, if you ask me."

"Yeah, I agree," Grace said. "But did you know Picasso and Igor Stravinsky were best friends?"

"Nope."

"They spent a lot of time together in Paris in the twenties and thirties, quite a colorful time. So many cultural icons rubbing elbows. I've used an earlier Picasso portrait of Stravinsky in my drawing class to teach technique. I wonder if the six at the Becker are very different?"

Burt chuckled. "You have a Picasso in your classroom?"

"It's a run-of-the-mill copy, you dweeb. The students turn the drawing upside down and cover it with a piece of paper. They expose about an inch at a time and draw the exposed lines. They continue inch by inch until they've drawn the complete picture. You should see their surprise after they turn it right side up. It's a wonderful drawing exercise. I dare you both to try it."

"Have you made AJ try it yet?"

"That's a great art date idea! Thanks, Burt."

Fred joined the conversation. "Do you think there's more Picasso portraits besides the six at the Becker?"

Grace narrowed her eyes and turned to Fred. "Interesting question, Fred." She paused, then hunched her shoulders. "Who knows? If Pablo drew six, perhaps he made others, prototypes. Or maybe he experimented with these hoping to create a new genre, like his blue period." She slid back in her chair. "So, how was your weekend, Fred?"

"So so. Browsed the bookstores looking for some new historical thrillers."

Burt looked up. "Doesn't your history curriculum include enough drama, with all the World War Two Nazi craziness?"

"You'd think, wouldn't you? But I appreciate seeing history through the eyes of a talented author."

"Did you find anything?" Grace said.

Did I find anything? Well, yes, I did. But it wasn't historical fiction.

"Nah. But I found some new zombie novels."

Grace chuckled. "Zombies? You? Really?"

"I'm kidding."

And wanting to throw everyone off a little. He'd found what he was looking for, but they didn't need to know what.

A gusty Santa Ana wind rattled the windows. The grove of eucalyptus trees danced in the late afternoon sun.

Burt sighed. "Time for another lecture."

"What's up this afternoon?" Grace said.

"Development of early musical notation of Gregorian chant," Burt said, punching a period in the air with his finger.

Grace attempted to muster some interest. "Sounds ... academic."

Fred cracked a smile. "Those monks, they sure knew how to liven up a party with some spunky tunes."

Burt launched into a lecture. "I'll have you know the Grammys created a category for chant! And in 1993, the album *Chant* peaked in the number three position of the Billboard 200 music chart and was certified double platinum!"

Grace laughed. "You're a nerd, you know that?"

"A nerd in the know." He punctuated the air again with his finger, stood, and left the room.

Grace stood and gathered her things. "I'm done for the day. Time to head home. How about you?"

"I need to work on some lectures for tomorrow. See ya."

"See you." Grace headed to the door.

Fred had work, all right. But it had nothing to do with a class lecture. Too many people were finding out too much. He needed a plan. It was time to make a phone call.

48

Scan or tap the QR code to see the website for Lines College.

CHAPTER 10

Her Arrival

Paris Train Depot, 1937

TODAY'S NEWSPAPER PLACED JOSEPHINE Baker's picture front and center with details of her morning arrival at the Paris train depot. Crowds of fans and curiosity seekers gathered to celebrate the arrival of the next flash from the American entertainment world. Josephine's flamboyant reputation preceded her.

Dottie led Emma to the arrival platform. "I haven't seen this much excitement since Marlene Dietrich came to town. And in trousers, no less."

Emma nodded. "The poor chief of police. Intent on arresting her for an outrageous fashion crime, a woman in men's pants. No one wanted to miss seeing that!"

Dottie chuckled. "And all it took was for her to step off the train with a smile, grab him by the arm, and with an air of confidence, parade him off the platform. There was nothing he could do."

Dottie had followed Josephine's career in America and admired the entertainer's tenacity in battling discrimination in show business. Emma reveled in Josephine's exuberance and vivacity, a perfect fit for her circle of friends.

Dottie clutched Emma's arm. "Emma, darling, you must invite her to your next soirée. The gang will simply love having her join us."

They elbowed their way through the crowd, edging to the front. Their cheeks welcomed the sun's warmth and their eyes squinted down the track, watching for the train.

Dottie saw it first and pointed. "Here she comes."

The shriek of the train's whistle filled the air, announcing its arrival. Slowing to a stop, steam spewed from its underbelly. Dozens of Parisians and members of the press surged forward. The steam dissolved into a sheer curtain, rising to reveal Josephine posing with her trademark smile.

"Hello, Paris!" Josephine said, waving to the crowd.

Josephine stunned her audience in her bell-shaped cloche hat, modest off-white flapper dress, over-the-shoulder floral African print scarf, and t-strap flats. Her ruby red lipstick magnified the smile she flashed for the cameras and a sea of smiling fans.

Reporters swarmed her with questions.

"Who are you staying with, Miss Baker? What are your immediate plans?"

"Where are you performing? When will you open?"

"Why did you leave America?"

Pushing past the reporters, fans delivered a sea of bouquets. Josephine received an armful, leaving the rest for her friend to carry. She stepped onto the platform and nudged her way through the crowd, immediately coming face to face with Emma.

Emma gushed, "Welcome to Paris, Miss Baker."

Dottie joined in. "Yes. And from one American to another, how you doin?"

"Ah, an American. Glory hallelujah! Glad to hear some real American English! Where you from?"

"Kansas originally, but I was in New York a few years ago and saw you on Broadway," Dottie said.

Josephine leaned in to make her point, flashing an even bigger smile. "Did you really? How about that! Well, I don't think Broadway will see me back anytime soon. No siree. Time for a fresh start here in good old Paree!"

Josephine's American career had stalled months ago over one thing she couldn't change—her complexion. Black was not welcomed on Broadway. Nothing new for Josephine. She'd heard it all her life—"White children, over here, black ones, over there." Even the great black athlete Jessie Owens endured inferior accommodations, traveling with his white track team. The demeaning power of one sign with two words—whites only.

"Miss Baker, a smile?" Josephine paused and smiled for the photographer.

Emma continued. "Miss Baker, may I introduce myself? I'm Emma Bernstein."

"Yes, Mrs. Bernstein. I've heard of you and your splendid soirées," Josephine responded, shaking Emma's hand.

Emma beamed at this acknowledgement and presented her calling card to Josephine. "Please consider this an invitation to join us soon to a welcome-to-Paris gathering at my home. Call me at this number and we will arrange everything."

The invitation delighted Josephine. She knew it was a golden ticket for an introduction to the best and brightest in the cultural life of Paris.

"How kind of you, Mrs. Bernstein. I will be gratified to give you a call."

Josephine turned to continue greeting other fans, pausing occasionally to answer a reporter. Just before stepping into a taxi, she turned, blew a kiss to the fans, and waved a final goodbye.

***

The crowds streamed out, emptying the depot. No one noticed the man casually leaning against the wall in a corner with his head tipped forward and a fedora slipped down, hiding his face. The cinder of his cigarette glowed with his last puff. He pulled it from his mouth and flicked it into a receptacle. Reaching in his right pocket, he pulled out a small notepad and pencil and wrote a few lines. Just the information his superiors needed.

CHAPTER 11

Music, Music, Music

Home of AJ and Grace Meyer, Irvine, California, 2022

Grace's classes started at 11:00 a.m. on Mondays, giving her some extra "me" time for her morning cup of tea and her devotions. Psalm 84 touched her soul on so many levels. The first few words, "How lovely is your dwelling place," lifted her spirit, the same way her eyes had lifted heavenward walking into Notre Dame Cathedral. Passing through the western-facade doors into the cathedral's majestic space, the vaulted ceiling drew her entire being upward, to the pinnacle of pure, sunlit colored windows to heaven. "My soul longs, yes, faints for the courts of the Lord."

Who would want to be anywhere else?

The artist in Grace found the Creator's beauty in places many others couldn't, and when that beauty led her into God's presence, she treasured the peace that passes understanding. Oh, to be like the mother sparrow, nesting her young in the very courts of the Lord. She clung to this incomprehensible peace, even knowing she would never nest her own young with AJ.

She finished sipping, reading, and praying. Dressed for the day, she grabbed her backpack and keys and headed to the car.

Grace zoned into auto-pilot mode, driving to work, still consumed by the evidence of twelve Picasso drawings she and AJ found in a box of random mementos from his grandfather. The discovery of a set of Picassos could rock the art world. And to assist in such a discovery wouldn't hurt her career, either.

Classical music from KUSC streamed through her car speakers, a relaxing piece by Edward Grieg. She mulled over the discoveries made through the years of art confiscated by the Nazis, found in barns, attics, storerooms, and private collections. She'd checked the online databases of missing art, but found nothing similar to the description of the twelve Picasso drawings in the photograph from AJ's grandfather.

A van advertising edible arrangements passed her on the right. *I should send one to AJ's work as a surprise.* She smiled.

Morning sun streamed through the eucalyptus trees lining the driveway to the Lines College faculty parking lot. Grace parked in her reserved spot and headed to the faculty lounge. Her mission today—find the meaning of the disjointed notes on the sheet of music from Grandy's box. Her photocopy showed only two lines of notes. Best not to reveal the reference to the Bernsteins or Stravinsky. She needed a premise for asking Burt about the music that wouldn't raise any suspicions. Perhaps claiming the sheet fell out of a book of piano music she retrieved from her small library. Or a book handed down from her father, of piano compositions by modern composers. Sounded plausible.

Walking down the hall to the lounge, she paused to read a new notice on the employee bulletin board: Reminder. Copy machines are for school purposes only. No personal copies allowed.

Really?

She continued into the lounge.

Fred and Burt, on their usual overlapping breaks, sat around the square coffee table to de-stress from their prior classes. Grace joined them, setting her backpack on the floor and plopping into one of the easy chairs facing the coffee table. She drank her tea from a travel mug, observing Fred and Burt.

Fred slouched in his chair and gazed off into the distance, sipping on his favorite bottled water. Burt skimmed through a professional music journal. Neither appeared very talkative. Grace took the lead.

"Hey, guys. What did you think about the memo from the administration? Kind of crazy, huh?"

Fred finished a sip. "They're getting stingy. No copies for personal use. You won't catch me doing that."

Burt looked up from his journal. "Somebody must be taking advantage of it."

Fred smirked. "Just don't get caught."

Grace retrieved the page of music from her backpack. Obviously a copy.

"What's that, Grace?" Burt said.

"A copy I made at home. Don't report me, guys."

"That's not why I'm asking. I'm not a snitch. Is it music?" Burt asked, looking at the page in her hand.

Grace stuck to her plan. "Yeah, I pulled out a piano book I haven't used in a long time and this fell out. Dad gave me the book, so perhaps he slipped it in."

Burt reached for it. "Can I take a look?"

She handed him the sheet. "That's why I brought it in. I thought you could make some sense of it. Seems kind of odd. Only two lines of notes."

Burt studied the music. "The first line of music is twelve notes. It begins with E flat and each note after is a half-step above the previous. The line contains all twelve chromatic notes of the musical scale. There's a notation above the second line of notes." Burt pointed. "It's French. Can you translate it, Grace?"

Grace rose from her seat, moved behind Burt's chair, and leaned over. Her eyes widened. She wasn't struggling to translate the French. She feared she had accidentally copied something she shouldn't reveal.

"*Rangée.* I think that's row," Grace said.

"Row one. I'd say this is the beginning of a composition someone planned to write in the twelve-tone technique." Burt waved his hand in the air, signaling success.

Fred sat up. "Can you explain for us non-musicians?"

Burt launched into lecture mode. "This style of composition appeared in the early twentieth century. Composers like Schoenberg, Berg, and Stockhausen wrote pieces with this technique. Even the great Igor Stravinsky wrote some."

The mention of Stravinsky grabbed Grace's attention. *Stravinsky really could have composed this music. After all, his signature appeared on the top of the page from Grandy's box.*

"Let me see." Fred reached out and took the sheet from Burt. "Not much of a composition." Fred handed the sheet back to Burt.

Burt raised his index finger. "Stick with me. In a twelve-tone composition, the composer arranges the twelve notes of the musical scale in a random order, creating what is called a prime row. Then, he creates three variation rows: backwards, inverted, and backwards and inverted."

Grace tilted her head. "Seems more mathematical than musical. Can you shed some light on this composition?"

Burt studied the music again. "This composer started, but didn't write much more." He pointed at the music. "It's likely he wrote the first line of notes down as a reference for the twelve chromatic notes he planned to use. He labeled the second line of notes as row one. Maybe that's his prime row."

Fred asked, "What about the brackets beneath the second line? Mean something?"

Grace panicked. *Oh no.* More secretive information she forgot to omit.

Burt furrowed his brow. "Well, putting brackets under notes is not typical of this style of composition. Here's two more French words. Grace?"

Grace hesitated. *Should I answer honestly? Would it give away something important?* "I think the words are *lot* and *key*."

Burt responded. "The composer labeled two groups of notes, not a usual practice. For them to mean anything, we need to assign numbers under each note of the scale in the first line. May I write on this, Grace?"

"Sure."

Burt wrote the numbers one through twelve under the first line of notes. "On this second line of notes, the composer used the word lot to group the first four notes. Using the numbers assigned from the first line of notes, these notes translate to twelve, four, five, and three. Then he used the word key to label the rest of the notes. They translate to six, four, seven, ten, nine, one, eight, and two. He used all twelve numbers of a twelve-tone scale from the first line. There you have it."

Grace tuned out after hearing the numbers twelve, four, five, three. Those numbers appeared in the letter to AJ's grandfather from the IBM Nazis with the same label, lot. *Was this a coincidence? How would Stravinsky have the lot number? And the label: key. Did Igor find the key to the computer tape referenced in the letter?* Her heart pounded faster and faster. She stepped back, put her hands on her hips, took a deep breath, and blew it out to regain composure.

"You okay, Grace?" Fred said.

Grace forced a smile. "Yes, fine." She turned to Burt. "So Burt, you don't know what lot and key mean?"

"Nope. Composers didn't bracket off groups of notes this way. Perhaps he, or she, grouped the notes to plan the composition."

"Interesting," Grace muttered, her thoughts still racing. *Lot and key. Same as in the Nazi IBM letter.*

"Or, some kind of code," Burt said.

Grace's anxiety jumped up a level. *Does he know something?* "Did composers write in codes?"

Burt set the music on the table and leaned back in his chair. "Sure. Bach is the most famous for doing this. He spelled his name in various compositions."

Fred narrowed his eyes. "But the musical scale doesn't have an H."

Burt grinned and pointed with his right index finger. "Not in English. But in German, B natural is the equivalent of the English H. Another composer, Brahms, included the name of his true love in a composition. 'Agatha.' He took way too many liberties to make that spelling work."

Fred leaned in. "Did any composer hide clues of any significance? Like the location of hidden treasure?"

Why is he so curious?

"Nope. Nada. Except ..." Burt left them hanging.

"What?" Grace and Fred said in unison.

"In a riveting thriller novel." Burt waved his hand. "The idea is pure fiction."

Grace picked up the music and stared at it. "So, I guess this music doesn't mean much."

Burt picked up his journal. "Sorry, that's all I've got. Seems the composer started something he didn't finish."

But Grace would pursue it, that's for sure. She put the music in her backpack and picked up her travel mug for another sip, her thoughts traveling a million miles an hour. *Did I find the key to the Nazi tape?* She couldn't wait to tell AJ about this. But first, time to give a lecture on early French impressionism.

Scan or tap the QR code to read Burt's blogpost about twelve-tone music.

Chapter 12

The Gap

Paris, 1937

Jacques Ponge began serving as a French intelligence officer in 1935. Within two years, he had developed an underground network for France's *Deuxième Bureau,* the Second Bureau. Thanks to his covert missions in Germany, he'd peeled back a foreboding veil and exposed valuable strategic counterintelligence focusing on Germany's post-war military aggression. Many personal assets qualified him for his undercover work. The strongest: his physique, with its husky, muscular, thirty-five-year-old frame, dark hair, and scarred forehead. Unfortunately, after multiple forays into Germany, his distinct appearance had drawn unwanted attention and too many second glances from uniformed Nazis on the streets of Berlin. His other agents continued without him, but having blown his cover, he needed to fill this unique gap.

Jacques sat at a wobbly table across from Ernest Hemingway in the dimly lit watering hole where he had pursued Hemingway two months earlier. After several rounds that night, Jacques had wooed Hemingway to assist in his efforts for the Second Bureau. Tonight, Jacques planned to pick Hemingway's brain on one issue—filling the gap. Jacque's right-hand man, Denis, joined him for tonight's rendezvous. Six empty glasses sat on the table and sultry tunes from an accordion-clarinet duo in the back of the bar slogged through the stale haze of cigarette smoke.

Jacques took a drag from his cigarette, then made a slashing gesture with the flick of his wrist. "There's no question Germany is violating the Treaty of Versailles. I've seen it all. The size of the navy, their tank and weapons production, the number of troops, but especially their air force."

Hemingway swirled the ice around in his glass of bourbon with one hand and held a half-spent cigar with the other. "It's worse in Spain. I can guarantee the krauts have plenty of planes there, even troops." He drew a puff of his cigar. "I've seen them." He exhaled. "I've even talked to those dirty bastards."

Working as a war correspondent in Spain, Hemingway provided firsthand dispatches of the Spanish Civil War for the North American Newspaper Alliance, NANA. He had invaluable information for the Second Bureau about Germany's latest weaponry.

Hemingway downed his drink, turned to the bar, and signaled for another round.

Jacques tapped his fingers on his glass and leaned toward Hemingway. "We've learned from some of our agents in Germany that the Reich has set up several covert operations and front companies. Finances for rearmament are running through a company called *Metallurgische Forschungsgesellschaft*, MEFO, a Society for Metallurgical Research. It appears to be a private company, but we have identified the Nazis who sit on the board of directors."

Denis leaned his head back, downed his shot, and slammed the glass on the table. "The French are exhausted from war." He gestured to the fellow patrons. "Look around. What do you see? One-armed drinkers, trying to forget."

Jacques stared at Hemingway. "We filled a million graves after the last war."

"One with my father's name, from battle," Denis said. "Another with my mother's name, for nursing those coming from battle, leaving an angry, unwanted boy at his aunt's house. If another war erupts with Germany, we'd be out armed two to one."

Jacques drew in another cigarette puff. "Article 98 of the treaty prohibits Germany from having an Air Force, yet they are using glider clubs as covers for training pilots."

"Well, they've done a damn good job at it," Hemingway said, attacking his next bourbon. "I've seen their dive-bombing techniques in Spain. Spot on their targets. You should see how they massacred Guernica. Complete demolition."

The bar tender delivered another round to the table. Jacques grabbed his drink and took a generous gulp. The soothing bourbon nectar flowed down, passing the burning frustration with the powers-that-be rising from his belly, bursting out like a geyser. "The Germans brazenly reoccupied the Rhineland on our border last year and our leaders did nothing." He pounded the table. "Nothing. We cannot trust them to protect us!"

Denis leaned in. "The French want peace and they think they'll get it by appeasing Germany. Last year's movement of Nazi troops to the border dimmed any hope of a continued peace."

Jacques picked up his cigarette. "Our picture of what is happening in Berlin is," he circled his hand in the air, "blurry." He turned to Hemingway. "To bring it into focus, we need additional agents to infiltrate deeper into the leadership of the Reich, at a personal level." He shrugged his shoulders and raised his arms. "But we don't have anyone suitable for the task."

Hemingway rubbed his chin. "I might have a humdinger of an idea. Are you aware of the arrival of one Josephine Baker?"

Jacques looked at Denis, then back to Hemingway. "Yes. As a matter of fact, we are. Why do you suggest her?"

"Well, she's outgoing, charismatic, flirtatious, and very easy on the eyes. And dare I say, seductive! I think she can help you out."

Denis turned to Jacques. "But do we know enough about Miss Baker?" He looked at Hemingway. "Can we trust her?"

"Trust. That's kind of an act of faith, ain't it?" Hemingway said. "This Yankee has a damn good sense of who to trust after what I've seen and experienced. As for

Josephine, she's a freedom fighter all right. She's had to fight hard for the freedom she has. She even left her home behind to find it."

The reporter in Hemingway approached life with a healthy dose of skepticism, always digging to get to the raw root of a story, and looking for the answers to who, what, where, when, and why.

"I've followed Josephine's story long enough to know she stands for the cause of freedom from unjust tyranny. She's struggled for her own freedom from the time she was a little girl, watching in horror the glow of Negro homes burning to the ground. That experience burned a drive for freedom into her soul."

Hemingway paused for a drink. "She's done a lot of traveling to perform in various countries. I'd say she's a shoe-in to perform in Germany, chum it up with some of those Krauts, and weasel out of them whatever she can. Have you seen her banana dance? Quite a costume. Twelve bananas hanging from her belt and very little on her top half. That'll drive them Krauts crazy! She'll have them eating out of her hand. Douse them with enough bourbon or whiskey, and their lips will be looser than a greased pig."

Jacques leaned back and folded his arms. "Do you think she will do this?"

"Tell you what," Hemingway said. "Let's start with an introduction and then set up a private conversation to lay it all out. I can't speak for her, but I'd bet my next bottle of bourbon she'll be more than happy to help bust them Krauts. I'll set up some kind of a social gathering with the Bernsteins. Emma is always looking for a reason to play hostess."

Jacques exchanged glances with Denis. He wanted Josephine to be the answer, but needed more reassurance.

"Get back to us when you have the date," Jacques said.

"Right, gents." Hemingway wobbled up from his chair and held onto the table to keep the room from spinning. "That's it for me tonight. Till next time." He gave a sloppy salute and took his time dawdling to the door, leaving behind a trail of cigar smoke and two patriots.

A melancholic tune from the musicians in the back floated by, an ethereal accompaniment to Jacques's thoughts.

Was this the right person to fill the gap?

The table had room for another round of drinks.

"Waiter."

Maybe the next bourbon would come with the answers he wanted.

Scan or tap the QR code to read Fred's blogpost about the attack on Guernica.

CHAPTER 13

About The Music

Lines College, Irvine, California, 2022

GRACE CLICKED ON THE next PowerPoint slide. She looked at her watch for the umpteenth time.

Ten more glacier moving minutes of lecture before I can leave and tell AJ what I discovered.

"Here you see *Impression, Sunrise,* painted by Monet in 1872. Often regarded as the inaugural Impressionism painting."

Words describing French Impressionism flowed automatically out of her mouth. But her mind continued mulling over the codes Burt had discovered in the mysterious sheet of music.

Is there a possible link between the Stravinsky music and the Nazi letter?

Click.

"In this closeup of the sun's reflection, you can see peach-like colored strokes with small ribbons of white. Monet achieved this by filling his brush with the peach color first and then passing it through white before pressing the brush against the canvas."

Were the words lot and key common terms in 1937? Why would Nazis and musicians both have used them?

Click.

Finally.

"Here are the dates for your term paper assignment. Don't forget, proposals are due next week. Have a good afternoon."

Racing home from work, Grace nearly ran a red light. She jerked to a stop in the driveway next to AJ's car, scooped up her backpack, and jolted for the door.

He's gonna love what I discovered.

Grace burst through the front door. AJ rushed out of his office and stared at her. "You okay?"

She smiled. "Wait till I show you what I found out."

AJ raised his hands. "About…?"

"The key." She opened her backpack and shuffled through the contents. "It's in the music. Burt found it." She pulled the copy of music out and unfolded it. "You gotta look at this. It's amazing."

She held the copy and pointed. "See, right there."

"But how…"

"Let's go sit in the living room and I'll explain everything."

They ended up on the couch with glasses of wine.

"Now, tell me what happened," AJ said.

Grace set her wineglass on the coffee table, next to the box of Grandy's bizarre mementos. "I showed the copy of the Stravinsky music to Burt and got excellent intel."

AJ grinned. "Intel? Listen to you, little miss secret agent."

She reached for the IBM letter in the Grandy box. "Look, here in the letter." She pointed. "The terms *lot* and *key*? They are in the music, too."

"Yes, we already knew that. So?"

"So, Burt filled in some important data." She loved using jargon like "data" from AJ's tech world.

"Burt explained the notes on the sheet. It's called twelve tone music, a composition technique used in the early twentieth century. And guess who composed music in this style?"

AJ shrugged his shoulders.

Grace beamed. "Stravinsky! He composed several twelve-tone pieces."

"So...."

"Here's the best part. This composition technique incorporates a unique numbering system."

She held the copy of music. "Burt translated the two groups of notes into numbers. Notice anything interesting?"

"Twelve, four, five, and three. Those are the lot numbers in the IBM letter." He stared straight at Grace. "Grace, this is amazing."

"Wait. There's more."

"Can't wait."

"Remember what the letter said about a separate communication?"

"The key."

"We know the word *key* is under the bracketed notes. Now we know the key numbers. They're right here. It's the key, AJ. We have the key!"

AJ took Grace's face in his hands and kissed her. "Grace, you're amazing." He looked at the music again. "Why would Stravinsky have the lot and the key to an IBM tape from the Nazis? Isn't this a little far-fetched?"

Grace took a sip of wine. "You mean more far-fetched than Nazis having IBM technology in the first place? How did that happen?"

"Did other composers put codes in their music?"

"I asked Burt. He offered a few examples of Bach and Brahms slipping names in their music."

"What about clues in art, Miss Professor? Did Picasso leave any?"

Grace picked up her copy of *History of Art* from the table. "Picasso put symbols in his paintings." She flipped through the pages and found the section on Picasso. "This is one of his most famous paintings, *Guernica*." She slid the book over to AJ.

"This is so … grotesque, even for Picasso. The terror in their faces. Like a brutal nightmare in a hundred shades of gray. Is this supposed to represent an actual event?"

"It's Picasso's startling interpretation of a savage attack by the Nazis on a village in Spain during the Spanish Revolution. Picasso put all kinds of symbolism in it but no clues, per se."

AJ closed the book and put it on the table. The living room smart plugs clicked and two table lamps turned on. "Does Burt suspect anything?"

"Don't think so. You know Burt. He got caught up in the academics of explaining music theory. But…." Grace looked down.

"What?"

Grace shook her head. "It's probably nothing."

"Tell me."

"It's just, Fred seemed interested in secret codes."

AJ took a sip of wine. "Why do you say that?"

"He asked if composers hid clues in their music about hidden treasure."

AJ set his wine down, folded his arms, and tilted his head. "Maybe a logical question, given the conversation?"

Grace pulled her knees up and rested her chin on them. "Yeah. Could have been."

AJ rubbed her back. "Kind of surreal, having the key to the Nazi tape. Wonder what's on it?"

"Gotta find it, first."

"True."

Grace leaned back and caressed his arm.

Time to ask the question.

"What about Grandy? Thought any more about where to learn about his IBM connection?"

Did he fear what he might find? A truth as dark and disturbing as the Guernica painting? Is that why he'd dragged his feet so far?

AJ lowered his head, took a breath, and turned to Grace. "Guess it's time to start on that, huh?"

She took his hand. "If you think you're ready. Where will you start?"

AJ propped his feet on the coffee table. "IBM is big on documentation. Chances are I'll find some archives to search through. I've got a connection at the IBM branch in Los Angeles. I'll start there since it's in our backyard."

"Can you work it into your schedule?"

He turned and grinned. "Have you forgotten who the boss is, dear? That's not a problem."

"Of course, boss. And a wonderful boss you are." Grace pulled his arm around her. "I hope your staff appreciates you."

"Not as much as you." He stroked her hand.

"Well, if anyone can solve the IBM mystery, it's you."

AJ kissed the top of Grace's head. "Thank you, Agent Grace."

Grace knew AJ still felt the sting from the initial shock of discovering his grandfather's potential involvement with the Nazis, a startling version of Grandy that didn't jibe with what everyone thought they knew about him. AJ needed answers.

We have the lot and key numbers. Where is that Nazi tape? What about Grandy? Can AJ handle the truth when he finds it?

Her morning devotion floated into her thoughts. "Blessed are those who dwell in your house, ever singing your praise."

Lord, wherever you are taking us, we will praise you.

Scan or tap the QR code to read Grace's blogpost about *Guernica* by Pablo Picasso.

CHAPTER 14

Lunch

Bernstein Residence, Paris, 1937

THE GEARS STARTED TURNING in Emma's head the day Josephine arrived in Paris. Emma adored planning special occasions, and what could be more special than an intimate gathering for her friends to meet Josephine?

Josephine became the talk of the town after her rave-reviewed premier performance at the *Folies Bergère.* She packed the house on her opening night with an audience of the social elite that included Dottie and the Bernsteins. Tuxedoed men escorting ladies wearing the finest Paris *haute couture* packed the room. Diamonds sparkled, champagne flowed, and the tinkling of glasses accompanied the greetings of, "Oh darling, you look marvelous. So good to see you."

Joyous sounds from the orchestra's snappy overture called everyone to their seat. The audience continued muttering, adding a layer of meaningless lyrics. The room lights dimmed. The crack and roll of a snare drum filled the air, timed with a spotlight hitting the stage. The crowd erupted with energetic applause and wide-eyed smiles, anticipating Josephine's entrance. Josephine walked out. Everyone jumped to their feet, whistling and whooping.

She instantly captured the audience with her larger-than-life ruby smile and slicked down spit curls. But it was the costume. Oh, what a costume. Groundbreaking, even for Paris. Twelve plastic banana peels hung from a belt around her waist, covering little more than the briefest of underwear. A necklace with multiple strings of oversized pearls, draped to below her breasts, the latter barely covered by a small, golden bra. The band began playing, she began singing, and her hips began swaying with her arms waving wildly in the air, and the occasional, seductive poke of her backside toward the audience. Song after song, the evening flew by, climaxing with her "Danse Sauvage" beckoning the audience to a lively conga line that snaked through the entire room, knocking over empty seats.

Two encores later, the audience left the theater, exhilarated and exhausted from the remarkable evening, and returned to their homes to find that tomorrow had arrived before them.

Emma organized a brunch for today's special event, giving Josephine the chance to sleep in before coming and also relax, prior to her evening show. Emma had spread the table with a menu perfect for the occasion. The multi-tiered serving stands presented fresh fruit and tea sandwiches adorned with fresh-cut flowers. Her *French Toile* china complemented the zingy yellow tablecloth. Tea service sat on the table next to the food. Everything artfully prepared for a relaxing buffet.

Once they arrived, Emma's guests enjoyed their preferred drinks from the bar, chatted, and awaited Josephine's arrival. The doorbell rang. Chattering ceased. Emma opened the door. Josephine's larger-than-life ruby smile announced her arrival, triggering a round of applause that rippled through the room. Josephine acknowledged the welcome with, "Y'all are too kind! Thank you. Thank you!" bowing her head as she greeted each guest.

Josephine graced her way through the "nice-to-meet-you" line, found a drink at the end, settled in one of the chair clusters, and started chatting with Emma and Dottie.

"We loved, just absolutely loved your show, Josephine," Emma said. "It's been a long time since I've had such an exhilarating night in Paris."

Josephine grinned and placed her hand on Emma's. "Then I guess Paris needs a little shaking up, right?"

Dottie leaned in. "And your costume. Amazing. Tell me, do you have trouble keeping it on? It looks so ... so delicate, shall we say?"

"A girl can't share all her secrets now, can she? I learned some costume tricks in my short, and I mean short, career on Broadway," Josephine laughed. "I don't mind saying, I'm famished. Mind if I grab some of what's on that beautiful table?"

Emma, embarrassed, answered, "Oh, of course, darling. How rude of me not to offer." Emma and Dottie accompanied Josephine to the refreshments.

Hemingway, with whiskey in hand, observed the guests from the side of the room. He'd lived in Paris long enough to know how to schmooze with any social class, but he always took his time before engaging. Jacques Ponges stood next to him, watching Josephine's every move.

Ernest turned toward Jacques and muttered, "I saw her show, Jacques. She is going to drive those krauts out of their everlasting minds. After she distracts and bamboozles them, it will be a cakewalk for her to extract the information we need from them."

"I can see her confidence in how she handles herself," Jacques said. "A polished act. Maybe she's doing an act right now for the Bernsteins."

Ernest sipped his drink. "If she is, it's a damn good one, don't you think?"

The two men waited for Emma, Dottie, and Josephine to finish eating before they approached the ladies.

Emma looked up. "Gentlemen. So glad you made it." She turned to Josephine. "Josephine, may I introduce Mr. Ernest Hemingway and a new friend who's come with him? Jacques, oh, please forgive me. I don't think I remember your last name."

"Jacques Ponges, madame," he said.

"Any friend of Ernest is welcome here, Jacques," Emma said. "If you will excuse us, Dottie and I need to greet some other guests. Josephine, I know I'm leaving you in good company." Dottie and Emma moved on to greet other friends.

Josephine gestured to the chairs, inviting the men to sit. "Nice to have another yank here, Mr. Hemingway. Do you write for the newspapers? Seems I've read some war correspondence by you, am I right?"

Ernest raised his eyebrows. "Why yes. Spent some time in Spain. Glad I'm here now, though."

"Nasty thing, war," Josephine shook her head. "Something America bull-dozed into my world, you might say. Just because of skin color. Isn't that a strange reason for a war? Certainly a sad reason to leave one's home." A smile returned. "But I'm glad I'm here now." She turned to Jacques. "What about you, Jacques?"

Jacques exchanged glances with Hemingway. "Let's just say I'm a patriot, a watchman."

"And what are you watching over?" Josephine said.

Jacques straightened up. "France and her sovereignty, Miss Baker."

"A noble cause," Josephine said.

Ernest leaned forward. "Am I correct in understanding you've done some performing in Germany, Miss Baker?"

"Why yes. Berlin, to be exact. Lot of those German Nazis come to my shows. Boy, can they drink! Kind of got out of hand a few times. Fortunate for me, the music hall managers watch out for their performers."

Ernest grinned. "I'd dare say you're the type who can take care of herself in those situations."

Josephine sat back. "You could say that. Don't mean to brag, but I've decked a few in my time."

The trio chuckled.

Ernest pulled a cigar from his pocket and lit it. He took a draw and continued. "Miss Baker, your love for freedom is evident in your decision to leave America for your own freedom. Jacques and I have a proposition we'd like to discuss with you, about freedom. But I think it calls for a private setting. Would you join us for a drink and a brief discussion about our proposal?"

Josephine made a crooked smile. "Why, Mr. Hemingway, you intrigue me." She threw both arms into the air. "Why not. If I'm anything, it's a woman of adventure. But let me make a polite goodbye to Emma and Dottie first. You go on ahead. After I grab my things, I'll join you outside." Josephine headed off to find Emma and Dottie.

Ernest looked at Jacques. "I told you she's got the stuff we need. Let's go."

***

Josephine met Ernest and Jacques outside and walked with them to a nearby cafe. She looked at her watch. Early enough to spend time with them and still rest up before tonight's performance.

The three sat around a table in the corner, ordered, and received their coffee. Ernest and Jacques explained the who, what, where, why, and when of their proposal.

Josephine leaned in, absorbing every detail. The two men finished. She sipped her coffee, leaned back, crossed her legs, folded her arms, looked at Ernest, and then at Jacques. She nodded. "Count me in."

This could be my role of a lifetime.

Scan or tap the QR code to read Grace's blogpost about Josephine Baker's Famous Dance.

CHAPTER 15

IBM Assignment

IBM Headquarters, Los Angeles, California, 2022

SOMETIMES, IMAGINING THE WORST possible outcome debilitates a person more than finding and facing the reality of an uncomfortable truth. For the last two weeks, AJ's imagination had shoved him down a slippery spiral, descending toward two dark tunnels of worst-case scenarios—what Grandy did for IBM and what IBM did for the Nazis. Darkness leading to two darker shades of dark. Grace's recent nudging had lit a torch, helping lead AJ back to the safety of a reasoned and analytical approach.

Emotionally, he wanted to cling to his pre-box version of Grandy. Intellectually, he knew he'd procrastinated long enough and needed to find the truth, uncomfortable or not. The best person to help him now—Merritt Nelson, head of IBM's Los Angeles branch.

AJ pulled out of the driveway and tapped the AM button. "Traffic on the 5 freeway is lighter than normal for your Monday mid-morning commute."

Cars zoomed by on both sides at acceptable, over-the-limit speeds.

"Watch out for minor slowing near the Long Beach freeway interchange. Otherwise, traffic into downtown is a breeze. This is Chopper Dave with your traffic update on the tens of each hour."

With confirmation of an easy commute ahead, AJ sat back, ticking through the list of items to discuss with Merritt.

He entered the underground IBM parking garage and pulled into the spot reserved for Merritt's guests, next to the elevator. The ten-floor trip delivered him to the reception area with its sleek, white reception desk, potted scheffleras, and walls peppered with modern art in coordinated colors. Video screens behind the desk displayed the traditional IBM logo, unchanged since 1972, alternating with the THINK campaign logo.

"Good morning, Mr. Meyer." Brenda smiled. "Nice to see you again. Mr. Nelson is waiting for you in his office. Go right in."

"Thanks, Brenda."

AJ entered Merritt's office, bright and airy, with potted plants in a variety of sizes and shades, complementing the sage green tufted rug in the center of the room. Further in, Merritt's glass desktop floated on four massive rough-hewed wooden posts. Behind the desk, a floor-to-ceiling window offered a clean-air-quality view of the Hollywood sign on the distant hills.

Merritt approached AJ with his trademark grin and welcoming handshake. "Hey, man. Good to see you. Coffee? Dark roast, just the way you like it."

"Great memory. Hit me with a cup." AJ placed his backpack on the floor next to the oval coffee table and sat. Merritt delivered two mugs, steaming with a rich aroma, set them on the table, and sat across from AJ.

"I haven't seen you since our roundtable discussion on network security last year," Merritt said. "You contributed some significant insights."

"I walked away with some, too."

The coffee mugs rattled on the glass tabletop. AJ raised his eyebrows.

"Just a minor tremor," Merritt said. "We get them so often we just ignore them. Besides, our building is on foundation rollers to cushion the impact."

AJ understood this, but he still woke from nightmares reminding him of the 1994 Northridge quake. Twenty seconds of terror for a ten-year-old.

"You've come a long way since sitting in my grad classes. Not surprising," Merritt said.

Only seven years and a few IQ points separated AJ and Merritt. They enjoyed a mutual admiration, transcending the teacher-student connection.

AJ gestured toward Merritt with his mug. "Thanks to a superb instructor." He took a sip. "Of course, I have to give credit to God, too. He's the one who gave me this crazy brain."

"Amen to that." Merritt turned and gazed at a framed picture of the giant California redwoods, captioned with the words, How lovely is your dwelling place, Oh Lord. "Easy to forget sometimes." He picked up his mug and sipped. "You didn't say much on your call about the reason for your visit. What's up?"

"Kind of on a personal journey," AJ said. "My mom gave me a box of things my grandfather left behind. Turns out he worked for IBM back in the day."

"No kidding. I thought he was a pastor." Merritt set his mug down.

"He was, part time."

Merritt leaned back, folded his arms, and raised eyebrows. "Interesting. Two generations of techie Meyers boys. Did your dad belong to the club?"

"Nope. He followed a different path."

That path included the summer of love, 1967, in San Francisco, and all the undelivered promises of the hippie lifestyle. By God's grace, members of the Jesus Movement from Southern California befriended him and walked with him on a path of redemption, ultimately leading him to the pastorate.

"I know IBM is meticulous about keeping documentation," AJ said. "If they have Grandy's, I mean, my grandfather's employment records, I need to find them."

Merritt smiled. "That's what you called him? Grandy? He must have been special, with a nickname like that. Do you know where he worked for IBM?"

"I have a letter addressed to him with a return address in New York, 590 Madison Avenue."

"That's where good old Thomas Watson worked. Mr. Think, himself. I wonder if your granddad worked in his office?"

Yes, wouldn't that have been something?

"Let me make a few calls and see if I can point you in the right direction."

"Perfect. I appreciate the help." AJ finished the last sip of his coffee.

"Besides, sounds fun to go digging through IBM's history," Merritt said. "Who knows what will turn up?"

That's what terrifies me.

"Fantastic," AJ said, setting his mug on the table. "What's happening around here these days?"

"Oh, the usual. Keeping up with the latest and greatest cyber criminals and what they're commandeering in the financial sectors."

"The world needs you, Merritt Nelson. Keep that cape on." AJ stood, grabbed his backpack, and slung it over his shoulder. "I should let you get back to rounding up the bad guys. Thanks for your time and the help."

"I've got a little free time this morning to start digging."

Don't dig too deep.

Thinking about his next steps on the drive home, a radio news bulletin blasted through. "The US Geological Survey is now reporting that this morning's tremor registered three on the Richter scale, centered near Ojai. We'll keep you updated with any further developments."

Earthquakes. So unpredictable. AJ hated unpredictable events.

He beat the traffic crunch on his drive back to Irvine, but he wondered what crunches waited further along his journey to finding the truth.

Scan or tap the QR code to read AJ's blogpost about security.

CHAPTER 16

Reporting to ERR

ERR Offices, Berlin, 1937

Bruno Lohse's time in Paris had delivered more than he'd hoped for on a first mission. He returned to Berlin with the smug confidence of a general returning from a victorious military campaign. Zero casualties and a generous measure of spoils. He had significant progress to include in his report to Alfred Rosenberg today at the ERR. The most important item in the report: a network of art suppliers throughout Paris with arsenals of art perfect for filling the Führermuseum. His shrewd recruitment of Dottie had yielded a profitable relationship with the Bernsteins, his doorway to a network he planned to target on future campaigns.

Before leaving Paris, he'd made choices of what to report to the ERR and what to whisk away secretly. He had catalogued the latter in his personal diary.

He'll never know these even exist.

Sitting in Rosenberg's waiting room, Lohse checked his Rolex. Five minutes until his nine o'clock appointment. The Nazis worshipped punctuality. Better for him to wait for Rosenberg than Rosenberg wait for him. Lohse once witnessed the tardy arrival of a subordinate. It didn't end well.

Five minutes past nine, Rosenberg's secretary answered the intercom. "Herr Rosenberg will see you now."

Lohse stood and smoothed the jacket of the Nazi uniform he reluctantly wore today. He'd thought it best not to dress as a civilian for this meeting.

No need to leave any doubts about my allegiance.

"Heil Hitler!" Lohse saluted upon entering.

Rosenberg returned the salute. Steam rose from his morning coffee and smoke drifted like a thin, twisted thread from the cigarette on his desk.

"Coffee?"

"Not necessary, Herr Rosenberg."

"Have a seat. I understand you have news from Paris."

"Yes. I've established a good foothold. I am now accepted in some of the most prestigious art circles in Paris. I've prepared an inventory for a first operation and recommend we commence immediately."

"Very good."

"I've established a connection with an Otto and Emma Bernstein."

"Jewish?"

"Yes."

"Any desirable pieces?"

"Many. I believe the acquisition will be easy. Their home security is pitiful and the view from the street and neighbors is negligible."

"Do you have everything you need for a team?"

"Not much is needed. The men you've allocated will be sufficient."

"I will review this with Göring. But I don't see why we won't move forward. Are you staying in Berlin for a few days?"

Why does Göring need to participate?

"Yes."

"I will give you final instructions before you leave."

"Very good." He stood and gave the obligatory, departing salute. "Heil Hitler!"

"Heil Hitler!"

Lohse left the office, smiling. With no one looking over his shoulder on this operation, he had a free hand in expanding his personal collection and with manpower supplied by the Reich, no less.

Were all the acquisitions going to be this easy?

He headed back to his gallery to meet with his brother. Rather, to conspire with his brother.

***

Lohse entered the gallery he and his brother owned on the trendy Charlottenburger Chaussee in central Berlin. Hans looked up from the desk. "Guten Morgen, Bruno!"

"Guten Morgen. Good news. Come, I'll share in the back office."

Bruno reversed the open sign in the window and locked the door. He followed Hans to the back office and closed that door. Turning to Hans, he paused, took a breath, and smiled. "It's all in place!"

"So soon?"

"Ja, ja!" His voice rose with excitement. "And what magnificent pieces we will soon own. Here's the list."

Hans looked. "All of these?"

"Ja. Maybe more."

"We should celebrate."

"When they are here, we celebrate. Now, we review the plan. Is the basement ready?"

"Yes. And the storage crates are exactly as you designed."

"Good. You should receive the shipment within two weeks."

"Does Rosenberg suspect anything?"

"As long as I supply him suitable quantities for the Führermuseum, there is no problem."

"And there are suitable quantities?"

"More than suitable. More than we could have imagined."

Bruno and Hans finished reviewing their plan before heading to a local cafe for a celebratory lunch. Bruno had learned how to prepare and successfully execute a plan by studying Nazi leadership. He'd also learned how to climb the ranks of the Reich, whether or not he agreed with their ideology. And he didn't. As for many in the Reich, membership served as a means to an end—personal profit and status. He'd found an easy success in achieving both. Everything in his plan continued to proceed perfectly.

Things do until they don't.

Scan or tap the QR code to read Fred's blogpost about Bruno Lohse.

CHAPTER 17

Gala Plans

Albert Becker Art Museum, Irvine, California 2022

With the Picasso drawings finally in hand, Brian Miller put his mind at ease. These deals can be tricky and he hadn't made such an exciting acquisition for the Albert Becker Art Museum in the dozen years he'd been curator. He usually acquired a single piece here and there, and by less notable artists. But now. Six pieces. All by Picasso. Brian took great pride in this accomplishment and decided it deserved a gala celebration.

His team had assembled around the oval walnut table in the conference room. Large posters of previous galas, artist bios, and flyers promoting local art exhibitions covered one wall. Another wall had a cork board with pinned notes from a previous planning session. An electronic whiteboard for high-tech brainstorming hung on a third wall, displaying the six Picasso drawings, subject for today's meeting.

The team included Lyle Bernstein, head of restoration, Suzanne Dupree in charge of PR and social media, and Paul Chin, historian and researcher. They sat around the conference table with their preferred beverages, various file folders, iPads, laptops, and good old paper and pencil.

Brian stood at the head of the table, beaming. "I don't need to tell you this is one of the biggest acquisitions in Becker's history. We are ever so grateful to the grandson of Igor Stravinsky for donating these six magnificent drawings by master Picasso. They deserve the best debut we can give them. Let's imagine it as an opening night on Broadway."

No one missed the New York reference. Brian had come to Orange County from a notable New York gallery. "Let's go around the table and just shout out your ideas."

Suzanne started. "I've found terrific social media material out there to make this sizzle." She distributed some preliminary sketches of her ideas.

Paul followed. "This takes us back to the heyday of Paris. Everyone loves journeying back to that period in history. So romantic."

Brian looked at Lyle. "Lyle, you with us?" Lyle looked up. "Have you got anything?"

"Um, well, they are very well preserved."

"Good. No rips, tears, holes?" Brian said.

"None of that. Whoever had them over the years took good care of them. Or they just sat around a long time."

Brian moved on. "Paul, have you considered where to place the display?"

"The gallery just past the entry hall always works well. The Los Angeles 1950s exhibit is just ending so that space is opening up. That's my suggestion. Yah."

"Of course," Brian said, as if it was an earthshaking idea. "But, that space is a little large. Do you think we can stretch out six pieces to fill it?"

"There's a big story to tell with this exhibit," Paul said. "The friendship between Picasso and Stravinsky, short bios of each of them, historical context of 1930s Paris. Gotta have all of that in there." Paul made no apologies for his love of that era in Paris. The carefree existence romanticized in endless books and movies. The calm before the World War Two storm.

"That's so you, Paul," Suzanne said.

"Can you and Paul coordinate and share content for the display and social media?" Brian said.

"Will do," Suzanne said.

"Here's a crazy, crazy idea. I totally love it." Paul couldn't contain himself. "I think you're gonna love it. Do you all know that there is an earlier Picasso drawing of Stravinsky teachers use in art classes?"

Brian raised his eyebrows. "Really?"

"Oh, Brian, come on," Paul said. "You should totally know this. The teacher flips the drawing upside down and only reveals a small portion at the top. Students draw the first part. Then the teacher shows the next part. The students draw about an inch at a time. When they've finished, they turn their drawing right side up and, *voilà*! They have a Picasso. So, what I'm thinking is, wait for it. Contest!"

"Contest?" they all said in unison.

"Come on." Paul raised his arms in the air. "How many students in this city have taken an art class and drawn this picture? You know, like, at least hundreds over the years. I bet many have kept them."

"Um, you think so?" Brian said.

"I've kept mine. Anyway, you know Grace Meyer in the art department at Lines College, don't you?" Paul said.

"Of course. She and AJ are great supporters of the Becker," Brian said.

"Check with her. I'm sure she'll agree."

"Let's go with that idea for now. Start working on the details of how we leverage it to stir up public interest. Suzanne, you up for that?"

"I love it. The gears are already turning," she said.

"Let's regroup in a week." Brian rubbed his hands together. "I'm warming up to this contest idea. We can have celebrity judges. The winner could cut the ribbon at the opening and..." Brian had entered one of his stream-of-consciousness grooves.

Suzanne broke him off. "We'll get there, Brian. I'll pull some ideas together for next week." She looked at Paul. "Want to help, Mr. Brainstormer extraordinaire?"

"I'm in," Paul said.

Brian smiled. "All right. Good work, people. Keep the juices flowing."

***

Returning to his office, Lyle continued struggling with the scheme that had consumed him during the meeting—stealing the drawings and returning them to the Picasso estate. But having no experience in such a heist, he could only imagine a worse-case scenario—stealing the drawings, being apprehended on his way out of town, surrounded by four police cars with lights blazing, and officers shouting over the sound of screaming sirens, "Lay the pictures on the ground, slowly. Step away, and put your hands up where we can see them."

What if I could remove them without getting caught, would I actually do it?

Did he have the guts to reclaim what he believed rightfully belonged to his family and return them to the Picasso family? After all, the Nazis had stolen them from his grandparents' home. Possession is nine-tenths of the law, isn't it? And the photograph of his grandparents standing in front of them at their home served as provenance, unless other evidence existed, such as a bill of sale. He'd never found one in his research.

What if someone else wanted these drawings?

Whoa. Where did that idea come from?

With one abrupt thought, a single, disturbing thread had mutated into a sticky, unwelcome, tangled web.

Scan or tap the QR code to see the website for Albert Becker Art Museum.

Chapter 18

First Assignment

Starlight Cabaret, Berlin, 1937

Josephine spent several sessions with Jacques and Hemingway, preparing for her first espionage trip to Berlin. Clearly, she was no novice.

"Growing up around white people sharpens your suspicions," she told them. "Heck, if I didn't know how to read a threat and deliver a powerful right hook, I'd never survived back in St. Louis."

With her street smarts combined with their training, Jacques and Hemingway declared her ready for this first mission.

Her goal—an encounter with Hermann Göring to discover potential military plans of aggression toward France. As the second most powerful leader in the Reich, Göring controlled the strategic planning of the most important campaigns, making him a key target for intelligence.

Jacques gave Josephine two important strategies: conversation starters to help Göring loosen his lips and how to leverage a fork in the road during the flow of a conversation.

"Don't you worry. Once I get him talking, I'll know what to do. You should have heard what I got out of Pablo Picasso after a few drinks and a few winks. Quite the womanizer."

On her previous trip to Berlin, Josephine performed to sell-out crowds, one of which included Göring and his friends. Remembering his reactions to that performance, she had no doubts that he'd enjoy an encore. Her banana dance had become the talk of Paris and Jacques made sure news of that performance had spread to Berlin and to Göring. Jacques's team had managed the publicity for tonight's performance and had plastered flyers at locations Göring frequented. Jacques left nothing to chance. Just like the Nazis.

Jacques provided Josephine with a small revolver, a last resort for any dangerous situations during the trip to Berlin. More importantly, he equipped her with a pen loaded with invisible ink. Recording the collected intelligence with invisible ink on sheets of staff paper ensured its safety and provided a plausible cover in the unthinkable event of the authorities stopping and searching her.

Josephine arrived in Berlin after an uneventful trip. Excited admirers greeted her at the station, just as they had in Paris. The warm welcome continued in her hotel suite, filled with dozens of long-stem flowers, a basket of fruit, a box with a variety of chocolates, and a colorful banner draped across the table reading "Welcome to Berlin, Miss Baker."

Resting before her performance, she lounged on the red velvet fainting couch, and reviewed the scenarios Jacques and Hemingway had drilled into her. The chilled champagne helped calm any anxiety that tried to creep in.

At the theater, more flowers greeted her in the private dressing room. She settled in and began her makeup routine. Reaching for the rouge on her table, she saw an envelope addressed to her. She smiled as she opened the card, thinking it might be from a fan of her last Berlin performance. It was. None other than Hermann Göring. She scored the first success of her mission. But reality set in, and Josephine's heart began racing. She took a deep breath and let it out, fending off the initial flash of fear.

If I could conquer those bigots in St. Louis, I can conquer this.
Knock knock. "Five minutes, Miss Baker."

Time for the next step. She gave her face one last touch of rouge, stood and adjusted her banana skirt, opened the door, and made the short walk to the stage entrance.

"Meine Damen und Herren, Miss Josephine Baker!" The band struck up her introduction. She walked from the stage wings into the flood of a spotlight and the roar of the crowd. It didn't take long for Josephine to click into the groove, the way many performers do, letting go and giving herself completely over to her audience. Conscious of her mission, she surveyed the audience as she moved around the stage.

She found him immediately. Not difficult, given he sat at the table closest to the stage and wore one of his flamboyant uniforms. Taking full advantage of the proximity, she seductively moved down to him, around him, caressing his neck, gyrating to the percussive punctuation of the band. At the end of her number, she made one last eye connection just as the band crashed a final chord. She froze in her final pose, locked in a gaze with his eyes. The crowd erupted with whistles and shouts of "encore." She broke her gaze and turned to walk back onto the stage, blowing kisses to thank the crowd for their applause. Exiting to the wings, she gave an alluring look over her left shoulder, followed by a seductive smile. He returned a smile and a wink.

In her dressing room, she collapsed on the couch, took a long drink straight from the bottle of whiskey, and instinctively licked her lips. A knock. *It's time.* She stood, glanced in the mirror, nodded to assure herself, then turned to the door and posed with her best smile. "Come in."

The door opened. "Miss Baker, may I introduce myself? Hermann Göring." She offered her hand, which he gently enveloped with his, and drew it up for a kiss. "I must say, what a thrilling performance you gave tonight! I've thought of your last performance often, but tonight's far exceeded it."

"You are too kind, Herr Göring."

"Please, Hermann." He replied with a smile that kept coming. "We are so fortunate you have returned to Berlin, if only for one night."

"Please. Come in. May I offer you some champagne, Hermann?"

"Of course."

She poured from the bottle chilling in the ice bucket and handed him the glass. "If you will bear with me, I'll just do a quick change while you enjoy your champagne."

He eyed the scant banana skirt as she moved behind her changing screen.

"It's so exciting to be back in Berlin. Such a lovely city. Such progressive attitudes."

"Yes. The Reich has brought many wonderful changes. And many more are on the way."

She returned from behind the screen wearing a loose-fitted, low-necked silk robe that revealed almost as much as her banana skirt. "I think I'll join you." She poured herself a glass and lounged on the fainting bed, pulling up one leg.

"Oh, my manners. Please have a seat, right here." She patted her hand on the foot of the bed. Time to look for a fork in the conversation road.

"Tell me, what is happening with the Reich? Exciting things? I love excitement," she said with a bit of a breath in her voice and emphasis on the word excitement.

"Why bore you with such mundane conversation?"

"Hermann, I find politics very interesting. We are all political, aren't we?"

"Political, yes. But let's discuss something else, such as your performance. How did you create such an amazing dance style?"

"I like to think of my dancing as art. More champagne?" She poured. "Do you like art, Hermann?"

"As a matter of fact, I have quite a collection. I like to think of myself as one who appreciates art." He stared into her eyes.

"Well, I have seen some interesting new art in Paris recently. Have you heard of Pablo Picasso?" Perhaps the mention of Paris could be a fork in the road that led to a discussion about plans regarding France.

"Ah, Paris. I've been many times. I've found some of my favorite pieces there. And, yes, I am familiar with Herr Picasso. Wouldn't mind one of his paintings in my home. That might happen soon."

Time to up the liquor ante.

She poured some bourbon into a glass and handed it to Göring.

"It's getting easier to pick up art in Paris these days. I've even got a plan in progress as we speak." He downed the bourbon. She poured more and kept the bottle handy.

"Do tell, Hermann. What kind of plan are you working on? I'm all ears." She fluttered her eyelids. He downed more bourbon and loosened his collar. She refilled the glass again.

"I have men in Paris as we speak looking for art you can't buy."

"What's the use if you can't buy it?" she asked with as much naïveté as she could muster in her voice.

"Oh, I really shouldn't be telling you this, but—"

She interrupted. "Oh, please go on. I'm sure it's ingenious." She ran her finger behind his ear.

"We've found a private collection in a salon with pieces I've decided I must have."

"This sounds exciting. What are they? I know a little about art."

Göring began describing painting after painting.

This can't be. It's almost the Bernstein's entire collection.

"And imagine a set of twelve portraits by Picasso. A major addition for my home. I will be the envy of all my fellow collectors."

No!

She forced calmness into her voice. "Are you just ... taking them?"

"Those Jews don't deserve them," he snarled. "What do they know about fine art? I'm doing the world a service by moving them to a place where true connoisseurs will appreciate them."

"So, tell me the plan, will you? I'm so intrigued."

Will he spill all the beans?

"It doesn't take much to fool those Jews. My man in Paris knows the night the family will be out of the house. Getting in and out will take no effort. He already knows exactly how he's going to do it."

I've got to warn the Bernsteins. Is there more?

"Any other big plans for Paris?"

"A day will come, perhaps this year or next, when the Führer will rule Paris. Perhaps all of France."

She tried to conceal her shock, listening to this ambitious rant.

"We are already on the border. It won't take much more. The French don't want another war. It will all be very amicable. You'll love it when we get there, my Josephine."

"How could I not?" She continued her charade. "But you don't know when it will happen? I want to be watching for you, mein Herr!"

"And I want to see you upon our arrival. You'll know when it happens. It will all be very peaceful and joining the Reich will make France a better place to live."

Maybe this is what Jacques wanted to confirm. Nothing very specific but a glimpse of the Nazi's plans.

"What a day that will be." She lifted her glass. "To France."

Göring snapped back into a formal posture, almost automatically. "To the Führer! Heil Hitler!"

Her instincts and his slurred speech told her she wouldn't get much more out of Göring.

"And now, Hermann, if you will excuse me, it's been a long day. Time to return to my hotel." She stood to prompt him. He joined her at the door.

"I enjoyed this time with you." He leaned forward and gave her a brief kiss on the cheek. "Good night, Josephine. Perhaps we will meet next in Paris."

"Why, yes." She smiled, struggling to speak with any sense of sincerity. "That will be lovely, won't it? Good night, Hermann."

Josephine closed the door, walked to her desk, and took out a page of music manuscript and the pen with invisible ink Jacques had given her. She recorded every detail of the conversation, although she had hoped there would be more. Setting the pen down, she looked in the mirror, seeing nothing but fear.

I must get back to Paris and warn the Bernsteins.

Scan or tap the QR code to read Fred's blogpost Josephine Baker Under Cover.

91

CHAPTER 19

Grace and Lyle Meet

Albert Becker Art Museum, Irvine, California, 2022

GRACE'S CURIOSITY HAD SOARED when she learned from Burt Mackey, music professor at Lines College, that the Albert Becker Art Museum now had six Picasso portraits of Stravinsky. Quite a coincidence considering the Grandy-revelations described twelve Picasso portraits of Stravinsky. If you believed in coincidences. Grace didn't. She believed in an omnipotent God who guided and directed events in her life for her good. The call from Lyle Bernstein, the conservation specialist at the Albert Becker Art Museum, inviting her to meet, delighted her. Nothing would keep her away from a chance to see the Picassos. And what about the coincidence of the name Bernstein on the black-and-white photo?

Lyle greeted her in the lobby. "Morning, Grace. Thanks for coming."

"Good morning, Lyle. You must be excited about the Picassos," she said.

"You have no idea. Let's go to the staff lounge." He led the way. "How's AJ?"

They walked past a wall of posters promoting previous exhibits.

"Oh, you know AJ. On top of everything. Keeping your museum safe."

Meyer Technologies provided security for the Becker along with other art and entertainment venues in the area.

"Well, look at that." Grace smiled, pointing to a brass plate on the tribute wall, acknowledging AJ and Grace's support.

Lyle opened the door for Grace to enter the staff lounge. "Have a seat." He retrieved some bottled water from the mini-fridge, handed one to Grace, and sat in the chair opposite her.

"I'm sure you want to see the Picassos."

"I've been dying to see them ever since I heard about them."

He smiled at her excitement. "You will. But I have something to ask you first."

He described the gala plans and came to his question. "What do you know about art teachers using a Picasso drawing of Stravinsky to teach drawing technique?"

"Well, I use it myself. The portrait's simple lines make it an excellent teaching example for drawing from observation rather than assumption. You see a straight line slanting down, you draw a straight line slanting down, not your idea of what a table or a window looks like."

"Do you think very many art teachers in the Southern California area have taught students using the drawing? Have very many students drawn the portrait?"

"Oh, hmm. Hundreds, I'd say. Several hundreds. Why?"

"As part of the gala, we thought having a competition would be fun. Anyone who drew the portrait could enter and have their drawing judged by a celebrity panel. By the way, how about joining the panel?"

"First, this is genius. It will draw a lot of attention to the exhibit. And second, yes, I'd love to be on the panel. Sounds fun. Now can I see them?"

Lyle grinned. "Let's go."

He led her to his restoration office and unlocked the drawers where he stored them. After putting on his protective gloves, he carefully removed them and placed them on his workbench.

Grace studied the first drawing, her eyes transfixed. Then the second, then the third, until she'd seen all six. "I'm speechless."

Just like the ones in the picture from Grandy, but only six.

"I felt the same way when I first saw them. Everyone knows about the earlier one art teachers use. Then these showed up. Six of them. Can't quite understand why six. And they're basically the same portrait, with only slight variations."

Six here. Where were the other six? How did they get separated? Who had them? Can AJ and I find the others?

She reached to pick one up, but Lyle intervened. "Sorry. They're still in process."

"Of course." She leaned in for a closer look and thought she saw something on the back bleeding through, but couldn't make out anything. "Any chance I could take a picture of them with my phone?"

Maybe these six are in the black-and-white photo.

"Just make sure the flash is off."

"Of course." She took several pictures to make sure she got the details she wanted. "When is the gala?"

"At least a couple of months away. We have some shifting to do in the gallery to prepare display space and we need time to create the historical displays and the marketing materials."

She took one last shot of the sixth drawing. "I will make attendance mandatory for my students."

"That's a great endorsement."

Grace continued studying the drawings. "Do you mind if I ask how you got these?"

"Not at all. They were a donation."

"From whom?"

"Stravinsky's grandson."

Did the grandson have the other six? If he did, why did he keep them and donate only six?

"Hmm," she said, not really sure what to think.

"I wonder when Picasso drew these?" she said. "I know he was in Paris in the thirties. I'm sure you know the large Guernica mural he created for the 1937 Paris Art Exhibition."

"Sounds like a possible time frame."

Here goes.

"Speaking of the 30s, did any of your relatives live in Paris back then?"

Lyle straightened one of the drawings. "Why would you ask that?"

Good question.

"I thought maybe ..."

"Well, that's them." He returned the drawings to the drawers and locked them up. "Thanks for coming in, Grace. Let me show you out."

Why was he rushing me out?

He walked to the door and opened it for Grace.

Her mind continued racing on the walk to the lobby.

"I'll contact you again about the contest, if you don't mind," Lyle said.

"Sure. Sure. Sounds wonderful." She looked behind her, momentarily deep in thought, then snapped out of it and smiled. "Thanks for letting me be one of the first to see them. Really appreciate that."

"Everyone will see them soon."

Grace walked to her car and drove off.

Is our quest for the twelve Picassos already half-way complete? What about the IBM letter addressed to Grandy? A biggy. And who were those people in the photograph?

She drove into the driveway.

How'd I get here so fast?

Scan or tap the QR code to see the announcement for the gala contest.

Chapter 20

Who Owns What?

Home of the Hoffmans, Paris, 1937

CLAIRE HOFFMAN OPENED HER oven door, releasing the rich aroma of butter and almond. She placed the tray of steaming breakfast croissants on the stovetop and leaned over to take in a satisfying whiff of her mother's recipe. The familiar scent sparked a flood of memories—some wonderful, of family and friends, and others, more monstrous. Memories of a world at war, a war that stole the simple joys of butter and almonds from an innocent girl. She'd become an unwilling twelve-year-old student of the horrors forged from the hands of politicians and soldiers.

Where does such hatred come from?

A question her Jewish ancestors had pondered since Egypt. A question with an answer as elusive as finding the meaning of life. With that war almost two decades behind her, Claire enjoyed a world filled with the sound of children's laughter instead of distant bombs. A world in which one can easily take peace and security for granted.

Fritz strolled into the kitchen with the morning paper tucked under his arm. "What is that glorious smell?" Claire stepped back from the stove to display her offering and smiled. Fritz made a beeline to the croissants. "Ahh, yes." He reached to take one.

She slapped his hand. He retreated. "Not yet. They just came out of the oven and need time to breathe, like a fine wine." She touched his shoulder and leaned up to kiss him. "Have a seat, dear."

Fritz opened the paper to the front page. Today's leading headline read, "A THOUSAND INCENDIARY BOMBS LAUNCHED BY THE PLANES OF HITLER AND MUSSOLINI REDUCE THE TOWN OF GUERNICA TO ASHES."

"It didn't take him long," Fritz said.

"Who, Fritz?" Claire brought two cups of espresso to the table.

"Hitler. His planes and bombs destroyed an entire Spanish village, Guernica. Incalculable number of dead. That slippery, mad man. Fanning the winds of war."

"Why is he helping Mussolini?" She brought a plate of croissants to the table and set them next to her favorite photo album and a small vase holding a white carnation. She sat, placed a napkin on her lap, and put a croissant on her plate.

"It says the order for the massacre came directly from a German named Hermann Göring."

"I thought we had the war to end all wars. Where is this heading?"

"Rightists have taken over a munitions factory on the outskirts of Guernica. I did business with that company during the war." Fritz lowered the paper and shook his head. "I don't like any of this."

Claire reached over and pushed the paper down. "Take a break from the news, dear. Here, have a croissant." She held out the plate, to entice him.

"With delight." He put one on his plate, set the newspaper aside, and spread a napkin on his lap. Claire sipped her espresso and looked out the window at her potted daffodils reflecting the morning sun and dancing in the breeze. Fritz picked up a croissant and passed it under his nose, let out an "ahh," and took a bite. With their son, Maurice, off to school, they had some time alone, time to talk about what she'd been holding in. Fritz finished half of the croissant and took a sip of his espresso.

"I can't imagine having a problem with Emma and Otto, dear. Can you?" Claire said.

"You still want to talk about this?" Fritz picked up the paper and turned to the financial section. "Money can change people, Claire. Greed often lurks below the surface of those you least expect. At its worst, greed leads to war."

She lifted her cup and looked at Fritz. "And where would your company have been, without a war?" She took a sip.

Fritz turned the page. "I'll admit war always brings misery, but every war needs guns and ammunition. It was our duty to supply France with what she needed. You haven't objected to the lifestyle our good fortune has provided."

This "good fortune" resulted from the Hoffman Munitions Company supplying critical weapons to defend France during the Great War. This "good fortune" opened doors to mingle with the wealthiest in France. This "good fortune" also provided freedom to pursue their love for art.

Claire picked up the photo from the recent Bernstein soirée. She smiled, pleased with how handsome they looked that night, standing in the foyer, in front of the twelve Picasso drawings. *How thoughtful of Emma to send the photo as a souvenir.*

"Do you think they're greedy? Emma is one of the sweetest people in Paris." She moved her plate and slid the photo album in front of her.

"She is now." He sipped his espresso. "Her life is one long party. She has everything she wants in duplicates. Take all that away, then you'll see her true colors."

The Hoffmans had agreed to initially showcase the twelve Picassos at the Bernsteins' home for the grand reveal and then, in a few weeks, move them to a gallery owned by the Hoffmans.

Claire turned a page of the photo album. "Pablo would step up for us if there were any question of ownership, wouldn't he?"

"I'm not so sure." He turned to the next page of the paper. "It's easy to assume he's our friend now. But look at his personal life. How many wives and mistresses has he gone through?"

"What are you saying?" She wasn't naïve about the lives of artists, but she needed to understand what he meant.

Fritz tilted the paper down and looked over it. "If he can flit from lover to lover, he could do the same to us, disregard us and conveniently forget we paid for his work." He set the paper down on the table and pointed his finger at Claire. "Picasso may be a gifted artist, but he's a lousy businessman. He never provides us with a bill of sale. We have nothing to support our claim of ownership."

Fritz took another bite of the cooling croissant. "The Bernsteins aren't our only concern." He took a sip. "We must think about the art we own hanging in other galleries." He picked up his napkin and wiped the buttered crumbs from his mouth. "It may be time to think about better security at these galleries to protect our investments."

Fritz folded the paper and put it down. They both picked up their espressos and gazed out at the small flower garden. The fresh, morning breeze moving across the garden entered through the open window and flowed over them.

Why isn't life as simple as a garden in full bloom?

Claire looked back at the photo album and focused on a picture of a young version of Igor and her, sitting on a park bench. "I've been thinking about giving the Picasso dozen to Igor."

"What?" He turned and glared at Claire.

"Yes." She nodded. "I think Igor should have them."

"Why? Because he's your cousin?"

"He is a very busy composer. Sitting for them took a lot of time away from composing. I think it's the right thing to do."

Fritz shook his head. "No, not all of them."

"Well, then, half. That still leaves six, a nice collection if you didn't know we had twelve to start with."

Fritz tilted his head. "You do remember how much we paid Pablo, don't you?"

"That doesn't matter. Igor's birthday is soon and this will make a special gift."

"But—"

"My mind's made up. I've thought about this ever since Pablo finished the first one. You know what great friends he and Igor are. Igor will always cherish them and it will remind him of the time he spent with Pablo during the sittings."

"You're sure about this?"

"Absolutely. It is the best gift I've ever been able to give him."

A far cry from the handcrafted birthday cards a young Claire made from scavenged paper, lettered in charcoal—the finest gift she could afford to honor a grateful mother. A young Fritz had his mother's gifts delivered from the finest department stores, but with all their good fortune, he never saw his family contribute to the poor house. War changes many things and the last war had softened his heart and loosened his grip on his wallet.

"You're sure it should be six?" he said with a smile.

She smiled back. "Nothing less."

He took her hand. "All right, six it is, my dear."

"Thank you, Fritz." She squeezed his hand.

"And I suppose a party is in order?" Although he kept a tight rein on their finances, he enjoyed hosting their friends with the best food and drink in Paris, a way for him to show off his wealth.

She grinned. "Of course. I've already started planning."

"I've no doubt."

She straightened up in her chair and reached for a notepad and pen. "Pablo must come. And Dottie. She adds so much. And I'd like to include Rabbi Josef. He's taken quite an interest in the Paris art world lately. And of course, the Bernsteins should be here. We want to keep in their good graces."

Perhaps the best strategy for this joint venture. No need to start a war.

Fritz sat back, enjoying her enthusiasm. "Do you think we can squeeze them all in?"

"Squeeze we shall. The joy shall flow out the doors, if need be," she said, making a sweeping gesture toward the front door.

Claire finished her invitation list and the last drops of espresso. She smiled, savoring the thought of hosting Emma in her home for a change.

Another breeze rustled the window curtains.

Had the Spanish winds of war drifted all the way to Paris?

CHAPTER 21

Pumping Fred

Home of AJ and Grace, Irvine, California, 2022

FRED'S CONVERSATIONS WITH GRACE and Burt in the Lines College staff lounge had piqued his curiosity. The discovery of the six Picasso portraits of Stravinsky, now at the Albert Becker Art Museum, came as a complete surprise, a welcome one. What about the numeric codes embedded in the music Grace showed them? Did the composer leave a clue to the whereabouts of the portraits, missing for eighty years? The mystery's trifecta of history, music, and art intrigued the three professors at Lines, especially Grace. Hence, her dinner invitation and request for a history lesson.

AJ and Grace welcomed Fred at the front door and led him through the entryway to the living room.

"Delightful home you two have," Fred said, surveilling the surroundings along the way. He stopped and pointed to a pair of framed oil paintings, portraits of AJ and Grace. "Are those some of your paintings, Grace?"

"Mine and AJ's. They're from our last painting date." She rubbed AJ's arm.

"Right. You mentioned that." He studied them, then turned to AJ. "Well done, AJ."

They followed the smooth jazz streaming from the Bose speakers in the living room.

AJ gestured. "Have a seat, Fred."

Grace brought a plate of hors d'oeuvres from the kitchen, placed it on the table next to a crystal bowl with floating gardenias, and sat next to AJ across from Fred. AJ poured three glasses of Chablis and passed them around.

Fred sat back and took a sip. "Grace said you guys have some history questions. What's up?"

"AJ is working on a family history project," Grace said.

"Sounds interesting. But could you hold that thought? I need to use the facilities."

"No problem," AJ said. "Around the corner, back toward the front door, and across from my office."

Fred followed AJ's directions, with a slight variance. He looked over his shoulder before entering AJ's office. He scanned the office to find anything that provided hints to why AJ and Grace wanted his help. Three items lay on the desk: the Nazi IBM letter, the sheet music, and the black-and-white photo. *What the heck is this all about?* He picked up the letter and began reading it. *Unbelievable.*

"Did you find it okay?" AJ's voice drifted in from the living room.

Fred's pulse quickened. He set the letter down before reading to the end and peered out of the office, making sure the coast was clear. He walked into the hall, answering, "Yup." Taking a calming breath, he headed back to the living room. He sat, picked up his glass, and forced a smile. "Now where were we?"

"Do you know anything about IBM's history during World War Two?" AJ said.

Fred furrowed his brow. *Did this have something to do with the items in AJ's office?* "A little. Anything specific?"

"I found some documents from my grandfather suggesting he worked for IBM, and I wondered what IBM did back then."

Grace passed the tray. "More cheese and crackers?"

"Sure." Fred put some on his napkin. "Well, Thomas Watson, the founder, conducted business all over America and in Europe before the war started."

"How about in Germany?" AJ asked.

"Yes. IBM had an international presence, especially in Germany. In those early days, customers used IBM's technology, and I use the word lightly, for basic data collection and processing. I'm sure you remember the eighty-column punch cards."

"Barely," AJ said.

"Customers used those cards to record and sort data with card readers, also known as tabulating machines."

"Did the Germans use them?" AJ asked.

Why all this interest in Germany?

"Probably. The Germans have a reputation for keeping thorough records, and using IBM cards simplified the process." Fred nibbled on a cracker.

"What sort of records did the Germans keep?"

Where is this going?

"Anything, I suppose. When the Germans began rearming before World War Two, they might have kept track of weapons, ammunition, that sort of thing. I think they used the cards and tabulators for train scheduling too."

Grace said, "So if you could count it, you could tabulate it?"

"That's an oversimplification, but yes," Fred said. "You could track an item's current and future location."

The wineglasses rattled on the table. Conversation stopped. AJ gripped both arms of his chair. Three long seconds of an earthquake tremor.

"Man, I hate earthquakes," AJ said.

Silence streamed through the Bose speakers, waiting for the disrupted WiFi to reboot.

AJ relaxed his grip, exhaled, and smiled at Grace. "Not the big one." He turned back to Fred. "So. IBM and the Nazis."

Why had he connected IBM with the Nazis?

"Did IBM have tape drives back then?" AJ said.

Tape drives? The letter mentioned a tape.

"We're not sure." Fred took time for a sip. "But Germany made so many technological advances during those years, it's possible. Did you know the Germans broadcasted the 1936 Olympics on live television?"

"Really?" Grace said.

"And think about all the brilliant German scientists the US recruited to develop rocket technology. Where would NASA be without them?"

The timer on Grace's watch beeped. "I think dinner is ready."

AJ smiled. "And I think I'm ready for dinner. Let's go."

Grace led the way to the kitchen, grabbed an oven mitt, and opened the oven door, releasing hot whiffs of garlic. She pulled the tray of bread out and placed it on the stovetop. Everyone served themselves buffet style, filling their plate with tonight's fare of a simple chicken salad on leaves of romaine lettuce with sides of mixed fruit and garlic bread.

After the leisurely dinner and superficial conversation, Fred glanced at his watch and set his napkin on the table. "Grace, thank you for a wonderful meal. If you will excuse me, I need to head home and make some preparations for a new lecture."

"Of course," she said.

They started for the front door. AJ stopped at their two portraits, hanging slightly crooked, and straightened each of them. Fred glanced into AJ's office at the mysterious items. Grace opened the front door.

"Hope I answered your questions," Fred said. "Let me know if I can be of any other help. Sounds like an interesting project."

Interesting, to say the least.

AJ smiled, leaning on the door frame. "You gave us plenty to think about."

"See you tomorrow, Grace."

"Night," Grace said, before closing the door.

Driving home, Fred's mind raced ahead of his car.

Is it just a coincidence? Both of us, looking for answers from the same time and place. Could those items on AJ's desk have anything to do with what I'm looking for?

CHAPTER 22

I Can't Get Out

Train Station, Berlin, 1937

JOSEPHINE WOKE EARLY IN her hotel room the morning after completing her first mission, pumping Göring for intel. Rain pelted the windows, filling the room with anxiety, urging Josephine to finish packing her suitcase that lay open on her bed, impatiently waiting for the last few items. No time to lose to return to Paris and warn the Bernsteins of the impending break-in Göring had described. Her trembling hands picked up the all-important sheet of music. One side seemingly blank, with her handwritten notes in invisible ink from Jacques. The other side, filled with music notation of a song from her act, to serve as a decoy. She folded the music and paused.

Should I hide this in my things?

She finally decided that leaving the decoy music in plain sight would raise less suspicion if the authorities searched her luggage. Nazis patrolled everywhere these days, especially at train depots and airports. She planned on using her tried-and-true approach—move with confidence and you can get away with murder, although that wasn't her goal today. She closed both bags and pounded the clasps shut with her clenched fist. Turning to the mirror, she picked up her hat and placed it on her head, adding the appropriate tilt. Two eyes in the mirror stared back at her, attempting to offer some encouragement. Two knocks at the door interrupted the failed attempt. She opened the door and greeted the bellboy, forcing her larger-than-life smile. He picked up her bags as she tucked her return train ticket into her purse and snapped it shut. They paraded through the lobby, passed under the dripping awning, and loaded her into a taxi.

Stepping out of the taxi at the station, a chaotic scene welcomed her. A large, boisterous crowd surrounded the ticket office. She trembled. *Something's wrong.* She fumbled in her purse for the ticket to confirm she had come to the correct departure location. Yes. But why such a clamoring crowd, angrily shouting at the ticket agent?

Josephine turned to the taxi driver. "Monsieur, please wait."

What is all the commotion about? This can't be good.

Pushing through the crowd, she made out bits of the cacophonous English, French, and German.

"But I have a ticket."

"My family needs me in Paris."

"I have important business to conduct. I can't wait two days."

Two days? Her chest tightened. *I can't wait two days either.*

Not with the urgent message she desperately needed to deliver to the Bernsteins. One way or another, she must warn them of the impending theft that loose-lips Hermann Göring had described, a warning far too important to wait two days.

Forcing a path through the pressing crowd, she reached the closed ticket window displaying a sign posted for her train.

"Today's Paris train is experiencing a delay due to a derailment. They expect to take two days to complete the repairs. We will honor tickets for today's scheduled departure then."

Josephine froze. The noise of the confused crowd faded into her jumbled thoughts. *Is there another way?* The committee strictly forbid any communication by telegraph or telephone. Too many eyes and ears these days watching and listening for secrets. But Jacques hadn't accounted for the unwelcome obstacle of mechanical failure in his plan.

Uncertain of what to do, she followed her fear back to the taxi, and pleaded with the driver, "Please, back to my hotel, quickly."

She checked in to a room and wore a pattern in the carpet, pacing and brainstorming. *Is there any other way to return to Paris in time?* As hard as she tried, every "maybe I could" ended with a big, fat, nothing. She didn't normally look for comfort from a bottle during times of despair. Today, it didn't take long to empty half of it. What else could she do but wait?

CHAPTER 23

A Fitting Word

South Coast Reformed Church, Irvine California, 2022

"THINGS SURE HAVE CHANGED since dad pastored here," AJ said, driving into the parking lot of South Coast Reformed Church.

Walking toward the church entrance, AJ greeted the leader of their weekly community group. "Hey, Joe. Sure enjoy our Wednesday nights at your house. Good to have a mid-week boost."

"And you always contribute rich nuggets for us to ponder," Joe said.

They met AJ's mother in the bustling lobby. Heading for the sanctuary entrance, they passed three portraits, prominently displayed. The first, Grandy's brother, John, who planted the church after moving to the land of Southern California orange groves in the post-war boom of the 1950s. The second portrait, AJ's father, Matthew, whose testimony of a journey from a 60s flower child to a minister of the gospel, exemplified the power of Christ to transform sinners to saints. The third portrait, Henry Hunter, the current pastor. Neither AJ nor his brother, Brett, felt called to pastoring the church, ending a family tradition.

Unless he and Grace experienced a miracle, another family tradition had ended. A loss he still grieved.

A smiling greeter handed them a bulletin and they entered the wide, curved sanctuary to find seats. Two large monitors on either side of the stage displayed a welcoming message, activity announcements, and online options for giving an offering.

The service unfolded, following the usual contemporary liturgy of a greeting, worship songs, a time of confession, and assurance of pardon. All paving the way to the sermon.

Pastor Henry Hunter, a slim, six-foot smiler, dressed in business casual, walked onto the platform and placed his iPad on the plexiglass podium. "Today we continue our series in Romans." He grinned and raised his hands in the air. "I know, I know, it's taking forever. But I hope you are seeing along with me how God showed Paul to pack so much into each verse."

AJ appreciated Henry's teaching approach. He found it deeply analytical and full of context and encouragement, a style that spoke to his innermost needs.

"Last week we looked at Romans 8:26-27 and learned Paul assures us that God hears the Holy Spirit's groans interceding for us and that He patiently yearns for us to conform to the image of Christ. Today we move on to verse 28. For you outliners, I've listed my three points in the bulletin."

AJ had studied last week's notes during his morning devotionals and read ahead to today's passage. He'd struggled during the week with the theme of all things working together for good, considering the Grandy revelations. His head understood the meaning of the verse, but his current distress contradicted what he thought he believed.

Pastor Henry continued. "You've probably encountered the question, 'How are you doing?' at some point. And you've probably answered, 'Not bad, under the circumstances.' Such a common response, especially when you are in the midst of difficult circumstances. But what are you doing under the circumstances? Are we controlled by our circumstances or do we live a life of confidence knowing, that for Christians, all things work together for good, for those who are called according to His purpose? Hold on to your seat while we dive in."

AJ fidgeted in his seat. He had dived in to the deep end when he opened Grandy's box earlier this week. He needed a lifeline.

"God is an amazing orchestrator, permitting or allowing circumstances in our lives to rip us from sin and prepare us for heaven."

Is my distress a matter of sin that God wants to rip out? Is this ordeal a preparation? Do I even have the right to ask that question?

"Let's be clear. Ultimate good is not always immediate good. The micro details are often confusing."

Is my confusion from this week's Grandy revelations normal? He clenched his fist.

"God is working through multiple events in our lives to curb our desire to control our lives."

Bingo. Control. His personal demon. An expectation that he personally had the power to control and keep everything in his life within acceptable and comfortable boundaries. Yet, he had no control over his infertility, struggling to accept that it served some ultimate good. On top of that, he faced the mysteries about his grandfather, also beyond his control.

"Stop playing it safe and trust Christ."

That was the main thing, right? *Do I truly trust Christ and believe that, no matter what is true about Grandy, God is orchestrating it all for His glory?*

"Trust and obey, for there's no other way." The closing hymn provided a final punctuation for today's message and a final challenge for AJ's self-examination.

Pastor Henry raised his hand toward the congregation and spoke a final benediction. "Go in peace."

Peace. That was what AJ craved and needed.

Members gathered their belongings and stood, joining a gradually crescendoing murmur of conversations. Grace headed to greet a friend in her small group, Evelynn left to deliver a gift to a new family, and AJ walked to the coffee bar to speak with Pastor Henry.

AJ gave Henry a generalized version of the recent Grandy revelations. "Can I call you this week? There's more I need to share, not to mention how today's message hit me between the eyes."

"I was aiming for the heart, but I'll take that," Pastor Henry grinned. "You know you can call me anytime. Or do you want to meet for one of these?" he asked, holding up his coffee cup.

AJ and Henry regularly met or spoke on the phone, enjoying a camaraderie that few men experience, a two-way street of transparent sharing and encouragement.

"I'll call you, and if there's time for a cup, we'll do it." AJ smiled and patted Henry on the back. "Thanks, Henry."

AJ saw Grace across the lobby and strolled to her with a spring in his step and a smile. "You're certainly perkier than during the sermon," Grace said.

"A happy heart makes a cheerful face and looking at you always makes my heart happy!"

"You're so sweet," she said, planting a kiss on his cheek. "But I'm so hungry. Let's go." She grabbed his hand and, with a slight tug, led him toward the car.

AJ's thoughts on the drive home flitted among confusions, expectations and hopes, and the desire to find some clarity. Clarity of what he honestly believed and about his grandy's secret life. Not to mention planning his next steps to get to the heart of that secret.

Chapter 24

The Big Plan

Paris, 1937

Louis had impressed Bruno Lohse with his credentials and experience at their first meeting. He came highly recommended from individuals Bruno trusted in Paris, a brief list when it came to art theft. Louis took this assignment seriously, knowing it could lead to more jobs with Bruno in the future.

Louis reviewed the plan with Bruno a day ago and through his own connections, he had assembled a team of three fellow Great War veterans looking for their next meal.

The team's evening briefing took place in a dank warehouse that smelled a hundred years old, not far from the target. With half of the streetlamps on the block broken, shadows provided a cover for those entering the building. Inside, a single-bulb fixture hung by a frayed wire over the crude table and chairs, providing barely enough light for the team to see each other.

Louis addressed the team. "We've all worked together before except for our new member, François. He'll fit right in, I assure you."

George ran the back of his hand over his two-day-old stubble and nudged Maurice. They turned to scrutinize the newcomer. François crossed his arms to resist the silent inquisition.

"We have a generous window of time to complete our mission. The target is a private residence. The occupants leave every Friday night like clockwork."

"A Jewish family?" George said, swatting a fly on his neck.

François turned his head quickly and stared at George.

"That's of no consequence," Louis said. "The mission is simple and clear cut—enter the house, collect a list of items, and bring them back to this warehouse."

François fidgeted in his seat. "What are the items?" A rat scurried across the floor.

Louis took a beat, staring at François.

Is this guy a little too curious? Seems a little anxious.

"You'll see the list Friday night. Any other questions?" Louis said.

Maurice blew his nose into a ratty, stained handkerchief. "Meet up time?" He tucked the handkerchief into what remained of his back pocket.

"Six p.m. here for the final briefing. All black, as usual, and face masks," Louis said. "Remember, you're part of this team because of your track record of skill and keeping your mouths shut. I expect the same for this operation. That's all. You're dismissed."

All three got up and walked across the damp, rough cement floor towards the door. George and Maurice waited for the rookie to exit the warehouse first. They gave him a head start and then followed him down the street.

This should be one of my easiest assignments yet, Louis thought. Lohse had suggested collaborating on future missions and Louis needed anything he could get. Just a guy wanting a pair of boots without holes—a veteran from the Great War who the government had forgotten to thank for his service.

CHAPTER 25

The Fakeout

Meyer Technologies Delivery Entrance, Irvine, California, 2022

THE VAN WITH TWO technicians approached the hut at the receiving dock of Meyer Technologies. Jake, the driver, opened the van window and smiled at the guard. "Delivery. Here's the invoice."

"Weren't you guys just here yesterday?" the guard said, looking at the invoice.

"Yeah, but they found a problem with those power supplies we delivered. The lot was defective. We need to install these new ones ASAP before the other ones cause any damage."

Jake's boss had replicated every detail of the real vendor for today's job, from the ID badges and uniforms down to the signage on the van. Made them look like the real deal.

"Go ahead. Guess you better hurry." The guard waved them through.

Jake parked the van. He and his partner exited and headed to the server room, following the floor plan they had memorized. But they weren't heading to the power supplies.

The plan called for tapping in to the servers that monitored security at the Albert Becker Art Museum. After finding the server, it didn't take long to attach the device to give them remote access to the system.

In less than fifteen minutes, they attached the device, returned to their van, pulled up to the exit, and waved to the guard. "You're all set. Think we got these in before you had any problems." Driving away, they gave each other a high five. How simple was that?

CHAPTER 26

Birthday Party

Home of Hoffmans, Paris, 1937

CLAIRE HAD COMPLETED PREPARATIONS for Igor's party the previous day, so they could observe Sabbath as closely as possible. They attended synagogue regularly and observed most high holy days. Tonight they attended synagogue but made a hasty departure.

By the time all the guests arrived, the tables displayed a feast that couldn't make Fritz prouder. But Claire was the real hostess. She'd made that clear to Fritz.

"Claire, how lovely everything looks," Emma Bernstein said. She always had gracious words for her friends.

"It's such a special occasion. Dear Igor's birthday," she replied.

"Where is that guy?" Dottie asked.

"He's found the wine over there." Claire pointed.

Igor wasn't alone. Ernest Hemingway, Robert Meyer, and Pablo stood next to him, drinking and laughing.

"What's this I hear about you leaving Paris, Igor?" Hemingway said.

"Academia beckoned and I have answered the call. I have an engagement at Harvard," Igor said.

Hemingway grinned. "You get around as much as I do."

"It won't be for a few weeks though. Still time to see what else Paris has to offer and spend more time with my friend Pablo," Igor said, grabbing the arm of a grinning Pablo.

Hemingway turned to Robert. "Robert, I understand you've been spending some time in Berlin. Anything happening we should be concerned about?"

Robert took a drink of wine before answering. "There are things that are bothering me, I must say."

"Such as?" Hemingway said.

"From my church sources, I'm hearing distressing news from rabbis in parts of Berlin. Since the Nuremberg Laws of 1935, the Nazis are defining Jews by genealogy not by religious practice. They are beginning to identify who is Jewish and who isn't by lineage."

"I've heard some of Hitler's early rhetoric about a pure Aryan race. Is this the start?" Hemingway said.

Fritz had approached and weighed in. "Hitler's a pig. Germany didn't learn anything from the Great War."

"My friend, Hitler has roused a sleeping giant and his support is swelling. I wouldn't ignore these warnings," Hemingway said.

"But we mustn't alarm the ladies tonight, must we?" Fritz said. "Claire is expecting this evening to be one of her finest. Let's help see that it is."

"Here, here." Hemingway raised his glass and Robert, Pablo, and Igor joined.

A clinking of a wineglass pierced the air. Claire continued clanging a spoon on her wine glass until the conversation in the room hushed.

"My dear friends. What a joy to find reasons to come together and celebrate. Tonight we celebrate my dear cousin, Igor."

Pablo squeezed Igor around the shoulders.

"You all know his friend Pablo drew a few portraits of him," she said.

Laughter rippled through the group clearly catching the understatement.

"All right, twelve is more than a few. I grant you. So, for a special gift for his birthday and before he leaves us for New York, I have something special for him. It comes from Pablo as much as from us." She lifted a flat rectangular package from behind her.

"Come, Igor."

He made his way forward.

"May these remind you, not only of your good friend Pablo, but also, of all your dear friends in Paris. Happy birthday." She handed him the package.

He took the package and carefully tore the paper. A large smile emerged on his face as he saw what was in the package. He held up one of the six portraits drawn by Pablo for everyone to see. The crowd broke out in applause.

Claire had packed them for travel knowing Igor was leaving soon and only one of the portraits was visible. He wouldn't know there were six of them until he unpacked them in New York.

"Thank you, my dear Claire. And you too, Pablo," Igor said. "What can I say? My life is so full here in Paris. But it's time for me to move on. This gift will always remind me of what we all shared together during this marvelous time in this place. Shalom, my friend."

"Shalom," Claire replied.

"Shalom," came from everyone.

A pounding at the door interrupted the shalom. Everyone turned. Josephine rushed in.

"I hope I'm not too late," Josephine shouted, panting heavily.

"Why, we just gave Igor his gift. Plenty of time to celebrate," Claire said.

"No. No. No. You don't understand," Josephine pleaded.

"Dear, sit down. Have some wine. Now what's this all about?" Dottie said.

She downed a full glass. "I tried to get back but the train was delayed. They're coming for your art." She pointed to the Bernsteins. "You need to do something, now!"

"Who's coming?" Otto asked.

"The Nazis. To your house," Josephine shouted, still sweating from running to warn them.

"How do you know this?" Otto asked.

"I got it from Göring himself. He gave me a description of the house and the art. There's no question it's your house and your collection. He specifically mentioned the twelve portraits by Picasso. You've got to do something!"

Claire remembered the conversation with Fritz just a few days before. He was right. The times were changing. Poor Emma. She must be horrified. Claire was definitely horrified.

"Did he say when they plan to do this?" Otto asked.

"He said his man had it planned on a night he knew you would be gone!"

"Otto! They knew we'd be gone to synagogue tonight. Do something!" Emma shrieked.

Hemingway stepped up. "Otto, we need to get over there immediately in case they haven't come yet. Fritz, we need you, too. The rest of you, stay here till we make sure everything's safe or—"

"We've lost everything to those damn Nazis?" Emma cried out in shock.

"Let's go. Robert, maybe you can send up a prayer for us. You too, Rabbi," Hemingway said.

The men rushed out, leaving a stunned gathering.

Scan or tap the QR code to read Grace's blogpost about the friendship between Igor Stravinsky and Pablo Picasso.

Chapter 27

What?

Meyer Technologies, Irvine, California, 2022

AJ HIT HIS USUAL jogging trail at his usual time. He got out of his car, shed his jacket, and joined a few other souls stretching in the parking lot before pounding the path into the rising sun. Free from any technology, he used this time to clear his mind and meditate on scriptures from his devotionals. Today's verse: Colossians 3:16—let the word of Christ dwell in you richly. Focusing on the mystery of God's word dwelling in him and transforming him, he nearly collided with an oncoming jogger. The jolt broke his focus and redirected every cell of his brain to last night's disturbing event—a breach into his company's systems.

AJ had meticulously built his company, carefully completing one building block at a time before moving to another. His peers admired this rising star in the tech universe who consistently implemented stable, progressive technologies. His company, Meyer Technologies, took up the entire fifth floor of the gleaming steel-and-glass high-rise in fashionable Irvine, California. The building, considered an architectural gem in Irvine's business corridor, achieved a fine balance between ultimate luxury and practicality.

The jog, shower, and a quick breakfast with Grace did little to ease his mind. The company he had so painstakingly built had suffered a breach for the first time in its seven-year history, with a JD Edwards award for each of those years. Last night changed all that.

"Let's just start at the top," AJ said calmly to the director sitting across the conference room table.

"Somehow, something disabled our monitoring systems, but only for five minutes. Exactly from 11:55 p.m. to midnight," Curt said.

Curt Matthews, one of AJ's top directors, wore a variety of hats. He'd been in the IT world five years longer than AJ and had more gray hair than black. His forty-year-old body couldn't compete with AJ's runner's physique but he still fit into pants with a 32-inch waist. AJ looked to him as his go-to guy on a wide range of topics. Plus, they just enjoyed hanging out together, inside and outside of work, fostering a comfortable working relationship.

"What was the extent of coverage?" AJ said.

How on earth did this happen? After all your testing?

"Kind of interesting," Curt said, looking at a report in his hand. "The monitoring system is segmented. We can analyze outages from a variety of perspectives. Last night's breach occurred in the arts division."

The arts division provided security monitoring for a variety of museums, concert halls, and other cultural venues. The breach not only rattled AJ, the tech CEO. It also rattled AJ, a patron of the arts in the community. He and Grace enjoyed and supported a number of art and music organizations.

"I don't know how this happened," Curt said, shaking his head. "We put this system through all of our quality assurance and system testing. We didn't find a single bug."

Grace Hopper, an early computer pioneer, coined the term *bug*. She found a moth trapped inside an electronic relay that had caused a system malfunction. After operators removed the moth, they taped it in the logbook with the notation, "First actual case of finding a bug."

"Well, testing only proves the presence of bugs, not the absence," AJ said. He'd worked around computers long enough to know, eventually, bugs show up. Computers only do what humans tell them, and humans are not perfect.

"Is it possible to pinpoint which venue?" AJ said.

"We are working on that. Of course, we could call each of the venues," Curt said.

"I'll do that follow up. Stay focused on the how, then let's search for the why," AJ said. "Keep me posted."

AJ rose from the table, signaling the end of the meeting. They both exited the glass-walled conference room to return to their respective offices.

Back at his desk in his office, AJ surveyed the landscape of the rolling south coast hills beyond his windows, tapping his fingers on his desk in a rhythmic pattern. A five-minute outage.

Who was behind this and what did they want?

Scan or tap the QR code to visit the website for Meyer Technologies.

CHAPTER 28

The Heist

Warehouse, Paris, 1937

Louis met with Bruno Lohse earlier in the day to review the plan one last time before conducting the operation with the team. Confident of Louis's qualifications, Bruno put him in charge of this simple plan. But simple things seldom are.

The list of paintings to steal seemed small enough for the team of four to quickly locate, remove from the walls, and stack in the van for transport. The route couldn't be simpler. So very easy. *I can handle this blindfolded with one hand tied behind my back.*

The team assembled at the warehouse precisely on time. Louis spread the crude hand-drawn map on the table.

"Who drew this piece of junk?" George snickered. "You can barely read the street names."

Louis ignored the crack and began the briefing. "This is the route to our target, just a few turns from here. On this block, we'll enter through a small driveway into a courtyard protected from view by a wall and bushes. The lock on the front door won't be a problem." He put another drawing on the table. "Immediately inside the front door, a set of twelve portraits are hanging in the foyer. François, you will remove them and load them into the van. George will collect the next five paintings in the hall past the foyer. Maurice and I will gather the rest in the salon."

He handed a list to François and one to George. "Look these over during the drive. Maurice, here's our list. Any questions?"

"That's it?" François said.

"Simple." Louis checked his watch. "The occupants are gone by now. Time to load up."

Louis took the driver's seat and tossed the map to Maurice who sat next to him. François and George entered through the side doors of the van and sat on the floor. Louis started the van, turned on the headlights, and drove off.

***

The team arrived at the target location in less than fifteen minutes. Louis drove into the curved courtyard as far from street view as possible. He turned the van around and parked facing toward the driveway for a speedy exit. The doors burst open and everyone approached the house.

Louis quickly demolished the lock, opened the front door, and the operation commenced according to the plan. Almost. George, Louis and Maurice headed off on their assignments. François began his work in the foyer. He looked at the wall and he froze. Instead of twelve Picassos, only six hung on the wall. With no other option, he took the six off the wall and loaded them in the van. Job finished but incomplete. It took the others only two trips in and out to complete the mission and regroup at the van.

"Sir, there's a problem," François said.

"What?" Louis snarled.

François looked down at the ground and back up at Louis. "I found only six paintings in the foyer, not twelve."

"Damn!" He paused then said, "Well, we don't have time for a treasure hunt. Everyone in the van." *How will I explain this to the boss?*

Louis drove out of the driveway, onto the street, and returned to the warehouse.

***

Bruno Lohse sat in a dark office at the back of the warehouse, waiting for the crew to return. The door opened and he watched the crew carefully bring in the paintings and place them on the sets of tables waiting for them. François finished laying his six Picasso pictures on the table, looked toward the darkened office, then turned away.

Louis examined the inventory and compared it to his lists. Aside from six Picassos, he saw everything on the list. He took a bag from under the meeting table and pulled out bundles of cash. "Payday, men." He handed a bundle each to George and Maurice. "Good work as usual." He moved to François and paused, staring into his eyes. "You did your job. Not your fault. Here." He handed the bundle to François who breathed a sigh of relief.

"Now, go enjoy yourselves. You've got plenty to spend on the wine and women of your choice."

George and Maurice headed toward the door, smiling and patting each other on the back. François followed quietly and closed the door behind him.

"Is that only six Picassos I see?" Louis turned to see Bruno sauntering toward the tables with his arms folded.

Quick on his feet, Louis said, "That you do. We found six. We brought back six."

"And I'm supposed to just take your word that you found only six at the house, and that no one has decided to add the other six to their own personal collection?" Bruno stood nose to nose with Louis.

Louis didn't know why they found only six. He couldn't care less about art collections. But he needed to convince Bruno. "You think I took them?" He chuckled and stepped away. "I don't know a Monet from a Mona Lisa. Come on." He hid his trembling hands behind his back.

Bruno paused. "What about the others?"

"There's no way any of them could have stashed them somewhere. I broke the lock, opened the door to the foyer, and saw six. It's the first thing we all saw."

126

Bruno walked around the table holding the six and picked one up to admire. He smiled and turned toward Louis. "I believe you." He set the drawing down and snarled, "Just not sure my boss will be happy about this." He walked to a table holding one of the other pieces and picked it up. "At any rate, you did your job."

Bruno set the piece of art down, looked at Louis, and reached into his coat. Louis froze. Bruno slowly pulled out an envelope and handed it to Louis. "It's all there, I assure you."

"Of course." Louis didn't even look.

Bruno strolled around the tables, looking at the haul. "I can take care of these myself." He turned to Louis with a wicked smile. "That's all," he said, gesturing to the door.

Louis tipped his head. "Yes, sir. Thank you, sir." He turned and grabbed his bag, stuck his pay envelope inside, and rushed for the door.

***

Bruno spent the next few hours carefully cataloging and packing the stolen art into specially made crates for shipment to Berlin. He recorded the critical information Dehomag needed for the computerized records—date, source, description of the art, lot number, key, and destination of the shipment. Bruno had chosen the destination for this shipment, a critical piece of information to store in the Dehomag computer records for finding these crates in the future. He opened his personal journal and duplicated the information. But the plan Bruno and his brother had created made this information a moot point.

CHAPTER 29

The Coach

Office of Derrick Edwards, Orange County, California, 2022

YOU DIDN'T TURN TO Google to find and hire someone with Derrick Edwards's resume. He worked in the shadows, yet the shady client had found him, a good fit for each other. His strip mall office, flanked by a mailing service and a chain drugstore, had a Newport Beach address. The parking lot sign read, "DE Investigations" in a plain, dull script. The office furnishings evoked the 1960s with a ruptured linoleum floor, peeling brown laminate desk, and industrial metal office chairs. At least the 2021 Los Angeles Angels poster alluded to the current decade, even if he still thought of them as the Anaheim Angels.

Derrick began his day with his usual morning gym workout. A youthful-looking 40, he worked hard to maintain his six-foot, 190-pound frame, still able to keep up with the twenty-year-olds at the bench press. By 8:30, at his desk, he mechanically sipped his latte, munched the Chick-fil-A egg-white breakfast sandwich, and scrolled through emails.

He tossed the sandwich wrappings to join five others in the trash, then opened the folder with the plans for his current client. He sat back and smiled. Batting a thousand had become a habit. Reviewing the plan, he savored each success.

Locate and hire an art detective. Check. First base.

Locate the art his client wanted. Check. Second base.

Breach the museum security system at Meyer Technologies. Check. Third base, despite requiring additional time, resources, and planning. This task had required assembling a team, investing in a van, and replicating the uniforms and badges of the hardware vendor that supplied Meyer Technologies. And, most importantly, purchasing the device for remote access to their systems. This phase took weeks to complete because of the hours of clandestine observations to discover what vendor supplied the servers at Meyer Technologies. Fortunately, Derrick's men had observed the delivery of new servers to Meyer Technologies and identified their make and model. This made selecting the correct remote access device a piece of cake. Ironically, Derrick ordered the device from the same vendor that supplied the servers to Meyer Technologies.

The dry run to disable the security system at Meyer Technologies a few nights ago went off without a hitch. Only days until the real deal, Derrick's confidence level soared.

His phone buzzed. The caller ID showed "Client." He didn't know the identity of his employer, but the healthy deposit the client had forwarded to his account provided the motivation he'd needed to accept the job.

"Derrick, give me some good news," the nameless voice said.

Derrick smiled and said, "Yes, well, I think it's great news." Clearing his throat, he forced the quiver of a healthy fear from his vocal cords. He knew from previous conversations that his client had a deep, personal motive pushing him like a pitcher throwing the last ball of a no-hitter. His client expected more than a pennant. He wanted the World Series.

"The breach test passed with flying colors. We are ready for the next phase."

"Have you identified the help inside Becker that you need?"

"Yes, sir, I have. A perfect candidate. His name is ..."

"Don't need to know," the client said. "That's your business."

"Of course. I have a recruitment plan in progress as we speak."

"You'll meet your next deadline?"

"Absolutely, absolutely," as if repeating it ensured success.

"You'll hear from me then."

A typical call with his client. Direct, concise, with a demand for success.

Derrick made the finishing touches to the recruitment plan. He had selected his target inside the Becker Art Museum—Lyle Bernstein, head of the art restoration department, a logical choice, given Lyle had possession of the Picasso drawings in his workshop for his review and any necessary restoration.

Derrick didn't know why his client wanted the set of twelve Picasso drawings, but when the art detective discovered the Albert Becker Art Museum had recently received six of the twelve, his client wasted no time engaging Derrick to steal them.

Derrick knew little about art, but he knew it served as a currency for collectors and bad actors such as weapons and drug dealers. He didn't know if his client fit either of these classifications. He didn't care.

Plan, succeed, repeat. What could be easier?

What could possibly go wrong?

CHAPTER **30**

And?

Home of the Bernsteins, Paris, 1937

A THICK FOG CLOUDED Emma's thoughts after Josephine burst into Igor's party, with the dire warning of an imminent break-in at her house. Otto and Fritz rushed off by car to the Bernsteins, but Emma feared they'd be too late. *What if someone has broken in already?*

The car screeched to a halt in the Bernsteins' courtyard. Otto and Fritz jumped out. They froze. The front doors hung wide open, exposing the houseful of darkness. Emma arrived right behind, accompanied by Hemingway. She shuddered with shock, staring at the black, blank wall in her foyer. It had held twelve Picassos, then six, now ... none. *Who would do something so heartless?* Strangers had entered her home and taken what belonged to her. Could she ever feel safe in her own home again?

Emma clinched Otto's arm. He led the funeral procession, passing one dead, blank space after another. One tear after another fell. That's where the Chagall used to hang. Next to it used to be the melting clocks of Salvador Dali. One used-to-be after another. Vacant windows peering into the abyss.

Otto guided Emma's limp body to a chair. He fetched a glass of water from the bar and handed it to her.

After several sips and minutes, she reached for Otto with her cold, pale hand and turned to him. "How did this happen, Otto? What are we going to do about … this?" She gestured to the barren walls. In a few scant hours, thugs had erased an entire collection that she had lovingly curated over several years.

Otto walked to the bar, poured himself a bourbon, and took a swig. He turned to Emma. "My dear. I'll tell you what we're going to do about this." He slammed his glass on the bar. "We're going to find these bastards and get our paintings back!"

Hemingway and Fritz had trailed Otto and Emma through the house, maintaining their distance in the room. Hemingway walked to Otto. "Then we need to act fast. It is possible that your paintings are already on a train heading out of the country."

Emma turned to Otto. "Is that true?"

"Everyone in Paris has seen our collection," Otto said. "The thieves can't show or sell any of the pieces in this city."

Emma furrowed her brow. "There are plenty of collections in Paris they could have stolen. Why ours? Is it because …" She struggled to even suggest this. "We are Jewish?" She looked into Otto's eyes, pleading for an answer.

A non-political, passionate art patron, Emma didn't ignore events unfolding in Germany. She'd read the reports about problems for the Jews. *Could that happen here? Had it already?*

Hemingway poured himself a glass of bourbon, crossed the room, and sat in a chair opposite Emma and Otto. "I have something I need to tell you."

Everyone turned and focused on Hemingway, waiting for his next words.

"Josephine didn't go to Berlin just to entertain. She had a special assignment."

Fritz gave Hemingway an icy stare. "An assignment? What kind of assignment?"

"A small patriot group in Paris is secretly tracking events in Germany from a military perspective. We are sending agents to Germany to bring back firsthand information. We don't trust reports in the newspapers to tell us everything that's happening there. Josephine just returned from such a trip and we need to hear what she has to report."

Blankness filled everyone's eyes.

Hemingway refilled his glass and continued. "There's nothing more we can do tonight. You all need some shut-eye. I'll help you secure the front door. Tomorrow we will listen to Josephine's report."

Emma raised her hands. "That's it? That's all we're going to do?"

Otto took her hand. "Emma, he's right. It's late. We'll deal with it tomorrow. Why don't you get ready for bed?"

"Not until you come with me."

"Yes, dear. Let me secure the door first." He turned to Hemingway. "I'll get my tools and meet you at the door." He headed off to find what he needed from the storage room.

Fritz walked to Emma and took her hand. "I know this has been a shock. I'll have Claire come over tomorrow." He turned and followed Hemingway to the front door.

Emma sat alone in the room. Alone and without her beloved art. Where was her Psalm 84 God? Her sun and shield? Why hadn't He shielded her from this?

CHAPTER **31**

Let's Meet

Becker Art Museum, Irvine, California, 2022

LYLE PULLED THE DOOR to his workshop open with one hand, holding his buzzing phone in the other. The screen didn't display a name from his contacts, just a number with a local area code appeared. He often received calls from various local professionals seeking his advice.

"Hello," Lyle said, struggling with the door.

"I'm trying to reach Lyle Bernstein," a baritone voice said.

"Speaking."

"Mr. Bernstein, my name is Matt Perkins. I'm a grad student at Lines College doing research on preservation techniques. I got your name from one of my professors as a potential source. You have quite a reputation at Lines."

"That's alway nice to hear." Lyle walked through the workshop to his office. "Can you give me some specifics of what you are looking for?"

"I'm writing about current techniques for evaluating new acquisitions. Specifically, how to determine an approach to repairing the art prior to display."

Sounded a little general to Lyle. But he liked to invest in someone interested in his field, especially from his alma mater. He sat at his desk. "I suppose I could help. I am under a bit of a crunch on a current project. How much time would you need?"

"I'd love an hour, but I can be briefer if that's too long, and I'll be glad to work around your schedule. Maybe on your lunch break near the museum, or coffee before work?"

"Coffee before work is best." Lyle preferred not to interrupt his day by taking lunch breaks. "How about tomorrow? There's a Starbucks near the museum."

"Yeah, I know that one. How is seven?"

"That works fine."

"Great! What's your favorite? My treat."

"Dark roast of the day will do."

"You got it. I'll watch for you at the door. I've seen your picture on the website. See you at seven."

"Sounds good. Bye."

Lyle's thoughts returned to stealing the Picasso drawings and giving them to the Picasso estate. A foolish move or a golden opportunity? If the first, he needed to weigh the pros and cons. If the latter, he needed a plan or a man with a plan. Where do you find one of those?

CHAPTER 32

What To Do

Home of the Bernsteins, Paris, 1937

HEMINGWAY'S PLANS FOR THIS morning's discussion banked on the likelihood the shock from the previous night's horrendous events had diminished and clearer heads prevailed. Regardless, he carried the brunt of guilt for deciding Josephine should maintain communication silence on her mission to Berlin, delaying her warning to prevent the break-in at the Bernsteins. And now both the Bernsteins and the Hoffmans had paid a price for his decision.

He arrived at the Bernsteins along with Jacques and Denis and settled in a chair, nursing a full glass of bourbon. Forget about coffee or tea for a morning drink, especially this morning. He lit a new cigar, took a puff and exhaled, sending the first wisps of smoke through the streaming sunlight, along with his regrets about Josephine's mission. Jacques and Denis sat next to him, discussing the recent events. The clinking of china and silverware drifted through the air. Ever the hostess, even in the midst of distress, Emma prepared coffee, tea, and pastries for the gathering. The doorbell rang.

Otto welcomed Fritz and Claire, arriving together with Josephine, Dottie, and Robert Meyer. "Please, come in," Otto said.

Dottie leaned in and kissed Otto on the cheek. "How is Emma holding up?"

"She'll be better now, with you here."

The men followed the ladies into the salon.

Dottie reached Emma first. "Emma, darling." Tears started forming in Emma's eyes. Dottie wrapped her arms around Emma. Pulling out of the embrace, the two women held each other's arms. A reassuring smile filled Dottie's face. "We'll get through this. I promise."

"Yes, I know. I'm glad you're here," Emma said, forcing her own smile.

Otto turned to the guests. "Please, everyone, help yourselves to some food and find a seat. We have much to discuss."

That's putting it mildly.

Claire gave Emma a polite nod from across the room and followed Fritz to a seat.

Hemingway sipped his bourbon and waited for everyone to settle in the circle of seats. Before he had a chance to speak, Otto started. "I think you owe us an explanation about Josephine's trip to Berlin and what it had to do with last night."

"Yes. There is a lot to unravel." Hemingway took a puff of his cigar. "First, it is important we keep everything discussed here this morning among ourselves. I don't say this to alarm you. We're all better off if we can agree to that. Any objections?"

He scanned their faces for any sign of disagreement and after a sufficient length of silence, he continued. "I mentioned a small group here in Paris monitoring events in Germany, the Second Bureau." He motioned to his left. "Jacques here is the group's leader. And Denis, next to him, is one of our agents. We recruited Josephine because of her unique cover as an entertainer and also because she is a damn smart lady."

Dottie held her hand to her mouth, gasped, and turned to Josephine. "Oh, honey. What did they make you do?"

Josephine smiled. "Darling, it wasn't nothing I hadn't done before. I just did that funny banana dance at a nightclub and had a few drinks with a damn Kraut in my dressing room afterwards. That was the simple part. The hard part was getting stuck in Berlin knowing they were coming for your art. It nearly killed me, stranded for two days with no way to warn you."

Otto slammed his fist on the arm of his chair. "It nearly killed you? Look what happened to us. Why didn't you telegraph or phone us?"

"She followed our orders," Hemingway said. "We sent Josephine to pump Göring for intelligence about Germany's military plans and couldn't chance anyone learning about her mission or the intel she got from Göring. We gave her strict instructions to avoid communicating with us over the telegraph or telephone. It wasn't safe. Unfortunately, this meant keeping the plan to break into your house a secret too. If the train delay hadn't happened, Josephine would have returned in time to stop it."

Josephine took Emma's hand. "I'm so sorry, Emma."

"You should be," Otto blurted. He stood and started pacing. "Maybe, just maybe, you should have disobeyed your orders. Now, look at what we've lost." He gestured to the barren walls. "Oh, wait." He turned to Josephine and snarled, "There's nothing there."

Fritz stood and advanced toward Otto, pointing to the foyer. "The Picassos may have hung on your walls, but we're the ones who paid for them." His bellowing escalated. He shook his finger at Otto. "You're not the only ones out of pocket, Otto."

Otto closed in, challenging Fritz, and fired a louder response. "Are you blaming me for this?" He shook his head. "You don't want to do that." He thumped Fritz's chest. "I'm warning you." Fritz and Otto froze in a defiant stare.

Emma covered her ears. "Stop it, all of you! None of this is helping. Sit down."

Otto broke the stare first, sat next to Emma, and took her hand. Fritz sat, took a cigarette from his pocket, lit it, and took a long draw. He leaned his head back and pushed out a mouthful of smoke, staring at the ceiling.

"We're all better off if we can work together on this," Hemingway said. "I don't know why they wanted your collections. It's the first time it's happened in Paris."

Claire turned to Fritz. "It's because we're Jewish, isn't it, Fritz? You just told me the other day we need to protect ourselves." She turned to Hemingway. "Is this what you meant? The first time it's happened in Paris, to Jews?"

"I think I can help." Everyone turned to Robert Meyer. "I travel to Berlin for my job. I belong to a church organization monitoring events there. It is a Protestant group, but we have strong relations with many Jewish leaders."

Fritz turned to Robert. "Have you seen how they're treating the Jews?"

"Yes." Robert paused. "For one thing, the Nazis have barred Jewish doctors from practicing medicine in German institutions. Jews can't serve in the military and most Jewish businesses suffer from boycotts."

Otto started pacing again. "That damn Hitler! It's all about his Aryan race theory. He's talked about it for years. We thought that's all it was, just talk. Now you tell us Jewish shop owners are losing business, doctors can't practice, and Jews can't even join the army. What's next?"

Emma looked up at Fritz. "But that's in Germany. We're in France. What does Hitler want with France?"

"Last year, Germany reoccupied the Rhineland," Hemingway said. "Troops are on our border now. That's why we send agents to Germany. We need to know the Germans' plans and prepare accordingly."

He damn well knew what Hitler planned to do after witnessing the German aggression in Spain and their decimation of Guernica.

"I will continue to pass on what I learn from my contacts," Robert said. "And the French Reformed Church will stand with you, no matter what happens."

"No matter what happens" doesn't sound very reassuring. Hemingway had hoped to steer the conversation clear of any dismal predictions about France. What hope could he offer?

"The Second Bureau will do everything we can to find information about your collections," Hemingway said.

Otto returned to his seat. "Shouldn't we call the police? We need to report this."

Hemingway needed to nip this in the bud. "You call the police, and you'll find yourselves in the newspaper. If you don't want to alarm your art clients, you need to keep this close to your vest. In the meantime, I suggest you do everything you can to secure your homes and galleries."

Was that reassuring enough? Was there anymore he could do? Damn Nazis.

Dottie broke the silence. "Emma, would you like some company today? How about we girls spend a day together?"

"Please, yes," Emma said with the hint of a smile.

Dottie started giving directions. "All right, Hemingway, you go do your planning and take the men with you. Otto, you need to properly fix your front door lock. You want your wife to feel safe in her own home, don't you? Of course you do."

The ladies gathered around the coffee, tea, and pastries. Hemingway led the men out to continue the discussion at a local cafe.

What more could he offer at this point? Where were those damn paintings? Why were the damn Nazis stealing art from Paris Jews? Damn it to hell.

CHAPTER 33

Really?

Conference Room, Meyer Technologies, Irvine, California, 2022

AJ SAT IN HIS office, reviewing Curt Matthew's breach incident report and marking items to discuss with a yellow highlighter. Curt's report detailed potential issues and procedures the company needed to address. AJ had his own list, starting with Hank, the guard at the receiving dock, one of AJ's first employees. He interviewed Hank the day after the breach and learned he'd followed the delivery protocol to a T. The perpetrators had done their research and gone to great length to reproduce the vendor's uniforms, delivery van logo, and ID badges. Everything looked identical to the real vendor who had delivered the previous day. Hank had no reason to suspect the fakes.

AJ asked the hardware engineers to check the power supplies the fake team claimed needed replacing. "Nothing suspicious," they said. Their diagnostics and their visual inspections found nothing wrong.

AJ met with Curt at a small, round table in his office. He preferred fostering an atmosphere encouraging a team effort instead of a hierarchical setting of boss-to-employee sitting across from each other at a desk. "We know now the breach affected the security systems at the Albert Becker Art Museum," AJ said. "Interesting. They were the only venue affected. I spoke to Brian Miller and asked him to investigate any problems the breach caused at the museum. We'll call him in a few minutes to see what he found. First, I have a few questions about your incident report."

AJ turned to the first page with highlighting. "You say here, on page two, that before installing the system, you ran through several test scripts looking for issues."

Curt looked at the report and turned to page two and read the lines AJ mentioned. "Yes." He looked up and pushed his horn-rimmed glasses up his nose. "The quality assurance group reviewed the scripts and approved them."

"Did any of the scripts include testing for power failures?"

"Well, all of our systems include code for responding to a power failure, so yes."

AJ sat back and folded his arms. "So why would someone sneak in power supplies?"

"I looked into those power supplies." He turned a few pages. "Look at page four." AJ turned to page four. Curt pointed to the middle of the page. "They're the exact model and series we originally installed. The hardware engineers examined them carefully. They found one tiny thing, but it could be an oversight."

AJ raised his eyebrows. "What tiny thing?"

"The label on the power supply showed the install date from two months ago, the original install date, instead of the date of the bogus delivery."

"So, it should show the date of the breach when they allegedly installed the new power supplies?"

"That's correct."

AJ started tapping his fingers on the table. He looked up at the ceiling, took in and thrust out a deep breath, and looked back at Curt. "That suggests one of two things." AJ pointed with one finger. "Either the phony technicians didn't follow the procedure to record the date correctly or"—AJ pointed two fingers—"they didn't actually replace the power packs at all and did something else to the servers."

AJ hadn't considered the latter possibility until he said it, thinking out loud. But he'd have to hold that thought.

"It's time to call Brian. Let me get him on speaker."

AJ made the call and set his phone on the table. "Brian, I have Curt here with me."

"Good morning, gentlemen."

AJ leaned forward and stared at his phone. "Did you find anything unusual at the museum after the breach?"

"No, not a single thing. We don't have any systems here that record downtime or breaches like you do there. Nothing seemed amiss in the museum. I talked to all the department heads, without letting the cat out of the bag. None of them found anything to report."

"Hmm. Has anything odd happened at the museum lately besides this?" AJ said.

"I wouldn't say odd. Extraordinary, yes. But not odd," Brian said.

AJ cocked his head. "Oh, what's that?"

"We recently received, through a donation, six amazing Picasso portraits previously unknown in the art world. This is a major boon for the Becker."

AJ nodded. "Yes. I heard about those. Congratulations, by the way. Are they valuable enough for someone to break in and steal?"

"They're priceless," Brian said. "But we have your security system protecting them."

AJ and Curt stared at each other's sullen face. AJ appreciated Brian's confidence in his systems, but he had to face facts. The breach lasted only five minutes. This time. Long enough for someone to break in and steal the Picassos if it happened again? What if the system went down again and someone actually stole something?

I need to get things under control.

AJ leaned toward the phone with his shoulders hunched and his hands clasped in his lap. "I appreciate that, Brian, and I assure you,"—he nodded, to punctuate his words—"we will continue working on our end until we find the cause of this outage. If you learn anything more, please call me."

"Sure will," he said. "Say hi to Grace for me."

AJ leaned back in his chair. "Will do. Thanks, Brian. We'll talk later." He ended the call and looked at Curt. "So, any thoughts?"

Curt took his glasses off, nibbled on the temple tip, then shook his glasses with each comment. "We've looked at software. We've inspected and tested the hardware. I'm a little stumped at this point."

AJ leaned forward. "Can you detect incoming wireless activity attempting to take over control of our systems?"

Curt straightened his papers. "Seems a little farfetched. Perhaps." He put his glasses on. "But if someone attempted to control our systems, why control them for only five minutes?"

"Yes, that is the question, isn't it? Look into the wireless thing and let me know if you find out anything."

"Absolutely. Anything else?"

"Nope. That should do it."

Curt headed to the door, stopped, and turned to AJ. "I know this is something we've never experienced, but we'll figure it out, AJ." Curt smiled. "I'm sure."

"Thanks, Curt. Keep up the good work."

Curt left the office and AJ walked back to his desk. He rolled his chair around to look out his window, into the endless blue sky. Clouds drifted across the horizon, dropping shadows on the hills in the distance.

Will we really figure it out? Lord, what's going on? I thought I had everything under control.

CHAPTER **34**

Dehomag Visit

Alexanderplatz Census Complex. Berlin, Germany, 1937

GERMANY'S WILLY HEIDINGER SERVED two masters, playing a critical role for both IBM and the Führer. He resurrected IBM's earnings in Germany and provided the Nazis with innovative technology, meeting their increasing need for computing power. Thomas Watson, IBM's CEO, and Heidinger entered a love-hate relationship. It began the day Watson acquired ninety percent ownership of Dehomag, IBM's subsidiary in Berlin, after Heidinger incurred massive debts during the German monetary crisis after the Great War. This left Heidinger a mere ten percent ownership, barely enough for him to continue managing Dehomag. But Heidinger had one thing Watson didn't have—Hitler's ear. With direct access to Hitler, Heidinger persuaded the Führer to purchase more and more of IBM's technology. This put Heidinger in a win-win position—building a robust computer infrastructure for the Reich and handing IBM accelerating earnings. Watson needed Heidinger as much as Heidinger needed Watson.

Heidinger had supervised the cleanup and organizing of every square inch of Dehomag prior to Robert Meyer's first visit. Thomas Watson's portrait hung next to Hitler's in the lobby. The IBM nameplate on hundreds of keypunch machines gleamed. Heidinger had communicated his expectations to every person in the complex. He needed and expected Meyer to send a favorable report of his leadership ability and accomplishments to Watson.

Heidinger arrived at the Adlon Hotel to meet Meyer exactly at ten o'clock. He entered the lobby and found Meyer, wearing a formal suit, with a briefcase in hand, waiting near the concierge. Heidinger wore a formal suit, too, but with one major difference—the swastika armband on his left sleeve.

Heidinger extended his right hand. "Welcome, Mr. Meyer. It is our pleasure to have you visit us today."

Robert accepted the handshake. "Good morning. Thank you for providing transportation to your facility. I sometimes have problems with the taxis in Berlin."

Heidinger smiled. "We can't have that, can we? Come. My car is waiting for us."

Robert followed Heidinger out of the hotel to the Mercedes-Benz, adorned with Nazi swastikas. Heidinger joined Robert in the back seat for the twenty-minute drive to the census center. The driver pulled out onto *Unter den Linden* across from the Brandenburg Gate and started driving the route Heidinger had plotted. No need to drive through any sections of Berlin with signs demanding the boycott of Jewish businesses. Far better to see the thriving businesses owned by exemplary Aryan German citizens—the Germany the world must see.

They passed numerous outdoor cafes filled with well-dressed patrons under the warm morning sun, shining on tables filled with cups of coffee, strudel, and copies of *Das Reich*, the Nazi's weekly newspaper. Heidinger pointed to scenes along the way. "Such a delightful day in Germany, no?"

Robert responded with a tepid, "Yes, it is." The drive took them past an endless display of red, white, and black swastika banners hanging from every building along the way.

The driver parked the car at the entrance to the massive warehouse structure. After stepping out of the car, Robert surveyed the building, slowly turning his head from left to right. Heidinger grinned with pride. "It is magnificent, isn't it?"

Robert turned to Heidinger. "Much bigger than I imagined."

"Come, come. Let's begin."

They walked into the lobby, flanked by offices on the left and right. Heidinger opened the door to the processing room. Robert stepped through the door. His jaw dropped.

"Quite a sight, isn't it?" Heidinger said.

A sea of workers filled every square inch of the cavernous room. Row after row, from wall to wall, keypunch operators sat elbow to elbow, hunching over their keyboards, their heads constantly turning between documents and keyboards. The clacking of keys smothered the air like a thick rumble of snare drums.

Hazy sunlight filtered in through smudged windows along the sides of the room, providing just enough light for the workers to read the documents. Long red swastika banners hanging on the walls interrupted the dullness of the room.

Heidinger began his tour speech. "This is where it all happens. Keypunch operators read the census documents and punch the information from each document onto a single card." He pointed to the operator next to him, oblivious to the visitor. "Each operator completes one hundred and fifty cards an hour. Impressive, no?"

A clerk passed them in the aisle, pushing a trolley loaded with stacks of new cards. Pointing to the cards, Heidinger said, "These just arrived from New York, thanks to your coordination."

Robert picked up a card. "Yes, I remember helping our staff prepare those for you."

They continued walking and came to an area identified by a sign reading "ERR," an abbreviation for Einsatzstab Reichsleiter Rosenberg. Hearing a loud exchange of words, they both turned to a heated conversation.

"Have you finished the cards from France yet? My superiors demand the reports now!" a red-faced command leader blurted, his back to Heidinger.

"Command Leader, sir, we've received them daily for the last month," the supervisor said. "The amount of cards is unmanageable." The supervisor pointed to a pile about to fall over. "We'll never get through that backlog."

"This is our highest priority." The command leader knocked the supervisor's chest with each snarl. "You...must...catch...up!"

The supervisor cowered. "Yes sir. I'll see to it. But sir, why are we dealing with data about artwork with all these census forms to process?"

The command leader slammed his hand on the desk. The supervisor jerked. "Do I need to remind you that your duty is to follow orders? Leave the priorities to those responsible. Now, *schnell*, on with it!" The clerk turned back to his stack of documents and continued his work. The command leader turned around, face to face with Heidinger.

The command leader's face snapped from surprise to military sternness and he saluted Heidinger. "Sir. I didn't expect to see you today. Just keeping everyone in line, sir."

"Yes. Good work. That's why I hired you." Heidinger turned to Robert. "We don't tolerate the questioning of authority and sometimes correction is necessary to keep workers on track."

Robert clasped his hands behind his back. "If I may ask, what art data are you processing?"

"This is a special assignment for the Führer. It is something I cannot discuss with you."

A puzzled look crept across Robert's face. Heidinger grinned and patted Robert on the back. "Just a project for tracking our art assets. That's all." He pointed to the right. "Let me show you the sorting machines."

Heidinger guided Robert to a room filled with IBM sorting equipment. Operators carried stacks of punched cards from a table and placed them into the sorting machines. The machines sorted the cards into separate stacks meeting specific criteria—city code, type of employment skill, or even by membership of a specific religion.

On the wall behind the sorters, a sign hung above a door with the word "*Nur Autorisiertes Personal.*" Robert pointed. "What is in that room?"

Heidinger banked on Robert not knowing the English translation.

"Just a storage area, is all. Shall we head out?" He gestured to the entrance.

They returned to the car. Heidinger smiled at Robert. "I trust you will write a favorable report to Mr. Watson."

"You are running an efficient operation, by all appearances," Robert said. "My report to Mr. Watson will state as much. Thank you for the tour. It was eye opening."

"My driver will take you back to your hotel, unless you wish to travel to a different destination," Heidinger said.

"Perhaps he can drop me at one of those cafes near the hotel," Robert said.

"Yes. He knows them well. It is getting to be time for lunch."

The driver closed the door after Robert entered the car, took his place in the front seat, and drove off.

Heidinger returned to the room with the sign reading "Nur Autorisiertes Personal," or in English, Authorized Personnel Only. German engineers had taken IBM's computing technology to a whole new level unknown by Watson in New York, and the machine in this room proved it. The giant, gray metal box reached from floor to ceiling. Paper tape on an eight-inch diameter reel passed through a small box to a matching spinning reel on the right. The box punched holes on the paper tape, recording data from punch cards stacked in a special card-reading machine. The paper tape recorded thousands of cards for later retrieval—a giant step forward in computing. If Thomas Watson knew about this technology, he'd be begging for it. But for now, the Nazis kept a lid on this secret.

Heidinger walked to the table, picked up the latest report and tapes for the ERR, and took them to his office. He set the tapes on a side table and put the report on his uncluttered desk. He began reading the report of the most recent catalogued items from Paris. The report included only six art pieces, all by the same artist, Pablo Picasso, taken from a Jewish patron. He grinned. How sad for those Parisian Jews.

He rocked back in his chair, hands behind his head, smiling, taking a moment for self-congratulations, knowing his superiors respected him for his skillful command of the computer operation. Turning to the vault, he dialed the combination, opened the door, took out the security log, and placed one tape inside. He opened the black hardback security log, flipped to a blank page, and entered the most important data: 12453, the TIN or tape identification number, and 647109182, the security key. The computer needed both codes to read the data on the tape. He returned the log to the vault and locked the door.

According to protocol, he prepared the second copy of the tape, including the TIN and security key, for shipping to an archive location. Having a desire for this particular catalogue of art, he took his personal diary from the locking desk drawer and made the same entry he made in the security log. It never hurt having an excellent source for his own art collection. Another good day for the Third Reich, IBM, and him.

Scan or tap the QR code to read AJ's blogpost about Dehomag.

CHAPTER 35

Who's Who?

Starbucks, Irvine, California, 2022

LYLE BERNSTEIN AND EARLY mornings didn't mix well. The gray, overcast sky didn't help much. He obeyed the obnoxious 6:00 a.m. alarm, showered, shaved, and dressed in time to meet with Matt Perkins, the graduate student seeking to drink from Lyle's well of knowledge and experience. With backpack slung over his shoulder, Lyle entered the agreed-upon Starbucks.

"Good morning, Mr. Bernstein. I'm Matt Perkins. I've got a table back in the corner for us. Your dark roast is waiting for you."

Matt led Lyle to a table and gestured to their cups. Both men put their backpacks on the floor, coincidentally, side by side.

Matt leaned forward. "First, Mr. Bernstein, I want to tell you how impressed I am with your work at the Becker. That 1950s Los Angeles exhibit was amazing. Your restoration work breathed life into those oils."

Lyle hadn't come for the flattery. He wanted to help this grad student, but he had a lot of work waiting for him.

Lyle took removed the lid from his cup and took a sip. "Glad you enjoyed them. Now, what can I help you with?"

"Word has it that Becker recently acquired a collection of intriguing Picasso drawings. Is that true?" Matt said.

Did everyone know about them? The Becker hadn't issued a press release yet.

Lyle looked up from his coffee. "Yes, that's true."

Matt grinned. "That must be exciting. Restoring art for a world premier."

Where is this going? Didn't this guy want help with a paper?

Lyle set his coffee down. Impatience filled his voice. "Matt, can we get on with the topic you called about?"

"We will." Matt pointed. "But first I need to tell you I know someone who is interested in those Picassos."

Lyle furrowed his brow. "You mean someone is interested in seeing them? They'll be on display soon, at the Becker."

Matt's grin vanished. He looked directly into Lyle's eyes. "No, I mean, someone is interested in acquiring them."

Lyle's body shuddered. *Something's wrong. Who is this guy?* He regained his composure, pretending he misunderstood what Matt had implied.

"Well, Matt. The museum recently acquired them. They're for display, not for sale."

Matt leaned back in his chair. He lowered his head and his voice. "Oh, he doesn't want to buy them. He wants to..."—Matt made air quotes—"have them."

"Then..." Lyle's mind started racing. This meeting had nothing to do with a graduate student research paper at all. Lyle's family had searched for these drawings for three generations. It never occurred to him that someone else wanted them.

"I think this meeting is over," Lyle said, reaching for his backpack.

"I don't think so, Lyle." Matt gently grabbed Lyle's arm. "Please, remain calm and everything will be fine. By the way, you have a lovely family."

A cloud of terror descended on Lyle.

Matt reached into his backpack, pulled out a photograph, placed it on the table, and smiled. "Such a beautiful wife and two happy kids."

Lyle's body tightened into a square knot. *Is this really happening in the middle of a Starbucks?* His neck muscles squeezed the words out of his throat. "What about my family? What are you going to do?"

A grim reaper's smile emerged on Matt's face.

"Absolutely nothing, if you follow a few simple instructions."

Words barely made their way out of Lyle. "Why should I? What's in it for me?"

"First, your family remains safe. And since my friend is very generous, you receive a tidy sum of money."

Matt slid a thick envelope across the table. Lyle lifted the flap—a mass of one-hundred-dollar bills. Lyle immediately closed the flap, nervous about flashing a bunch of cash in public.

"That's the first half. A security deposit, shall we say? Complete the job and you'll see the rest and your family."

This is insane. Am I dreaming? He forced a breath into his tight chest. "All right. What do you want me to do?"

Matt handed him another envelope. "Here are the instructions. Follow them and everything will be fine." He spoke in the tone of a reassuring parent.

Lyle opened the envelope and scanned the instructions.

"Easy, right?" Matt said.

"Yes, easy," Lyle repeated in a monotone voice, putting the instructions back in the envelope.

He had to think fast. Taking the two envelopes, he reached down to put them in his backpack. His hand scrambled inside his backpack, shaking and searching for something. *Is that it? Yes.* He found what he wanted, cupped it in his hand, pulled it out of his backpack, and put it in an open pocket on Matt's backpack. *Quick enough not to raise suspicion?*

"And I have your assurance no harm comes to my family?" Lyle said.

"No need for that to happen. Just follow the plan." Matt picked up his backpack, stood, and looked down on Lyle like a predator gloating over his prey. "We'll be in touch. No worries. Hope you enjoyed the coffee." He slung his backpack over a shoulder and casually strolled out of Starbucks.

Lyle reached for the photo of his family but his trembling hand knocked over his cup, flooding coffee over the picture, drowning his family in dark roast. A morning coffee with Matt Perkins at Starbucks had shattered his entire world.

CHAPTER 36

The Beautiful and The Useful

International Exposition of Arts and Technology, Paris, 1937

"*Amigas, rapidas.* Quickly," Picasso encouraged his two friends. "The opening speech by French President Albert Lebrun is about to begin."

Picasso led Dottie and Emma through the crowds to the viewing area of the Palais de Chaillot for the opening of the International Exposition of Arts and Technology in Modern Life. Rushing to their seats, they turned their heads to a buzzing coming from a dirigible floating above, in the clear, blue sky. Settling in their seats, the murmurs of a multitude of languages engulfed them.

Picasso surveyed the crowd of world travelers and smiled. "So many countries and so much peace and joy. At least here, at least today."

Dottie said, "So exciting. I know something wonderful is in store."

"Si. Yes. From the useful to the beautiful. As the great French Victor Hugo said, 'The beautiful is as useful as the useful. Perhaps more so.'"

"Why, Pablo, you are so well-versed in our culture," Emma said, touching his arm.

"Profound ideas, whether for the eye or the ear, always find a way to travel across lines on a map," Picasso replied.

The president stepped to the podium, acknowledging the roar of welcoming applause from the international audience. Following his warm greetings and recognition of the myriad of groups responsible for the exhibition's preparations, his voice boomed for the finale of his speech. "And it is with great pleasure I declare the 1937 International Exposition of Arts and Technology in Modern Life officially open."

The roar of acclamations in French, Spanish, German, Russian, Italian, and a dozen more languages turned to mumbling, as the crowd streamed to various pavilions.

"Come. Let me be your guide today," Picasso said. He knew the layout well, traveling through the exposition, day after day, preparing his mural in the Spanish Pavilion. Turning toward the promenade, he led them to their first stop, the Peace Pavilion.

Dottie tilted her head back, taking in the towering column. "Kinda reminds me of the Tower of Pisa, round and tall. Interesting star on top."

Emma faced the three letters around the base. "PAX. Did they misspell that?"

Picasso explained. "It's not French, dear. The French is *paix*. PAX is Latin for peace, a universal word not to be owned by any one country. We are all one people regardless of how we say the word *peace*."

"Oh, if that were only true," Dottie said, looking at Emma and locking arms with her.

Picasso continued the promenade, past food booths decorated with bunting and flags in the vendor's sovereign colors. He stopped at the most spectacular view of the entire exhibition. On the left stood the German pavilion—a monolith topped with an eagle clutching a swastika wreath. On the right, the Russian pavilion, rising to the sky, crowned with a working man and a peasant woman standing together, clutching a hammer and sickle. The two pavilions stood as powerful and resolute as the two forces they embodied. In the distance between the two, Mr. Eiffel's tower punctuated the scene—a French exclamation point separating Germany and Russia.

Emma turned her head toward the Russia pavilion, then to the German pavilion across the street, pointing her finger back and forth. "It's almost as if they are dueling."

Picasso looked back and forth at the two pavilions. *Perhaps they will someday.*

Dottie walked closer to the German pavilion and stretched her neck to take in the structure's height. "Dottie, what a pleasant surprise." She turned around. Bruno Lohse.

"Emma and Señor Picasso too," Lohse said. "I'm delighted to see you all. Quite something, isn't it?" He turned to the German pavilion and smiled. "Designed by one of Mr. Hitler's favorite architects, Albert Speer."

Picasso pointed to the eagle on top. "Almost as if Germany is taking in all of France, yes, Herr Lohse?"

Did I make my point clear to the German?

Dottie chuckled. "Oh, Pablo. It's only an eagle." Lohse grinned and joined her chuckle.

Dottie's naïveté worried Picasso. *Perhaps seeing my mural depicting the Nazi's atrocities in Guernica will open her eyes.*

Lohse spread out his hands in a welcoming gesture. "Germany is here to celebrate with the rest of the world at this grand exhibition. Señor Picasso, I am so very eager to see your mural in the Spanish Pavilion."

Dottie lit up. "We're heading there now. Care to join us?"

He is in for a rude awakening.

"Why not," Lohse said.

"Great. Pablo, lead the way," Dottie said.

Music from a distant band floated through the air along with mist from waterspouts, shooting up from reflecting pools on either side of the promenade.

Dottie wiped the spray from her face. She took in a long sniff of something that woke her stomach. She followed the rich aroma, which led to a German vendor standing behind his cart. Steam floated from a tray of pretzels. "Let's have a pretzel."

"I could use a snack," Claire said.

Picasso turned away. *No infernal German pretzels today.*

Picasso looped his arms with Dottie and Claire. "Ah, but you must try these tamales from my hometown." He guided them to the Spanish vendor across the promenade, and turning back, he smirked at a perturbed Lohse.

They walked on to the Spanish Pavilion, far more modest than the German skyscraper. In fact, the boxlike structure comprised a mere three levels. Picasso led them to the entrance and paused, allowing them time to read the slogan on the wall. WE ARE FIGHTING FOR THE RIGHT OF THE SPANISH PEOPLE TO DETERMINE THEIR OWN DESTINY. He continued to the room displaying his mural and the work of other Spanish artists.

Picasso originally planned to portray an artist's studio for the exhibition. This radically changed after he read the news reports describing the bombing of Guernica, Spain, earlier in the year. Supporting the Nationalist Army in the Spanish Civil War, Nazi aircraft dropped high explosive bombs, creating a firestorm in the center of town on market day. During the three-hour bombardment, the city suffered devastation, resulting in the death of a third of the population. Outraged by the slaughter, Picasso used this opportunity to expose the atrocity, not only for posterity, but for an international audience to witness and report back to their home countries.

"Thirty-five days I agonized to show the world an ocean of pain and death. How I abhor the military caste."

Dottie, Emma, and Lohse stood with Picasso, scanning the expansive mural from side to side, aghast, sucked in by twenty-five feet of grisly images portraying the horror of the German attack. Black and white tones of ashes. Grotesque faces. Mouths gaping open, bellowing, wailing, pleading. Unblinking eyes, forced to stare at the oncoming flames of death. Arms reaching up, desperate for a mother's comforting embrace.

"The world must know and remember," Picasso said.

"Oh, Pablo. This is ... gruesome," Emma said.

"Yes. War is gruesome. Right, Mr. Lohse?"

Dottie wiped the mascara running down her cheek and turned to Bruno. "Bruno, are the people in Germany aware of this?"

"Absolutely not. This is almost too unbearable to take in," Lohse said.

Almost too unbearable? What part of it is bearable?

Picasso turned to Lohse. "And yet, there it is."

How will the world perceive the mural—beautiful or useful?

The surrounding crowd had grown to fill the room. An eerie silence belied the number of people gasping at the abomination.

Emma turned away from the mural, dabbing her eyes with a damp handkerchief. She clutched Dottie's arm. "I need to leave now. This is too much, too much." Dottie and Emma slogged their way through the crowd, away from the mural.

"Yes, this is too much," Picasso said, looking directly at Lohse. "Too much."

"This shouldn't happen to anyone, anywhere," Lohse said, returning Picasso's stare.

Did he really mean it?

Picasso turned his back to Lohse.

Is he an opportunist art dealer oblivious to his government's ideology? Perhaps. Hard not to condemn him guilty by association.

"I believe it's time for me to return to my pavilion," Lohse said.

Yes, go back where you belong.

Lohse trudged toward the door, stopped, and turned back for one last look, then disappeared into the crowd.

Inside the pavilion, Pablo watched the horrified, speechless visitors.

Do they understand this mural? Do they understand who the Nazis really are? If it could happen in Spain, where else?

Scan or tap the QR code to read Grace's blogpost about the International Exposition of Arts and Technology

Chapter 37

Blink, Blink

Lyle Bernstein's Office, Albert Becker Art Museum, Irvine, California, 2022

AFTER HIS TERRIFYING ENCOUNTER with Matt Perkins, Lyle weaved through the crowd of anxious Starbucks addicts and shoved aside a lone coffee junkie blocking the door. Laser focused on his car, he charged across the wet street. Honks and brake screeches entwined with the ringing in his ears. He fumbled for the key fob in his pocket, unlocked the door, and thrust his backpack and trembling body into the front seat. His gasping subsided, but the adrenaline rushed through his fingers and whitened the knuckles of two stiff hands locked on the steering wheel. He pried them loose and grabbed his phone. Tapping the screen, he launched the app to locate the AirTag he'd stashed in Matt's backpack. The tag's location and movement sprang to life. The first whoosh of relief.

Where are you going, Matt Whoever?

Lyle turned on his wipers, pulled out, and followed the route of the blinking dot in the app. He battled the thick, going-to-work traffic for fifteen minutes. *Why does a little Southern California rain turn everyone into a crazy driver?*

The blinking dot in the app stopped moving. He looked up from his phone and slammed his brakes. Didn't need to rear-end a Tesla this morning. He took a cleansing breath, checked his side mirror, and edged to the curb. The app showed the location of the AirTag—across the street. He slid down in his seat and studied the scene—a small strip mall with three buildings, including a mailing service, a chain drugstore, and an office with a window sign: DE INVESTIGATIONS.

Is that it?

He double-checked the address in the app. It matched. He surveilled the office for several minutes. The office door opened. Matt Perkins walked out and reached to unlock a car parked in front of the office. *It's him.* Matt turned and stared straight across the street, sizing up Lyle's car. Lyle shrank below the window level, his shirt sticking to the seat and his heart racing. After an eternity, Matt turned back to his car, entered, and drove off. Lyle sat up and wiped his forehead.

Calculating the timing of the events since leaving Starbucks, Lyle figured Matt had been inside the office for only a few minutes. *Enough time to give a report to someone on what transpired at Starbucks? A boss of some sort?*

Lyle scooted up and surveyed the area. No sign of Matt. Lyle headed to his office at the Becker.

He parked in the empty garage, grabbed his backpack, and headed in. Hurrying through the lobby, he glanced at the clock—at least another hour before anyone else showed up. He entered his workshop and headed to his private inner office. Shutting the door, he set his backpack down and collapsed into his desk chair. Time to breathe.

He grabbed the half-empty bottle of water on his desk and chugged the contents. Opening his laptop, it sprang to life. He logged in and headed straight to Google.

The search took .0143 seconds to find DE Investigations. Bingo. The website, an amateurish single landing page with a crude logo, displayed the business name,

DE Investigations, and address—a match to the AirTag app. At the top, the name of the business owner, Derrick Edwards.

Lyle rocked in his chair. *Is Derrick Edwards Matt Perkins's boss or partner?*

He turned away from the screen and picked up the sea-shell framed photo of his wife and children frolicking at the beach, a living color version of the family Matt Perkins threatened to harm. He ran his fingers across the picture, offering his three most treasured possessions a promise of protection. Could he follow the instructions, protect his family, and hang on to the six Picasso drawings?

He replaced the photo and pulled out Matt's instructions. There must be a way. He studied them until ... *Eureka.* A loophole in the plan. An open door to a workable scheme, but only if he mustered more courage than a mild-mannered art professional should ever have to muster. The loophole wasn't enough. He needed something more—eyes or ears inside the DE Investigations office to discover the details of their plan.

He turned back to Google and combed through articles describing miniature listening devices capable of transmitting over several miles.

What the heck am I doing? I'm not this person.

Within an hour, Lyle had loaded his Amazon shopping cart with everything he needed. He clicked on the Buy Now button and ... boom. Done. With same-day delivery, he'd completed phase one. If his plan worked, the six Picasso drawings had another adventure waiting for them.

The blast of lights coming on in the workshop jarred Lyle away from his newly hatched James Bondian assignment.

"You here, boss?"

Lyle slammed his laptop shut and bolted out of his office.

"How come the lights were off?" Diego rubbed his forehead. "Are you okay?"

Lyle leaned against the doorway, slowed his breathing, and forced a grin. "Doing some pesky administrative work. Easier with no one else around. You're early."

"Five minutes. Surprised?" Diego elbowed Lyle, walked to his workstation, and set his backpack on the table. He scooted into his chair, opened his notebook, and multitasked the rest of the conversation, staring at his screen. "You sure you're okay? You look really stressed."

Was it that obvious? "I'm fine. Got some budget numbers stuck in my head. I need to go back and finish up."

"Oh. Got it." Diego brought up his email. "I know how much you love budgets." Delete. Delete. "Good luck."

Lyle entered his office, closed the door, and opened his laptop. He Googled a nearby bakery and placed an online order for chocolate chip cookies. Pickup in an hour. On to ordering shipping supplies, a notecard, and a lot of luck.

**Scan or tap the QR code to see the website for
DE Investigations.**

CHAPTER 38

Armbands

Madison Square Garden, New York, 1937

A WEEK HAD PASSED since Robert Meyer's trip to Germany for his first meeting with Willy Heidinger, manager of the IBM subsidiary in Berlin. On his tour of the facility, Robert passed areas labeled *Nur Autorisiertes Personal*. He had picked up bits and pieces of German, an asset for his work, and knew the translation: AUTHORIZED PERSONNEL ONLY. Heidinger had kept him away from that area, but why? This troubled him, but not as much as two other issues: Hitler shifting his government progressively to the extreme right and Thomas Watson holding fast to conducting business-as-usual with the Nazis.

Watson assigned Robert to attend tonight's political rally at Madison Square Garden. "The newspaper described the rally as a pro-American event, but the key speaker is a German, Fritz Kuhn," Watson told him. "Find out why he's here. He could be an important contact for us."

Police directed Robert to a parking lot several blocks from the Garden. He walked around the corner and joined the torrent of New Yorkers streaming into a swirling pool of confusion in front of the auditorium. Hundreds of police on snorting horses formed a line to hold back thousands of fist-raising protestors, barking at those coming to the rally.

A bullhorn blared, "Be American. Stay at home!" An orchestra from a local Broadway show played the national anthem to encourage the self-proclaimed patriots.

A protestor broke through the line and planted himself in front of Robert, eye to eye. "Dirty Nazi." He shoved Robert's left shoulder, half-spinning him backwards, his hat flying. The protestor snarled, "Leave."

Robert regained his balance and ran his hand over his head. "Leave?"

The protestor pushed past Robert to assault another confused citizen, leading the flow of a dozen others who'd broken through the police line. Robert kneeled to retrieve his hat. The chaotic mob pressed around him, rocking him from side to side. He reached for his hat, but the ebb and flow of the crowd sabotaged his aim. Steadying himself with one hand on the ground, he grabbed his hat with the other. He stood. Panting. The rapids of demonstrators flowed around his body, jostling back and forth. Holding the hat brim with both hands, he clutched it to his chest.

What am I doing here?

He forced his way through the havoc and entered the auditorium.

A full body portrait of George Washington flowed from the ceiling to the floor behind the stage. Banners with stars and stripes flanked the Washington portrait. Next to them, something Robert never expected to see in New York—pennants with Nazi swastikas. Swastikas everywhere, even on the arms of most audience members.

How could anyone here, in America, in good conscience, hang Uncle Sam's red, white, and blue next to Hitler's red, white, and black?

He sat next to a gentleman slightly older looking, but certainly of a different persuasion. The armband.

The man turned to Robert. "Are you a follower of Herr Kuhn?"

"Follower?" Robert said.

"Yes. He leads the German American Bund." The man thrust his chest. "My son attends their camp. He's receiving such important training."

Robert scratched his left cheek. "From a German?"

The summer camps run by the German American Bund existed from coast to coast and accepted boys as young as six years old to receive training in archery and antisemitism. They learned how to pitch a tent and how to salute with "Sieg Heil." Modeled after the Hitler Youth program in Germany, Bund leaders sought to establish a Nazi ideology in America that included a pro-Hitler, anti-semitic, isolationist agenda.

"Ladies and gentlemen. Please stand for the national anthem."

A light rumble filled the hall from twenty-thousand chairs scratching the floor, commingling with the orchestra's introduction. Armbanded voices competed enthusiastically with voices sans armband. A procession of young men wearing brown shirts and Nazi armbands marched solemnly in step through the auditorium, carrying American and German flags. They climbed the stairs and spread across the full width of the stage.

The man next to Robert pointed to the front, turned, and shouted above the singing, "That's my son, leading the line across the stage."

"The one holding the Nazi flag?" Robert said.

"Yes."

That's a source of pride?

The singing soared to a conclusion. "And the home of the brave." A roar of "*Sieg Heil*" bellowed through the crowd. All but a few in the audience raised their right arm in a rigid salute toward the speaker approaching the podium.

A chill ran up and down Robert's body.

Fritz Kuhn stepped to the podium. He wore a military-style khaki jacket with a black tie and black pants. The black leather belt and shoulder strap emphasized the military appearance. And, of course, the armband.

"You all have heard of me through the Jewish-controlled press," he said in a thick German accent. "Wake up! You, Aryan, Nordic and Christians, and demand that our government be returned to the people who founded it. It has always been very much American to protect the Aryan character of this nation." The roar of the audience fueled the fire in his belly.

Who are these people? Robert looked around. Average New Yorkers, nicely dressed. Men in suits and hats. Women in fine dresses. People you'd expect at a Pro-American Rally. Probably church goers. But cheering on this revolting rhetoric? Had they forgotten Jesus was a Jew? That there is neither Jew nor Greek in Christ?

Kuhn's flagrant oratory grew more offensive the longer he spoke. "If George Washington were alive today, he'd be friends with Adolf Hitler." Robert shut his eyes for a beat, opened them, longing to wake from this dream, this nightmare.

Kuhn made his final vile remarks. Robert followed the euphoric crowd out the door, confronted by the throng of protesters still shouting and surging against the horse-mounted police, weary from holding them at bay for three hours. Robert headed for an edge of the danger and found a safe path out and back to his car.

He closed the front door of his home haven, put his hat on the rack, and dropped his keys in the bowl on the entry table. His wife called out from the bedroom. "How was the rally, dear?"

What was he going to tell her? Did he understand himself what he'd witnessed?

"Just a political rally, Doris. You know New Yorkers. People excited about their causes. Politicians with lots of hot air."

He needed to talk to Thomas Watson.

CHAPTER 39

Bases Loaded

Office of Derrick Edwards, Irvine, California, 2022

DERRICK EDWARDS MADE A quick stop at his office to deposit his backpack after his performance as Matt Perkins in his Starbuck's meeting with Lyle Bernstein. On to the gym.

How easy was that? I should go on the stage.

After his workout, he picked up his egg-white muffin breakfast sandwich and coffee. Munching and drinking at his desk, he started his daily routine—scanning news websites, reviewing Google alerts, and attacking his email inbox. With that mundane routine completed, he unlocked the side drawer of his desk and pulled out the file folder containing the plans for his current and most important nameless client. The handwritten label on the folder read: PICASSO.

He pulled out the page filled with brainstorming bubbles, comments, and what-if lists, connected by a tangle of multicolored lines. Next to this, he placed a typed numbered list. Time to check off the latest completed task: Bribe Lyle Bernstein. Check. The next task had Lyle Bernstein's name with the assignment:

Prepare the Picassos for the heist at the Becker Museum. Completion date—two days from today.

Derrick leaned back, fingers interlaced, and smiled.

You're batting a thousand, Derrick.

His phone buzzed. The caller ID showed Client. Perfect timing for an update.

"Status," the voice on the other end demanded.

Derrick grinned. "I have recruited an accomplice inside the Becker."

"He'll be ready in time for the next step?"

"Yes. He assured me all the—"

"I don't care what he assured you. What I do care about is what you can assure me. And I'm waiting for you to assure me that everything is in place."

"Yes, sir. It is. In fact, I'm meeting this afternoon with—"

"I don't care." Click.

The curtness of the client had startled Derrick in the early days of the project, but he'd grown accustomed to it. With his plan under control, he headed out for an extended lunch break.

***

Returning to his office, Derrick found a package leaning against the door. He stuck it under his arm, unlocked the door, and entered. He hadn't ordered anything recently, and strangely, the package had no sender information. He sliced through the packing tape and opened the box. A batch of chocolate chip cookies wrapped in cellophane. An envelope lay on top. He opened it and pulled out a card, thick for a note card. The handwritten note read: To Our Success. If his client sent this, it was out of character. But Derrick had a weakness for chocolate chip cookies, and these looked fresh. He set the notecard on his desk and took a bite. Just the right crunch and an ample portion of chips. He set the box on the back of his desk and organized his folders to prepare for this afternoon's meeting.

Derrick had selected two expert contractors from his arsenal to conduct the challenging operation. They had worked for Derrick before and proven themselves worthy. With the expected promptness, Duke and Butch arrived on the dot.

Sitting next to each other across the desk from Derrick, they scanned the pages he'd given them to review.

"Everything's in place," Derrick said. "The test outage at the Becker Art Museum went off without a hitch, and I have my inside man in place now."

Duke lit a cigarette and took a drag. "You're sure about him?" He exhaled the smoke over Derrick's head.

"Don't worry. He has enough at stake." Derrick rolled the baseball back and forth on his desk. "Did you visit the Becker and familiarize yourself with the layout?"

"Yeah, but we couldn't see any of the office areas," Butch said.

"Look at the map on the second page. You can see the complete layout. It's pretty basic. Two routes split off from the lobby. One to the galleries and the other to the employees' area. That's your way in to the offices. Each one has a label. The restoration office has a name plate with Lyle Bernstein's name. It's the third office on the left."

"How will we know what item to pick up?" Duke said, flicking ash on the floor.

"Look at item six for the description of the package," Derrick said.

Duke found item six. "That's clear."

The plan is very clear, very simple, very perfect.

"Butch, you head off southbound on your motorcycle with the decoy bag. Duke will turn northbound with the real package. The delivery destination is at the end of the list, along with the password for the courier picking up the package."

"Denny's on Sand Canyon?" Duke raised his head. "Are you serious?"

"It's open late, fewer people, and you won't look suspicious drinking coffee while you sit there. All you have to do is wait for the courier to find you and give you the password."

Duke looked down at the instructions. "Never too late for breakfast?" He looked up and snickered at Derrick. "What kind of password is that?"

"Just make sure you're wearing this Angel's hoodie so the courier can find you. He'll be wearing one too." Derrick handed the hoodie to Duke.

"Any questions?" Derrick said.

"Guess not," Butch said.

"Got it," Duke said.

"Good. Report back when you have completed your tasks." Derrick stood. "Good luck."

The two contractors folded their instructions, stashed them in their jackets, and left.

Derrick leaned back in his chair, munched on another chocolate chip cookie, and tossed his Angel baseball in the air over and over.

Play ball.

Chapter 40

What's Up?

Cafe La Rotonde, Paris, 1937

Josephine Baker's first mission to Berlin for the Second Bureau yielded mixed results. She had extracted intelligence from Göring about the imminent plot to steal the Bernstein's art collection, but a train delay and orders to maintain radio silence foiled a timely warning and led to a heartbreaking loss for the Bernsteins. On the plus side, she had allured Göring with her feminine mystique and firmly established a rapport with him. He remembered their connection in Berlin fondly enough to pursue her for an evening out on his current trip to Paris.

After receiving Göring's invitation, Josephine alerted Jacques about the opportunity to gather more intelligence. The unexpected contact with Göring opened the door to pry more military plans from the Nazi and clarify Germany's intentions toward France.

But as a friend of the Bernsteins and the Hoffmans, Josephine also wanted to pump Göring for more details about the recent theft of their art. He'd gone into great detail in Berlin about the plan and now that it had actually occurred, she wanted to find out what happened to the stolen pieces. Perhaps another flow of liquor could lead to a flow of clues to recover the art.

Jacques and Hemingway met with Josephine and formulated a plan of attack for this evening. Jacques stressed that Germany's military presence in the Rhineland posed the greatest threat to France. "Above all, you must press him about the next phase of their Rhineland occupation."

Hemingway agreed. "Yes. How the international community allowed the Germans to occupy the Rhineland without any resistance is beyond me. You'd think the Treaty of Versailles was null and void."

"If they violated that part of the treaty unopposed, there's no telling what they'll do next," Jacques said.

"Of course," Josephine said. "Maybe I can get an idea of the number of troops and extent of military equipment."

Jacques pressed her. "Also, find out if there are any other high-level Nazis in Paris other than Göring and Lohse and why they are here."

"I'll do my best," Josephine said. "If this goes as well as my Berlin assignment, I won't have trouble pumping this out of him. You can bet on that."

For the evening encounter, Josephine decked herself out in her most provocative gown with a daring neckline and a slit longer than her legs. The ensemble of a flowing satin number in ruby red, matching black jade earrings and necklace, and a white fur wrap created a nod to the red, black, and white swastika colors and a subliminal suggestion of ideological approval. She finished with a little extra rouge, just the right amount of Chanel Number 5, and luxurious eyelashes, maximized to draw him in to her gaze.

Exiting the taxi, Josephine entered the glow of lights from the Cafe La Rotonde marquee over the front door and the lines of colored neon lights framing the entrance. A perfectly lit stage for entrance of a star. And Josephine knew how to make an entrance. She flashed her larger-than-life ruby smile to the tuxedoed doorman and entered the lobby.

With a beaming smile, Pierre, the owner, reached out with wide open arms. "Miss Baker. Welcome back."

Josephine leaned in to kiss Pierre on the left cheek, then the right. "Quite a crowd tonight, Pierre."

"But you are the most special. Let me take your wrap."

She surrendered her white fur and glided toward the *maître d'*, allowing ample time for heads to turn, fingers to point, and voices to whisper.

The maître d' sprang to life. "Bonsoir, Mademoiselle Baker." She held her hand out for his welcoming kiss. "So nice to have you joining us at the Cafe La Rotonde. Your host, Herr Göring, is right this way."

"Thank you, André."

He guided her to the table where a smiling Göring stood to welcome her. "Good evening, Josephine. You certainly know how to make an entrance. May I say how beautiful you are looking tonight?" He walked around the table and pulled out her chair. Josephine sat and Göring leaned in behind her, slid her chair toward the table, and took a sniff. "That perfume suits you well."

Good. Time to initiate my flattery assault.

"Now, how did you know this is my favorite place in all of Paris?"

Hermann smiled and held up the wine bottle. "The French are excellent at making wine and we Germans are very good at gathering intelligence, ja? May I pour you some?"

"Please do. I see you didn't wait for me," she said, slowly sipping.

She needed more than wine to loosen him up. He'd downed half the bottle. A good start, but she'd need to shift him to something harder, soon. She sipped most of the glass and set it down.

Göring poured more. "Thirsty tonight?"

"Yes, I'm working on new songs for my act and my throat is as dry as the Sahara after all that rehearsing." She signaled to a waiter.

"Please bring my friend your best bourbon." She smiled at Hermann.

"And for you mademoiselle?" the waiter asked.

"I'm happy with the wine, thank you," Josephine said.

Hermann leaned in and raised his eyebrows. "You do like taking command, don't you?"

Staring into his eyes, she said. "I can't have my host drinking wine when I know he's craving something else." She held his gaze longer.

"Ah, Josephine. You are one of a kind."

The various dinner courses came and went. Josephine made sure the rounds of bourbon came and went, too, over and over. And on his insistence, a chilled bottle of champagne arrived at their table. Josephine masterfully manipulated the direction of the evening's conversation, bouncing from her nightclub act to news from the United States, and even the appearance of Hitler on the cover of *Time* magazine in 1933, thoroughly stroking Göring's ego. He spilled plenty of German beans.

By the last drop of champagne, Josephine had sucked every bit of intel out of Göring she and the Second Bureau had wanted to retrieve. Time to execute an exit.

"Hermann, I've had such a delightful evening. Perhaps the fates will continue to smile upon us for more times together in the future," Josephine said.

The free flow of liquor had done its job. "Jo, darrrling, you puuuut things sssso el-e-gant." He stumbled around the table and slid out her chair.

Josephine rose, offered her hand for a kiss. "Good night, Hermann. I'll treasure everything we've shared tonight. Everything."

He kissed her hand. "Good night, my dear Josephine."

With a smirk, Josephine strolled to the lobby, retrieved her wrap, and hailed a taxi. Not only had she weaseled out the information Jacques wanted, she also had something to help her friends, the Hoffmans and the Bernsteins.

CHAPTER 41

Your Package Has Been Delivered

Lyle Bernstein's Office, Albert Becker Art Museum, Irvine, California, 2022

DEHYDRATED, UNCAFFEINATED, AND STARVING, Lyle shifted his focus between the gala update meeting in progress with Brian Miller at the Becker and the threat by Matt Perkins to kidnap his family. He'd gobbled up his morning with the time spent planning his surveillance of Perkins and rushing home to put a more important plan in place—sending his family out of Matt Perkins's reach.

***

A blank expression froze on his wife's face.

"We'll have a relaxing getaway. The four of us, in the mountains." Lyle faked a smile and forced artificial calmness into his words. "I'll join you for the weekend." He fumbled for some random clothes in the dresser and threw them next to the suitcase on the bed.

"Lyle, this isn't like you." Cheryl pulled a strand of hair behind her ear. "We haven't even talked about this. What's going on?"

Yes, what is going on? I'm in this way over my head.

Suppressing the anger and fear brawling in his belly, Lyle slowed his words. "Take the kids out of school early. They deserve a break."

Cheryl picked up a shirt, clutched it to her chest, and bit her lip. "Lyle. You're scaring me. Please tell me what is happening." She stared, waiting.

How much should he tell her? She deserved to know something. How could he condense everything that had happened in the last four hours and still get her out the door?

"I promise to explain everything when I join you in Big Bear." He haphazardly stuffed more into the suitcase. "Until then, you need to trust me. Here's the key to Uncle Seymore's cabin. I've texted the address. Once you have the kids, the drive should only take two hours. Send me a text when you're on your way."

He helped her pack the car. She threw her arms around him and whispered in his ear. "I trust you. Whatever is going on, trust me to handle it along with you. Please?"

He pulled her closer, stroked her hair, and promised her with a kiss.

She left to pick up the kids. He returned to work in time for his meeting with Brian.

***

"Lyle, are you with us?"

Lyle turned his focus back to the meeting with Brian. "Sorry. Where were we?"

"Question is, where were you? Everything okay?"

"I'm fine." Lyle's right knee bounced like it was keeping up with a freight train.

"The Picasso drawings. How's the progress?"

"I've completed the scans." He wiped his brow with the back of his hand. "I'm working on eliminating any mold. Not much. And minor water damage." He forced his knee to a halt. "The last step is adding the UV protective glazing."

"By the way, you're keeping them locked up at night, right?"

Lyle rubbed his eyes. "Of course. I'm the only one with a key."

"You think you're on track for the opening date?"

Lyle's phone buzzed. An alert from the delivery service: *PACKAGE DELIV-ERED.*

Lyle pushed away from the table and shot out of his chair. "Brian, this is urgent. I'll get back to you." He bolted for the door. "Everything's fine with the Picassos."

Good thing I'm not Pinocchio.

He raced to his office, thrust open the door, and brushed past Diego.

"You okay, boss?"

Lyle ignored Diego, entered his office, slammed the door, and closed the blinds. He switched on the receiver, clicked the recorder, inserted an earbud, and waited.

A thud. Rustling. *The box of cookies?*

His phone buzzed. His body jerked. His wife's text message: *Have the kids. On our way. Love you.*

More rustling in the earbud and then ... nothing.

The knock at his office door nearly launched him out of his chair. Diego entered. Lyle yanked the earbud out.

"Boss, I wanted to double check—"

Lyle snapped. "Not now, Diego. Come back later."

"It'll only take—"

"Not. Now."

Diego left. Lyle put the earbud back in. A scraping noise. A voice.

That recorder better be getting this.

"Everything's in place. The test outage at the Becker went off without a hitch, and I have my inside man in place now."

Matt Perkins's voice. Or Derrick Edwards's? Lyle shuddered hearing him described as the "inside man."

"You're sure about him?" A different voice.

"Don't worry. He has enough at stake. Did you both visit the Becker and familiarize yourself with the layout?"

Both? There's two others with Matt/Derrick?

Lyle's office phone rang, twisting his nerves into a tighter knot. He held the phone to the ear without the bud.

"Hey, Lyle. This is Suzanne. I'm working on the social media for the Picasso display. Do you have any scans I can use?"

In the earbud, "You can see the complete layout. It's pretty basic. Two routes split off from the lobby. One to the galleries and one to the employees' area."

They've scoped out everything.

Over the phone, "Lyle, you there?"

"Yeah. Sorry. Scans? Uh, working on it."

In the earbud, "Each one has a label. The restoration office has a nameplate with Lyle Bernstein's name. It's the third office on the left."

They know where my office is.

Phone ear, "When can you send the scans?"

Bud ear, "How will we know what item to pick up?" "Look at item six for the description of the package."

Does it match the description in the instructions I got at Starbucks?

Phone ear, "Lyle, when can you send the scans?"

"Oh, um...Scans. Right. Next week okay?"

Bud ear, "The delivery destination is at the end of the list, along with the password for the courier picking up the package."

He needed to hear this.

Phone ear, "Okay thanks. I'll get—"

Lyle hung up.

Bud ear. "It's open late."

What is? What's open late? I missed it.

Lyle pressed his hand against the bud and listened to the rest of the conversation. "Good luck," followed by prolonged silence. He listened to another five minutes of silence and clicked the recorder off.

He locked his office door and forwarded his office phone to voice mail. His trembling hands reached for the digital recorder. He steadied his hand, tapped the rewind function, the play function, and began listening. He held his breath. "Everything's in place." *Phew.* The recorder captured the entire conversation, including the delivery destination and password he missed during the live conversation.

He let out a long sigh and melted into his chair, quivering from the four hours of adrenaline rush. He closed his eyes and transitioned into his karate breathing technique. Hands in the Sanchin position, inhale through the nose, exhale through the mouth. Yes. The wall of tension raised by the morning's nerve-racking horrors, fell brick by brick. Another breath in through the nose, out through mouth. His sensei's words comforted him. "Do not think you have to win. Think rather that you do not have to lose."

I do not have to lose those Picassos.

The last tension brick fell, making room for an ascending faith in his plan—recover the Picassos in the heist, store them in his safe place and, in due time, return them to the Picasso Estate.

He licked his sandpaper lips and looked around his office—nothing to drink, let alone eat. He stood. The room wobbled. He grabbed his desk until it stopped. Steadying himself, he walked out of his office.

"Diego. Sorry for earlier. It's been a rough day."

Diego looked up from the workbench. "Must have been. I've never seen you look so white."

"I need a snack."

In the break room, he washed down a crumbling granola bar with a tasteless cup of coffee. He pulled out his phone and called his wife. No ringing. No connection sound. Just silence. He tried again. Chilling silence. *Hadn't the cell providers removed the dead zones in the mountains a few years ago?*

One more time.

Stone.

Cold.

Silence.

The wall of tension started rising.

CHAPTER 42

This Little Light

Second Bureau Meeting Location, Paris, 1937

THEY SHOULD BE HERE by now.

Jacques Ponge paced back and forth in the Second Bureau's secret location, waiting for the others to arrive to hear Josephine's report on her recent encounter with Göring. He stopped to throw the butt of his cigarette on the floor next to the other two and smashed it with his boot. Time for the fourth. The windowless office adjoined other nondescript storefronts along the abandoned block. A wire hung from the ceiling with a crude fixture holding a single light bulb, providing a dull glow over a scraggy table and chairs. Over the course of their meetings, the walls had heard more than enough to send everyone to prison, but Jacques had picked this unassuming location to ensure that didn't happen.

Protocol dictated the members stagger their entrances to the room and approach the location from different directions to avoid any undue attention. A block away, Hemingway paused and leaned against a crumbling stone wall. He relit his cigar and enjoyed a few puffs, the glow of his cigar barely visible in the moonless dark. He checked both directions, strolled on, and entered the room. Denis approached from the opposite direction and entered. Dottie and Josephine made their way down the block, arm in arm, chatting and laughing.

Five glasses of wine greeted the members. Two bottles waited. *Enough for tonight?*

Jacques cut the anxious pleasantries short. "Josephine. Please. Your report."

Josephine set her glass on the table, crossed her legs, and settled back in her chair. "I gotta tell you all. Herr Göring is such an easy mark. He just can't hold his liquor or his tongue. I did my homework and prearranged with my dear friend André, the maître d', to keep the drinks coming with a little something extra in them."

She paused for a drink of wine.

"By the end-of-evening champagne, he was spilling the beans right and left." She rubbed her hands together and faced Jacques. "Where do you want me to start?"

"The Rhineland," Jacques said, jiggling the cigarette loosely held by his lips.

Josephine leaned her head back. "Let's see. What did he say?" She wagged her finger in the air. "Oh yes. He said, 'You could've blown me over with a feather.' The Nazis couldn't believe how easily they moved their German troops into position. And with no reprisals. He said Hitler deemed it a defensive move, but if the French had even mobilized, he would have retreated."

Jacques slammed his hand on the table, shaking the glasses. "Damn. Such pathetic French leadership. The German Foreign Office told our ambassador in Berlin they'd only send two thousand troops."

"Now they're up to fifty thousand," Josephine said.

Hemingway raised his eyebrows. "Fifty thousand?"

"Fifty ... No!" Jacques shot up from his chair, knocking it over. "What other lies are they spewing? What about plans beyond the Rhineland?"

"Just that they promised Britain and France a pact of nonaggression for twenty-five years," Josephine said.

"There. More lies." Jacques started pacing and lit another cigarette. The smoke floated into the haze hovering overhead.

Josephine continued. "Göring said their success in the Rhineland resulted from a double-edged sword strategy—a show of force coupled with peace proposals."

Jacques stopped pacing and addressed the group. "And what good will come from those peace proposals? Hmm?" He shook both arms in the air. "When will the rest of the world see this man for what he is—a mad tyrant?"

Hemingway stirred the air with his cigar. "The Germans think he's a messiah saving them from their despair after the Great War. His support grows by the hour." Hemingway's cigar contributed to the growing tobacco fog.

Josephine raised an eyebrow. "Göring said Hitler is in an apocalyptic mood after the Nazis' successes in the Spanish Civil War. Hitler's convinced the Reich will be the master of all of Europe one day."

Jacques waved his hand in the air, disturbing the nicotine cloud. "There it is. His true goal."

Josephine downed the rest of her wine. "Göring also mentioned he's leaving Paris soon."

Jacques stepped toward Josephine. "And when is that?"

"A week from tomorrow, Thursday, on the 10:00 a.m. train to Berlin, in a private car."

"Very good." Jacques continued pacing. "This is excellent. He may be our first target."

Hemingway dragged the cigar from his mouth. "Target?"

Jacques stopped pacing in front of Hemingway. "If we have an opportunity to eliminate the Nazi's second-in-command, we cannot pass it by."

"My friend, let's give more thought to this," Hemingway said. "We can't allow hot-tempered emotions to force impulsive decisions. Consider the repercussions of such an action."

Jacques shook his fist in the air. "If our political leaders won't resist, we must."

"And we shall. But not tonight and not tomorrow. We have a week to calculate the best plan of attack." Hemingway gestured to a chair. "Please, have a seat."

Jacques cocked his head toward Hemingway, took a breath, and sat.

The cigarette and the cigar continued to contribute to a layer of gloom hanging over the group.

"Anything else, Josephine?" Hemingway asked.

"Not politically. But I got some details about the art theft at the Bernsteins."

Dottie straightened up and turned to Josephine. "What, Jo? What did you find out?"

Josephine looked down, then at Dottie. "Lohse was part of it."

Dottie stamped her foot, shook her head from left to right, and shrieked, "No, no, no."

"I'm sorry, Dottie. He planned the whole thing."

Dottie threw her glass against the wall. "Bastard Kraut. It's all my fault. I'm the one who introduced him to Otto and Emma. What a dope."

Josephine took Dottie's hand. "Hey now. None of us had any suspicion. You can't beat yourself up over this."

She wiped a tear. "But I sure want to beat him up. Ha. You can be sure of that."

Hemingway mugged a smirk to Dottie. "I think we may have an opportunity here, Dottie."

"An opportunity for who?" Dottie dabbed her nose. "What on earth are you talking about?"

"Do you believe you can do what Josephine did?" Hemingway said.

"What, spy on Germans?" Dottie shrank into her chair. "I, I, don't know. I'm not Jo."

"But you are a flirt," Josephine said, elbowing Dottie.

Dottie cracked a small smile. "Is that all it takes?"

"Hear me out," Hemingway said. "Lohse's countenance always brightens when he's with you."

"In retrospect, I'd say that's because I've been useful to him," Dottie said.

"He may still see you that way," Hemingway said. "Can you arrange a morning coffee with him?"

Dottie dabbed the mascara drips. "I think so. He's often at the cafe where we first met."

"Good," Hemingway said. "All you need to do is follow Josephine's example."

"What, ply him with liquor?" Dottie snickered. "Don't think that's gonna happen at morning coffee."

"No honey," Josephine said. "Use your charm. Don't booze him. Shmooze him."

Dottie shrank. "You're gonna have to give me a few lessons before I'm ready for this."

Josephine lifted Dottie's chin. "Honey, you're a natural. You'll do great. So, Ernie, what are you thinking?"

"You need to tap into his love of art and the tragedy surrounding art theft. If he is a true art aficionado, you'll make a connection that may open the door to discovering what happened. It'll be a high-wire act, that's for sure."

Jacques spoke up. "Find out if any other Nazi agents are prowling around Paris."

"I'll do my best, friends." She smiled. "Never thought of myself as a spy, but if you think I can do it, count me in."

Jacques and Hemingway, with cigarette and cigar, prepped Dottie for her mission. Josephine added her hints here and there.

"How soon can you arrange this?" Jacques said.

"I'll look for him at the cafe tomorrow morning. The sooner the better for me to get this over with."

"Good," Jacques said. "We will reconvene after Dottie's meeting and plan our next steps."

Jacques stood and raised his glass. "Friends, join me in a toast."

The others stood and raised their glasses.

"*Vive la France*," Jacques called out.

The four responded. "Vive la France." They drank in unison, set their glasses on the table, and made their exits, staggering them in the same way they arrived.

Jacques sat alone with an empty cigarette pack. The cloudy haze strangled the dull glow of the single light bulb.

How much longer will France's light shine?

Scan or tap the QR code to read Fred's blogpost about the real Second Bureau.

CHAPTER 43

More Clues

Home of the Client, Irvine, California, 2022

THE CLIENT USED SEVERAL sources to gather information for his quest, but he relied on Derrick Edwards for much of his intel. Derrick had located six of the Picasso Dozen and performed a successful test to disable the security systems at the Albert Becker Art Museum. Derrick continued proving his worth with this successful track record. The Client counted on him to continue his winning streak on the next assignment.

The Client discovered from another source that AJ Meyer and his wife possessed evidence about the Picasso drawings. Meyer had a copy of the black-and-white photo showing the twelve Picassos, like the one in the Client's family photo album. Along with the photo, Meyer had two other curious items the Client wanted—a letter referencing an IBM tape from the Third Reich and a musical composition by Igor Stravinsky.

Yes, Stravinsky posed for all twelve drawings. Did the Stravinsky composition relate to the drawings? And the reference to the IBM tape from the Nazis. What could a Nazi tape have to do with Picasso, Stravinsky, and twelve drawings lost for eighty years? Coincidence all of these items sat on a desk in the Meyers' home?

Recovering the drawings remained the Client's primary focus, but he couldn't resist pursuing the disparate set of artifacts in the Meyers' home.

The Client dialed Derrick's number. "Derrick, give some good news."

"Everything's set at the Becker for tomorrow night. I've prepared my team, and you should have your merchandise tomorrow."

"I have an additional assignment for you."

"Yes, sir. How can I help you?"

"A small break-in and surveillance job. Home of AJ Meyer. I want pictures of three things—a letter from the Nazis about an IBM tape, a sheet of music by Stravinsky, and an old black-and-white photo. You will find them in the office in the house, just past the front door."

"Do you want it left undisturbed?"

"Yes. I can't afford to raise any suspicions."

"May I ask how this relates to our primary mission?"

"No."

"Timing?"

"My source tells me they are gone on Wednesday nights from 7:00 to 9:00 p.m."

"Got it. And how do you want to receive the photos?"

"The usual cloud file."

"Yes, sir. Got it."

"That's all for now." Click.

The Client had researched the background of the Picasso Dozen starting with tidbits from his family. He learned Picasso and Stravinsky shared a friendship in 1930s Paris. Stravinsky came to America and Picasso stayed in Paris through the Nazi occupation. The trail of the Picasso drawings grew cold after that.

Nazis and an IBM tape. Sure, the Nazis looted from the best French art collections. Perhaps someone discovered the Picasso Dozen in loot plundered by the Third Reich. But an IBM tape? And Stravinsky music?

He'd have to wait another few days for the intelligence recovered by Derrick's team. But in twenty-four hours, he'd be holding six of the Picasso Dozen, regaining half of his family's investment.

CHAPTER 44

Choices

Home of Robert Meyer, New York, 1937

ROBERT MEYER AGONIZED FOR seven days about the outrageous Nazi rally at Madison Square Garden before setting up a meeting with his boss, Thomas Watson. *Did Mr. Watson understand what the Nazis stood for?* The disturbing image of a sea of red, white, and black swastikas mingled with the red, white, and blue American flags still tormented Robert along with the one-armed salutes punctuated with frenzied shouts of "Sieg heil."

How could citizens of a country that proclaims all men are created equal take a vile stand against one group of people because of their religious roots? Especially Jews, God's chosen people, a people God calls "the apple of My eye," an expression of protection. Hitler's fiery anti-Semitic rhetoric drove an ever-widening wedge between Jews and non-Jews, leading to boycotts. The number of humiliated businesses identified with a yellow Star of David grew larger in between each visit Robert made to Berlin.

Is that what the radicals at the New York Nazi rally wanted for America? Unthinkable.

Robert hesitated to speak to his wife about the rally, but the more it gnawed at him, the more he felt compelled to discuss it. With their son, Matthew, at school, now was a good time.

"Have you read the news report about the Madison Square Garden rally?" Robert said.

Doris picked up Robert's empty breakfast plate from the table. "Yes. Are the news descriptions accurate?" She carried the plate to the sink.

"They are. So many people packed in the auditorium. One inflammatory speech after another, riling the audience to a fever pitch." He picked up his coffee cup for a sip.

"The news described it as wild enthusiasm." She dipped the plate in the sudsy water and washed it.

"Far more than that. The complete opposite of what Scripture calls us to do—stir up one another to love and good works. Those speakers stirred up the crowd all right, into an anti-Semitic frenzy." He grabbed his napkin and wiped his mouth.

"Sounds like the events in Germany." She rinsed the plate.

"I've thought a lot about Germany since the rally. And about my job with IBM."

Doris stopped washing dishes at the sink and turned to him. "What, dear? What about your job?"

Robert rubbed the back of his neck. "On my trips to Berlin, I'm seeing more and more public signs of hatred towards the Jews. Now, I'm hearing the same rhetoric at the rallies in America." He tightened his grip on his napkin. "Worse, I'm suspicious the Third Reich uses IBM equipment to promote their anti-Semitism."

Doris walked to the table and sat eye to eye with Robert. "And what are you thinking about your job?"

Robert gestured upward with his hand. "What I am *praying* about my job is what God would have me do. If IBM is contributing to something evil, I can't be part of it."

Doris dried her hands with her apron. "Does that mean finding another job?"

"It might." Robert took her hand. "But our hope is not in this job or that job. God has always been faithful in meeting our needs. He's the same yesterday, today, and tomorrow. Our real job is to glorify God in all we do."

Doris smiled. "He has been faithful to us. And you have been faithful to Him." She patted his hand. "He will show you the way." She leaned forward and gave him a tender kiss.

***

In the reception room of Thomas Watson's office, Robert picked up last year's April edition of *Time* magazine, still sitting on the side table, as if it were a prized possession. A picture of Hitler giving the one-handed salute filled the cover. Robert turned a few pages to find the international news section.

Adolph Hitler was reasonably happy last week. Behind him was a Germany so united on paper as to leave no outside doubt that he was its one and only master. Before him was a ring of sovereign powers who could not make up their common mind what to do about this fuzzy-lipped little man who had just spat in their respective faces. Once again, Germany had a real army, with more than half a million men cocked and primed to strike at a minute's notice. Once again, a tough, hard-hitting German navy was in the making. Once again, the Rhineland, sacred soil to every German, was back in the Fatherland's military hold, with German guns and German gunners muzzling the frontier. And once again, Germany was virtually friendless in an angry world.

The *Time* article echoed the same news the Second Bureau used as a rallying cry to warn France what might be coming. Seeing the story in black and white in a reputable American magazine magnified the reality of Hitler's threat. If Hitler so brazenly defied the international community by rearming and reoccupying the Rhineland, what other ambitions did he have on his agenda? Could any government trust his peace treaties? What more did he plan to do with the Jews to make way for his pure Aryan race?

The secretary's intercom buzzed. She pressed the receiver button. "You can send Mr. Meyer in now." She relayed the message and Robert entered Mr. Watson's office.

Robert walked to Mr. Watson's desk where a framed item caught his attention. He'd read about it, but seeing it in person sent a shiver down his spine. A German cross surrounded by four eagles hovering over swastikas hung from a red ribbon. Robert had read the report of Mr. Watson's visit to Berlin earlier this year, where he received the cross from Mr. Hitler himself. *What kind of person proudly displays such an item in light of events in Germany?*

Mr. Watson stood to greet Robert. After pleasantries, he asked Robert about the purpose of the meeting.

Robert clasped his hands together. "Sir, it's about the rally you sent me to attend at Madison Square Garden."

Watson smiled. "Yes, quite the spectacle, from what the papers reported."

"Indeed." Robert planned his next words carefully. "Is IBM comfortable doing business with Germany?"

"Being comfortable isn't really a concern in the business world, Robert."

"No, sir. Perhaps a wrong choice of words."

Lord, give me wisdom.

"Are you concerned at all about how the Nazis are using our equipment?"

Watson folded his arms and leaned back. "Why do you ask?"

Robert edged forward on his chair. "On my last Berlin visit, I witnessed the Nazis using our equipment for census collection."

"Yes. We've been involved in census work for several years with many countries."

Robert stroked his chin. "But I've heard rumors the Nazis plan not only to identify their entire population but also to classify each person by religion." He leaned forward. "Does that concern you?"

Watson spread his hands apart and smiled. "Why should it?"

Robert shot back. "Sir, we've all read reports in the papers about the Nazis' dealings with the Jews. I've seen some of it myself. And it's getting worse."

"We must be careful about accepting everything we read in the American press." Watson sifted through papers on his desk and picked one up. "I received this official letter from the manager of Dehomag. He states, 'The stories of cruelty toward German Jews are untrue and you must not believe any unfounded rumors.'" He set the letter down. "There. Nothing to worry about."

"But can we ignore so many reports?" Robert shook his head. "It's not a handful anymore."

"Robert. I appreciate, as a pastor, you may have a certain perspective on this. As a businessman, I have a business perspective. I don't have to agree with everything a business partner does." Watson pointed with his right index finger. "But I can cooperate with leaders in the things I believe in. We do business in seventy-eight countries and they all look alike to me."

Robert froze. His focus shifted from Mr. Watson to what passed through the air over the New York skyline. The window pulled him like a magnet. He stood, speechless, transfixed by the view. It took a moment for Mr. Watson to swivel his chair around and take in the sight—the mighty Hindenburg airship floating over the forest of skyscrapers.

"Quite a view, isn't it?" Watson said. "First trip from Germany this year. She came over ten times last year."

"Not much room for passengers," Robert said, gesturing towards the gondola clinging to the belly of the beast.

"That's the control cabin for the captains and crew operating the ship." Watson stood and pointed. "The passengers' quarters are inside the bottom of the hull. An amazing achievement by the Nazis. I wouldn't mind traveling on it one day myself." Watson turned to Robert. "Now, is there anything else you'd like to discuss, Robert?"

The swastikas on the airship fins caught Robert's attention. Another incursion of Nazi swastikas into America.

"Robert?"

He turned away from the Hindenburg and peered at his boss. "I'm sorry. What?"

"Is there anything else?"

Robert walked back around Mr. Watson's desk. Three items glared at him—a small swastika flag next to a small American flag, a picture of Mr. Watson wearing the German cross, and a stack of documents stamped with the swastika.

Robert tightened his lips. "No, sir. You've made yourself perfectly clear."

"Wonderful. Keep up the good work. Proud of how things are moving forward in Berlin."

Robert turned and trudged out of the office. The Nazi's Hindenburg floated onward. Thomas Watson reviewed this year's income statement and smiled.

Scan or tap the QR codes to read Fred's blogposts.

Hitler on the cover of Time

The Hindenburg in America.

CHAPTER 45

History Lesson

IBM Headquarters, New York, 2022

AJ's RED-EYE TO NEW York arrived as the sun awakened the East Coast horizon with a golden hue. The plane descended into La Guardia, floating over the sea of high rises. AJ woke from his intermittent sleep and floated into consciousness.

He'd traveled to New York many times for work wearing his tech CEO hat. On this trip, he wore his Sherlock Holmes hat, searching for details of his grandfather's IBM history. The clues from Grandy's box of mementos provided few details for plotting this investigation. Time to put his powers of deduction to work sorting through IBM's vast ocean of records.

His friend, Merritt, in the Los Angeles IBM office made a few calls after AJ's visit. He learned that, yes, employment records dating back to the 1930s existed in the New York office and they welcomed AJ to come and search through them. As for locating the backup tape mentioned in the Nazi letter, another story. But the people in New York promised to assist in the search.

During the flight, AJ reviewed his notes from last week's sermon by Pastor Henry on Romans 8:28. Control, his number one issue. Not a new revelation from the sermon. A long-term struggle. "God is working at curbing our desire for control through multiple events in our lives," Pastor Henry said. AJ had faced difficult situations throughout his life, relying on his intellect to lead him to an answer. But intellect hadn't led him to any answers for his infertility, yet. Did the generations of the Meyers end with him, because of him? He tried everything science offered. Nothing worked. Could God do a miracle? Yes. Would God do a miracle?

Looking ahead to the end of his family line pained him. Looking back at his grandfather's possible complicity pained him even more. Pain versus pain. Infertility versus an ancestor's entanglement with the most heinous regime in all of history. Could he find peace with both pains? Or either?

***

After that recent sermon, AJ met Pastor Henry for coffee. Pastor Henry listened patiently as AJ laid everything on the table about his infertility and the Grandy revelations.

"AJ, I had no idea about the infertility," Henry said. "Are you doing okay?"

AJ forced his focus up out of the blackness of his coffee. "You know, it just dawned on me. You're the only one, besides Grace and the doctors, I've talked to about this. It's been tough. I think I've worked through it and then something brings it all up again." He lowered his head. "And I feel helpless all over again."

"How's Grace doing?"

AJ nodded. "She took it hard at first." His shoulders slumped. "We both cried a lot, to be honest." He raised his head. "But talk about a namesake. She's shown so much grace."

"That's so good to hear."

AJ straightened in his chair and took a sip of his coffee. "I have a few questions about your sermon last week. One thing hit home. 'Ultimate good is not always immediate good. The micro details are often confusing.' How are we supposed to handle those confusing details?"

"We can't see what God sees. We can't see our future or how God will use the hard circumstances we face today." Henry smiled. "But we can trust God is always good all the time."

"My head understands that. But when the rubber meets the road, that's where I struggle."

"You're not alone, AJ," Henry said. "Everyone struggles. We're human and we're still in the flesh, fighting fleshly desires, wanting to control our life when we get anxious. Jesus talked about having anxiety about the future. You know what advice he gave us?"

"What?"

"He said, 'Seek first the kingdom of God and his righteousness and all these things will be added to you.' He's telling us to seek salvation, first, as the most important thing in life, and then trust God to meet all our needs."

"That's hard in our I-want-it-now society."

"True. But maybe this will help since you're a runner. Paul exhorts us to run the race with endurance, with a steady determination to keep going, regardless of the temptation to slow down or give up. That's how God calls us to live our lives."

"I get that. That's helpful."

"In this life, everything is not good all the time. But God is always good all the time. He is willing and powerful to cause all things to come together for good. Let God be God, AJ."

Let God be God. Simple but not easy.

***

AJ deboarded and made his way to a taxi that delivered him to 590 Madison Avenue. He checked in with the receptionist and waited in the twentieth-floor lobby for a staffer who led him to Jayson Parry's office.

"Merritt told me about your journey with your grandfather. Said you wanted to search for his employment records," Jayson said.

"Yes. In the mid-thirties. Do you have records from that period?"

"We do. In fact, I already located records for a Robert Meyer. That is your grandfather, correct?"

AJ raised his eyebrows. "Yes. You did? May I see them?"

"Of course. But I need to warn you. They are incomplete. Here."

"Incomplete?" AJ took the file and studied the details. "I see what you mean."

"Oddly, there's no record in the file of his end date."

"No one knows when he stopped working for IBM?"

"Correct. Plenty of commendations for his work, though. Seems that Thomas Watson thought highly of him and especially his work in Berlin."

In 1930s Berlin, IBM only worked for the Nazis.

"And no payroll records that show when they stopped paying him?"

"Unfortunately, no."

AJ flipped the papers back and forth, willing the missing information to appear. He closed the file and attacked the next subject. "There is another matter I need help with."

"I'll be glad to help if I can."

AJ pulled the Nazi IBM letter out of his backpack. "I found a letter addressed to my grandfather regarding a backup tape the Nazis sent from Berlin to IBM's New York office in 1937. Can you help me find this tape?"

Jayson leaned forward and furrowed his brow. "May I see that letter?"

AJ handed the letter to Jayson and waited.

Part-way through, Jayson waved his hand. "Well, this is incredible, I must say."

"That's what I thought. Does IBM have an archive for tapes this old?"

"I—I need a minute to reread this." Jayson sat back and read through the letter again. "Wow. Um, well." He set the letter down and looked at AJ. "You know, this is a pretty delicate matter, the IBM connection with the Nazis, that is."

"I imagine so."

Jayson leaned forward on his desk. "Who else knows about this?"

"Just my wife. Why? Is there a problem?"

Jayson took in a deep breath and let it out. "First, I will help you. Second, it's in your best interest to keep this information as private as possible."

Why?

AJ cleared his throat. "Do you know where to look for the tape?"

"I do. Few people in the company know about the archive. I'm part of a task force reviewing allegations of IBM's involvement with the Nazis. So, yes, I'm very interested in finding this tape."

"Will you help me locate the tape?"

Jayson nodded. "I will."

And can I trust you?

"I think I know where to search for it, but it may take a week to locate it. I'm sure you can appreciate the potential volume of tapes I'll need to weed through to find it."

"Is data accessible on such a tape after all this time?" *And will you try to get your hands on it before me?*

"We'll have to see after I find it."

"Can you ship it to me?"

"Of course. Happy to do it." Jayson smiled. "Is there anything else I can help with?"

"Finding the tape is my primary concern. Thanks."

Jayson and AJ made some superficial closing remarks to one another walking out of the office.

AJ headed to the elevator, descended to the street level, and stepped into a waiting taxi. During the ride to his hotel, he looked through Grandy's file once more. He still found nothing to show when Grandy stopped working for IBM. Did Grandy continue working in Berlin through the holocaust by the Nazis? Was Grandy complicit in any way, shape, or form? He didn't find the answer he was looking for in the file. But maybe he'd find some answers on the tape if they found it.

Was something a little off with Jayson?

Was he ready to let God be God?

CHAPTER 46

My Card

Cafe Le Livre, Paris, 1937

DOTTIE BEGAN WALKING PAST Cafe Le Livre the day after the Second Bureau meeting, hoping to encounter Bruno Lohse. Returning home from that meeting and thinking about what they expected of her, she manufactured a thousand reasons why she could never execute their plan. But thanks to coaching by Josephine, the initial fright of the assignment had faded.

"Honey, first, keep in mind why you're doing this," Jo said.

The friends sat in Josephine's living room, sharing afternoon tea.

"Okay. Well, I'm helping my dear friends, Otto and Emma, find their stolen art."

"Good. And for the Second Bureau?"

Dottie put her hand to her cheek. "That's what terrifies me. He wants to find more Nazi thugs in Paris, but I'm no Joan of Arc."

"Now hold on, dear. Let's take it down a notch." Jo took Dottie's hand. "No one's going to burn you at the stake. Maybe this will help. Have you heard of Esther in the Bible?"

Dottie looked up for the answer. "Wasn't she a queen?"

"Yes. But not until she did some bold things for God. Like you, Esther found herself in a challenging situation resulting from God orchestrating a complex web of events. But because of her obedience and boldness, God did a great work for the Jewish people. I think you're like Esther. God has put you here for such a time as this, with an assignment only you can complete."

A smile spread across Dottie's face. "An assignment from God?" She snorted a giggle. "You sure about that?" She nibbled on the shortbread.

"Sure as I'm sittin' here. So, let me give you a few more tips." Josephine reached for a bottle of rum, opened it, and added more than a splash to each of their cups. She took a fortifying sip and licked her lips. "Remember, Lohse first connected with you because you were useful to him. Appeal to that. Ask him about the art he's interested in. Flatter him on his good taste. Men's egos are so fragile, they just love our attention."

Dottie finished half her cup. "They are such saps, aren't they?" Josephine added more rum.

The coaching session continued with several more rounds of rum-tea to help bolster Dottie's courage and prepare her for such a time as this.

"Gosh darn it, I'm gonna give it my all and trust God," Dottie proclaimed with a raised fist. "After all, it's His assignment, right?"

At least that's what Josephine said.

On the third morning of Bruno-watch, Dottie found Bruno sitting outside at the Cafe Le Livre reading the paper.

Time to put on my Queen Esther crown.

She shook off her hesitations, pasted on her jovial Yankee smile, and approached him. "Well, look who's here. Fine day for a latte, isn't it?"

Bruno looked up from his paper. "Dottie." He smiled. "What a wonderful surprise. Please join me."

He stood and offered a chair. "I've looked forward to meeting again since seeing you at the expo. Would you care for a latte?"

"I'd love one." She leaned in and smiled. "Thank you, Bruno."

Bruno signaled a waiter and ordered. "The expo was extraordinary, wasn't it?"

Dottie gave a sparkling smile. "So many wonderful artists from all over the world. Did you have a favorite?"

"The magnificent murals." Bruno oozed delight with enthusiasm uncharacteristic of a stoic German, speaking with his hands as much as his mouth. "Such bold shapes and colors, especially Robert Delaunay's."

Schmooze him. "You have such wonderful taste, Bruno."

"Unfortunately, not the taste of my clients." He tapped his cigarette on the ashtray.

"And what would interest them?" Her eyes beckoned an answer.

He peered off into the distance through the smoke of his cigarette. "Mostly French masters. Impressionists. Some clients are interested in Chagall, even Dali."

Dottie opened her purse and stared into it, aimlessly rifling for nothing. "My friends, the Bernsteins, had works by both Chagall and Dali."

"Oh, yes. I remember seeing them at the soirée." He turned and smiled. "Thanks to your kind invitation."

The waiter delivered Dottie's latte.

"But something unfortunate happened." She snapped her purse shut and shot him a nonchalant gaze. "Someone stole them."

Someone like you.

She set her purse down, picked up the latte, and sent a piercing inquiry over the top of her cup.

"Yes. I heard about that." Bruno crushed the life out of his cigarette in the ashtray. "Very unfortunate."

Dottie brushed her bangs across her forehead. "How did you learn about it?"

"The art world is close-knit, is that how you say?" He circled his hand in the air. "Comings and goings of art spread quickly among dealers."

The beep, beep, beep of a car horn rang from down the block.

Dottie picked up her napkin. "Did you, um, hear anything about what happened to them or who stole them?"

Easy does it. Stay calm. She dabbed her lips with the napkin.

"It is quite a mystery. None of my contacts have a clue what happened." He shook his head. "I'm sorry for your friends." He tilted his head back, took a long draw from his cigarette, and took his time to exhale.

Two yapping poodles tugged their owner down the sidewalk.

Dottie shifted in her chair. "You might remember the Picasso drawings in the foyer. They stole them, too."

"Most unfortunate." A cold, disinterested blankness filled his face.

Time to shift gears.

Dottie finished her latte and set the cup on the table. "That was delicious." She put both hands on the table and leaned forward with a perky smile. "Bruno, can I ask you a silly question?"

"Of course."

"Have you ever dealt with any Nazis in your business?"

He chuckled half-heartedly. "Sometimes, in Berlin." He tapped his cigarette on the ashtray. "It is something I have little control over."

Dottie raised her eyebrows. "Do they ever"—she leaned forward and whispered—"tell you things?" She sat back and grinned.

Bruno squinted. "What kind of things?"

Dottie animated her words. "Oh, I don't know. I'm not a political person, but it seems that Mr. Hitler has big plans for Germany."

"He talks a big talk. That is true."

Dottie spoke with another exaggerated whisper. "Do you think there are any Nazis in Paris?"

Bruno leaned forward, smiled, and whispered back, "Probably at the German embassy." He laughed heartily.

"Do you think there are, oh, this is going to sound more silly, Nazi spies in Paris?"

"You idiot." A clanging commotion erupted at the table next to them. The waiter had tripped and spilled the customer's coffee, drenching the tablecloth and splashing the gentleman's coat.

"Pardonnez-moi, monsieur."

Bruno turned back to Dottie. "Why would you worry about something like that?"

Dottie smiled and gave the air a "golly gee" slap with her hand. "Oh, maybe an overactive imagination." *And training from my reporter days to get to the truth.*

Bruno deployed an impish grin. "Well, if there are, I don't know about them. I'm here for my art business." He looked at his watch. "In fact, it's time for me to meet a client."

Bruno stood, opened his wallet, pulled out some francs, and laid them on the table. Something else fell from his wallet to the ground. Dottie slyly moved her shoe to cover the item.

"It was so good seeing you again, Dottie." Lohse smiled and tipped his hat. "Enjoy your day."

"Thanks for the latte, Bruno."

Bruno walked off.

Dottie's foot froze in place.

Bruno turned the corner.

Dottie picked up the card.

About the size of a five franc note.

She unfolded it.

Gasp!

Dottie looked around.

She carefully refolded the card.

And put it in her purse.

Dottie walked off in the opposite direction of Lohse.

Clutching her purse with the prize inside, she smiled.

CHAPTER **47**

Something Borrowed

Home of AJ and Grace, Irvine, California, 2022

DUKE AND BUTCH CARRIED out myriads of missions for Derrick Edwards, with Duke usually taking the lead. They preferred the larger jobs with larger payouts such as the upcoming art heist. But nothing wrong with a shorter grab-and-go. Derrick would pave the way by remotely disarming the security system at AJ's home—such a shaming event for the head of a tech company.

These jobs had their benefits and their challenges. In this case, Duke knew what to look for but not where, exactly. Three items. A letter from the Nazis about an IBM tape. *What's that about?* A sheet of music by Stravinsky. *Who cares?* An old black-and-white photo. *Hope there isn't more than one.*

Duke and Butch made a trial run by the house the prior day to scope things out and take photos of the house, yard, and neighborhood. They also watched the traffic and determined the type of vehicle that would blend in the best.

Duke's headset squawked at 7:05 p.m. "You guys all set?"

"Yeah, boss. We got this. Just getting ready to drive up and park. Is the security system down?"

"Affirmative. You're all set."

"We're pulling up now. Looks clear. We'll contact you from inside."

Duke and Butch pulled up close to the front door to minimize exposure. The car had a dummy license plate, in case anyone tried to ID it. They exited the car, approached the front door, and *voilà*, it opened without a challenge.

A lamp on an entry table lit the hallway, showing the way to the office. Entering the office, they found no window exposure to the street. Duke turned on the desk lamp and started going through the drawers. Butch searched for a file cabinet.

Duke opened the center desk drawer. Nothing there. He moved to the top right-side drawer. Unlocked. A neat arrangement of pens, paper clips, tape—normal desk stuff. The second drawer held a set of files. Duke started fingering through them.

Butch called out. "See any keys in the desk? The file cabinet's locked."

"Hang on." Duke went back to the center desk drawer. Nothing. Top right drawer. Nothing. Was the owner gonna make this hard? Scanning the desktop again, Duke noticed a small bulge in the lower right corner of the desk blotter. He picked up the corner and found the key. "Here you go." He tossed Butch the key. The owner made it too easy.

"How's it going in there?" Derrick said over the headset.

"It's only been five minutes. Give us a chance, will you?" Duke blurted. He opened the drawers on the left side.

Butch pawed through the top drawer of the file cabinet. "Okay. Here we go." He pulled out a file folder. "Looks like everything's here. And there's more notes and stuff too." He handed the folder to Duke.

Duke took the Nazi IBM letter out of the envelope and laid it on the desk to photograph. He snapped several photos, tucked the letter back in the envelope, and laid it aside. Next, the black-and-white photo. Duke snapped the front and the back. He placed it next to the letter. And finally, the sheet of music. The additional pages in the file included handwritten notes and printouts of emails. *Could be helpful to the client.* Duke photographed all the pages.

"Done. Put everything back." Duke said.

Butch slid the items back in the file folder—the pages, emails, letter, photo, and the sheet music.

"Hold on," Duke said.

"What now?"

"You sure that's the order you found them?"

"Think so. Why? Do you think it matters?"

"It might. Looks like this guy is pretty OCD from how neat his desk is."

"You guys find everything?" Derrick squawked over the headset.

Duke glared at Butch. "Yes, we got it all. Cleaning up."

"Good to hear. I'll be waiting for the photos."

Duke stood toe to toe with Butch. "Man, how can you not remember the order of a few pages?"

"I—I ... come on. What's the big deal? Let's finish up and get out." Butch backed away and put the folder back in the file drawer.

"You sure you got the folder in the right place?" Duke snarled.

"I'm sure. You're a real pain sometimes, you know." Butch locked the cabinet and threw the key to Duke.

Duke put the key under the corner of the blotter, closed all the drawers, and gave the desk a once over. Everything looked good. "All right, let's get out of here."

They returned to the car. Duke clicked the headset. "Okay, boss. You can turn the security system back on."

"Ten four." Derrick said. He rearmed the system at 7:30 p.m.

Duke checked the mirrors, backed out, and drove off to Derrick's office.

Did Butch put things back in the file in the wrong order? If he did, Derrick didn't need to know about it, right? After all, they got everything Derrick wanted for the client. That's all that mattered. Right?

CHAPTER 48

Two Masters

Reformed Church of Brooklyn, Brooklyn, New York, 1937

Robert Meyer had only a few years under his belt serving as a pastor, but God had gifted him with two important aptitudes. Some pastors excelled as skillful teachers of the Bible, others as shepherds of their congregation. Robert commanded a rich blending of both in his ministry. How are they to hear without someone preaching? Who will protect the flock if not the shepherd?

Now this shepherd needed shepherding himself.

Robert stood at a fork in the road after his recent meeting with his IBM boss. Mr. Watson chose to believe the Nazis didn't have a "Jewish problem" and that the Third Reich treated the Jews no differently than other German citizens. Robert knew otherwise. On his work trips to Berlin, he had witnessed the gradual lifting of a fog hiding the cruel actions toward the Jews by Hitler and the Third Reich. The increasingly degrading and punishing acts had progressed beyond business boycotts. Jews could no longer hold public office or civil service positions. The Nuremberg Laws prohibited Jews from working for the press or radio. Stock exchanges and brokerages no longer employed Jews. In short, the Nazis had stripped the Jews of their German citizenship and basic rights.

The census data that the Nazis collected and processed on IBM equipment specified an individual's religious affiliation. Robert had seen the punch cards in person on his recent visit to Dehomag. Column 22 on the punch card recorded a person's religion code. Hole one in that column indicated Protestant, hole two, Catholic, and hole three, Jew. IBM tabulating machines sorted and grouped the cards by religion code for additional processing, lumping Jews into one stack. In light of the increasing marginalization of the Jews, the potential for using census data to take further punitive actions against the Jews terrified Robert. He had to choose. Work for a company that supplied equipment to a regime tightening a noose around the Jews. Or quit.

Continuing to work for IBM thrust him down a path complicit with compromise. Quitting called him to trust that, one way or another, God would provide for his family. Robert knew he didn't need to face this dilemma single-handedly. He'd meet with his elders after today's service, present his predicament, and seek their guidance.

Robert had prepared a special message for today's service in response to the Hindenburg tragedy this past week. The memory of sitting in Mr. Watson's office watching the mammoth airship drift peacefully through American airspace still haunted him. Swastikas floating unchallenged over Manhattan stunned him and emboldened his challenge to Mr. Watson. Hours later, the mighty German engineering feat lay, defeated, in a heap of twisted metal and ashes. Miraculously, sixty-two of the ninety-seven passengers and crew survived the exploding fireballs. Several members of his congregation worked at the Lakehurst Naval Air Station and sacrificially conducted rescue operations, battling the explosions and flames.

Gertrude Hagaman sat three rows back from the front clutching a handkerchief drenched from three days of relentless lamenting. Her bloodshot eyes pleaded. How could God allow such a thing to happen?

"Where was God in all of this, you might ask? He was there with the ground crew, where our own Allen Hagaman sacrificed his own life, saving the lives of others. A true picture of sacrificial redemption. God was there with the fire crews, the emergency equipment and the ambulances treating the survivors. In disasters like this, we see the uncertainty of life. We should grieve with those who grieve and also remember not to take our lives for granted. Martin Luther said, 'When you look around and wonder whether God cares, you must always hurry to the cross and you must see him there.' Look to the cross for your hope and your salvation."

"Before we conclude today, I have some updates on events in Germany from our dear brother, Dietrich Bonhoeffer. You may remember meeting him a few years ago during his time at Union Theological Seminary."

Robert picked up a letter.

Dear Pastor Robert. Greetings in the name of our Lord and Savior, Jesus Christ. I write to you today humbly requesting your prayers for our church and our country. Our churches are under increasing pressure from the Nazi government. Taking collections during our services is now illegal. Pastors are arrested for standing for the Gospel and against National Socialism that lifts Hitler up as a demagogue and a false messiah. Gestapo officers often attend services and monitor activities. They have closed our seminary at Finkenwalde, forcing us to conduct classes on the run. While there is suffering, we, along with Paul, "consider that the sufferings of this present time are not worth comparing with the glory that is to be revealed to us." Suffering is the badge of true discipleship. When Christ calls a man, he bids him come and die.

Robert closed the service with a prayer for Dietrich followed by a benediction. "The Lord bless thee, and keep thee: The Lord make his face shine upon thee, and be gracious unto thee: The Lord lift up his countenance upon thee, and give thee peace. Amen."

In his study, Robert met with his elders. He explained his work with IBM, the use of computing equipment by the Nazis, and the ostracizing of the Jews he'd observed in Germany. "Proverbs tells us there is safety in an abundance of counselors. I appeal to you today for your wisdom and guidance."

Matthew, the head elder, spoke first. "Robert, I think you already know your answer. You are shining the light of Christ on the darkness of the Nazis' evil acts. Ephesians 5:11 tells us to take no part in the unfruitful works of darkness, but to expose them. You are doing just that."

"Perhaps you have an opportunity to share the gospel with Mr. Watson," Elder Mark said. "He knows of your church work, correct?"

"He knows I'm a part-time pastor. But our conversations are solely business related so far."

Elder Luke said, "Robert, have you thought about the loss of income if you resign? How does Doris feel about it?"

Robert smiled. "You know the gospel of Doris. There's nothing God can't do. As for the income, I am seeking God's direction on how to provide what we need."

"We have an emergency fund to help you get by till you find something," Elder John said. "Can we all agree on using that?"

"Yes," Arthur said. "We can work those details out later. Do you have your answer now, Robert?"

"Yes, I think it's very clear."

"Gentlemen, let's pray for our brother," Elder Arthur said.

They stood and surrounded Robert, each placing a hand on his shoulder.

"Our loving, Heavenly Father, we thank you for our brother Robert and the call you have on his life. We rejoice in the fruit of his ministry that brings you glory. Your Word says if anyone lacks wisdom to ask and you will give generously. We ask you today for wisdom, to light the way of Robert's future. May these trials produce steadfastness in Robert, that he may lack for nothing. And we ask that you go before him as he meets with Mr. Watson, and shares the love of Christ, for your glory. Amen."

The men removed their hands and stepped back from Robert. Arthur said, "We'll all be praying for your time with Mr. Watson. And for God's provision."

"Thank you," Robert said. "I believe God will provide."

Robert remained in his office after the elders left. He opened his Bible to Matthew 6 and read the passage of God's promise to provide. "But seek ye first the kingdom of God, and his righteousness; and all these things shall be added unto you. Take therefore no thought for the morrow: for the morrow shall take thought for the things of itself. Sufficient unto the day is the evil thereof."

Robert closed his Bible.

Dear Lord, help my unbelief.

CHAPTER 49

Putting It Together

Home of the Client, Irvine, California, 2022

THE CLIENT SAT IN his home office, monitoring everything happening during the break-in at AJ's home in real-time, thanks to the bugs planted a few weeks earlier. Conversations he'd heard between AJ and Grace had already provided loads of information about the Picasso Dozen. He learned an IBM tape held the key to something important. Why else would AJ fly all the way to New York to ask someone at IBM about it? The Client's contact in New York would be answering that question soon.

Within hours of the break-in at the Meyers' home, Derrick had uploaded the photos to a secure cloud account and messaged the Client. The Client previewed them on his laptop, choosing which ones to print. The first picture he printed showed a letter addressed to Robert Meyer at IBM in New York. Dated March 5, 1938, the letter included a Nazi swastika at the top and described a tape sent from Berlin to New York for archiving. The tape had a lot number, 12453. The letter explained that a separate communication included the key necessary to access data on the tape. Would he find the key in the rest of the photos?

The second printout showed musical notes scribbled on a sheet of staff paper. Another source had told the Client about the cryptic music but couldn't explain it. On the top of the page, a line of French, loosely translated to: "a tribute to Picasso." The next line, maybe a signature? He picked up a magnifying glass. First name, perhaps Igor? Last name looked like it started with "Str." He turned to his laptop and googled "Igor Str." The first line that popped up: "Igor Stravinsky, a Russian composer with French nationality." Interesting. Stravinsky had posed for all twelve of the Picasso Dozen. Had he written the music that appeared below his signature?

He turned back to the staff paper and studied the two lines of music with brackets and French labels. The first group of numbers labeled "lot" in English, matched the lot number in the Nazi letter: 12453. The second set of bracketed numbers, labeled "key," showed 6 4 7 10 9 1 8 2. The key needed to access the tape?

At the bottom of the staff paper, a handwritten line read, "For my dear friends, Otto and Emma Bernstein." The Client pounded his fist on his desk. Those names dredged up painful memories of the source of the feud lasting three generations. Time had come for him to set things right in his generation.

He put the music aside and picked up the printout of the front and back of a black-and-white photograph. On the photograph's backside, some handwriting: "1937, Paris, Bernsteins." That disturbing name again. The front of the photograph showed the twelve Picasso portraits, proof they existed. Tomorrow he'd scoop up six of them. And the other six? Where?

The next printout displayed the word "TAPE," circled in the middle of the page. Additional circles filled the rest of the page and contained names, item descriptions, details from the Nazi IBM letter, the key, and the lot from the music. Arrows from these circles pointed to the "TAPE" circle in the middle. Everything AJ pieced together indicated the tape held something important. Any chance it still existed after eighty-four years? If the tape existed, where could he find a machine capable of processing the data? Perhaps his New York contact could locate one.

The next printouts he pulled off the printer included a series of emails. One referred to AJ's visit to the IBM office in Los Angeles. Another mentioned a visit to the New York branch. The emails provided specific names and contact information to help the Client continue his investigation of the tape.

The Client put all the papers in a folder, closed it, and set it aside. He picked up his phone and called Derrick for one last status of the art museum heist. "Status?"

"Everything's set."

"And you're sure of your man inside the Becker?"

"Yes, sir."

"I'll expect the package tomorrow night."

Click.

In twenty-four hours, he'd have his hands on half of a collection that rightly belonged to his family.

If everything went according to plan.

CHAPTER 50

Thy Will

IBM Headquarters, New York, 1937

DRIVING IN TO NEW YORK CITY to meet with Mr. Watson, Robert Meyer mentally rehearsed his upcoming conversation with his boss. He hadn't planned just a resignation speech. He believed he had an appointment to bring the good news of the gospel to one of the most successful and influential businessmen in the country, perhaps the world. Thoughts of David versus Goliath came to his mind. Not that he thought of Mr. Watson as an evil enemy, but one who sat in a seat of great power, financially and politically. With Watson's keen interests in international affairs, President Roosevelt considered him an unofficial ambassador and often called on him to entertain foreign dignitaries.

Robert first met Mr. Watson in Endicott, New York, at IBM's leadership training institute. On his first day of training, Robert walked up the path to the training center, paused, and gazed above the front door at the THINK motto in two-foot-high brass letters. He approached the five steps leading up to the front door. The entire IBM philosophy reached out to him, step by step. Step one,

THINK. Step two, OBSERVE. Steps three through five: DISCUSS, LISTEN, and READ. Mr. Watson's advice to all employees: inform yourself and learn.

The training at Endicott indoctrinated Robert into IBM's company culture of dressing in impeccable suits, vowing to avoid alcohol, and singing the praises of Mr. Watson at company functions.

Thomas Watson is our inspiration,
Head and soul of our splendid I. B. M.
We are pledged to him in every nation,
Our President and most beloved man.
His wisdom has guided each division,
In service to all humanity.
We have grown and broadened with his vision.
None can match him or our great company.

Another song particularly disturbed Robert—the song praising William Heidinger, manager of Dehomag.

Our I. B. M. in Germany is led by Hermann Rottke,
That's why we're growing all the time,
In the Fatherland where flows the Rhine.
All praise to Willy Heidinger—a Continental Pioneer,
And all our stalwart German leaders fine,
Each year they increase sales of our great line.

Robert struggled to sing these songs. They smacked of idolatry. He could barely tolerate extolling Mr. Watson. But Robert abhorred praising Nazi leaders as "fine," an issue on which he completely disagreed with Mr. Watson.

Robert had driven the entire route into New York immersed in thought. Making a right turn, he passed a church, and before he knew it, he was praying. "Lord, grant me wisdom, and may the Holy Spirit remind me of what truths to present to Mr. Watson from your Word. Amen."

Robert walked into the office. Mr. Watson's secretary greeted him. "No need to sit down. He's waiting for you." Robert entered Mr. Watson's office.

"Good morning, Robert. Come, have a seat. Now, what's this all about?"

Robert took a moment to find his starting point. "Thank you for taking the time to see me so soon after our previous meeting."

"Not at all. Your work in Germany is very important to me."

Robert shifted in his seat. "At our last meeting, I mentioned my concerns about the Nazis' treatment toward the Jews."

Watson furrowed his brow. "I thought we cleared that all up, Robert."

"You presented your thoughts on the subject and the comments in the letter from the Dehomag managers. They present an entirely different picture from what I am seeing firsthand. The Third Reich is segregating and punishing the Jewish people, using IBM's equipment to accelerate the process. In good conscience, I cannot be a part of a company that contributes to this. I've thought about it. I've prayed about it." He took a breath. "I have decided I can no longer continue my employment with IBM."

Mr. Watson sat for a moment with a poker face. His distinguished good looks and gray hair gave him a fatherly appearance of a kindly man of wisdom. He leaned back in his chair, taking his time to respond. "You're a pastor at a church in Brooklyn, correct?"

"First Reformed Church."

"I often attend Brick Presbyterian myself. Reverend Paul Wolfe is the pastor. Splendid fellow. Always encouraging us to good works."

The many plaques of adulation in Mr. Watson's office affirmed his donations to a variety of charities.

"But of course, good works have nothing to do with our eternal destiny."

"Come now, Robert. Of course they do." Watson chuckled. "God loves a cheerful giver. Isn't that right?"

"Yes. He does. But that's not what saves us. Jesus came to seek and save the lost."

Watson cleared his throat. "Jesus was a good, moral teacher."

Please, Holy Spirit, bring the light.

"Sir, I hope you will carefully consider he was more than a moral teacher. Jesus said, 'I am the way, and the truth, and the life. No one comes to the Father except through me.'"

Watson straightened the papers on his desk. "Perhaps a decision for another day."

"Sir, we never know if we have another day. The victims of the Hindenburg crash didn't."

The mention of death killed the flow of discourse between the two men.

Is any of this reaching Mr. Watson's heart?

"Tragic accidents happen every day." Watson shifted a pen on his desk. "Now, back to your resignation. You've done great work for us in Berlin. But in light of your current concerns, I think it is best you resign. Please submit a written resignation letter. I'm sure I can count on your cooperation while we transition your responsibilities to another employee over the next two weeks."

Robert nodded. "Yes, sir. I will do all I can to help."

Both men stood. Mr. Watson led Robert to the door and reached for his hand. "Good luck, Robert."

Robert shook. "Thank you, sir. Please, think about what I said."

Driving home, Robert prayed.

Lord, may you work in his life and bring him understanding and conviction to find his salvation in you. And by the way, where do you want me to work next, Lord? Amen.

CHAPTER **51**

Come And Get It

Albert Becker Art Museum, Irvine, California, 2022

LYLE BERNSTEIN WRESTLED WITH sleep the night before heist day. He lost. Tossing and turning in bed without his wife, his thoughts splintered in a hundred different doomed directions, all shrouded in fear. At least his family was safe. He had finally spoken with Cheryl and confirmed she and the children had arrived safely in Big Bear. Their continued safety depended on him perfectly executing a series of tasks, precariously built one upon the other, like a house of cards that could come crashing down if any one card faltered.

He dragged his limp body to the bathroom and reluctantly faced the mirror. The bags under his eyes and his stubble convinced him to take time for his morning shaving routine. Today of all days, best he look as normal as possible to avoid any unnecessary scrutiny. He threw on some clothes, grabbed his bag, and headed out.

Driving to the office, an endless stream of doubts pricked his thoughts. What if. Over and over and over and—...

Where'd that red light come from?

He slammed his brakes, barely avoiding a collision.

Whoa. I need coffee.

He made a quick detour to grab a cup. Five sips later, he pulled in to the empty parking garage at the Becker.

What time is it, anyway?

His watch told him 7:09. Hours to go. Hours to contemplate the slim chance of pulling off the heist tonight.

Making his way to his office, his watch told him 7:10. Hours to go. He took the checklist from his locked desk drawer and started reviewing the items he must complete by the end of the day. First, properly wrap and pack each Picasso drawing to protect them during transport. He double-checked the supplies for the job: acid-free tissue paper to cover the portrait, acid-free painter's tape to secure the paper, bubble wrap to surround the tissue layer, and cardboard to reinforce the corners and layer between each portrait. He had everything. The only problem, he couldn't start preparing the drawings with Diego in the office.

The backpack for transporting the drawings had arrived earlier in the week, sent by Matt/Derrick. According to the instructions Lyle received at the blackmail meeting, Matt/Derrick had delivered a backpack constructed of black polyester fabric measuring 22 inches wide, 28 inches long, and 18 inches deep. All six sides contained sponge padding to protect the drawings. The back had adjustable shoulder straps and a cross strap.

The minute hand on the office clock moved slower than traffic in a downpour. Diego dragged in. Late. Lyle poked his head out of his office.

"Morning, boss." Diego inspected Lyle. "You okay? You look a little, uh, not right."

"I'm fine. Missing the family. I never sleep well when they're gone."

"Oh. Right. So, I could use some extra time off this afternoon. I have a project due tomorrow. Anyway, can I leave early today, say, at lunchtime?"

Perfect.

"I think that will work. We're on track with our projects."

"Thanks, boss."

Lyle remained in his private office the rest of the morning, rotely reviewing the checklist. Lunch time arrived, taking Diego with it. Time to jump into action.

Lyle locked the door to the workshop, removed the Picasso drawings from the locked drawers, and placed them on his workbench. These drawings had already taken a momentous journey, starting in Paris with his grandparents, surviving the Nazis, making their way across the Atlantic, and crossing from the east coast to the west coast. Would they survive the next leg of their journey?

A sudden jolting interrupted his preparation. The room swayed. Lyle grabbed his worktable. Pencils rolled across the tabletop. It stopped. He took a deep breath and waited for more. It didn't come. No alarms kicked in except for Lyle's adrenaline. He launched the radio app on his phone.

"Well, folks, here in the studio we just felt a pretty good jolt. A little rocking and rolling. Seems to be over. We'll bring you an update as soon as we hear from the US Geological Survey."

Lyle didn't need a geological disruption to his day. He took a drink of water and walked around his office to shake off the anxiety and continued the packing.

Lyle added cardboard panels in the front and the back of the bundles in the backpack and between each portrait. He zipped up the backpack and lifted it to check the weight. Maybe thirty pounds. But that didn't matter to him.

"Folks, we're getting news from the USGS. The quake a few minutes ago was a 2.5 on the Richter scale. They think the center was near Corona. We've received a variety of reports on the impact. Mostly, descriptions of doors and chandeliers swaying. No reports of broken windows or other building damage. We'll keep you posted."

An omen of things to come?

Matt/Derrick's plan directed Lyle to leave the backpack on his project table, making it easily visible. The thug's job: walk in the office, strap on the backpack, and walk out, in less than a minute. Once that happened, the Picasso Dozen was in play, and out of Lyle's control, a thought that terrified him.

Just stick to the plan.

He knew the pickup point and the password. His next step: arrive at Denny's before the real pickup courier.

***

Duke and Butch rendezvoused at a gas station five blocks from the Becker at 11:45 p.m. "Are you all set to knock out the security?" Duke asked over the comms.

"Yes, I've checked the connection with the system," Derrick said. "You boys set?"

"Ten four. Time check?"

"11:46. Mark."

"Got it."

The nonexistent traffic at this time of night in the high-rise section of Irvine made it easy to pinpoint the duration of their drive to the Becker and minimize their presence on site.

At 11:57, Duke gave Butch a thumbs up and they headed off on their Harleys. At exactly midnight, they drove in to the circular entrance to the Becker and parked their bikes. Duke looked at various cameras and security sensors. No blinking red lights. Derrick had control of the security system.

Butch wore the decoy backpack and remained with the Harleys. Duke entered the museum and walked the route he'd memorized from the plans. He entered the employees' wing, reached the third office, and verified the name, LYLE BERN-STEIN. Opening the door, he found the black backpack on the worktable. He strapped on the backpack, retraced his route, and exited to his bike.

"Heading to drop-off point now." Duke reported over the comm. He took off northbound and Butch, the decoy, turned southbound. From a distance, Duke and Butch looked like clones of each other.

***

Lyle had parked at Denny's at 11:30 p.m. He wasn't taking any chances in case the pickup occurred earlier than planned. Sitting in the car wearing an Angel hoodie and sunglasses, he squirmed as each minute passed more slowly than the one before.

What am I doing? This is completely crazy.

The headlight came into sight, followed by the rumble of the motorcycle. Hunching down, he followed its path. The driver parked near the front door.

The backpack.

Lyle's heart raced.

The driver dismounted, slipped the backpack off, and entered Denny's.

This is it.

Now or never.

For the sake of my family and Picasso's family.

Lyle waited a minute. He got out of his car and traipsed into Denny's. The thug sat off to the right in a booth. Lyle dipped his head and moved to the booth. The thug looked up. Lyle's throat tightened. He pushed the words out. "Never too late for breakfast, is it?"

A waitress walked up to the table holding a coffee pot. Lyle froze. She refilled the cup and left.

The thug stared at Lyle for a moment. He gestured to the backpack. Lyle picked it up, slung it over his left shoulder, and walked out to his car. His heart pounded faster.

His fingers fumbled with the key fob. Upside down. Turn it over. Find the darn button. The backpack slipped off his shoulder. Breathe. He set the backpack upright in the backseat, closed the door, and got in the driver's seat. Strap on the seatbelt, press the start button, and slam the car into drive. He checked the rearview mirror.

No!

The thug mounted his motorcycle.

Lyle flew out of the parking lot, making a reckless right turn onto the highway. He glanced at the rearview mirror. The image sent a shock down his spine. A single headlight flashed out of the parking lot. Lyle clinched the steering wheel with a death grip. His eyes darted back and forth between the rearview mirror and the road ahead. The single headlight turned left.

The thug?

Sweat fogged his vision.

Two lights or one light behind me?

He cleared his eyes with a swipe of his hand.

Two lights.

The skirmish between navigating the road ahead and surveilling for motorcycles behind him twisted Lyle's nerves tighter with each mile. One twist short of them snapping, he pulled into his driveway, exhausted. He clicked the garage door remote, drove in, and clicked the remote again, nearly crunching the back of his car with the garage door.

He sat.

Frozen.

Staring into the void.

An adrenaline buzz ran through every nerve in his body accompanied by a soundtrack of high-pitched ringing. He shook his head to break the trance and stepped out of the car.

A noise outside the garage.

A motorcycle passing the house?

He waited.

My mind playing tricks.

He grabbed the backpack and entered the house.

In his home office, he'd prepared a locked cabinet to store the Picassos. He set the backpack in the cabinet, locked it, and collapsed in his office chair.

Tomorrow, he'd call his wife and let her know it was safe for them to come home. And tomorrow there'd be a lot of explaining to do at work and at home.

CHAPTER 52

Close But No Cigar

Cafe Le Livre, Paris, 1937

DOTTIE HEADED DOWN THE block from the cafe after her morning espionage coffee with Bruno Lohse. She had grilled him about possible Nazi agents sleuthing about Paris. What did she get?

A big fat nothing.

Except for the slip of paper that had fallen out of Lohse's wallet.

Plenty of promising information on that card.

She stopped at the corner and waited. A bus pulled away and out of nowhere, Hemingway and Jacques crossed the street and headed toward her.

Why are they here?

"Morning, gents." She grinned. "Not here by accident, I assume."

Hemingway tossed his cigar butt in the gutter. "Thought we'd catch up on the morning news is all. Let's take a stroll."

Hemingway and Jacques flanked her, looping their arms in hers. The trio crossed at the next corner, entered a park, and meandered down a curvy path through the sculpted shrubbery.

"You guys following me this morning?" Dottie said.

A flutter of leaves crossed their path.

"Only for your own good," Jacques said. "We've tailed Lohse since Josephine reported he was part of the Bernstein's art heist."

"And?" Dottie asked.

"So far, nothing of any substance. He visits art galleries and dines with French and Germans, seemingly nonpolitical," Hemingway said. "What did you learn?"

Dottie shook her head. "Nothing as far as Nazi contacts. He didn't give up a thing. Just talked about his clients and the type of art he's looking for in Paris. But wait till you see what I got."

Hemingway guided them to a bench. A frisky poodle pulled a young boy past them, followed by his mother.

Dottie pulled the card out of her purse and showed it to Jacques and Hemingway. "This fell out of Lohse's wallet when he paid the check. He didn't notice it fall, so I covered it with my foot until he left." Dottie unfolded the paper, about the size of a five franc note. "It lists the six Picassos and names the Bernsteins. Then some kind of codes." She held it for Hemingway and Jacques to see.

ERR

Date: 12 April 1937

Source: Bernstein, Paris, France

Description: Six pen ink portraits of Igor Stravinsky by Pablo Picasso

Lot: 12453

Key: 647109182

Destination Depot:

Hemingway took the card and examined it. "Lot and key. Some kind of cataloging system? But no destination listed. And what is the ERR?"

The distant midday bells of Notre Dame chimed.

"I've heard rumors the Nazis created an agency to collect art for Hitler," Jacques said. "The name is Einsatzstab Reichsleiter Rosenberg, ERR."

Dottie huffed and shook her head. "Please. I can't stand listening to all this German in Paris lately." A breeze rumpled her dress. "It's vulgar." She smoothed her dress and turned to Jacques. "Do you think the ERR stole the Bernsteins' art and took it to Germany?"

"We don't know." Jacques took the card from Hemingway, copied the information on a notepad, and handed the card back to Dottie.

"Put that back in your purse," Hemingway said.

A teacher led twelve rowdy boys past them.

"Come. Let's walk through the quad," Hemingway said.

Hemingway led them into the area empty of other strollers. They huddled in a circle. "This card may hold the key to finding their art. But it's only a key. There must be something that needs this key."

"I'll show this to some of my German contacts," Jacques said. "Maybe they can find something helpful."

"In the meantime, keep the card in a safe place," Hemingway said.

Dottie turned to Hemingway. "But I need to show it to the Bernsteins."

"Fine. But afterward, they must put it in their safe. I don't know how, where, or when, but the information on that card is critical in finding the Picasso drawings," Hemingway said.

***

At the Bernsteins' home, Dottie made phone calls to the Hoffmans, Stravinsky, and Josephine, urging them to come hear her update. Even for an impromptu gathering, Emma took time to prepare afternoon tea for the group. Her coping mechanism. When life is out of control, control what you can.

The group arrived and Josephine walked up to Dottie. "How did you do, my dear? Did you nail him?" She nudged Dottie with her elbow.

"Thanks to your advice, I kept my calm. But so did he. Not sure I nailed him, but I got some interesting information about the Picassos," Dottie said.

"Excellent!" Josephine said.

The women helped themselves to tea. The men wanted information. Otto called the group together. "Please take a seat. Let's hear what Dottie has to say."

"That Lohse is one smooth character. It was hard to pretend I didn't know about his involvement with the theft. And when he told me he knew about it, he didn't flinch. He said the news had spread among the art dealers in Paris."

Otto and Fritz exchanged glances. "That's news to me," Otto said. "None of the galleries we deal with know about it."

"That's true," Fritz said. "We all agreed to keep it confidential within this circle. I haven't heard a word from any of our galleries."

"If that's true, Lohse is lying," Otto said. "If he knew about it, he must have been part of it."

Dottie opened her purse and pulled out the card. She smiled. "But wait till you see this." She opened the card and held it up. "When Lohse paid for the coffee, this fell out of his wallet. I hid it with my foot until he left."

Josephine grinned. "Excellent work, dear."

Otto unfolded his arms and leaned forward. "May I see it?"

Dottie handed him the card.

Otto's face hardened. He flicked the card with his fingers. "This has our name on it and lists the six stolen Picassos."

Emma straightened in her chair and turned to Otto. "What? Let me see."

Emma took the card from Otto and drew it closer to her face. She shook the card with each "No, no, no! What does this mean?" She fixed her wondering eyes on Otto, waiting for an answer.

Dottie answered instead. "Jacques and Hemingway think it is some sort of inventory card."

Fritz said, "Inventory?" He walked to Emma. "Let me see it." He took the card. "What does this lot and key mean? And who or what is the ERR?"

"Jacques told me the ERR is the name of a Nazi agency in charge of finding art for Hitler," Dottie said.

"Damn!" Fritz slammed his fist on the table. "That Lohse may not wear a uniform, but he sure is in thick with the Nazis."

"And if the Nazis have our art, it's probably somewhere in Germany by now," Otto said, slowly shaking his head.

"At least you have the key and lot information," Josephine said. "What would a lot mean as far as art is concerned?"

"Perhaps they packaged the six drawings together, and the lot number identifies the package," Fritz said.

"But the key?" Otto said. "I can understand labeling a group of pictures to inform the recipient of the number of pieces to expect in a package. But if they receive the package, who needs a key?"

Stravinsky had quietly listened to the news. "May I look at the card?"

Fritz handed him the card. Stravinsky put on his glasses and studied the contents. He reached into his coat pocket, pulled out a small notepad and pencil, and scribbled something on the pad. He returned the notepad and pencil to his pocket, took off his glasses, and handed the card back to Fritz. "Interesting. Thank you."

Why would Igor, a musician, want this information?

Dottie turned to Otto. "Hemingway said you should keep this locked in your safe."

Fritz tightened his grip on the card. "I'll put it in my safe." He tucked the card in his pocket and scowled at Otto. "No one's broken into my house so far."

Otto clinched his jaw. "So far."

Somewhere a church bell chimed six o'clock. Somewhere six innocent Picasso drawings lay captive in lot 12453.

Chapter 53

It's Like This

Office of Derrick Edwards, Irvine, California, 2022

Derrick Edwards sat in his office at 1:00 a.m., fidgeting with insignificant items on his desk, halfway through a six-pack. Why hadn't he gotten an update since Duke left the Becker art museum with the package of Picassos?

He had built fail-safe steps into his plan to trigger confusion for anyone trying to track the package. Step one: Duke steals a backpack with the drawings from the Becker and transports it to Denny's. Step two: a courier gives a password to Duke at Denny's, grabs the backpack, and delivers it to the Client.

According to the plan, Duke should have made it to Denny's and completed the handoff to the courier by now and the courier should have delivered the backpack to the Client. No one had checked in since Duke left the Becker.

Derrick picked up his comm and radioed Duke. *He better answer.*

"Yeah?"

"What the hell is going on? Where's the package?"

"Everything's good, boss."

"What exactly does that mean?"

"The courier picked up the package, like you planned."

"What courier?"

"The one in the Angels hoodie with the password."

Derrick froze. *Holy shit. What happened?* Someone had sabotaged his very clear, very simple, very perfect plan. But who?

"Did you see the guy when he drove off? Can you ID his vehicle?"

"Didn't think I needed to. What's going on?"

"The guy you gave the package to was not our courier."

Silence. Then, "What the..."

"Exactly."

"I don't know what to say, boss. This guy came straight over to my table. Had on an Angels hoodie, looked at the backpack, and gave me the password."

Great. There'll be hell to pay.

Derrick called the courier.

"Yes?"

"Did you get the package?" Derrick said, picking up a baseball on his desk.

"Nope."

Derrick's hand tightened on the baseball. "What do you mean? You should have made contact an hour ago."

"I went to Denny's just like you told me."

"And?" His knuckles turned white.

"I looked all around. No one there with the package you described. So, I left."

Derrick slammed the ball on the desk. "You left?"

"Yeah. What else was I supposed to do?"

"How about call and ask for instructions, like a thinking person, you ape. You can forget about a paycheck."

"But—"

Click.

Derrick hurled the baseball at the Angels poster.

The shock from his failure escalated. His ears began pulsing with each heartbeat. A dark fog engulfed his thoughts. He struggled to process what to do next.

The buzz on his phone jerked him out of his quandary. The Client. His chest tightened.

Where do I even begin? He tapped the green circle.

"What the hell are you trying to pull? Where's my package?" the Client snarled.

"If you give me a minute, I can explain."

"I doubt it. I thought you had a foolproof plan."

So did I.

The pulsing in his ears crescendoed and muddied his thinking.

Did Duke make off with the goods? Or the courier?

Surely, he was paying them plenty. Neither of them had experience in selling or trading black-market art. Who had outsmarted him?

Derrick closed his eyes, took a deep breath, and blew it out. "Let's call this a hiccup. I'm sure I will get to the bottom of things."

"A hiccup? This is a total failure, you imbecile. Did you vet your team?"

Derrick resented this inquiry. He might as well be strapped to a chair in an abandoned warehouse with a blinding light shooting in his eyes.

"Of course, sir. I don't think they are the problem."

"You don't think. That's the problem. Has anything strange happened to you recently?"

It came to him in a flash. *The cookies.*

"I was surprised when you sent me cookies last week."

"Cookies? Why would I ever send you cookies?"

"That's what I wondered. They came with a notecard that said, 'TO OUR SUCCESS.'"

"You idiot. I didn't send those. You've been hacked. Check that card for a bug."

Derrick retrieved his bug wand and scrambled through the items on his desk to find the notecard. He passed the wand over the card. The entire row of red dots lit up.

Damn. How did this happen? And who made it happen?

"And?"

"You're right. The card is bugged."

"How the hell could you not notice it?"

"The notecard is barely thick enough to—"

"Enough excuses." A breath blasted through the phone. "Listen carefully. You will investigate every individual who had any part in this plan. Your thugs, your insider at the Becker, and their friends and families. Understand?"

"Yes."

"Do you have the sender's information from the cookie delivery?"

"There wasn't any."

"More excuses. I want results. And if you can't deliver, you can forget about any more payments. Do your job or else." Click.

Derrick wondered if his career had just ended, or worse. The Client had connections with professionals who did the "or else" thing without leaving a trace.

Derrick cleared a spot on his desk, grabbed a legal writing pad from his side drawer, and set it in front of him. He opened his next bottle of beer and downed half of it.

He started planning an investigation of anyone involved with the heist. The longer he worked, the longer the list grew. Frustration and fatigue chased him through the night. It finally subdued him.

***

The morning sun pried Derrick's eyes open. He lifted his groggy head from his desk, pushing the piercing light away with his hand. Memories of last night's failure grew from an ember to a raging fire, stoked by the memory of his livid Client's threat.

Or else!

CHAPTER 54

Planning the Boom

Hoffman Munitions Company, Paris, 1937

JACQUES PONGE HAD MANY skills useful to the Second Bureau. None of them included bomb building. Fritz Hoffman's munitions company had plenty of bomb experience. With Göring's upcoming departure from Paris, the Second Bureau had an explosive opportunity and needed Hoffman's expertise. At first, Fritz had resisted the idea of participating in a radical response to Germany's aggression in the Rhineland. But Hemingway and Jacques had persuaded him something must be done. Now.

Eliminating the Nazis' second-in-command with a bomb would send a clear signal: France is not afraid to resist Germany. If France's politicians and military leaders refused to respond to the Nazis' aggression, the people would rise to the challenge. With Germany already fighting in Spain, who else would stop Hitler from expanding the war to France? If Hitler formed an alliance with General Franco, Germany and Italy would hem in France on the north and the south.

Preparing for today's meeting with Fritz Hoffman, Jacques obtained the rail schedule and route for Göring's trip to Berlin next Thursday. After studying the rail map, he chose the location for the bomb: east of the Canal de Saint-Denis, where the woods provided a cover for the bomb team. With map in hand, he headed to Fritz Hoffman's munitions company.

***

As owner, Fritz had little involvement on a daily basis of running Hoffman Munitions Company, but occasionally, he made unannounced appearances at the headquarters. The framed awards and government commendations on his office walls testified to his company's role in France's military victories in the Great War.

Before Jacques arrived, Fritz met with Henri, his explosives expert and a trusted confidant. Behind closed doors in his office, Fritz explained the plan and discussed explosive options. After agreeing on the best option, Fritz raised a more important issue.

"I am working with an inexperienced group of patriots who share our concerns for the future sovereignty of France. I need someone with your experience to assist them in executing this plan."

Henri leaned in. "And you want to know if I'm willing to be that someone? Am I willing to do whatever it takes to keep those Krauts out of France again?" Henri folded his arms and leaned back in his chair. "Compared to some things we did twenty years ago, this is nothing. You can count me in."

Fritz nodded. "Thank you, Henri. Let's hope this isn't the beginning of the next war to end all wars."

Fritz opened the door to the reception area. "Jacques, please, come in. He closed the door behind Jacques.

"Jacques, may I introduce you to Henri? My explosives expert and fellow patriot."

Henri and Jacques shook hands, sizing each other up. Henri with a warm smile. Jacques with a set jaw.

"Do you have the rail map?" Fritz said.

Jacques pulled the map out of his messenger bag and laid it on the desk. Fritz and Henri gathered around.

Jacques pointed to a spot on the map. "After the train leaves Gare de l'Est, it curves to the east. Past the Canal de Saint-Denis is a wooded area. Good cover for the team while they wait for the train. This is our spot."

Fritz studied the location. "I agree. The ties lay on a firm foundation in that area. The blast should cause minimal damage to the tracks."

Henri said, "I know this area." He pointed. "The tracks are close enough to the woods for laying the fuse cable. Looks easy if everything goes well."

"If?" Jacques straightened up and locked eyes with Henri. "Why shouldn't things go well?"

An awkward tension filled the air.

"I meant nothing by that. Just an expression," Henri said.

Fritz turned to Jacques. "Henri is as zealous about this mission as you are."

"The Germans stole my brother's life," Henri said, with a somber face. "I hate them. It's time they have a taste of their own medicine."

"I'm sorry." Jacques placed his hand on Henri's shoulder. "Thanks for joining the cause."

Henri nodded. "France's cause, my friend. When is the attack?"

"Next Thursday," Jacques said. "The train leaves the station at 10:00 am. It should pass the target area within thirty minutes. We need to plant the bomb and lay the fuse cable the night before, under cover of darkness."

"We can plant the dynamite in the track, so it is undetectable," Henri said.

Jacques said, "Good. Someone should remain at the site overnight to assure no one removes the dynamite. If someone removes it, we need a second set of supplies."

"Yes, I agree," Fritz said. "We must ensure the success of this effort."

Fritz sat in his chair and folded his hands. "No doubt the authorities will launch an investigation afterwards. We can't leave any evidence that leads the investigation here."

"Our dynamite is no different from our competitors," Henri said. "If investigators find any residue, which is unlikely, it won't point them to your company, Fritz."

"Mr. Göring is an enormous man. Better take that into account, Henri," Fritz said, leading everyone in a much-needed chuckle.

Fritz walked to a side table and poured a round of sherry for the three. "Gentlemen, a toast to the success of sending our message to Herr Hitler and the Third Reich." They clinked glasses and downed their sherry.

Fritz took a long breath. "I don't need to tell you we are about to cross a line, a dangerous one. I pray to God there aren't many more lines ahead."

All three stared into their empty glasses. Fritz broke their contemplations. "I'll let you two work together on the final arrangements. If you need anything from me, ask. Good luck."

Jacques folded his map and tucked it back in his messenger bag. He and Henri left. Fritz closed the door after them and sat at his desk, facing the blue, white, and red striped flag in the corner. Freedom, equality, and brotherhood. A trinity of causes, worthy of his support, again.

He picked up the framed photo on his desk of Claire, sitting in a field of flowers with a picnic basket next to her. Her smile radiated pure joy.

Would his bomb steal that joy from her, and the rest of France?

CHAPTER **55**

The Morning After

Albert Becker Art Museum, Irvine, California, 2022

THE 6:30 A.M. ALARM startled Lyle Bernstein from a deep sleep. After the adrenaline crash following last night's heist, he'd slept more soundly than any night since his family left for Big Bear. Gradually gaining consciousness, the previous night's activities came into focus. Or was he waking from a dream? A nightmare? He yawned and rubbed his eyes open. Sitting on the edge of his bed, he scratched his morning stubble and replayed the tape of last night's events. He executed his plan, recovered the Picassos at the Denny's pickup location, and locked them in his home. Today, he had a new challenge. What to say at work? How many lies would he have to tell?

He arrived early at the Becker to beat everyone else to the scene of the crime. Entering the staff parking, Lyle passed two parked cars. A bolt of shock ripped through his body. Why was Brian here so early? And Diego? He's always late. His phone rang, startling him and sending a reflexive stomp on the brakes. He hadn't paid attention to his phone all morning.

Several missed text messages.

All from Brian.

Brian's caller ID showed on the screen.

Lyle's vibrating finger tapped the green circle.

"You okay, Lyle? I've tried reaching you all morning."

"I'm, I'm, yes, I'm okay. Parking now."

"Get to your office as soon as you can."

"Yes. On my way."

Lyle pounded the steering wheel.

So much for beating everyone else to work.

He took a deep breath, a futile attempt to calm himself, but enough to find he had stopped his car in the middle of a drive lane. He pulled into a parking spot and headed to his office.

Lyle sprinted through the lobby and turned the corner. He stopped dead in his tracks. Several museum personnel crowded outside the door to his office turned in unison toward him. *This doesn't look good.* He blinked to make them disappear. They didn't. He slinked past them and entered his office to find Brian and Diego examining the locks on the drawers where he stored the Picasso drawings.

Brian turned to Lyle. "I have some horrible news. Someone broke in and stole the Picasso drawings last night."

Lyle couldn't move. *Do I look suspicious? Time for a poker face and the first set of lies.*

"What?" Lyle said.

"Somehow, our security systems went offline last night. The Picassos are the only things missing. Odd, isn't it?" Brian said.

Lyle cleared his dry throat. "I don't know what to say. I'm sure I locked them before I left last night."

Lie number one.

"Diego and I examined the locks. No sign someone jimmied them. Whoever picked them is an expert. Who has keys to these drawers?"

"Only me. I keep them locked in my desk drawer and I'm the only one who can unlock that."

"Let's make sure the keys are there," Brian said.

Brian and Diego followed Lyle to his office. He unlocked and opened his desk drawer.

"Here they are." Lyle picked up the keys and showed them.

"Well, that settles that," Brian said.

***

A second outage at the Becker. How? AJ telegraph-tapped the steering wheel on his drive to the art museum.

What happened?

Two calls had come in quick succession. First, Curt's call informing AJ about last night's system outage. Second, Brian's call confirming the security systems at the Becker had gone offline. And, worse, intruders had stolen art from the museum this time. Brian and AJ shared a decade of friendship, but how many system failures could their friendship endure?

Control, slipping through his fingers.

Control. An illusion.

Lord, give me your peace and wisdom. Help me work through this hopeless situation.

***

AJ met Brian, Lyle, and Diego in the conference room at the Becker. He greeted them and headed for the coffee carafe on the side table for his first cup of the day. Maybe caffeine would bring clarity.

"Here's what we know," Brian said. "Someone broke in last night, undetected because of the system outage, and walked out the door with six valuable portraits by Picasso. We've gone through the entire gallery and nothing else is missing. Why they only took these six pieces is puzzling. They could have taken several more."

"This may not be my place, but who else knew you had the Picassos?" AJ said.

He already knew the answer, but he wanted to hear Brian's response.

"The entire staff had agreed to hold off on any publicity. I guess it slipped out somehow," Brian said. "Lyle and Diego, have you mentioned them to anyone?"

"Not me," Diego said, holding up his hands.

243

"As a matter of fact, I showed them to Grace," Lyle said. "I talked with her about the gala idea of soliciting drawings from the public. She told me a music professor at Lines College knew about them."

"Well, the cat's out of the bag," Brian said. "That doesn't help us much now. The drawings are gone and we have to deal with that. Lyle and Diego, that's all for now. I'll talk to you later."

Lyle and Diego left the conference room.

"Brian, I'm not sure what to say. I learned about this just before you called me," AJ said.

"I understand, AJ. I have to answer to a board. This is twice now. I'm not sure our museum is safe."

"Is there any video footage?"

"No. The outage knocked out the video recording."

"I see." AJ telegraph-tapped the table. "Brian, I promise I'll sort this out. We will run a complete system test at our site and I'll send my best technicians out to check everything here. Can I have forty-eight hours to investigate?"

"Okay. If you can't find a reason for the outage, I need to consider other security options," Brian said.

"Thank you, Brian. I'll send updates on everything we find."

Driving to his office, it dawned on AJ that yesterday's earthquake could be a factor. His staff had run their normal diagnostics but found nothing wrong in the aftermath. Is it possible something occurred at the museum after the earthquake? Slim chance, but he needed to grasp onto something.

Lord, I know you send out your commands to the earth, even if they're earthquakes. My faith is a little shaky right now. Help my unbelief.

***

Lyle sat in his private office, overwhelmed by the events of the last twenty-four hours. His mind-fog blocked him from determining what to do with the drawings now sitting in his home.

He had followed Matt Perkins' instructions to a "T" and decided it was safe for his family to return.

He made the call.

They'd arrive home this evening.
He had a lot of explaining to do.

245

CHAPTER 56

Ashes, Ashes

Paris, 1937

Driving to the Hoffman Munitions Company, Jacques relayed to Hemingway the details of his meeting with Fritz and Henri the previous day.

"Don't get me wrong. I'm grateful for Hoffman supplying the equipment, but I disagree with him putting Henri in charge. It's our mission."

"Learned a lot about that in Spain," Hemingway said. "Gotta be careful about letting things get under your skin. Wise to respect someone like Henri, who has experience in blowing up things."

Jacques focused on the dimly lit road and considered Hemingway's comment. Yes, they all had the same motivation: push back on the Germans before they crossed another red line.

He turned the corner, drove to the back of the Hoffman Munitions building, and parked next to the loading dock. Henri met them at the door and led them to a room with the supplies for their mission.

Jacques and Hemingway examined the eight sticks of dynamite, two spindles of cable, and two detonators.

Jacques turned to Henri. "Is this enough for our objective?"

"We've done this hundreds of times," Henri said. "I've included double in case anything fails. Jacques, load the cable, and Hemingway, you load the detonators. I'll load the dynamite."

Each man loaded his assigned item into a canvas bag and zipped it up.

"That's it. Let's go," Henri said.

They loaded the canvas bags into the truck and grabbed a seat. Jacques drove the team on to their destination for tomorrow's attack on Göring.

"I've timed the trains over the last week," Jacques said. "Each day, the train arrived at our target location thirty minutes after leaving the depot. Tomorrow, Denis will radio us when the train leaves, so we will know the approximate arrival time."

Hemingway gazed out the window. "Weather is decent. Let's hope it holds up tomorrow."

"Shouldn't make a difference," Henri said. "Rain or shine, these explosives worked every time in the last war."

Leaving the city, the streetlights grew scarcer until the only light on the road came from the truck's dull headlights. Jacques pulled into the woods adjacent to the tracks. They opened the bags with the dynamite and the cable and began their assigned tasks. Henri, having the most experience, fastened the dynamite against the track. Hemingway and Jacques laid the cable from the tracks to the woods. Tomorrow, they would connect the cable to the detonator. They finished by covering the dynamite and cable with dirt, rocks, and debris.

Henri made a final inspection of their work. "Yes. This will do."

***

Jacques's sleep came in short bits. Some filled with gloomy images of failed train bombings. In the first nightmare, Jacques thrust the detonator just as the train passed over the dynamite, but nothing exploded. In the second nightmare, images of a laughing Göring, the size of a dirigible, floated over the train. He pointed a gun straight at Jacques. With a menacing laugh, Göring pulled the trigger. Instead of a bullet, a rod extended out with a small flag displaying the word "BANG."

Jacques woke in a sweat with half memories of foreboding nightmares. All he remembered for sure: the dynamite never exploded. He washed the thought away at the morning sink and focused on a victorious blast for France.

Jacques rendezvoused with Hemingway and Henri and drove the team to the bombing location. From the woods next to the tracks, Henri used the binoculars to check the dynamite and the cable.

"Everything's good," Henri said. "Time to connect the detonator."

He took the detonator from the canvas bag and connected the cable.

Jacques checked his watch. Göring's train would depart the station in thirty minutes.

***

Denis perched himself against a wall at the Paris train station, maintaining a visual of the rail carriage adorned with swastikas. Several porters had come and gone from the carriage, but no Göring yet. There would be no mistaking when he arrived. Göring's vanity always played to the crowd, especially during arrivals and departures.

Looking down the platform, Denis recognized the gentleman walking toward Göring's car. Bruno Lohse. *What is he doing here?* Bruno entered Göring's carriage. *Strange.*

At 9:45, a hubbub came around the corner. Sure enough, Herr Göring and a small entourage, engaged in jovial conversation, walked to his carriage and boarded.

Denis alternated his attention between Göring's carriage and the clock on the station wall. The minute hand moved to twelve. A whistle blew. The conductors hopped on to their respective cars. Steam flew. Wheels began turning. The train departed exactly on time.

"The train just left the station," Denis reported to Jacques over the radio transmitter. "Göring's car is twelve past the locomotive."

***

"Message received," Jacques said, acknowledging Denis. "Won't be long now."

Jacques, Henri, and Hemingway played a waiting game, filling the time with cigarettes, cigars, staring at watches, and constant glances through the binoculars.

At 10:25, Hemingway picked up the binoculars. "There's smoke."

Jacques's sweaty hand grabbed the binoculars. Henri took his turn.

"This is it. Time to nail the bastard," Jacques said.

The minutes ticked down. Chugging came into earshot. Louder and louder. The locomotive passed them, sending dust and debris airborne. They started counting carriages. By the tenth, the carriage covered in swastika banners appeared down the track.

Nine. Ten. Eleven.

The nightmare of a bloated Göring floating over the train flashed through Jacques's mind. He shook his head to clear the image.

Twelve.

Henri pushed the detonator.

A deadly boom. A flash of flames. Shrapnel of wood splinters darted through the air. Thick smoke engulfed Göring's carriage. A blast of heat shot over Jacques, Henri, and Hemingway in the woods. Flames pushed black smoke higher, sending a cloud that surrounded the trailing supply car, still attached to the remnants of Göring's carriage and the cars ahead. Naively unaware, the locomotive pushed on down the track. The injured supply carriage spewed a gloomy trail of lifeless soot in its wake.

Stunned, the trio stood in frozen silence, staring down the track until the train vanished.

"It's finished." Henri gathered the detonator and what remained of the cable. "Time to make haste, gentlemen."

After checking for any witnesses, they loaded into the truck and left.

***

The afternoon edition of *Paris-soir* featured a picture of what remained of the rail carriage carrying Göring to Berlin. Jacques, Henri, and Hemingway had gathered in Fritz's office to learn what the world would now know. The article described the near total destruction of the carriage carrying Göring and his guests back to Berlin.

Fritz read aloud to the others. "'If Göring had not been away from his car, strolling through the train and engaging other passengers, he would have died along with Bruno Lohse, a well-known art collector from Berlin. However, Göring survived without injury.'"

Fritz slammed the paper down. "Damn social butterfly."

"We accomplished nothing," Jacques said, pounding his fist.

Hemingway turned to Fritz. "And now we read your art thief, Lohse, is dead."

Fritz stood, walked to the window, and looked down on the munitions factory. "That bomb may have destroyed our collection, along with Lohse."

How would he explain this fiasco to Claire and the Bernsteins? Not only had he failed to assassinate Göring, but far worse, his bomb may have reduced their valuable art collection to cold, black, anonymous ashes, mingling them with swastika cinders and scattering them along the Berlin-bound tracks.

CHAPTER 57

Let's Get Together

Home of AJ Meyer, Irvine, California, 2022

AJ LIVED FOR ORDER and control. Lately, the twin illusions refused to submit to his commands. Other twins, unforeseen and unwanted events, had launched attacks on the twin worlds of his personal and professional lives. Nothing an analytical brain couldn't manage. Right? But so far ...

AJ met with Curt Matthews at his office all afternoon, searching for causes of the system outage at the Becker Museum. Instead of finding answers, every hypothesis led them into a labyrinth of confusion. The day ended with more questions than when it started.

Failing to conquer his professional challenge, he diverted his attention to his personal challenge of the Grandy mysteries. In his home office, he unlocked and opened the top drawer of the file cabinet and pulled out the folder containing his Grandy research.

He turned the pages, looking for an email printout. *What? Everything's out of order.* The IBM letter, not in the front. The photo, sheet music, notes, and email printouts all mixed up. His chest tightened.

Who did this? Grace? She'd never do such a thing. Would she? He carried the folder to the living room.

"Honey, I found something odd in my file on Grandy. You haven't rearranged my papers for any reason, have you?"

Grace grinned. "What? Disturb your perfectly refined, controlled filing system? I'd sooner die than do such a thing. Why?"

"Someone's rearranged the pages."

He sat next to Grace and held the folder open.

Grace leafed through the pages and turned to AJ. "But if it wasn't you and it wasn't me, then..." She sank into the cushions.

"That's what I'd like to know." He closed the folder. "If we've had an intruder, the security system didn't detect him."

Grace fingered her necklace. "Have you checked the security system?"

"I will now that I know you're not the guilty party."

Dread swept over AJ. A stranger had invaded his home and handled the evidence that could incriminate his grandfather and shame his entire family.

AJ carried the file back to his office, opened the cabinet housing the home security system, and started investigating. He started a system diagnostics cycle and waited for the results. The test returned a green confirmation for each component. He armed the system and walked outside to check the cameras in the front yard. Grace followed. AJ approached the house from several directions to test each camera's motion detection. Every approach triggered a system warning text message as it should. He punched the code to unlock the front door, opened it, and waited. Another text message arrived, followed by a phone call from an agent at Meyer Technologies. AJ put the call on speakerphone.

"Mr. Meyer, this is William from the home security department. We received an alert for a sensor triggered at your home. You didn't disarm the system within the required time. Is everything all right?"

"Yes, thank you. Just testing my system. But I need some information."

"Of course. How can I help?"

"Search through the history and see if you can find any strange combinations of disarming and rearming my system during the last three days."

"Yes, sir. Please hold while I check," William said.

AJ and Grace walked to his study, sat, and waited in curious silence for an answer.

William came back on the line. "Mr. Meyer, thank you for holding. I found something odd. This past Wednesday night, someone armed the system at 6:30 p.m. Then it was disarmed at 7:05 and rearmed again at 7:30."

"You said that happened Wednesday night?" AJ said.

"Yes, sir. Nothing unusual since then. Do you want us to come out and check the system?"

"Under the circumstances, yes. And you better check my house for bugs."

"We'll send someone right out."

"Yes. The sooner the better."

"Very well. A technician will arrive in ten minutes."

"Thank you," AJ said.

"Of course."

AJ took Grace's hand. "Someone broke in Wednesday night. They knew we'd be away at our small group. Someone's watching us."

Helplessness had attacked AJ again. The first attack, two years ago, brought personal grief from the discovery of his infertility. The next three attacks came in rapid succession over the last two weeks. Family shame, if Grandy's involvement with the Nazis proved true. Professional damage from his company's unsolved system outages. Failure to protect his wife and home resulting from the break-in. Hemmed in on four sides, the power of AJ's intellect failed to rebuff the relentless Helplessness. *Lord, how much more?*

Grace tightened her hand around AJ's. Her voice quivered. "AJ, what's going on?"

That's what he wondered. AJ had lived a life of uninterrupted personal and professional successes until the first attack by Helplessness. AJ's struggle with "why me, God?" had yielded a repetitive cycle of two seasons. One season filled with trust and contentment. The other, with doom, resulting from the sporadic and fruitless cravings for "there must be something I can do." Idols of control and self-reliance, always the enemies of trust and contentment. Enemies he defeated when he turned to God's Word for reminders. Reminders that God leaves nothing to chance in our lives. That nothing can separate us from God's love. That suffering is a drop and God's grace is an ocean.

The three recent deliveries by Helplessness had come so close together, AJ hadn't yet regained his status quo of order and control. Cracks had weakened his foundation of confidence. Had they also undermined Grace's faith in him? If these foreboding cracks had shaken his confidence, what about hers?

AJ turned to Grace and found the answer in her eyes. He wrapped her in his arms.

Grace curled up. "Have you checked your office? Is anything missing?"

"Nothing. The rearranged file is the only clue someone's been in my office."

Grace stroked AJ's hand. "This may sound like a long shot. What if our break-in has something to do with theft at the Becker?" She sat up and faced him. "I mean, isn't it odd our break-in happened so close to the break-in at the Becker?"

She may be an art professor, but she also had the sensibilities of a good detective. And AJ needed all the sleuthing help he could get.

Her face brightened. "Oh, and there's the Picassos." She pointed with both index fingers at invisible words in the air as she spoke. "I think it's more than a coincidence that right after we started investigating Grandy's clues, someone stole the Picassos from the Becker."

AJ looked through the file again. "Everything is still here."

"But they've seen everything about Grandy."

"Not to mention my email correspondence with individuals helping me."

AJ put the file back in the cabinet and turned to Grace. "So, to be clear. The value of these twelve, or six, Picassos, is enough for someone to engage in cloak-and-dagger stuff and steal them?"

"Worse has happened by art thieves."

He couldn't allow anything worse to happen. He yearned to regain order and control of this situation before anything more happened. But how?

AJ telegraph-tapped his fingers. "There's some strange connection with our break-in and what's happened at the Becker. "

"What if we talk with Brian, tell him everything we know about the Picassos from Grandy? Maybe we can team up with him to discover what's behind all of this."

AJ's arm stiffened around Grace.

"AJ, what's wrong?"

Brian's concerns about AJ's ability to solve the system failures had come through loud and clear. He needed answers and AJ wanted to find a solution before their next meeting. So far, he had nothing. An underwhelming offering, making for an awkward encounter with Brian that Grace had just proposed. AJ needed a solution to arrive within the next twenty-four hours. In the meantime, he could only presume upon Brian's patience and long-standing friendship.

"No argument from me."

***

AJ and Grace met Brian in his private office at the Becker. AJ described the list of items Grandy had left him and explained what they'd learned from the photo and the sheet music. He finished with the news that someone had broken into their house and seen his files.

"We think there's a connection between the theft of the six Picassos from the Becker and the break-in at our house," AJ concluded.

"Twelve Picassos in the photo Grandy left you? Hmm," Brian said. "We got six of them. Well, we had six. Wonder where the other six are? Wonder where my six are now?"

Brian locked eyes with AJ and opened his mouth to make another comment. He paused and offered an affable smile instead.

The awkward moment had reared its ugly head—the subtle reference to the theft resulting from AJ's system outage. Thanks to Brian's civility, he stopped short of indicting AJ, offering an olive branch with his silence.

AJ cleared his throat and put on an optimistic smile. "We're doing everything we can, Brian. I promise."

Brian nodded. "Of course."

Grace refocused the conversation. "Don't you think it's odd—you lost your six Picassos about the same time someone broke into our house and discovered clues about all twelve?"

"It seems more than a coincidence," Brian said.

"If we work together with you, we'll have a better chance of finding out what's happening," Grace said. "AJ is making progress with his resources. You can assist with your connections in the art world. There's got to be more information out there about these Picassos."

"Right," Brian said. "But let's step back and examine the facts. The six Picassos came to the Becker as a gift from Stravinsky's grandson. Stravinsky must have brought them to America when he moved here in the late 1930s. If there's twelve, why did his grandson donate only six? If the other six stayed in Germany, it's possible the Nazis stole them during the occupation. The name 'Bernstein' on the back of the picture suggests the couple was Jewish. The Nazis plundered art from many Jewish collections."

"One thing I haven't figured out—how my grandfather was involved," AJ said. "Clearly, he knew the Bernsteins and saw the twelve Picassos. He had connections with the Nazis, possibly through his work for IBM. And now, you suggest the Nazis stole the other six. Is it too wild to think Grandy knew something about the theft?"

"AJ, remember when we talked with Fred?" Grace said. She turned to Brian. "He's a history professor at Lines College. He said the Nazis kept records on everything. Brian, if they were such fanatical record keepers, did they keep records of the art they plundered?"

"I know they did," Brian said. "We have detailed records in Hermann Göring's own handwriting."

Grace turned to AJ. "If the Nazis used IBM equipment to keep census records, is it plausible they used their punch machines to keep records of the art they stole?"

"It's absolutely possible," AJ said. "They'd only need a punch card designed for collecting information about art. For example, a title, description, name of the artist, where it came from, and where they sent it. Maybe a few other tidbits."

"Is there any way the punch card tidbits could be put onto a tape?" Grace said, raising her eyebrows.

AJ stood up, started pacing, and shaking his right index finger. "Of course." He took Grace's head in his hands and kissed her forehead. "Have I ever told you how smart you are?"

"Yes, and I love it when you do," Grace said with a smile.

"So, here's a wild scenario. The Nazis steal the Bernsteins' art. They catalog it, record it on punch cards, and make a tape of all the punch cards."

"But could such a tape be any good after this many years?" Brian said.

"If someone stored it properly," AJ said.

"Do you think that's the tape mentioned in the letter to Grandy?" Grace said.

"I do."

The three sat in silence, taking in the significance of Grace's suggestion.

Grace slapped the table. "Well, then, we gotta get the tape."

AJ smiled back at Grace. "Yes. We definitely gotta get the tape."

"So, where is the tape?" Brian said.

"I made a trip to a New York IBM office several days ago. The manager is looking for the tape in an archive as we speak. I'm hoping to hear from him any day now."

Brian let out a gasp. "Whooo. This is big. Finding the other six Picassos could put the Becker on the map. It will be the greatest event for the gallery since it opened."

"I appreciate your enthusiasm, Brian. But let's take this one step at a time," AJ said. "If the tape even exists, I still have to find the equipment to read the tape, somewhat of a challenge, given how old the technology is."

"If anyone can do it, you can," Grace said with an admiring look.

"I assume we'll keep this among the three of us for the time being," Brian said.

"Of course." AJ turned to Grace. "Right, my dear darling art professor? No more discussions at the college?"

"Nope. Nada. Nothing." Grace made a zipper gesture across her lips.

"Contact me after you get the tape," Brian said. "I'll be on pins and needles till you do."

"I think that makes three of us," AJ said. "And let us know if you turn up anything from your connections."

"Of course. I can't thank you enough for coming forward with this, AJ, and you too, Grace."

Walking to the car, Grace said, "Do you think the tape has information about the location of the Picassos?"

AJ turned and smiled at Grace. "We'll have to wait and see."

Waiting. His second least favorite thing, right behind not being in control.

CHAPTER 58

Lots and Keys

Berlin, Germany, 1937

ON THE BERLIN BOUND train, Josephine collected her thoughts, traveling over the same tracks Göring's train traveled the previous week. The failed assassination of Hermann Göring triggered two powerful responses from her friends. First, Jacques's disgust that Göring had survived, sabotaging his revengeful message he wanted to send to the Nazis. Second, shock the Bernsteins and Hoffmans endured, uncertain whether the bomb had blown their art collection to smithereens. No actual proof existed of the collection's destruction. But it seemed plausible Lohse had shipped the stolen art on the train under his personal supervision.

Hanging on to a sliver of hope their art had survived, the Hoffmans and Bernsteins called on Josephine to travel to Berlin. Her mission this time: pursue Göring to discover the meaning of the mysterious lot and key numbers on the card Dottie had recovered from Lohse. If their art had survived, their recovery relied on the significance of these numbers.

One reward Josephine received from her previous schmoozing with Göring included his Berlin office phone number. After checking into her Berlin hotel, she dialed the number. His voice came through the receiver. She smiled across the phone line.

"Mein Hermann, this is your lovely Josephine. How are you today?"

"Josephine? Ah, today, now I'm wonderful, hearing your voice. But the line is so clear. Where are you, my kitten?"

"In my favorite Berlin hotel, thinking about you."

"Berlin? Are you performing in town? I read nothing about it."

"I'm here on a break from French society. Sometimes it is so, oh, I don't know—"

"Rude?"

"I'd never say that, Hermann. While I'm here, shall we find a time for dinner together?"

"Tonight?"

Good, he's eager to meet.

"Your enthusiasm overwhelms me. My hotel dining room?"

"Yes. At eight."

"I'll meet you in the lobby."

"*Auf Wiedersehen.*"

Wonderfully easy. No reason to think she couldn't accomplish her mission tonight.

***

Josephine knew how to take command in a power struggle. With his German punctuality, he arrived at 8:00 p.m. Forcing him to wait for her, at 8:06 pm, she descended the curved marble staircase, captivating Hermann Göring. Her low-necked, bejeweled red evening gown competed for the prize of best dressed with his custom-tailored white uniform, adorned with medals and the Knights Cross hanging from his neck. Sparkles reflected from both of them as they walked through the lobby to the hotel restaurant.

"Ah, Herr Göring, *guten Abend.*" The maître d' smiled, holding two menus. "Your usual table is ready. Right this way."

Music from the string quartet accompanied their walk to a table in a secluded corner.

Settling into their seats, Josephine smiled and lobbed her first barrage of compliments. "Gardenias. How did you know they are my favorites?"

"Never underestimate a man of the world, Josephine," Göring said, grinning.

The evening proceeded from cocktails to the main course. Josephine endured his small talk but steered the conversation in her direction.

"We should celebrate your recent success," she said.

"Which one? I have many."

"Surviving that horrible train bombing. I worried so when I read the report in the papers. Did you suffer any injuries, Hermann?"

"Not at all. I was several cars up the line when it happened."

"Poor Mr. Lohse. He wasn't so lucky."

"No. He wasn't. And an enormous loss for me now."

"Oh?"

"Why, he was my best art collector for the Reich. He had quite a knack."

He sure did.

"But your collection, is it still growing?"

"Ah, yes. We will have the finest collection in Europe one day."

"With so many pieces of art from so many places, how do you keep track of it all?"

"We Germans are very good at keeping track of things. It's in our genes."

Josephine forced a laugh, disguising the knot in her stomach. The Nazis' ideology of promoting an Aryan race and eliminating the Jews repulsed her. A bitter reminder of the prejudice she left behind in America and a concern she carried for her friends in Paris.

"When our agents acquire a group of paintings, they give the group a number, a lot number."

Ah. The lot number. The group of paintings stolen from the Bernsteins has a lot number.

"Interesting. What else happens?"

"Our Führer insists we keep records of everything. He is progressive in technology. So, thanks to IBM in your United States, we record everything on what they call punch cards."

Josephine leaned forward, licking her wine glass. "This is so fascinating. What happens with these punch cards?"

"At our computer center, the clerk groups the cards for one lot together and records them on a tape of paper."

"Sounds fantastical."

Göring's excitement for the process increased with each of Josephine's questions.

"Yes. Machines punch little holes in special arrangements for each letter of each word. It looks like gibberish, but that's when the magic of the computer comes in. The technician places the tape on the computer, enters a key, and the computer translates the little holes into words and sentences and prints them on paper. We record where every piece of art came from and where it went for storage."

There. A key for a computer to process a tape with information about a group, or lot, of artwork. That must be the lot and key recorded on the card Dottie recovered from Lohse. If Josephine could find that tape, she could find the art, but only if she could also find a computer to process the tape.

"This is all so amazing, Hermann. Who on earth figured all this out?"

"Believe it or not, IBM gave us almost everything we need. Our engineers made a few changes to adapt it for our purposes."

Maybe Robert Meyer knew something about this through his work for IBM.

"My head is so dizzy listening to this."

"Yes. We take great pride in our accomplishment. We can catalog anything. Including people. In fact, soon, we will have recorded our entire population census on punch cards. We'll have records of everything about everybody on these cards."

Josephine shuddered at this prospect. Knowing everything about everybody—a step toward a totalitarian control of a population.

Josephine grinned. "You Germans. Leading the world in so many ways."

Göring leaned forward, nodding, "You understand, don't you, Josephine?" He sat back and continued, making large gestures with his hands. "Our superior race will lead the entire world into the future."

Josephine's inner being quivered, frightened by his prediction. She sat across from evil itself, doing her best to belie her true hatred of everything the Nazis stood for.

She endured the rest of the evening, finally welcoming its finale.

Göring escorted her through the lobby to the stairs. So many garish swastika banners. Josephine paused, extended her hand, and reluctantly received a kiss from Göring. She forced the evening's last smile and ascended the stairs.

Having the intel she'd come for, she only needed to make her way back to Paris. That should be no problem, right?

CHAPTER **59**

Line by Line

Home of AJ Meyer, Irvine, CA, 2022

GRACE SAT IN HER favorite easy chair, bathed in the Saturday morning light. With her Bible resting on her lap, she sipped the last of her coffee. Today's devotional focused on the Sermon on the Mount in Matthew 5:14. "You are the light of the world." Light. Such a basic element. The first element God created to dispel the darkness. How amazing that Jesus calls us the light of the world, a creation of God. Not any light, but *the* light, to show our good works that others might see God and glorify Him. What an honor Jesus bestows upon us.

Lord, may your light show the way for AJ as he deals with all that's happening in his life. And thank you for today's beautiful sunshine.

The morning light filled the den for today's date with AJ. Another art date. With their ongoing focus on the Picasso pictures, Grace planned a date to draw their own version of the famous Picasso portrait of Stravinsky, one line at a time. Sure, AJ could learn to draw the picture by watching a YouTube video. But where's the fun in that, when he has his very own art instructor to show him in person?

Grace began moving the furniture to make room for their easels. AJ entered the den. "And it's furniture moving day because—"

Grace looked up with a "you're really going to like this" smile. "It's art day. Help me make some more room."

"Art day? More room for what?" AJ said, moving a chair.

"You and I are drawing our own version of Picasso's early portrait of Stravinsky. How about that!" She pushed another chair toward the wall.

"What? Aren't there enough of those Picassos in our life, even if they're all missing?"

"It'll be fun. Here, help me move the couch."

AJ helped Grace slide the couch across the floor. She stood and analyzed the new arrangement. "Good, plenty of light from the French doors."

"Can I at least get another cup of coffee before we draw these forgeries?"

"Copies, not forgeries. And yes, go tank up."

Walking to the kitchen, he shouted over his shoulder. "Might need a bagel too."

"Go," she yelled back, smiling.

Grace walked to the closet and retrieved the easels. Creating art together on these dates offered Grace a small measure of consolation for something they'd never create: a human life. How heart wrenching, that doctor's visit two years ago. The doctor slid the report across the desk and gave them time to absorb the shocking words waiting for them. Confirmation of AJ's infertility bullied them both into a period of mourning—months filled with emptiness and colored with sadness, especially for AJ. Grace had found peace, believing their sovereign God and Savior had a divine purpose that would bring Him glory. AJ's struggle continued in ebbs and flows.

AJ returned from the kitchen, munching on an everything bagel and sipping from a cup of coffee. "Whu ihhh ahh thsss?"

Grace snickered. "Don't talk with your mouth full, you ninny."

He took a drink. "What is all this?"

Grace had placed two painting easels to catch the light from the French doors. Each of their easels had a piece of drawing paper taped down. On a tripod between the easels, a blank paper hung from a clipboard.

Grace spoke to the smart speaker. Sweet, gentle orchestral sounds filled the room.

"Today we will copy a picture Picasso drew of Stravinsky in 1920, earlier than the twelve in Grandy's photo. He drew those in 1937. We'll use a technique called upside-down drawing."

"Let me see the picture," AJ said.

"Nope. That's part of the lesson. I put the picture under the blank sheet of paper on the clipboard. I will expose a little of the picture at a time. At the beginning, all you will see are lines. Oh, and the picture is upside down too. Hence the name."

Grace unclipped the cover paper on the tripod, moved it down a few inches, exposing the top of the upside-down drawing. She fastened the cover paper in place with blue tape.

She pointed to the exposed lines. "That's what we draw first."

AJ scrunched his eyes and pointed. "I can't even tell what that is. It looks like a bunch of random lines."

"That's the point. A true artist draws the lines he sees, not a preconceived object."

They faced their easels and picked up their pencils. AJ let out a teenager's huff and started. With Erik Satie's *Gymnopedie Number 1* floating in the background, they made their first marks.

Grace's teaching persona kicked in. "Did you know, the first word Picasso spoke was *piz*, short for *lapiz?*"

"And that's—"

"Spanish for *pencil*. Kind of interesting, even as a toddler, his first word had something to do with drawing, like it was God's purpose for him."

"Was he a believer?"

Grace moved the cover paper down another two inches.

"Still doesn't look like anything."

"Patience. Keep drawing what you see. Picasso's family practiced Catholicism, and they baptized him as a Catholic. But he rejected his beliefs in his twenties. His hormones rebelled, demanding freedom from any moral standards. Both he and Stravinsky sowed their wild oats."

"Must have made for some colorful discussions when they were together in his studio."

"Imagine. Two creative geniuses, enjoying a conversation together."

AJ flashed a smile at Grace. "You mean, like us?"

Grace chuckled. "Of course, dear. Like us."

She moved the cover page down farther.

"Ooh, I think I see fingers," AJ said.

"No. They're not fingers. Their lines. Focus on the lines."

They drew more lines. The *Elvira Madigan Piano Concerto* by Mozart accompanied them.

"Do you think the tape in Grandy's Nazi letter is connected to the lost Picasso drawings?"

"Wouldn't that be something?"

"Oh, come on, AJ. Is that all you've got?"

"Of course it's staggering, thinking that all the clues from Grandy are leading us to a lost art collection the Nazis stole. Who wouldn't want to be part of a story like that?"

"Story? You think it's a story?"

"Is this one of those 'there's no right answer' questions?"

"No. Really. Don't you think it's possible?"

"Of course it's possible. I'm all about following the clues until there's nothing left to follow. And we still have a lot to follow."

Grace uncovered the last part of the upside-down portrait. "We're almost done. Last section."

"Now that looks like a head."

She repeated her mantra. "Lines. They're lines."

They drew their last lines.

"Time to turn them right side up," Grace said.

"Hey. Look at that." AJ tilted his head. "It kind of looks like a person in some sort of chair, almost. Those hands look a little funny, though."

Grace slid next to AJ and fist-bumped his shoulder. "You did it, Mr. Arteeest."

"Not as well as you. But, still, it was fun."

He took her in his arms, stared at his drawing, then hers. He let out a discouraged teenager's sigh.

She snuggled into the warmth of his arms.

Oh, Mr. Meyer. It is a joy to create with you. You are the light of my life. Thank you, Lord, for this wonderful husband. And what's our next step to find those Picassos?

Scan or tap the QR code to read Grace's blogpost about upside-down drawing.

CHAPTER 60

Plunder Thunder

ERR Headquarters, Berlin Germany, 1937

ALFRED ROSENBERG SAT IN his office at the Berlin ERR headquarters contemplating the repercussions of the recent death of Bruno Lohse. According to the latest computer report from Dehomag, Lohse had obtained a small collection from a Jewish Paris family, Lot: 12453, and assigned a storage location for the collection. The recent train bombing left the collection's current location and even its existence open to speculation. Had Lohse taken the collection on the train with him or not?

With Hermann Göring's art world connections, Rosenberg found an immediate replacement for Lohse. Walter Hofer had the skills and experience on par with Lohse's, if not superior. His international connections, in France and Italy, provided opportunities not only in the art world but also in the worlds of politics and munitions. With the recent Rome-Berlin Axis agreement between Italy's Mussolini and Hitler, Hofer's connections made him a valuable asset to the Führer.

Rosenberg walked to the reception area and greeted Göring and Hofer, waiting for this month's status meeting. Rosenberg led them to his office and closed the door.

"Please, take a seat. We have much to discuss."

The trio sat around a circular oak table with refreshments in place.

"Herr Hofer, welcome. Hermann told me of your many qualifications."

A mid-forties, average-built Walter Hofer wore civilian clothes. He neither owned a Nazi uniform nor belonged to the Nazi party. But his usefulness to the mission outweighed the technicality of party membership.

"Thank you, Herr Rosenberg. Such an honor to serve the Führer," Hofer said.

Rosenberg lit a cigarette, took a long drag, and let out a stream of smoke. "What about this resistance in Paris, Göring? What do you know?"

Göring shifted in his seat. "Resistance, yes. But the ERR was not the target."

"Oh? What was?"

Göring slammed his fist on the table. "It was my rail car they bombed." His face reddened. "I was the target, of course."

Rosenberg exhaled another long drag. "And yet, here you are. The French must be growing weary of our Rhineland occupation. But that's none of our business."

Rosenberg picked up the computer report. "This collection from Paris that Lohse acquired, Lot 12453. Did it make it on the train with Lohse?"

Göring crossed his arms and leaned back. "Lohse entered the train before me. I didn't see what he brought on board and it wasn't with the luggage when we arrived in Berlin."

Rosenberg locked eyes with Göring. "Perhaps we need tighter security for our shipping procedures."

Göring folded his arms. "If you wish."

"Now, Herr Hofer, let's talk about Italy. I understand you have a wealth of connections," Rosenberg said.

"Yes, sir. And I have ideas for expanding our mission," Hofer said. "While we continue building the Führer's collection, I believe the art we acquire can serve another purpose."

Rosenberg crushed his cigarette in an ashtray. "Yes? And what would that be?"

"Germany faces challenges in the financial sector with the Reich's limitations on foreign trade," Hofer said. "But the ERR can lead the way in overcoming this obstacle."

"And how is that?" Rosenberg said.

"By using art for currency," Hofer said.

Göring chuckled. "Preposterous."

"Go on," Rosenberg said.

Hofer continued. "I have connections in Italy's black market that accept art as payment for, shall we say, valuable wartime assets."

"What are you suggesting?" Rosenberg said.

"We all know what Hitler wants. The Rhineland occupation is only a steppingstone. He wants much more. But he needs more weapons. We can help him get what he needs without breaking the German bank. There's more than enough art in Europe to build Hitler's art collection. We can exchange the pieces he rejects for weapons."

Rosenberg and Göring exchanged glances.

"What munitions connections do you have?" Rosenberg said.

"I can introduce you to the appropriate parties," Hofer said.

"You will give me your contacts and I will take further actions myself," Rosenberg said.

"But..." Hofer said.

"As soon as possible. Understood?"

"Of course." Hofer's shoulders slumped.

"The Führer's Art Exposition opens in two weeks. He approved the selection of pieces himself and will give the opening speech. Our presence and support are paramount."

"His preferences have emerged for some time now," Göring said. "Romantic art elevating the Aryan race and the glory of the Fatherland. Rather narrow minded."

"A style he aspired to as an artist but never quite achieved," Rosenberg said. "Have you seen any of it, Hofer?"

"Hitler's art? No."

Rosenberg walked to his desk and returned with an album with photos of Hitler's art. He opened the album for Hofer and Göring.

"He painted this still life in 1912."

Göring and Hofer examined the crude drawing of flowers in a vase. The work of an amateur.

Göring turned the page. "He drew many of these postcards while he lived in Vienna. Rumor has it he made more money painting houses than from his art."

The embarrassing works of a talentless artist proved why a younger Hitler failed twice to gain acceptance into the Vienna Academy of Fine Arts. And why, as Führer, he hired Schulte Stratthaus to find, confiscate, and burn every piece of art he had created in his youth.

Rosenberg closed the book and returned to his desk. "You shall never speak of these to anyone. Our Führer's destiny is leading Germany to greatness. We should admire and emulate his appreciation for art. Hofer, I expect to have those contacts by tomorrow. We need another Paris agent to speed up the work in France. Göring, see to it. That's all. Heil Hitler."

Göring and Hofer responded. "Heil Hitler."

The concept of art as currency captured Rosenberg's interest. Swapping art for munitions to build Germany's war chest—another path toward gaining favor with the Führer.

CHAPTER 61

Lost and Found

Meyer Technologies Offices, Irvine, California 2022

AJ's copy of Picasso's Stravinsky portrait from his upside-down drawing date with Grace greeted him each day in his office, a fond reminder of the joy he shared with her. Their art dates knitted them together, creating something, even though they couldn't create a new life. How he loved this wonderful woman, a gift from God. Talented, beautiful, and dedicated to following Jesus along with him.

Curt Matthews burst through his office door. "I found it."

"And good morning to you too. Found what?"

"How they breached our systems."

A burst of joy flooded AJ. "You found it?" An answer to his anguish of failing his friend and client—twice. He walked from his chair and patted Curt on the back. "You've made my day, Curt."

"Don't know why our diagnostics didn't pick it up. That's another story. But look."

Curt held a flash drive for AJ to see.

"A flash drive. So?"

"Pretty small, right?"

"Yes, very small." AJ smiled. "Are we going to keep playing twenty questions?"

"Well, that's what caused the outage."

AJ bent in closer and pointed. "That thing? Where did you find it?"

"Here's the thing. We ran diagnostics, but they didn't identify any problems. So, we made a visual inspection of the servers controlling the Becker's security system. But look how small this thing is. It barely protrudes from the port. We looked right past it on our first inspection. So, I did a test to check every single USB port on every single server. You can imagine how long that took. But, bingo, I found it."

AJ took the flash drive from Curt but dropped it on the floor. He picked it up and held it closer to examine it. "How'd you remove it from the port?"

"It took tweezers to get this baby out."

"I bet. Have you analyzed it yet?"

"Oh yeah. Interesting. Never seen anything like it," Curt said, with a wave of his hand.

"What does it do?"

"It contains a built-in receiver. Someone sent a signal that released a virus, a very specific virus that affected only the systems for the Becker's security."

AJ stroked his chin. *Who outside the company could have that kind of coding information?* "And now?"

"I looked at the code on the drive and the code in our system. Everything's fine if we keep the flash drive detached from the server."

"Any way to find out who made this?"

"China." Curt nodded. "Probably China."

AJ grinned. "Well, yes. But who wrote the code?"

"AJ, we live in a world of hackers. They're a dime a dozen. I can put this code out on the dark web and wait for someone to respond, but it's a long shot."

AJ fingered the flash drive again. "Can I assure Brian Miller at the Becker Museum we've found the problem? Their system has failed twice, and our reputation and my friendship are at stake."

"Interesting about the twice thing. They could only execute the code twice to disable the security at the Becker."

"Guess that's more confirmation we're in the clear."

"For the Becker, yes. But—"

"But what?"

Curt paused. "The flash drive also contained code that disabled your home security system."

AJ tapped his fingers on his desk. "You're sure?"

"Yes. It only ran one time. But you already know that."

And as a result, AJ had no idea who had discovered the files in his home office with details about Grandy's history and the mysterious Nazi tape.

"Thanks, Curt. Say, have I given you a raise lately?"

"Been a while."

"Watch your paycheck."

"Thanks."

Curt left. AJ stared at the tiny flash drive in his hand. So small, yet the cause of so much chaos. At least he'd solved one mystery.

AJ's phone rang. "This is Jayson Parry at IBM in New York. I have some good news for you."

"I'll take it."

"We found the tape you're looking for. Boy, was it buried. I didn't know our archive vault had tapes this old."

"Did you look at the condition of the tape?"

"It's in good condition for its age. IBM is top-notch at archiving tapes. Something else surprising, though. Your tape wasn't the only one we found with swastikas. We found dozens. Quite a mystery you've unleashed."

AJ nodded to himself. *Yes, my whole life is one mystery after another. What about these other Nazi tapes, Grandy?*

"Can you ship the tape to me?"

"I'll ship it to Merritt in the Los Angeles office through our private inter-company courier system."

"That works. When can I expect it in Los Angeles?"

"How is two days?"

"And you're sure it's secure?"

"Yes."

AJ fingered the tiny flash drive. *Nothing's 100 percent secure.*

"Great. I'll check with Merritt on Wednesday. Thanks, Jayson."

"Of course. Have a good day."

A good day. Yes. A great day. Good news on two fronts. He'd discovered the cause for the outage of the Becker's security systems, and he made a giant step forward in solving his Grandy mystery.

***

"I just called and told him I'm shipping the tape," a voice on the other end said.

The Client smiled. AJ may think he's one step ahead, but the Client's well-placed assets keep leapfrogging him farther ahead.

"And you're shipping the tape to Merritt in Los Angeles?"

"Yes."

"Very good." The Client entered the account and payment information on his laptop and hit enter. "Your wire transfer is on the way." Click.

The Client believed this tape held clues for finding the missing Picassos. He'd lost six of them after the botched heist from the Becker. Serious money down the drain, thanks to that idiot Derrick. *Wonder where those ended up?* A challenge for another day.

He owed it to his grandparents and to himself to find these Picassos, his inheritance from their wise investment as art patrons. The amount he'd spend paying assets to help him recover the Picassos—a drop in the bucket compared to the millions he'd pocket.

The Client checked his watch. Time to go to his real job.

CHAPTER 62

Cashing In

Grazioli Munitions Headquarters, Milan, Italy, 1937

SIPPING HIS ESPRESSO, ALFREDO Grazioli, president of Grazioli Munitions, finished reading the morning paper. He laid it aside and picked up the telegram he'd received last week from Hermann Göring requesting a meeting. Grazioli knew of rumors this Nazi worked directly for Adolf Hitler to build an art collection, but that didn't explain why he wanted to meet with a munitions company.

He sipped more espresso and admired his own collection hanging on his office walls. The Botticelli, his father had obtained before Alfredo's birth. The Miro and the Picasso, his own additions, reflecting his preference for modern art.

A knock interrupted his art gazing.

"Come in."

The production manager entered, carrying a stack of papers. "Your report, Mr. Grazioli. As of last night." He handed the report to Grazioli. "Is there anything else?"

Grazioli took the report and started scanning it. "No. Not for now. That's all."

The dismissed manager left the office. Grazioli continued reading the report. FM-37 submachine guns, 100%.

BM-17 grenades, 100%.

LM-52 flamethrowers, 98%. They'd catch up on production for this item with no problem.

He laid the report on top of previous versions on the corner of his desk.

He unlocked the bottom drawer on the right side of his desk, pulled out a ledger book, and put it on his desk. The figures on these pages held more important details than his inventory report. The book contained, line by line, each art exchange transaction he'd completed and his current available credit. Far more valuable, the directory of black-market agents specializing in exchanging art.

The use of art in lieu of cash, now a reliable alternative currency, avoided the usual governmental scrutiny of international exchanges. Grazioli's father had mastered the process, taking him on as an apprentice. He honed his technique over the years, expanding his reach far beyond that of his father.

***

After the last ERR meeting, Albert Rosenberg pondered Walter Hofer's convincing presentation on exchanging art for arms. The more he considered the concept, the more merit he found in such a scheme, and the bolder he felt ahead of his presentation to the Führer.

Göring joined Rosenberg for the presentation to Hitler. The Führer flashed a rare smile over the idea of building his war chest through such a unique means, especially if it avoided spending Reichsmarks from Germany's coffers. With Hitler's approval, Rosenberg sent Göring on his first diplomatic foray with Italy.

***

Göring entered the Grazioli Munitions Headquarters at 10:00 a.m. Glass display cases in the reception area housed various samples of the company's munitions, from bullets to grenades to submachine guns. The receptionist knocked on Grazioli's office door, entered, and announced, "Signor Hermann Göring."

Grazioli walked out and greeted Göring with an enthusiastic handshake. "*Bene, bene. Willkommen*, Signor Göring." He guided Göring into his office.

"Please, have a seat," Grazioli said, gesturing to the guest chair. Göring sat and placed his briefcase on the floor.

"I trust your trip was comfortable, yes?" Grazioli said, attempting introductory small talk.

"Longer than I'd like, but we had fair weather for our flight."

"Bene. Espresso?" Grazioli offered, smiling through his thick, black mustache. "*Danke.* Please."

Grazioli had prepared extra espresso this morning in hopes Göring would welcome the fraternal conversation that accompanies the rich Italian elixir. Steam floated from the cup he delivered to his guest.

Reaching for the cup from Grazioli, Göring looked past him at the collection of art. "I see your taste in art is like a smorgasbord, Signor Grazioli. Do you favor any over the others?"

Grazioli's smile grew bigger and he began waving his hands at his collection. "The traditional masters have much to offer. I am particularly drawn to more modern works, especially those by Signor Picasso, here. The colors, the shapes." He shook his two fists. "Makes me feel alive."

"Unusual. Finding an art gallery in a business office, no?"

Grazioli turned to the opposite wall with framed pictures, chronicling explosions from weapons his company manufactured. "Ah. But in a world filled with so much ugliness, we all need beauty, no more so in a building full of bullets and guns. A contradiction of creation"—he pointed to the wall of art—"and destruction," he pointed to the wall of explosives.

Grazioli returned to his desk. "Your telegram mentioned an opportunity that would be of mutual interest. Shall we discuss?"

Göring set his cup on the desk, reached into his briefcase, and pulled out a stack of papers. "I believe, even more so, after seeing your wonderful collection, we have an opportunity that will benefit us both. The Führer authorized me to engage your company for the supply of certain munitions, shall we say, for defensive purposes. In exchange, I have resources I'm sure will interest you."

Grazioli sat forward. "And what would those be?"

"Here is a list of some of them." Göring handed a sheet to Grazioli.

Grazioli scanned the list, and seeing one particular item, raised his eyebrows.

"I'm sure a man of your resources and experience can accept items such as the ones on this list, as payment in full," Göring said.

Grazioli sat back and smiled at Göring. He began mentally calculating the value of the listed items. "Signor Göring, we are, what is it they say, birds of the same feather? Where shall we begin?"

Göring pulled another paper from his briefcase and handed it to Grazioli. "These are the items I propose for our first transaction."

Grazioli read through the list. Reasonable volume. And all in stock, according to this morning's report. "Yes. This is a good start." He laid this paper next to the listing of art proposed as payment. "I will put this order on hold while I determine a fair payment from your list. Of course, I will need time to work with my financial advisors." By which he meant his black-market contacts.

Göring looked Grazioli dead in the eyes. "I believe we understand each other perfectly."

Grazioli returned the stare. "Perfectly." Then, breaking the seriousness of the stare with a smile, "More espresso?"

Göring picked up his briefcase and stood. "Thank you. No. It is urgent I return. My plane is waiting."

Grazioli walked around his desk and offered his hand. "Be sure to send my regards to the Führer."

"I await your response regarding payment."

After Göring's departure, Grazioli returned to his desk and picked up the list of art Göring had proposed as payment. His eyes kept returning to one particular line item. *Yes. That works very well as payment, to me. And I have just the place for it.*

CHAPTER 63

Rewind

IBM Headquarters, Los Angeles, California, 2022

AJ's RECENT VICTORIES HAD propelled him in an encouraging direction. Curt had discovered the causes of the two system breaches at the Becker and the outage of AJ's home security system: a pesky, teeny flash drive. IBM had located the Nazi tape described in Grandy's letter. But one failure clung heavily on him—the void of evidence to vindicate Grandy and clarify his IBM connection with the Nazis. Investigating IBM's employment records for Grandy failed to answer questions regarding his work in Berlin. Should he interpret the absence of any mention by Grandy of his work during World War Two as an effort to conceal nefarious involvement with the Nazis? Is lack of proof lack of truth? Did a ticking bomb of proof exist out there somewhere he hadn't, or couldn't, find?

And the tape. Even if he'd found the tape described in the Nazi letter to Grandy, what shape was it in? And where the heck could he find a machine to process the information on the tape? Did such a machine exist?

Driving to the IBM office in Los Angeles, AJ listened to Pastor Henry's latest podcast.

"Today we are looking at Romans 9:20-21. 'But who are you, O man, to answer back to God? Will what is molded say to its molder, "Why have you made me like this?" Has the potter no right over the clay, to make out of the same lump one vessel for honorable use and another for dishonorable use?'"

Ouch! Had he spoken back to the Molder in the darkest days of grieving his infertility, days filled with nothing but helplessness? Questioning God, "Why have you made me infertile?" Accusing God of making a mistake?

"Whose will is bigger and better?" Pastor Henry said. "God's will or our will? God is God, and we are not."

The simple but hard truth for a believer. God's sovereignty. He's either sovereign or He isn't. Over all things or over nothing. *Lord, you know my heart. Prone to wander. Please, take my heart and seal it for your glory.*

AJ pulled into the parking structure of the IBM building. In the elevator to Merritt's office, he refocused on the mysterious tape he would soon hold. Another victory to add to his recent wave. He entered Merritt Nelson's office wide eyed.

"Come on in, AJ. Bet you're anxious to see it," Merritt said. He led AJ to the package, sitting on a table.

Canvas straps with buckles secured a square, worn pasteboard carton. In bold black stenciling: LOT 12453. The unmistakable red, white, and black Nazi symbol. *Unbelievable.* Images of the Nazi letter and the Stravinsky music flashed through AJ's memory. After 85 years, Grandy's clues had paid off. *Here we go, Grandy!*

"Go ahead, AJ. Open it," Merritt said, grinning.

A wave of euphoric anticipation washed over AJ. Everything else in the room faded into nothingness. AJ took a deep breath. He undid the buckle, pulled back the canvas straps, removed the lid, and lay it aside. There. In 3D. Paper tape wound around a metal reel. AJ dipped his fingers into the box and gingerly lifted the reel out. He rotated the reel. The end of the paper tape dangled in the air. Light filtered through dozens of holes in random patterns on the tape, meaningless to him, but not to a machine. He wound the tape back on the reel and placed it back in the box.

The nothingness faded back to the real-time fullness of the room. AJ remembered to breathe but the tape continued its hypnotic hold on him. "So this is it," he said.

"Yup. Gotta tell you, AJ. Jayson said this astonished the guys in New York. Ends up, they found several other tapes with swastikas on them, too. Crazy, huh? No one had looked in that section of the archives since, well, probably the forties or fifties. You may have opened up a can of worms."

More Nazi tapes? AJ broke free from the tape's hypnotic spell and put the lid on the carton. "They can have the rest of the worms." He grinned. "This is the only worm I want."

Merritt crossed his arms. "So what's going on, AJ? On your last visit you wanted help to find your grandfather's employment records. Next thing I know, there's an ancient-of-days tape plastered with a swastika sitting in my office." He raised his eyebrows. "Care to explain?"

AJ tapped his fingers on the table. "It's complicated." He wrapped the straps around the carton. "I'm still piecing everything together. I promise when all is said and done, I'll fill you in." He fastened the buckle.

"Guess I'll have to wait. But there's something you need to know about this tape. I learned this from Cliff Dewitt, one of our old timers who's still around. Turns out you will need a key to read what's on this tape."

A key. Well, I have a key, thanks to Grandy. The sheet music signed by Stravinsky had provided the lot number and the key. That had to be the key to the tape.

"Cliff has a lead on a machine to read the tape. I told him you would be here today and pay him a visit."

AJ picked up the carton and smiled. "Merritt, what can I say? This is beyond amazing. I owe you."

"No problem. But let me know what this tape leads to. I'll tell Cliff you're on your way to his office."

***

Past official retirement age, Cliff Dewitt had garnered a wealth of historical knowledge few of the bright up-and-comers cared about. None of them had a clue about punch cards like the one in a gold frame hanging on the wall in Cliff's office.

"That is the first card I ever punched back in the day," Cliff said. "Part of a COBOL program I wrote as a student."

"I studied punch cards. Never punched one, though," AJ said.

"Not surprising for your generation." Cliff turned toward AJ. "Anyway, Merritt showed me your tape. Fascinating, I gotta say. He told me it had something to do with your grandfather."

"That's right. Story for another day, if you don't mind. Merritt said you might know where to find a machine to process this."

Cliff grinned. "Sure do. The Technology Historical Society. Located in Des Moines, Iowa, of all places. I'm a charter member, which comes with some perks."

"Perks like accessing a vintage tape machine?"

"Yes, perks like that." Cliff smiled.

"You wouldn't be interested in taking a trip to Des Moines, would you, Cliff? All expenses paid?"

Cliff's face lit up. "When do we go? This is exciting stuff for an old-timer like me, operating some old technology that still works, not to mention getting a peek at something the Nazis left behind."

"Well, let's keep that part to ourselves, if you don't mind. I'll work on the travel arrangements and coordinate your time off with Merritt. How's your schedule?"

"Name the day, and my bags are packed," Cliff said.

"Great. Looks like you and I are off on a technological adventure together, Cliff. I look forward to your company."

***

The Client's phone buzzed. "Yes?"

"He just met with me. He has the tape."

"Good."

"He invited me to travel with him to the Technology Historical Society. They have a machine to process the tape."

"Even better."

The Client had picked well. An IBM dinosaur who couldn't resist the lure of participating in unlocking a piece of history. A nerd version of Indiana Jones. The contact at the Technology Historical Society nailed it when they recommended Cliff.

"Your first payment is on its way. The rest will come after Des Moines."

AJ Meyer, keep it up. Thanks to you, we'll both know what's on that tape.

CHAPTER 64

Pure Art

The Great German Art Exhibition, Munich, Germany, 1937

HERMANN GÖRING SAT ALONGSIDE other high-ranking Nazi officials scanning the sea of faces listening to the Führer's speech. The opening ceremonies for the Great German Art Exhibit in Munich drew a crowd of cheering Germans, as did any event featuring an appearance by the beloved leader. The Reich always made sure of that.

Crowds had gathered early in the morning, vying for the best location along the parade route for a glimpse of the Führer. Young and old, many in traditional nineteenth-century German peasant garb, lined the street, pressed together several layers deep. Military horseback brigades strewn with Nazi flags opened the parade, followed by civic and political groups marching in tight formation. Then came the unique entry in the parade. Hand-picked blond, muscular men clothed in Teutonic garb held poles supporting a large circular, foil covered representation of the cosmic ash-tree Yggdrasil from Norse mythology. The sun reflected from the foil, creating a spotlight effect on the convertibles next in line, carrying Nazi officials. The crowd's roar grew louder with the arrival of the last car, a Mercedes-Benz W 150 convertible. The impressive vehicle carried the Führer and those he trusted most, including Hermann Göring and Josef Goebbels, head of the Reich Ministry of Public Enlightenment and Propaganda.

The Führer stepped out of his car to the accompaniment of a military band, drowned out by the engulfing waves of "Sieg Heil" from the elated onlookers. With a continual smile, he paused, turning from side to side, acknowledging the masses with his trademark salute, joyously returned by the crowds.

Hermann Göring and Josef Goebbels followed Hitler from the car to the stairs covered with a red carpet. The group reached the top of the stairs, turned, and took in the horizon of adoring countrymen and women.

Two milestones fueled Hitler's enthusiastic speech today. The first milestone: the dedication of the initial public building designed and built for the Third Reich: the *Große Deutsche Kunstausstellung*, or Great German Art Exhibition building, exemplifying classic, Greek colonnade architecture. The second milestone: the premier of a series of planned annual art exhibitions promoting pure Aryan art. The exhibition displayed only art that Hitler and his censors deemed "German." The Reich had classified modern art as "degenerate" and forbid displaying such filth in national museums.

Hitler concluded his opening speech. "I have come to the final inalterable decision to clean house, just as I have done in the domain of political confusion, and from now on rid the German art life of its phrase-mongering. But with the opening of this exhibition, the end of German art foolishness and destruction of its culture will have begun. From now on we will wage an unrelenting war of purification against the last elements of putrefaction in our culture."

Classifying art as either acceptable or unacceptable, Hitler had declared his first war.

Hitler and Josef Goebbels led the entourage du jour into the much-anticipated exhibit hall. Hermann Göring followed and kept in earshot of the Führer and Goebbels.

Adolf Ziegler, the organizer of the exhibition, walked side by side with Göring. "You have no idea of the difficulty working with Hitler," Ziegler said. "Three days ago, he ranted over some unfinished pieces he wanted displayed. He demanded so many last-minute changes."

Göring continued listening to Hitler with one ear and Ziegler with the other. "Herr Ziegler," Göring said, "one must be careful of such statements in public. Destinies are so transient these days." With the other ear, he listened to the Führer compliment Heinrich Knirr's portrait of the leader, painted for the opening.

"Yes. Realism as the gods intended," Hitler said, pointing. "See the beautiful German landscape in the background?"

Continuing the promenade behind Hitler, Göring investigated every display. He'd come today hoping to find the pieces Bruno Lohse had plundered from the Parisian Jews, especially the Picassos. Göring held onto the hope that Lohse had not taken them on the train the resistance had bombed outside of Paris. Or somehow they had survived the bombing. In either case, he had to find them. He'd prematurely offered them to Signor Grazioli in exchange for Italian munitions to fill Germany's war chest. Fortunately for Göring, Grazioli had not yet estimated the value of the items Göring had offered, giving him more time to locate them.

Göring turned the corner and entered the next gallery, nearly bumping into the Führer, conversing with Josef Goebbels.

"Mein Führer, your exhibition stands as an example to our people, shining a light on true German art and exposing the Jews' degenerate art," Goebbels said. Hitler smiled and nodded. The Reich had confiscated much of the "Jews' degenerate art" and thrown it together in a humiliating exhibit across town.

Goebbels is such a hypocrite. They all owned "degenerate" art in their personal collections, whether by Jews or Gentiles. Every high-ranking Nazi had their share of secrets. The trick: keeping one step ahead, discovering the secrets of others before they discovered yours.

Göring followed the Führer through the remaining rooms of the great hall, examining every surface of every wall, hoping to find even one piece on his list.

He left the exhibit empty handed, desperate for another strategy for finding the missing art.

***

Hitler's entourage boarded the plane for the trip back to Berlin. At cruising altitude, Goebbels opened a chilled bottle of champagne and poured three glasses.

"To our Führer's success today, leading the German people to yet another victory for the Aryan race. Heil Hitler," Goebbels and Ziegler raised their glasses. Göring joined the toast, feigning a smile. The Führer credited today's victory to Goebbels's efforts. But a day was coming when the art complex and collection he was building in Linz would far outshine Munich's exhibition. He'd be the recipient of even greater accolades from Hitler. He needed fewer train bombs and less disappearing art.

Scan or tap the QR code to read Grace's blogpost about the Great German Art Exhibition of 1937.

CHAPTER **65**

What Are You Reading?

Technology Historical Society, Des Moines, IA, 2022

AJ SET HIS ALARM to rouse him in the morning, two hours earlier than normal. Catching the 6:45 a.m. flight at John Wayne Airport meant leaving the house by 4:30 a.m., which meant packing tonight.

Grace handed AJ a few pairs of underwear and socks for his carryon. "I still can't believe they found the tape from Grandy's letter," she said.

"Yes," he said. "Nearly miraculous."

Odds a tape from 1938 still existed: extremely low. Odds of locating it: even lower. AJ had beaten both those odds, thanks to IBM's tape archiving. Why hadn't IBM's HR department protected Grandy's employment records with as much diligence?

AJ crammed the underwear and socks in his bag. "I must admit when Jayson Parry called with the news, I got a little tingle. This whole thing is like a National Treasure movie."

"Well, Benjamin Gates," referring to the main character, "you still have a way to go." Grace smiled and handed him his pj's. "Do you think the machine in Des Moines can read the tape?"

A fortunate turn of events, meeting Cliff Dewitt at the Los Angeles IBM office, a guy who *just happened to know* the whereabouts of a machine to read the tape. God's favor in the midst of this mystery? Or something, or someone else, behind it?

"After talking to Cliff, I called the museum in Des Moines. They assured me they have the machine I need. One odd thing, though."

Grace looked at AJ. "What?"

"The guy I talked to at the museum told me how excited they were to have someone come and use one of their machines. In fact, they'd received another call asking about the same machine."

"But that would have been Cliff, wouldn't it?"

"I asked, and they said, yes, Cliff had called," AJ said. "But someone called before Cliff, asking about it."

"Did they say who?"

"No. They said the caller had asked if they had this type of machine and did it still work. After the museum representative confirmed, yes they did, the caller told them thanks, and hung up."

Grace froze, fingering her necklace. "That's kind of strange, don't you think? What are the odds someone else is interested in that machine?"

AJ took a T-shirt from the pile on the bed. "I don't know. Main thing is I'm finding out what's on that tape in less than twenty-four hours. And then we're off on the next leg of our National Treasure adventure. Take that, Mrs. Benjamin Gates." He smiled, threw the T-shirt at Grace, leaned over the carry-on, and kissed her.

***

The direct flight carrying AJ and Cliff landed in Des Moines a few minutes before its scheduled 1:40 p.m. arrival. They departed in their rental car less than thirty minutes after landing. The drive to the museum lasted twenty minutes, delivering them to the parking lot ten minutes before their appointment. AJ found great satisfaction when plans worked out so precisely.

George Nimitz, the porky museum manager, greeted AJ and Cliff in the lobby. He smiled as wide as the Iowa prairie and his handshake wiggled on and on. "I can't tell you how excited I am. We don't receive many requests here, you know, to use our machines. So, welcome. Come on in."

George led them through the museum, passing tables loaded with machines of various sizes, shapes and odd designs, each labeled with a name, date and short description.

"Here it is. We shoved some tables out of the way while you're here. We wanted to make it easier to use."

A small group of volunteers huddled around AJ, Cliff, and George and watched AJ inspect the equipment. On a long oak table with a varnished top sat three machines in gray metal casings, each with an IBM nameplate. The first rectangular box measured twelve inches deep, ten inches wide, and ten inches tall. On the side of the box, a spindle protruded horizontally to hold the reel of paper tape.

"The tape reel clicks onto the spindle," George said, pointing, "and travels over this conducting plate. These spring wires above the tape make contact with the conducting plate through the holes on the tape as it moves forward. An electrical signal from each contact flows to the processor."

AJ and Cliff walked around, studying each part as George explained the tape reader's operation.

"The cables coming out of the back connect to the other two components that work with it." He pointed to a box resembling a typewriter. "These keys send commands to the tape machine. And this"—pointing to the third box—"is a very early version of a computer printer." The roll of paper in the printer measured six inches wide, much narrower than today's standard 8 1/2 inch-wide paper.

AJ opened his backpack and pulled out the box. "All right, gentlemen. Here it is." He set the box on the table, unbuckled the straps, and lifted the lid. The group bunched closer in to see the piece of history.

AJ slowly lifted the reel of paper tape out of the box. George's eyes grew as large as saucers. "I, I, wow. Will you look at that? It's not every day you see a swastika in Des Moines." His laughter jiggled his belly.

Cliff took over from George and guided AJ. "The reel goes here on the spindle, with tape rolling from the top." AJ placed the tape on accordingly. "Now, gently pull the end of the tape and feed it under the spring wires until the first holes rest on the conducting plate."

The onlookers whispered among themselves, watching the process unfold.

"Okay. Now we power up all three units." Cliff flipped the power switches for each unit. The printer came to life, triggering a collective surprised gasp from the huddled observers. It printed a single sentence and stopped. The printed line read: "Enter access key." The tape moved forward to the next set of holes.

"Holy cow. It's working," George announced, pointing to the printer, as if no one else had seen what had happened.

Cliff turned to AJ. "Got a key, AJ?"

AJ unfolded a piece of paper he'd removed from his backpack. *Let's hope Mr. Stravinsky gave us the right code in his sheet of music.*

AJ stepped to the keyboard. He took a deep breath. He typed: 6 4 7 10 9 1 8 2. and hit the enter key.

The room plunged into darkness. Stony silence. Every nerve in AJ's body started firing. Everyone else froze, shocked by the cause and effect of AJ entering the key and the sudden loss of power.

Emergency lights kicked on.

"Damn fuses," George said, breaking the tension. "I thought we fixed them all."

One by one, light from phones started illuminating the area.

"Come on, Pete. Let's go fix 'em." George led his co-worker to the back of the building.

Five minutes later, the room lights came on. The tape started rolling and the printer came to life.

AJ stood in front of the printer and watched the report appear on the paper, line by line.

Start

ERR

Date: 120437

Source: Bernstein, Paris France

Description: Six pen ink portraits of Igor Stravinsky by Pablo Picasso

AJ stared transfixed, almost not believing his eyes. ERR. An acronym for some organization? A European formatted date? April 12, 1937. The Bernsteins, the name on the black-and-white photo. Stravinsky portraits by Picasso. But why only six? The photo showed twelve.

The next line printed.

Lot 12453 key 6 4 7 10 9 1 8 2

The same lot and key in the Stravinsky music from Grandy.

Another line printed.

Destination

AJ held his breath, waiting for the next revelation. Where had these drawings ended up?

The printer paused. All eyes turned from the printer to the tape. It had stopped turning.

Had he come to the end of the trail?

Cliff reached for the tape. "These machines need a little coaxing sometimes." He gave the tape a gentle tug. The reader came back to life, and the reel turned another turn.

Waiting for the next printed line seemed like an eternity for AJ. The address, the most crucial piece of information he needed for recovering the drawings. The printer started clicking.

Hans Lohse

Who was he?

Charlottenburger Chaussee, 68, Keller

Berlin

And there it was. The destination of six missing Picassos. A rush of questions flooded AJ's brain. After 85 years, could the drawings still be at that address? Was it a home? What was at that address so many years ago? Could the building at that address survive the Allied bombings? If so, had anyone already found the drawings?

The printer continued.

Portrait 1 of Stravinsky by Pablo Picasso 1937

Portrait 2 of Stravinsky by Pablo Picasso 1937

Portrait 3 of Stravinsky by Pablo Picasso 1937

Portrait 4 of Stravinsky by Pablo Picasso 1937

Portrait 5 of Stravinsky by Pablo Picasso 1937

Portrait 6 of Stravinsky by Pablo Picasso 1937

End

The tape stopped. The printer stopped. The last line on the report hinted that the machine had processed all the data on the tape.

The audience of volunteer techie nerds broke into applause, acknowledging the success of retrieving data originating with the Third Reich. AJ grinned, shook hands with Cliff, and then with George. In his elation, he shook hands with every volunteer.

"Whew. That was nip and tuck there for a while," George said. "Thought we were goners with that outage and the hardware failure. Someone must be looking after you, AJ."

With Cliff's help, AJ rewound the tape. He packed it back in the box and returned it to his backpack. He moved to the printer, turned the platen to advance the paper, and carefully tore off his printout.

The edges of the printout had small rips because of its age. "I've got a packing tube you could use if you'd like," George said. "Might help protect that paper. Looks a little fragile." He came back a minute later and handed a tube to AJ. AJ rolled the paper, slid it into the tube, and placed the tube in his backpack.

AJ handed a check to George. "Here's a donation for the museum." AJ chuckled and patted George on the back. "Maybe you can fix those fuses. Thanks for your time and use of your equipment."

On the drive to the hotel with Cliff, AJ started mentally reviewing a list of what if's and what's next. Clearly, a trip to Berlin topped the list of what's next.

AJ set his backpack on the table in his hotel room, plopped on the bed, and called Grace.

"I've been waiting for your call all day. Did it work?" she said.

"Berlin, here I come."

"Wait. You got an address?"

"Yup. The reports listed six of the Picasso drawings of Stravinsky. Even said they had come from the Bernsteins in Paris. Can you believe it?"

AJ gave Grace a complete rundown of the afternoon events. They celebrated together until AJ nearly succumbed to the adrenaline drain and the time change.

"I'll see you tomorrow, Mrs. Gates."

"I love you, Mr. Gates."

***

Cliff entered his hotel room, set his bags down, and slumped into the easy chair. He opened the photos app on his phone and reviewed the pictures he'd taken of AJ's report when AJ wasn't watching. He selected three of the photos, attached them to a text message, and tapped send.

He called the Client. "Did you receive the photos?"

"Yes. Do they show everything from the printout?"

"Yes. We had a minor blip when the—"

"Don't care. You'll receive the rest of your money tonight." Click.

Scan or tap the QR code to read AJ's blogpost about Technology of Yesteryear.

CHAPTER 66

Bullets and Bombs and Art, Oh My

Cafe Vittorino, Milan, Italy, 1937

AFTER WORKING TWENTY YEARS at the Hoffman Munitions Company, Remy Paquet earned the position of Mr. Hoffman's protégé, which allotted him a substantial raise. A forty-year-old bachelor Frenchman, Remy shared Mr. Hoffman's love of art and owned a handful of framed pieces hanging in his modest apartment—copies the art wannabees created of originals by the art gods. Remy filled his free time roaming the museums, galleries, and studios in Paris, a ritual he'd begun after the Great War to combat the ugliness the Germans left behind. He traveled as often as his bank account allowed. With the healthy deposit from his raise, he made a long-awaited trip to Milan.

Today he sat, mesmerized, absorbing one of the most famous paintings in history, Da Vinci's *The Last Supper*. The symmetry of Da Vinci's masterpiece pulled Remy into the last meal the disciples shared with their Rabbi. Christ sits in the absolute center, surrounded by His disciples in animated arguments, reacting to His prophecy. "Truly I tell you, one of you will betray me." *What a heartbreaking moment for Jesus.*

After a contemplative hour soaking in Da Vinci's gift to the world, Remy walked to a cafe, ordered a coffee, and waited for his reunion with a former co-worker, Yves. Da Vinci's scene lingered, and Remy imagined himself sitting next to Jesus, hearing the Lord teach His disciples to love one another. *The world needed these words more than ever.*

"Remy." His friend, Yves, rushed toward the table with arms wide open. Remy stood and received the embrace. "How are you, my friend?" They broke their embrace and held each other's shoulders.

"No worse for wear, *mon ami*," Remy said.

They drank, ate, reminisced, and laughed until the sun slipped below the treetops. An icy wind swirled around their table, and Yves's warm countenance faded.

"Yves, what's wrong?" Remy said.

Yves crossed his arms and leaned forward. "Something strange is happening at Grazioli's company."

Remy leaned in. "Are you okay?"

Yves waved off the concern. "Yes, yes. I'm fine. It has nothing to do with me. It's about Signor Grazioli." Yves sat back in his chair. "He had a visitor from Germany recently. One Herr Göring."

"Göring?" Remy tilted his head. "What did he want?"

"He's after weapons for Germany." Yves gestured with his index finger. "Here's the strange part. He wants to trade art to pay for them."

"What?"

"Göring gave Mr. Grazioli a list of pieces he proposed to exchange for a munitions order. I saw the list."

A gust of wind swirled the late afternoon leaves around their feet.

"You saw Göring's list?" Remy said. "I don't understand."

Yves sipped his coffee. "Remy, I heard about the art theft in Paris, friends of the Hoffmans. A family named Bernstein."

"That's true," Remy said. "But how did you hear?"

"The news circulated through all of my art friends." Yves lit a cigarette and took a drag. "From what I heard, the Hoffmans commissioned Picasso for some of the art the thieves stole."

Remy leaned in. "But what does Göring's visit have to do with this?"

"The list Göring gave Mr. Grazioli includes the drawings by Picasso, portraits of Igor Stravinsky."

Remy shook his head. "No. No. This is terrible. This news will devastate Mr. Hoffman."

"I considered calling Mr. Hoffman myself," Yves said. "Now that you're his protégé, it's better you tell him, and in person. Will you do that?"

Mr. Hoffman had confided in Remy, an understanding fellow art aficionado, about the theft. Losing the Picasso drawings of Stravinsky had grieved Mr. Hoffman, whether for a financial loss or because of an emotional connection with the art, Remy didn't know.

"Of course I'll tell him." Remy stood and buttoned his coat. "I'm leaving by train tonight. He won't like this, Yves, but it's only fair he knows."

Yves stood and embraced his friend. "God be with you, my friend."

Remy broke the embrace but held his smile. "Seeing you has brought me joy. But now I leave a friend behind and take sad news home with me."

They departed in opposite directions. Yves to Mr. Grazioli's office and Remy to the train station, carrying a suitcase and disheartening news for Mr. Hoffman.

***

"Is Yves sure the list included Picasso's Stravinsky portraits?" Fritz asked.

"Yes, six of them," Remy said. "He saw the list."

Fritz Hoffman sat in his office across from Remy along with Hemingway and Otto Bernstein. Remy recounted his conversation with Yves at the Milan cafe. Fritz tightened his lips, took a deep breath, and exhaled his exasperation. "As alarming as this sounds, it offers hope that at least the drawings survived the bombing of Göring's rail carriage. If Göring's offering them to the Italians, he must have them in his possession."

"Or forgeries," Hemingway said, puffing on an ever-present cigar.

Fritz and Otto stared at Hemingway. "Forgeries?" Otto said. "How would that even be possible?"

"We have evidence Lohse stole the drawings," Hemingway said. "We don't know how long they stayed in Paris or if he took them somewhere. Is it too unbelievable to think he paid someone to make copies?"

"Otto, you and I both know how many forgers live in Paris," Fritz said.

Otto nodded. "Unfortunately."

"It's a fact of life in the art world, a fact that complicates our job as art dealers and brokers. So, yes, there could be forgeries," Fritz said.

"What do we do now? Wait?" Otto said, his face downcast.

"Fritz, how's your relationship with Grazioli?" Hemingway said, puffing away.

"I can't question Grazioli about his dealings with the Germans, if that's what you mean," Fritz said.

"Sounds like Yves is your best inside man at Grazioli's," Hemingway said. "He may be your one and only shot to find out what happens next."

Fritz sat back and tapped his fingertips together. "Remy, thanks to your friendship with Yves, it looks like you'll be returning to Milan."

"Sir, I'm not a spy," Remy said.

"No, you're not. You have a helpful connection with Yves," Fritz said. "I think we can count on his help. He is as concerned as we are about the Germans plundering the art world and cashing in for weapons."

Remy squirmed in his chair. "What am I to do?"

"We will work that out tomorrow," Fritz said. "I appreciate your bringing me this information. Now, go home and get some rest."

"Yes, sir. Thank you." Remy left the office.

"I need to tell Jacques this news," Hemingway said. "If Göring is after munitions for Germany, Germany is preparing for military action against France."

"Yes. Which means I may be ramping up my production for France's defense, again," Fritz said.

How dare that bastard Göring! Stealing French art to buy Italian bombs for dropping on France.

CHAPTER 67

Enough Is Enough

The Client's Office, Irvine, California, 2022

THE WALL IN THE Client's office resembled a scene from a CSI show. Strings crisscrossed, connecting colored index cards, Post-its, and a big question mark. A pushpin held the 1937 black-and-white photo from his grandparents at the top of the clue board. The photo showed the twelve Picasso drawings from 85 years ago before they had wandered off into history. Evidence of the twelve drawings in the photo had launched the Client's quest thirty years ago. Two generations of the Hoffman family before him had hunted for them, but to no avail. His grandfather, Fritz, had failed to find the drawings after the break-in and theft at the Bernsteins' home. His hunt continued after fleeing the Nazi occupation of France. Nothing. The Client's father inherited Fritz's gallery business and moved it from New York to Los Angeles but never found the drawings either.

His grandparents had discussed the useful business relationship they had with the Bernsteins. The Bernsteins' soirées attracted an array of artists, writers, composers, and most importantly, buyers. Buyers for his grandparents' commissioned works such as Picasso's Stravinsky portraits. The Hoffmans' patronage of Picasso had paid off for years. They commanded top dollar selling his pieces to collectors, an ongoing arrangement they trusted to bring continued profits.

The break-in at the Bernsteins introduced a complication to the symbiotic relationship between the Hoffmans and the Bernsteins, the patron and the exhibitor—a blurring of the clarity of ownership. Because thieves stole the art from the Bernsteins' home, their descendants may attempt to claim ownership based on possessory interest. The Client had no evidence he competed with living descendants of the Bernstein family to find the drawings, but he'd read news reports of vicious disputes between contending family descendants in similar situations. More reason to expedite his mission.

Below the photo at the top of his clue board, the Client had placed a card with the number twelve in bold, black writing. *Why on earth had Picasso drawn twelve portraits?* He painted several pieces in his Blue Period. Had he planned a Twelve Period but gotten no further than these?

A string stretched down from the number twelve to a card labeled "ART DETECTIVE." Below that, a card with the number six indicated the detective found only six of the twelve drawings. The next card down showed "BECKER," the location where the detective had found the six drawings. The next series of cards below listed "EDWARDS," "TEST," and "MISSION," with a last card filled with a large question mark. That question mark cost the Client thousands of dollars, thanks to the bumbling Derrick Edwards. Things started off well with a promising plan to steal the drawings from the Becker. Now, he might as well draw a giant red arrow back up to the number twelve under this grandparents' photo and start over.

Another string stretched down and right from the photo to a card labeled "MEYER." The next two cards below displayed "BUG" and "RETRIEVE." Thanks to planting a bug at the Meyers' home, the Client had gathered information to direct his next steps. Below "RETRIEVE," the Client had taped two things: a picture of the Nazi IBM letter to Robert Meyer and the Stravinsky sheet of music. The next two cards lay side by side, one labeled "IBM LA" and the other "IBM NY." They both pointed down to the word "TAPE" inside a thick circle.

The final two side-by-side cards in this line contained an address in Berlin under a large number six.

He admired AJ's diligent pursuit of the same priceless art works his family had sought for generations. AJ's art professor wife—no slouch either. Her intuition had led to some golden finds. The latest conversation between AJ and Grace provided the information he needed to plan his next step. Thank goodness, they hadn't found the last bug device.

"Are you sure you don't want me to come?" Grace said.

"I've got Brian by my side. Two of us should be able to handle things. We're meeting tomorrow to plan the trip. He's already working with a contact in Berlin."

"You think you'll be safe?"

"What kind of question is that?"

"An honest one. AJ, think about it. The theft at the Becker. The break-in here, at our own home."

"I'll be fine. You'll be fine. The home security system is fine. I made sure. I'll be praying for you and so will my mom and Pastor Henry. He knows all about what's going on."

Praying? How the heck was that going to help? Chanting some feel-good words to an un-listening imaginary deity? Wasn't AJ more intelligent than those religious wackos?

The Client started a list for his next steps. First: engage his agent and send him to Berlin. Second, if worse came to worst, prepare some leverage, something to hold over AJ in case AJ beat his agent to Berlin. After the last conversation between AJ and Grace, planning that leverage just got easier.

The Client had considered going to Berlin himself but decided to stay and manage the mission from his office. He had the communications technology to maintain reliable contact with his man on the ground. More importantly, if he set his leverage plan in motion, he needed access to Grace.

He made the call.

"Yes?"

"I'm ready to engage your services."

"Very good. And the terms?"

"As we've discussed previously. Travel and expenses in addition to your fee upon delivery of the items."

"Acceptable. Any potential complications? Do I need to be armed?"

Good question. What kind of danger could a techie and an art nerd pose? Better prepare for any possibility.

"Yes. But no fatalities, understood?"

"Understood."

"I'll text your boarding pass, hotel arrangements, the description of items, and their location. I expect immediate confirmation after locating the items and delivery two days after you collect them. Nonnegotiable."

"Agreed. Anything else?"

"No. But let me be clear. Any future business depends on the success of this mission." Click.

The Client stared at his clue board, deciding where to add the next card: "ACQUIRED-6 PICASSOS." Time to refocus on finding the six pieces from the bungled Becker heist. Maybe he should pray about it like that sap, AJ. That's a laugh.

CHAPTER 68

I Know It When I See It

Degenerate Art Exhibition, Munich, Germany, 1937

Fritz Hoffman had achieved his business success for two reasons: his keen instincts and his analytical skills. His instincts told him the missing Picassos could be anywhere. His analytical skills urged him to expand his investigation beyond the French border into Germany. After all, his most likely suspects, Hermann Göring and the formerly alive, Bruno Lohse, lived there. Combing through the Paris art circles yielded nothing helpful for locating his stolen investment. Over the last two weeks his protégé, Remy Paquet, had continued investigating the art for munitions swap between Göring and Grazioli's Italian munitions company. Time for Fritz to take on Germany.

News of two art exhibitions in Munich had made a splash in the Paris press. The Nazis had assembled both exhibitions, but for two different purposes. The Great German Art Exhibition displayed pure Aryan, German, traditional art by pure Aryan, German, traditional artists blessed by the Führer. The Degenerate

Art Exhibition dismally displayed un-German, progressive art condemned by Hitler, calling it an insult to the German psyche.

Otto and Hemingway joined Fritz in his living room to discuss the news about the exhibitions.

"Look at this," Fritz said, handing the paper to Otto.

The headline screamed at Otto, "DEGENERATE ART EXHIBITION IN MUNICH."

"What kind of word is that to describe art?" Otto said.

"What kind of word describes the Nazis is a better question," Fritz said.

"Of course Hitler had to give a speech," Otto said. "Listen to this. 'If they really paint in this manner because they see things that way, then these unhappy persons should be dealt with in the department of the Ministry of the Interior, where sterilization of the insane is dealt with.' Sterilization? He's mad."

Hitler's mention of sterilization referred to the 1933 "Law for the Prevention of Offspring with Hereditary Diseases." Any of the nine hereditary conditions decided a person's fate of sterilization. Jewish bloodline did not appear in the list. Yet. Artistically, Hitler had sterilized an entire classification of art.

Otto continued. "The Führer acknowledged Wolfgang Willrich's book, *The Cleansing of The Temple of Art* for his inspiration."

Hemingway, seated across the living room, perked up at the mention of a temple. "Interesting he would make a biblical reference."

Otto and Fritz turned to Hemingway.

"It refers to the temple in Jerusalem," Hemingway went on. "I'm sure you are both familiar with the temple from your Jewish upbringing. On two occasions in the New Testament, Jesus railed against the money changers and merchants selling animals for offerings on the temple grounds. They gouged the Jews coming to offer their sacrifices. Jesus said, 'Ye have made it a den of thieves.' He purified the temple from their abuses, running them out with a whip."

"Just reinforces Hitler's messiah complex, if you ask me," Otto said.

Fritz slapped his knees. "We need to go to Munich."

"What?" Otto said.

"I think we can agree that Herr Hitler would classify Picasso's art as degenerate," Fritz said. "Maybe, just maybe, our drawings are prisoners in that exhibit."

"Unlikely," Hemingway said. "But possible, I guess."

Fritz stood and paced around the room. "Unlikely or not, I can't sit around waiting for Remy and the Italians. This is my next best hope." He stopped and turned to the group. "I'm going and you can join me or stay here and do nothing."

"Thatta boy, Fritz. You've got spunk." Hemingway waved his cigar. "You can count me in." He turned to Otto. "What about you?"

Otto turned to Hemingway, then to Fritz. He smiled. "I'm not sure how Emma will take this, but yes, I'll join you."

***

The trio turned into a quartet after Hemingway told Jacques about the Munich trip.

"If I even have a chance to look Göring in the eye before I shoot him," Jacques said. "I'm going."

Hemingway raised a hand. "Hold on. That's not the purpose of this trip. We're searching for the Picasso drawings. If you want to come and take a reading on Germany's military plans, that's fine. But that's it. Understand?"

Jacques challenged Hemingway's stare. "Yes. I understand."

***

A gray sky shrouded Munich's Institute of Archeology housing the Degenerate Art Exhibition. Fritz led the quartet through a dark, narrow hallway into the first exhibit room. His eyes locked onto a sloppily hand-painted slogan hanging crooked above a group of partially framed paintings. "NATURE AS SEEN BY SICK MINDS." He glanced at Otto and signaled toward the slogan with his eyes. The crudely painted, demeaning, red six-pointed Star of David on each artist's nameplate screamed JEW.

A dull, low mumble filled the air. Visitors, stunned by a gruesome crucifix on the wall, shuffled into the next room. Fritz recognized works by Klee and Kandinsky. He stepped to the next item and froze. A Picasso. Not one of the Hoffmans'.

307

Fritz pulled Otto in close and whispered. "If they have this one, maybe ours could be in the next rooms. Come."

The tease of the Picasso lit Fritz's hopes on fire. He pushed against the crowd, but the packed curiosity seekers resisted his efforts. Inch by inch, his hope burned hotter.

Entering the room, Fritz turned to Otto. "You take the right side. I'll take the left." They moved to their respective positions and started scanning up, down, and across. The sluggish pace of the crowd provided the time they needed to search every square inch. Statues with misshapen body parts. Portraits of war veterans with gaunt nightmarish faces and severed limbs spurting blood. A crudely painted tangle of bodies, squeezed together by the sides of the frame. Fritz's fired-up hope dwindled by the time they reached the next room.

Fritz walked through the door. His entire body stiffened. He grabbed Otto's arm. Standing in the middle of this room, his monster—Hermann Göring.

Hemingway and Jacques stood across the room in hushed conversation. Hemingway turned back to Göring. Jacques's face turned crimson. He slowly pulled his arm out of his jacket. Little by little, he exposed a pistol. Horror ripped through Fritz. He hadn't come for this. He tried to push out a scream. Silence came out of his gaping mouth. The crowd pinned his arms to his sides. How could he signal Hemingway? Oh, God. No. Not this.

Hemingway turned. He spotted the gleam of Jacques's pistol. With deliberateness, Hemingway forced Jacques's hand down to the side. The crowd blocked Fritz's view. Did Hemingway have control of the gun? Hemingway restrained Jacques's arms and shoved him through the mass to the exit.

Throughout the entire pistol incident, Göring continued conversing with the celebrity-seeking crowd. *What an egotist.* Fritz gritted his teeth. The Nazi trash, in his flashy white uniform and jeweled medals. Ironically, amidst the dull, oppressive art, Göring was the only thing lighting up the room.

Fritz and Otto searched the room for their Picassos but came up with nothing but disappointment to take back on the train to Paris.

***

Göring couldn't care less about today's chattering crowds seeking his attention. He'd come seeking six things and he left with none.

Scan or tap the QR code to read Grace's blog on the Degenerate Art Exhibition.

CHAPTER 69

Something Old, Something New

Becker Museum, Irvine, California, 2022

AJ SET HIS BACKPACK on a chair in the Becker Museum conference room. Brian Miller closed the shades to cover the wall of windows. No need for curious eyes to peer in while they made their final plans for the trip to Berlin. How ironic. The curator of an art museum taking part in an art heist.

"That must have been something. Seeing the printer come to life," Brian said, moving to a seat at the table.

"You should have seen those old boys." AJ chuckled. "You'd think they'd won the lottery when those machines started humming."

"Pretty amazing, finding the equipment you needed in working condition. Ever think it's a little too amazing?"

AJ paused and tilted his head. "What are you getting at?"

Bryan shot a crooked smile. "Come on, AJ. Hasn't it all been a little too easy? Finding the tape from 85 years ago and locating someone who just happened to know where to find a working tape reader? It's like you're walking down Easy Street. Way too easy."

AJ pulled a file folder out of his backpack and smiled. "You just need to know the right people in the right places. We've got work to do."

AJ pulled two pages from the file folder, an original for himself and a copy he handed to Brian. "This is the printout from the tape. Check out the address. Of course, I mapped it online, but nothing came up."

"Yikes. Not helpful."

"Right? Kind of freaked me out a little." AJ's speech accelerated. "So Grace enlisted the help of Fred, a history professor at Lines College. Since the address pointed to a location that presumably existed in 1938, we thought he could shed some light on what's located there today."

"Did he?"

"Yup." AJ's explanation picked up more speed. "Interesting story. On June 17, 1953, a strike action by construction workers in Berlin grew to a million-person uprising against the Soviet occupation of East Berlin. In commemoration of the uprising, the government renamed Charlottenburger Chaussee. Now it's *Straße des 17. Juni.*"

"But even if an art gallery existed at this address in 1938, would it have survived the Allied carpet bombing?"

"Excellent question." Giddiness flowed from AJ's chest to his fingers as he handed the next page to Brian. *I may be walking down Easy Street, but boy, does it feel good.* "I used Google Earth to zoom in on the property. Look. It's a cafe now."

Brian studied the page. "Cafe Viktoria. A real place?"

"Yup. Not much online about it." AJ tapped his finger on the printout. "But it exists."

Bryan looked up from the map. "But why would someone send stolen art to a cafe?"

"Fred gave us a little backstory of the area. During the Third Reich, this section of Berlin thrived with cultural centers and art galleries."

Brian picked up the sheet with the address. "What about this *Der Keller* in the address?"

"That's German for basement."

"Let's hope this cafe still has one."

AJ pulled out another paper and handed it to Brian. "This should answer that question."

Brian glanced at it and shook his head. "How'd you get this?" The page contained full schematics for the cafe building, including a basement.

AJ raised his eyebrows. "Right people at the right places."

Brian put the paper down, fidgeted with his hands on his knees, then looked up at AJ. "Let's talk about the pink elephant in the room."

Whoa. Where's this going? AJ sat back and folded his arms. "Okay. Shoot."

"Your security systems for the Becker failed twice. The second time, someone stole art from my museum. Someone hacked your own home security, broke into your house, and went through your Grandy files. People are watching you. AJ, as a friend, I have to tell you. I'm concerned. Aren't you?"

Ouch. Everything he said is true. Grace told him some of the same things. *Is this a warning, Lord?*

AJ leaned forward. "Brian, how long have we known each other?"

"What, seven, eight years?"

"That's about right. Grace and I have faithfully supported the Becker every year."

Brian squinted. "Is this about payback for your donations?"

AJ shook his head. "No, not at all. I'm saying we have history together. We've been there for each other. Let's be there for each other with this. If we find these Picassos, they're going straight into your museum. You know that, right?"

A semi-smile formed on Brian's face. "Yeah. I do. I just, I don't know. I just wonder if all these coincidences are a warning to watch for trouble in Berlin. That's all."

"You have contacts in Berlin to call for help, right? So if anything happens, we're covered."

"I hope," Brian said. He wagged a finger at AJ. "But I want you to know, one thing they didn't teach me in art management—how to search for buried treasure."

"Arrr, matey. The searching's already done. We're going to collect the booty."

"As long as the owners of Cafe Viktoria don't mind us taking something that's in their basement and walking out the front door without as much as a thank you."

"Who said we're not saying thank you? Or that we're walking out the front door?" AJ said.

He handed more pages to Brian. "Here's the itinerary and your tickets. I'll see you at the airport tomorrow."

"All right, Sherlock. See you there."

"The game's afoot, Dr. Watson."

Walking to his car, AJ pondered the coincidences Brian mentioned. Were they more than coincidences?

CHAPTER 70

The Envelope, Please

Home of the Hoffmans, Paris, 1939

THE GLOW OF CANDLES filled Claire and Fritz's living room. A festive banner with a farewell greeting in Russian hung on the living room wall. Claire's fanciest tablecloth covered a buffet table. Plates of chocolate-dipped macaroons, madeleines, and lace cookies surrounded a vase filled with freshly cut roses. Steam floated from the silver pot of French press coffee. Sherry, bourbon, and Cointreau awaited those who preferred them to coffee.

Igor Stravinsky's upcoming departure for America filled Claire with a measure of joy and two measures of sadness. Joy for the glorious new opportunities waiting for Igor. Sadness over losing a dear friend and her closest relative, other than Fritz, in the wake of losing the Picasso drawings.

Fritz walked in and embraced Claire. "It looks wonderful, darling."

Claire rested her head on Fritz's chest. "As it should. Igor deserves a special send off. I hope Harvard appreciates him as much as I'm going to miss him."

The group of invited friends had grown closer after the break-in at the Bernsteins two years ago. Nothing else binds friends together like a common enemy. For them, the wretched art-whoring Nazis.

The friends burst through the door in one jovial entourage, clattering in lighthearted conversation.

Dottie finished describing a scene from a movie starring her friend Mae West. "And then Mae says, 'Why don't you come up and see me sometime, hmm?'"

Josephine cracked a smile. "Leave it to Mae."

"Welcome, friends," Claire said.

Josephine led the group, turning this way and that. "My, Claire, everything is so lovely."

Pablo and Igor staggered in, arm in arm, singing in unison, *"Savez-vous planter les choux À la mode, à la mode? Savez-vous planter les choux À la mode de chez nous?"*

Their friends cheered, "Bravo. Bravo." Igor and Pablo wobbled a bow.

Dottie turned to Claire. "What do the words mean?"

"'Do you know how to plant cabbage?' A silly children's song," Claire said. She turned to her guests. "Welcome, welcome. It seems Igor and Pablo began celebrating without us." A chuckle flowed through the room. "Everyone, please help yourselves to the refreshments."

The partygoers oohed and ahhed over the offerings on the table. Side conversations emerged, as happens on these occasions.

Robert Meyer, with coffee in hand, approached Hemingway with bourbon in hand. "I heard about the train bombing."

"Yes. Unfortunate results," Hemingway said.

"Are things heating up for the Second Bureau?" Robert said.

Hemingway nodded. "Unfortunately. All depends on Mr. Hitler. He's already moved into Austria and Czechoslovakia. If he dare take one step out of the Rhineland into France, it's a powder keg."

"I've seen what's happening to the Jews in Berlin," Robert said. "If the Germans invade France, I fear for the French Jews," Robert said.

Igor approached Robert and Hemingway. "May I have a word with Robert?" Igor said.

"Of course." Hemingway headed off to give them a moment.

Igor pulled an envelope from his coat jacket and leaned in close to Robert. "Please take this." Igor handed Robert a sealed envelope addressed to Robert Meyer. "Put this in your jacket. This is very important. You must get it to America for me. I beg you." Igor turned, smiled, and walked back to Pablo. Robert put the envelope in his coat pocket.

Dottie wandered over to Robert. "Well, don't you look perplexed. Everything okay?"

Robert fingered the envelope in his coat pocket. "Yes." He turned toward Igor, then back to Dottie. "Everything's fine."

Fritz, Otto, and Hemingway had grouped together. "That damn Göring," Fritz said. "If he came for our collection, there's no doubt he'll hit up others in Paris. Everyone I talk to is worried."

"I've heard some dealers are shipping parts of their collection out of the country," Otto said. "They're sending pieces to New York under the guise of displaying them at the World's Fair next year."

"Seems kind of drastic, don't you think?" Hemingway said.

"Not when you know the value of our collections," Fritz said. "If the Germans come to France, that may be our best option."

Clink, clink, clink. Claire tapped her wineglass. "Friends, thank you for coming to celebrate our friend and my cousin, Igor." Claire turned to Igor. "Igor, you made quite an entrance to the Paris music world with your *Rite of Spring* ballet. Who knew ballet music could cause such a riotous ruckus in an audience?" Chuckles rippled. "But Paris loves you, anyway. And we love you as a dear, dear friend these many years. That is why with sorrow we say goodbye and with joy we wish your good fortune." Claire raised her glass. "To Igor." The crowd echoed. "To Igor."

Igor smiled at his friends, raised his right arm, circled it in the air, and bowed in a regal gesture.

"My dear friends. How good to be with souls who love and pursue beauty, a desire God has infused in us all. To create, there must be a dynamic force, and what force is stronger than love?" He held his hand to his heart. "This love we share travels with me, as will my fondest memories of Paris. And as we say in Russia, *da vstryechee*, until next time." He kissed his hand and waved to his friends.

Pablo approached Igor and planted a kiss on his right cheek. "*Hasta la proxima vez*. Until next time, mi amigo." Igor caressed Pablo's face with his wrinkled hands and shared an endearing smile.

Claire revered the affection expressed between the two friends. A tear flowed, followed by another. Would history ever truly understand the deep bond shared between these creative gods? Would the future show kindness to the friends celebrating together tonight?

CHAPTER 71

So Long, Farewell

Home of AJ Meyer, Irvine, California, 2022

A FAMILIAR AROMA GREETED AJ as he opened the front door. Walking toward the kitchen, he took a big whiff. "Olé. Enchiladas tonight." Grace turned from the stove and puckered for a welcome home kiss. AJ fully engaged.

"Wow. Aren't you Mr. Cheerful," Grace said, handing him napkins to place on the table.

"Yes, indeedy. This Benjamin Gates is about to find his national treasure."

Grace pulled the tray of enchiladas out of the oven and put them on top of the stove. "How's the plan for Berlin? Got a perfect version, not that I'd expect anything less." Grace elbowed AJ.

"We made a few tweaks today after going through everything."

"And our home security system, is it all *tweaked* too?" Grace said with air quotes.

AJ walked to Grace and embraced her. "Honey, you know it is. Curt found the bug in our system that caused the outages here and at the Becker. It's gone. Poof."

"And this?" she held out her necklace.

"Safe and secure from all alarm, as always." He tapped her nose with his index finger.

The table started shaking. The plates and silverware rattled. Water rippled in the glasses. The chandelier swayed. The doorbell rang.

AJ and Grace gripped the table, waiting for more.

The shaking stopped.

They relaxed their grip. Grace looked at AJ. "The doorbell."

AJ walked over and opened the door.

"Did you feel that?" Brian said, staring at AJ.

"We did. Come on in."

"Felt like a, um, maybe a three," Brian said. "What do you think?"

AJ led Brian to the kitchen. "About that. Like the recent ones."

Grace greeted Brian with a smile and a hand on her hip. "Hey, Brian. Feel that rocking and rolling?"

"Yeah." He looked up. "Something, huh?" The chandelier steadied. He looked down at the bottle in his hand. "Oh, here's a little something for tonight." He handed it to AJ.

"Orange County Zin?" AJ said, raising his eyebrows.

"Yeah. It's from a vineyard in our own backyard, Newport Beach Vineyards. Thought I'd make you guinea pigs and see if it's good enough for a museum event."

"Always glad to support the Becker, Brian." AJ took the bottle to the counter, opened it, and poured a glass for each of them.

"I propose a toast." AJ raised his glass. "First, to my partner on a journey through history, my dear Grace."

Grace and Brian clinked glasses with AJ's.

"Second, to our dear friend and art purveyor extraordinaire, Monsieur Brian." Another joint clink.

Grace got in the action. "And to my two brave art heroes. May they return victorious."

A final clink.

AJ took his first sip. "Mmm. Nice, Brian. I'm hungry. Let's eat."

They served themselves buffet style and gathered at the table.

"So, Brian, if you find the six Picassos, will you resume your plans for a gala?" Grace said.

AJ turned to Grace with furrowed brows. "What do you mean, if?" He cracked half a smile.

"All right, Mr. Confidence. *When* you find the six Picassos," Grace said.

"Well, yeah. I mean, it would be great if we had all twelve," Brian said. "But I'm happy to have six." He turned to Grace. "These are delicious."

"But imagine if you had all twelve. Quite a discovery." AJ looked at Grace. "Honey, have any other artists created a collection of the same subject?"

Grace circled her fork in the air. "There's Andy Warhol's Campbell soup cans. He did thirty-two canvases."

AJ perked up. "Thirty-two? Why so many?"

"One for each of the Campbell soup flavors at the time. Other than Warhol, no one else."

Coffee and churros followed the enchiladas.

"AJ tells me you have a contact in Berlin in case you need help." Grace crunched on a churro. "Are you sure you can trust them?"

AJ frowned at Grace. "Honey, really?"

"It's okay, AJ," Brian said. "A colleague from my previous job in New York works there now. I trust him with my life."

Grace turned to AJ and took his hand. "I need to know my hubby's in good hands."

"I can understand that. AJ and I have reviewed our plan at least a hundred times."

"A hundred and one after today," AJ said.

"We got this, Grace," Brian said.

"That's all I need to know," Grace said. "More coffee, anyone?"

The three talked for two more hours, recounting the events leading up to tonight.

Brian brought the conversation to an end. "Time for me to head home and finish packing."

AJ and Grace walked with Brian to the front door. "Thanks for a delicious meal, Grace. I promise to take care of AJ."

"I know you will, Brian." Grace gave him a hug and a cheek kiss.

"See you at John Wayne tomorrow, AJ."

"Good night, Brian."

AJ and Grace walked past the dirty dishes and headed to the couch in the living room.

Grace snuggled into AJ's arms. He stroked her hair. "Honey, everything's going to be fine. Okay?"

"AJ, I'm sure it will. There's been so much craziness leading up to this. You understand, don't you?"

"Of course I do." AJ cracked a smile. "I bet you just can't stand being away from me for four days."

Grace grabbed a pillow and pounded AJ's stomach. "Take that."

AJ retaliated and a pillow fight and laughing match ensued until they collapsed, breathless. After catching their breath, they headed upstairs. The dishes never made it to the dishwasher. Lord willing, tomorrow AJ would make it to Berlin, 5,700 miles away. Drifting to sleep, he remembered something. Something important.

CHAPTER 72

Panic

Home of the Bernsteins, Paris, September 3, 1939

ROBERT MEYER'S TRAVELING TO Berlin ended two years ago after resigning from IBM in 1937. But even observing Germany's aggression from afar, he and the rest of the world witnessed the dark events illuminating Hitler's grim intention: domination of all of Europe. In 1938, Hitler marched his troops into Austria, and without firing a shot, proclaimed it a federal state of Germany. With the 1938 Munich Agreement, the allied powers of France, Great Britain, and Italy virtually handed all of Czechoslovakia over to Hitler, hoping to appease him and maintain peaceful relations. Two days ago, Hitler invaded Poland.

Amid these troubling developments, Robert continued traveling to France and assisted church leaders forming the French Reformed Churches. He'd completed several meetings this week, some of which addressed a potential German invasion. Robert chaired a committee tasked with building a network to provide safe harbor for the French Jews. As wise men such as Edmund Burke have said, the only thing necessary for the triumph of evil is for good men to do nothing. If the churches didn't help, who would?

Sunday afternoon, he attended an early worship service in Paris, along with Dottie. After the service, the ushers opened the doors to a disturbing cacophony. News boys barked out a headline, "*La guerre est déclarée*. War is declared."

The church-goers started leaving the church.

"*La guerre est déclarée*. War is declared."

They froze, grasping the gravity of the headline.

Dottie grabbed Robert's arm. "Robert, did you hear that?"

The crowd's mumbling crescendoed into collective gasps and punctuated exclamations.

Robert rushed with others to buy the extra edition. He held the front page for Dottie to see.

"Since daybreak on September 1, Poland has been the victim of the most brutal and most cynical of aggressions. Her frontiers have been violated. Her cities are being bombed. Her army is heroically resisting the invader. In rising against the most frightful of tyrannies, in honoring our word, we fight to defend our soil, our homes, our liberties."

"What does he mean, 'in honoring our word?'" Dottie said.

"After Hitler invaded Czechoslovakia, France and England pledged mutual assistance to Poland in the event of a German invasion. Hitler invaded two days ago."

They turned back to President Daladier's announcement.

"The responsibility for the blood that is being shed falls entirely upon the Hitler Government. The fate of peace was in Hitler's hands. He chose war. We are waging war because it has been thrust on us."

The congregation's stunned reaction deteriorated into a panicked scramble to cars and buses to return to the safety of their homes. Robert and Dottie joined the hastening departure and headed for the Bernsteins.

What comfort could he offer his dear friends? Their dread of Hitler had grown from a tiny seed into an invasive weed since the Nazis invaded the Bernsteins' home. With this gruesome turn of events, fear of a German invasion of France soared. Such an invasion threatened the French Jews with the same dreadful fate the German Jews now suffered. Robert's work with the Reformed church network took on a new urgency, especially their plans to protect the French Jews.

After the break-in at the Bernsteins, Robert's cordial friends enjoyed a weekly Sunday evening ritual at the Bernsteins, coming together to eat, drink, and discuss world events, meaning Hitler.

Dottie and Robert entered the living room and joined their friends. They stared blankly at the radio delivering a message from President Daladier.

"Every one of us is at his post, on the soil of France, on that land of liberty where respect of human dignity finds one of its last refuges. You will all cooperate, with a profound feeling of union and brotherhood, for the salvation of the country. Vive la France!"

Fritz turned the radio off, sat, and stared at the floor, listening to the silence with the others.

Jacques spoke first. "The world should have prevented this in 1936 when Hitler sent his troops to the Rhineland. Not a single world leader raised his hand against him." He stood and started circling the room. "It's been one appeasement after another by Daladier, along with Chamberlain."

Fritz held up an issue of *Time* magazine. "Man of the Year, they said." He turned to the cover story and read.

"But the figure of Adolf Hitler strode over a cringing Europe with all the swagger of a conqueror. Not the mere fact that the Führer brought 10,500,000 more people under his absolute rule made him the Man of 1938."

"Swagger of a conqueror." Fritz looked up. "Disgusting."

"Some of those German immigrants are stirring up discontent here," Dottie said. "I talked with a German Jewish mother at the market. She made it clear the French aren't doing enough to stand up against Hitler. The poor woman held her palm up and said, 'These are the callouses from scrubbing the sidewalk with a toothbrush for the SS.' She rolled her sleeve up, showing burn scars on her arm. 'This is from saving a few precious items from our synagogue engulfed in scorching flames. Maybe you should do more than sip your French wine and eat croissants.'"

"The international community made it clear at the Evian Conference last summer. They've shut their door to Jewish immigrants," Hemingway said.

"Getting visas is impossible," Otto said. "Look what happened to those nine hundred Jews who sailed on the St. Louis liner. They sailed for two weeks to Cuba. When they arrived, the Cuban government turned them away after invalidating their landing certificates."

Emma shook her hands in the air. "And what are we to do the day Hitler comes for us?" Her voice trembled. "France is helping other Jewish immigrants, but who will help us when the Nazis march in, or fly in, or however they'll come?"

"I may be able to help," Robert said.

Everyone turned to Robert. "I'm working with other Christians in France, behind the scenes. We are planning networks to help you, in case you need to leave."

His friends' silence invited more encouragement.

Robert picked up his Bible. "Listen to what David wrote when he suffered distress in the midst of fleeing violence." He turned to Psalm 28:7 and read. "'The Lord is my strength and my shield; in him my heart trusts; so I am helped and my heart exults, and with my song I give thanks to him.'"

Robert closed his Bible and smiled at his friends. "May you all find the same shalom that David found in his time of trouble."

And may all of Europe one day find shalom again, Lord.

Scan or tap the QR code to read Fred's blogpost about Hitler, Time magazine's Man of the Year, 1938.

CHAPTER 73

Ding Dong

Lines College, Irvine, CA, 2022

GRACE CLEARED HER CLASS schedule Monday morning between 11:00 a.m. and 12:30 p.m., the time of AJ's layover in New Jersey. She sat at her office desk at Lines College, gazing at her upside-down drawing of Stravinsky, a reminder of last week's art date with AJ. Stiff from last night's spontaneous pillow fight, she stretched her arms and smiled. What a joyful, silly outburst.

AJ's ID popped up on her phone.

"Hey there, beautiful. How's your day going?"

"You're in good spirits for rising so early. Everything going well so far?"

"So far, so good. Just enough time for a quick bite and to call you to say how much I love you."

"It's only been eight hours, goofball." She fingered her necklace.

"I didn't want to wait till we got to Berlin. It'll be late your time when we land."

"Better get some rest on this flight."

"Gotta go. They're calling our flight. I'll call from Berlin. Love you. Bye."

"Bye."

After her lectures, Grace worked later than usual, grading papers. She wrapped up her work and entered a food order for home delivery. She drove home, plopped her briefcase on the entry table, hightailed it to the bedroom, and changed into her sweats just in time. The delivery message popped up on her phone. She grabbed her phone and headed to the front door.

She opened the door. A smiling young man held a brown bag with the logo of her restaurant. "Order for Grace Meyer."

"That's me. Hang on." She started digging in her pocket for a tip.

"Here, let me hold your phone for you."

"Thanks."

She handed him the phone.

Everything turned black.

CHAPTER 74

By the Skin

Paris, June 5, 1940

ROBERT SPED INTO THE Bernsteins' driveway and screeched to a halt. Thank God for providing a truck large enough to transport all of them out of Paris. The Hoffmans and their two children sat on wood benches in the truck bed enclosed with canvas.

Robert rushed into the house and shouted, "Please, you must hurry! The streets are almost impassable."

The horror of German bombs falling on Paris forced the Bernsteins and the Hoffmans into the unthinkable decision. Chaos and panic spread throughout the entire city. Mass departures began filling the roads heading south of Paris. The Nazi attacks on northwest France and on the Maginot Line blocked French troops from reaching Paris to defend the city. Paris. A hopeless, sitting duck.

Robert Meyer had coordinated rescue plans for the Jews with the French Reformed Churches and the IRC, the International Rescue Committee, in case of the unthinkable, Paris falling to the Nazis. The organizations planned escape routes, potential sanctuary locations, and networks for obtaining visas.

"Robert is here. We must leave. Now," Otto yelled. "People are clogging the streets."

Emma dashed from room to room, scouring for one last treasure to cram into their one suitcase. One suitcase to preserve a lifetime of memories.

"Otto, I can't do this." She collapsed into a chair. "Why is this happening?"

The dire bulletins blared on the radio. "French forces lost more ground today at the Maginot Line. The Nazis continue their march south to Paris. Roads out of the city are nearing a standstill."

"How will we even get out of Paris?" Emma screamed. She turned toward Otto and pounded his chest. "What about all of my family's things? Why didn't we leave sooner?"

Otto took Emma in his arms. Her rage melted into sobbing. "No one expected this to happen so fast," he said

"What about everything in our home?"

"They're only things, my love. We have each other and our collection, safe in New York. We'll start a brand-new life with our friends. It'll be safe there. I promise." He stroked her hair. "Now, please, hurry and finish packing your bag. I'll get the children."

Emma dabbed her cheeks with her grandmother's lace hanky, tossed it into the suitcase, and slammed it shut. She forced the suitcase down the stairs against its will and trudged over the Italian marble floors through the foyer that once showcased her Picasso Dozen. Gone. Some to America with Igor. The others? Who knew? She kissed the front door goodbye, turned, and skulked to the truck that was here to bully her from her home against her will and take her to who knew where.

A breathless Dottie sprinted up the driveway. "I was afraid I'd miss you, my darling." She embraced Emma.

Robert interrupted their goodbye. "Please. We must go."

Dottie kissed Emma's cheek. "Until next time, my dear friend."

Robert carried Emma's bag to the back of the truck. He lifted the flap. Emma froze. Such crude bench seats to carry her away from Paris.

A buzz rumbled in the distance. Everyone turned toward the sky. A squadron on the distant horizon approached in formation, but whose?

Robert took Emma's arm and helped her up. Otto thrust the luggage in and hoisted their two children. Fritz grabbed their young son and daughter and guided them to a seat. Such terror for a six and eight-year-old. Otto jumped in. Robert closed the canvas cover, scrambled to the driver's seat, and slammed the door.

He turned the key. The engine chugged twice. It didn't start. He turned the key again. The engine failed again. And again. His passengers gasped.

Dear Lord. Please, give us your favor in our time of need.

He turned the key. The motor revved to life. His passengers cheered behind him.

Blessed be your name.

He turned right onto the street, opposing the fleeing mass. The IRC agents warned to take this route to avoid the roads clogged with weary refugees.

A few miles out, progress halted. Robert ran to the back and opened the flap. "What is it?" Otto said.

The frightened friends stared at Robert. "The road is blocked. Fritz, Otto, out. I need your help."

The two men followed Robert to the front of the truck. A broken tail wing from a downed French Air Force fighter and a tree limb formed a V and blocked the road, making it impossible to continue.

Robert pointed to the limb. "Otto, take that branch. Fritz, you and I will take this one. Now push."

The limb shifted.

Aircraft buzzed in the distance.

"Everyone to this side and try rolling." The three grunted together and pushed the top of the limb. It rolled a short distance, then hit a snag.

Robert wiped his brow. "Again."

The limb rolled over the snag toward the side of the road. The trio shoved and rolled two more times.

An airplane roared louder.

"If you angle the truck, I think you can make it past the tail wing," Fritz said.

Robert jumped in and started the truck. He backed up to adjust the angle of the truck's approach and shifted into first gear. Fritz and Otto stood on either side, guiding him. Robert drove forward, forcing the limb out of the way.

The metal of the plane's tail scraped against the other side of the truck. Robert didn't hesitate. He inched forward. A long screech pierced the air. The truck survived the bilateral assaults and made it past the obstacles. Robert leapt out and followed Fritz and Otto to the back. They hopped in and he closed the flap. He bolted to the driver's seat and put the truck in gear.

On the horizon, black trails of smoke spewed from a fighter plane, spinning down from the sky. The plane met the earth and shot a fireball to the heavens.

Robert drove on, taking a detour around the fiery crash. Safe this time. But hours of driving lay ahead to escape the threatening reach of the Nazi invasion and deliver them to the safe harbor of the IRC's network.

Chapter 75

And The Winner Is

Berlin, Germany, 2022

AJ AND BRIAN LANDED in Berlin at 7:15 a.m., fifteen minutes behind schedule. The captain announced the all-clear for cell phones and AJ tapped Grace's entry in his favorites list but the call went straight to voicemail. Chatting with someone? Surely she'd take his call after seeing his caller ID.

AJ froze, staring at his phone.

"Everything okay?" Brian said.

"Grace didn't answer. Maybe..." He trailed off, tapping his fingers, searching for a reasonable explanation. "I'll try again from the luggage carousel."

By the time they checked into their hotel, he still hadn't spoken to Grace. He'd sent a text telling her he arrived safely. No text from her. The nine-hour time difference didn't help. It was after midnight in Irvine, so she'd be asleep. Right?

AJ and Brian threw their bags in their rooms and rushed back to the lobby. AJ hailed a cab and handed the driver the address he'd decoded from the Nazi tape. They traveled past a mixture of modern and older buildings, some that had survived the war. A hopeful sign. The Victory Column stood tall ahead of them, pulling them forward on their route. Had Grandy traveled on this road and passed by the Victory Column on his way to…? So many unanswered questions. For now, he clung cautiously to the same hope and anticipation that his ten-year-old self clung to, expecting that special Christmas present, but unsure it was his until he opened the gift. The cab turned a corner onto *Straße des 17. Juni* and a view opened of the Cafe Viktoria, a far better gift than his ten-year-old self could imagine.

The cab parked at the tree-lined curb and AJ and Brian stepped out. "Cafe Viktoria!" He turned to Brian. "Eureka! We found it. Come on."

They walked in, ready to investigate the premises. *Wonder if the basement survived the war.*

Cafe Viktoria resembled other European eateries in repurposed buildings with a past. A box, rectangular shape with replastered walls sprinkled with framed art, and exposed ventilations ducts clinging to the ceiling. Gray aluminum tables and chairs added a chic accent.

The maitre d' greeted them and led them to a table perfect for scoping out the surroundings. A waiter arrived, took their order, and left.

Brian smiled. "Where do we start, Sherlock?"

"I'll check the back, see if I can find a way to the basement."

AJ walked toward the back of the cafe and entered a hallway, where he found a restroom on his left and a door on his right. Next to the door hung a framed black-and-white photo of a storefront with a sign that read: Lohse and Lohse, Kunsthändler. Lohse! The name on the report from the Nazi tape. AJ's chest vibrated. Another Eureka!

He squished against the wall, allowing a waiter to pass. With the coast clear, he opened the door, stepped in, and closed the door. He flipped on a light and walked down a set of stairs.

At the bottom, he stepped into a room filled with shelving units loaded with restaurant supplies. Between two of the units, he found a door covered in dust. He turned the handle, but the door wouldn't budge. Twisting the handle with one hand and pushing with his shoulder, he shoved the door open. A dankness from the past spilled out.

He moved his phone flashlight around the room, empty except for cobwebs and layers of dust. Decades' worth. An encouraging sign. He examined the wall in front of him and the wall to the right. Nothing notable. But something strange about the wall on the left: a wire protruded out of the plaster. He moved his light closer. What's on the other end of this wire? Something behind the wall? He swept his light across a wall, revealing a door-shaped outline. Pounding against the wall returned a hollow echo. This required a sledgehammer, at least.

AJ exited the room, closed the door, and headed up the stairs. He cracked the door open to the noise of the bustling kitchen and peeked out. No one watching. He turned the light off, closed the door, and returned to the table.

"And?" Brian said.

"Where's my breakfast?" AJ said with a sheepish grin.

"Come on. What did you find?"

AJ described his discovery. He leaned in and whispered. "All we need is a sledgehammer."

The waiter arrived, interrupting the whisper, and served their order. "Will there be anything else, sirs?"

"No. Danke," AJ said.

Brian picked up his breakfast croissant. "Have you reached Grace yet?"

"Not yet." He took his first bite. "With the time difference, she's still asleep."

What was with her phone, anyway? How come she hadn't answered his text?

"Right. That's probably it," Brian said.

They finished eating and headed back to the hotel. On their way, they found a hardware store and purchased a sledgehammer for tomorrow's planned excavation of the alleged hidden room.

In his hotel room, AJ picked up his phone and opened his favorites list.

His phone buzzed.

Grace's caller ID appeared.

He answered.

"Finally," AJ said, smiling. "I was worried about you. Everything okay?"

An electronically altered voice replied. "Absolutely."

AJ's entire body stiffened. "Who is this?"

"Doesn't matter. But here's what does matter. If you want to see your wife again, do exactly what I say."

AJ struggled to take in air. "Go ahead."

"Tomorrow, after you retrieve the package, my agent will meet you. You will hand it over to him. Then I'll set your amazing Grace free."

"How do I know she's safe?"

"Say hello to your hero."

"AJ, it's me. I'm fine. Grace be with you."

"Proof enough for you?"

"You won't get away with this."

"Just hand over the package and everything will return to normal. Understand?"

AJ's fingernails jabbed his fisted hand. "Yes, I understand."

"That's good." Click.

AJ paced, tugging his hair and grasping for control.

Lord, help!

He placed a call.

A voice answered. "Yes?"

"Initiate Operation Necklace."

"Yes sir. Immediately."

He never imagined he'd ever launch Operation Necklace. Thank God Grace had given him the code words.

CHAPTER 76

Passing Through

Le Chambon-sur-Lignon, France, 1941

EACH TIME ROBERT MEYER visited the rural farming community of Le Chambon-sur-Lignon, he met first with the village leader, Pastor André Trocmé. Robert had forged a strong bond with Pastor André over the last four years, working together to establish the *Église Réformée de France*, the Reformed Church of France. Thanks to Pastor André, Robert had found a safe haven for his Paris Jewish friends, the Bernsteins and the Hoffmans.

Pastor André had nurtured a seed of generosity in this southern pastoral French community, a seed that blossomed into an asylum garden for the Jews escaping imprisonment by the Nazis. According to the German-Franco Armistice of 1940, the occupying Germans controlled the northwestern part of France and had already filled concentration camps with over 40,000 French Jews. Le Chambon-sur-Lignon fell inside the sovereign southeastern Vichy zone governed by the French and free from Nazi occupation.

Today, Robert brought a gift for Pastor André and his wife, Magda. He joined them in their living room, bright from the helpful sun, and handed a package to Pastor André. "I thought this might bring some cheer your way."

Pastor André opened the package. A box filled with chocolates and coffee, scarcities these days.

Pastor André and Magda gasped. "This must have cost a fortune," Pastor André said. "Thank you, brother Robert. To be enjoyed on a special occasion, certainly." He put the lid on the box and handed it to Magda.

"A special occasion, yes," Robert said with a fading smile.

"Special" had taken on a new meaning for the Bernsteins and the Hoffmans since leaving Paris. Safety at the top of the list. Soirées at the bottom. But how could one complain about life in Le Chambon-sur-Lignon? A life free from the death sentence handed to the Jews who didn't make it out of Paris.

"I don't know how it can get any worse, Brother André," Robert said. "The Germans plan to deport 100,000 Jews from France over the next three months. God only knows where they'll end up."

Pastor André looked down, holding his hands and shaking his head. "Dear Lord. Your chosen people." He turned to Robert and took his hand. "Our homes are open, but Robert, the town is about to burst."

"Yes, I know, and I am grateful." Robert clasped Brother André's hand between his. "It's impossible to help Jews cross the Vichy line." Robert released Brother André's hands and sat back. "I'm working on the next phase to help your refugees make their way on to the next leg of their journey."

His refugee friends from Paris needed a visa for the next leg, but a tedious and backlogged application process made this nearly impossible to accomplish. And with the current international climate, who would open their doors?

Robert laid out his plans for the refugees with Brother André. The most critical task, getting visas, required a miracle. The two servants concluded their time in prayer for the refugees, the townspeople, and peace for France.

Robert left Pastor André's and walked down the street to visit the Hoffmans and the Bernsteins. On his way, he passed a group of farmers returning from a day's work in the mushroom fields, their backs warmed by the afternoon sun, singing as they walked.

Sowing in the morning, sowing seeds of kindness,
Sowing in the noontide and the dewy eve;
Waiting for the harvest, and the time of reaping,
We shall come rejoicing, bringing in the sheaves.

Robert joined the joyful chorus as he walked to the home of the family hosting the Bernsteins. Franz and Heidi Schumacher had converted their home library into a private room for their guests. A year after leaving their luxurious Paris home, the Bernsteins had found a new simpler contentment, even in these strained living conditions, buoyed by the graciousness of their hosts. The Hoffmans had found similar accommodations with another generous family. These Christians, these angels, fostered a warm, accepting fellowship with the new residents. They had provided a school for the children and a place for Jewish services. The community's acts of self-sacrifice puzzled the two families at first, but hearing Pastor André's readings from the Christian Bible shed some light on what motivated them.

Robert turned the corner and strolled down the flower-lined sidewalk. Half a block away, he spotted Otto and Emma Bernstein on the Schumachers' front porch. With smiles worthy of welcoming an old friend, they walked down the porch steps to greet him.

"Robert, so good to see you," Otto said, shaking Robert's hand. Emma reached up and gave him a kiss on the cheek.

"Come, join us inside. The Hoffmans are here," Otto said.

Robert entered the home and greeted Fritz and Claire.

"It's been three months," Claire said, welcoming Robert with a kiss. "How we've missed you. Please, sit."

Everyone waited, anticipating Robert's routine on these visits. He took a seat, opened his shoulder bag, and pulled out a variety of letters and documents.

"Mail call," Emma said, giddy as a schoolgirl. She clapped. "I can't wait."

"Yes. And the first one is for you, Emma," Robert said, handing a smile and a letter to Emma.

Emma smiled back, taking the letter. "It's from Dottie," she said. Emma opened it, sat back, and started reading to herself.

"Fritz, this is for you," Robert said.

Fritz took the envelope and opened it. The more he read, the more his face tightened.

Claire cuddled his arm. "What is it, Fritz?"

Fritz held the letter for Claire to read. "The Germans traded some of our collection for munitions with the Graziolis."

"What?" Claire gasped, reaching to hold the letter herself.

Fritz turned to the others. "One of my employees, Remy, is still in contact with Yves, who works at Grazioli's. Yves said Grazioli shipped munitions to Germany after agreeing to receive specific pieces of art as payment. The list included some of our stolen art."

Emma looked up from Dottie's letter. "Did the list include the Picassos?"

"No," Fritz said. "Yves says none of the paintings on the list arrived. In fact, Göring has sent nothing to Mr. Grazioli."

Otto walked over to Claire and looked over her shoulder. "Does this mean Göring is double crossing Grazioli? Promising but not delivering?"

Fritz took the letter back from Claire. "He doesn't say. We're as much in the dark as before." He put the letter down and held Claire's hands. Otto sat next to Emma and wrapped her in his arms. The unhelpful sun filled the room with a grim shade of gray.

Heidi Schumacher entered the somber scene and turned on a light. She smiled and gestured with welcoming arms. "Claire, Emma. May I help you prepare for Shabbat?" An offer of encouragement more than a request. Heidi walked over to Emma, sat, and took her hand. "We'll use my lace tablecloth tonight and serve on my special dishes."

Robert stayed through for the evening Shabbat meal. Rations saved through the week made up a modest meal served on Heidi's hand-painted china. They burned the precious, dwindling candle long enough for one chorus of "Shabbat, shalom." Though small and brief, that bit of light reminded everyone at the table that God was still the light of the universe, however dim that light seemed tonight.

Scan or tap the QR code to read Fred's blogpost about the real Le Chambon-sur-Lignon and Pastor André Trocmé.

CHAPTER 77

Final Approach

Cafe Victoria, Berlin, Germany, 2022

THE RING FROM AJ's phone gradually pierced through his semi-conscious fog, pulling him out of the jet lag induced sleep.

"Yes?"

"AJ, are you all right? It's 10:30. Time to go," Brian said.

AJ shot up in bed, gasping for air and scanning his unfamiliar surroundings. Where am I? Five dreadful seconds of disorientation ticked down. Finally, Berlin. Picassos. Grace. Kidnapper.

Last night had drained him mentally, physically, and spiritually. The call from Grace's kidnapper, numerous calls to his office, checking on her tracker's location, pleading with God for Grace's safety, and the final assault of irresistible sleep.

AJ checked his phone. Twenty identical text messages, "Tracker active."

He rushed through a morning bathroom routine and foraged through his suitcase for something suitable to wear. He pulled on a shirt. Without warning, it started.

His chest tightened and his breathing accelerated.

Quickening heart-beats thumped in his ears and tingles shot through his hands.

A body numb from jet lag, in full rebellion.

Is this what a panic attack feels like?

He sat on the edge of his bed with pants in hand, closed his eyes, and focused on his breathing. Slow deep breath in, slow exhale out. Again. Again.

Control, AJ. Get yourself under control.

Words filled his mind. "Do not be anxious about anything, but in everything by prayer and supplication with thanksgiving let your requests be made known to God. And the peace of God, which surpasses all understanding, will guard your hearts and your minds in Christ Jesus."

Thank you, Lord.

He gained control of the rebellion. For now.

His phone dinged with an incoming text message.

"Tracker active."

A knock at the door.

He opened it.

Brian walked in.

"Man, I was worried you would miss the main event. Everything okay with Grace?" Brian asked.

"So far, yes." AJ turned to pack his bag with the sledgehammer and other supplies for the day. "The authorities have a fix on a location. I'll know soon."

Brian grabbed AJ by the shoulders. "She's fine. You put an amazing procedure in place. Have some faith, AJ."

Yes, Lord. Give me more faith.

"I think that's everything," AJ said. He checked the room one last time. "Let's go."

***

The same maitre d' from yesterday greeted them. "Welcome back to Cafe Viktoria, sirs."

"A table toward the back, please," AJ said.

The maitre d' led them to a corner table close to the restrooms.

"Perfect," AJ said. "Two coffees, please."

"Very good," the maitre d' said. On his way to the coffee bar, the maitre d' caught the eye of a customer and nodded toward AJ and Brian.

AJ set the canvas bag against the wall.

"Good thing they're not very busy. Fewer observers to worry about," Brian said.

"Right," AJ said, finger-tapping the table.

"Good to know they've located Grace."

On the taxi ride from the hotel, AJ received word the authorities had located Grace using the coordinates from the tracker in her necklace. They had surrounded the location but hadn't conducted the rescue yet.

"Yes. It's good." AJ said, checking the other customers in the room.

The waiter arrived and served their coffees. "Are you ready to order?"

"Not yet. A few minutes, please," AJ said.

The server left.

"I think it's time," AJ said, looking straight into Brian's eyes.

They took a quick sip of coffee, stood, and pushed in their chairs. AJ picked up the canvas bag and headed to the basement door. He checked for onlookers, then opened the door and entered. Brian waited and followed him a minute later.

Brian met AJ at the bottom of the stairs and followed him to the next door. "It's over here. Time for the flashlights."

AJ reached in the canvas bag and pulled out two headband flashlights and handed one to Brian. "Through here."

AJ forced the door open and they entered the room. Brian closed the door. They walked to the wall with the door outline.

AJ pulled out the sledgehammer and tapped it against the wall a few times, listening for the best spot to attack.

"Here goes." He made his first swing.

Thud. Several thick chunks of plaster jumped off the wall.

He took another swing. More chunks danced.

The third slam smashed a hole through the wall.

"Do you see that?" AJ said, pointing.

Brian aimed his headlamp at the hole.

"Here goes." Brian stepped back and AJ readied for a harder swing and a louder thud.

The hole grew to a foot in diameter.

"Almost there." Time to open that special Christmas gift.

AJ grunted and slammed the wall four more times and created an opening large enough to crawl through.

"Eureka!" AJ threw the sledgehammer to the floor. He dipped his head through the hole and angled his shoulders to scrape the rest of his body into the room.

Brian followed his lead.

AJ turned his head, shining his lamp from side to side.

There, a table with a package on top.

His hands trembled.

He turned to Brian. "Do you see it?"

Brian followed AJ's light to the table. "It's ...it's ..."

"I know. Let's go get it." AJ and Brian approached the table and examined the package.

The box measured 22 inches wide, 28 inches long, and 18 inches deep. Plenty of room for the Picassos.

AJ brushed a layer of dust off the package and found some handwritten lines.

Hans Lohse

Charlottenburger Chaussee, 68, Keller

Berlin

"The same address from the report," AJ said. "This has to be it."

Time of truth.

Brian helped AJ cut the aged twine wrapped around the box. They removed the next layer, some sort of lightweight canvas, and found a wooden crate fastened with nails.

AJ grabbed a small crowbar from the canvas bag and worked it under the front edge. He gave the bar a yank. The edge budged with a screech, creating a larger space for the bar. One more push and the plank sprang free. AJ removed the remaining top planks in quick order.

Inside the crate, they found six tubes. AJ pulled out one tube. He took a knife from his pocket and sliced around one end and pulled out the rolled-up contents. Brian helped him unroll the item and lay it on the table.

Their flashlights brought to life, for the first time in 85 years, a Stravinsky portrait by Pablo Picasso.

A voice behind them interrupted. "I'll take that."

CHAPTER **78**

Get Out Of Town

Vichy Region, France, 1942

"I DIDN'T EXPECT THIS," Robert said, craning his neck.

The line to the U.S. Consulate in Marseille stretched for blocks, one weary sojourner after another, desperate to get a coveted exit visa. The gentleman ahead of Robert stretched his arms with yesterday's newspaper in one hand.

"We must pray and wait for God to provide. He's been faithful through this entire journey," Arthur said.

Robert Meyer traveled to Marseille with Arthur Sparks, his head elder, on this mission. With so much at stake for Robert's Jewish friends, the board insisted Arthur go with him as an added measure of safety.

Today's rigid plan depended on a timetable with little room for delay. Procure the visa signatures, drive to Le Chambon-sur-Lignon to pick up their two refugee families and return to Marseille in time to board the Lisbon-bound freighter. No room for error.

Morning mist floated over the harbor and a stream of dock workers hustled onto waiting ships. The damp coldness weaved its way through Robert's coat and scarf on his walk with Arthur from the hotel. A truck loaded with food and supplies sat around the block, ready to whisk them to Le Chambon-sur-Lignon. First, they needed the visa signatures, but their feet hadn't budged.

Lord, please, show us favor.

Receiving a visa signature required proof the refugees would not become a public charge, dependent on the United States government for financial support. After prayer and fasting, Robert's congregation pledged the support for both families. Only two hurdles remained: getting visa signatures and traveling to Le Chambon-sur-Lignon and back to Marseilles in time to board the freighter bound for America. The first hurdle seemed impossible, considering the lack of motion in the line.

"Pastor Meyer."

Robert turned. A man wearing a consulate uniform approached him.

"I'm walking to work and who do I see, but my dear Brother Robert. How I've missed you since you last spoke in our church."

Robert and Luis Fronge shared a warm embrace, long enough for Robert to whisper in Luis's ear.

"I can help. Follow me," Luis said.

Luis led them to the front steps of the consulate and motioned for them to stand off to the side.

"Wait here."

Dear Lord. Thank you for your servant, Luis. Guide him.

Luis came out the door five minutes later and gathered the two men close to him.

"Here's everything you need for your friends. Quick, put them in your bag."

Robert put the priceless papers into his briefcase and locked it.

"We can't thank you enough, Luis. God bless you," Robert said.

"You'd do well to leave this way," Luis said, pointing to a route diverting them away from the pressing crowd.

With their penultimate step completed on time, Robert and Arthur rushed to the truck and headed out on their six-hour drive to Le Chambon-sur-Lignon.

***

On the day of their departure from Le Chambon-sur-Lignon, Pastor André Trocmé hosted the Bernsteins, Hoffmans, and their host families for a farewell breakfast in his home. Suitcases lined the hallway, carrying less than what they'd carried from Paris. Entwined hearts had become heavy and hopeful at the same time.

"*Boker tov*, my friends," Pastor André said to the fellowship of guests and hosts. "Today is a sad day for us, but a day of joy for you. Sad for us, as we will miss the joy you take with you to America. Joy for you as you find freedom and security in America."

The breakfast feast Magda provided filled the table with her finest Gruyère cheese omelettes, fresh fruit from the village garden, and home-baked bread. Stories from the last year passed back and forth.

The phone rang in the hall. The stories stopped. Magda excused herself to answer the call.

"Yes, he's here. One moment. André, come, quick."

Dread delivered by past phone calls descended upon the friends as André strode to the telephone.

"Yes? How far? You know what to do. I'll take care of our guests."

André returned to the table and delivered the expected, worrisome message.

"They're coming."

Radicalized Nazi sympathizers had returned to search for Jews in the village. Although the village had executed their evacuation plan many times, hiding their guests in the forest, each invasion stretched their faith, trusting God to protect them.

"Not today," shouted Fritz. The families squeezed hands, looking to Pastor André for hope.

Pastor André spoke with calm authority. "Take your bags with you out the back door and load as much as you can into my car. Franz, bring your car and take the rest. My friends, the God of Abraham, Isaac, and Jacob, is watching over you."

In panicked silence, the families gathered their bags and headed out the back door. Franz arrived in quick order. With military precision, the men loaded the luggage and the families. Pastor André kissed his wife, jumped in the car, and led the small caravan to the usual forest hideout.

The drivers parked their vehicles and helped the men unload the luggage.

The families huddled, shocked and shivering, under the late morning sun, waiting for some hope from Pastor André. The rapid succession of frightening events had stunned his refugees.

Pastor André took his binoculars and surveyed the village. He put the binoculars down and turned to face his friends. They stood proudly, fearfully defiant, wearing their bravest faces and finest clothes to make room in their suitcases for priceless photos and irreplaceable family memories. How much longer can they wander through the wilderness until they carry empty suitcases?

"Friends. I must return to my home. My absence will raise suspicion. Franz will stay and wait with you for the all-clear signal. If Robert arrives before, I'll send him on to you. God delivered Daniel from the lion's den and He will deliver you, my friends."

Franz and the trembling refugees stood in the shadows as Pastor André drove off without them.

***

Weary from the strenuous drive from Marseille, Robert squinted, concentrating on the dark road leading him into Le Chambon-sur-Lignon. He parked in front of Pastor André's home and jumped out.

Pastor André shoved his front door open. "Robert." He pointed. "They're waiting in the forest."

"A raid?" Robert said.

"The traitors left hours ago, but our friends feared returning to the village."

"Jump in, my friend."

Pastor André joined Robert and Arthur in the truck and led them to the forest hideout. Before reaching the group, Pastor André jumped out and ran ahead.

"It's Robert," Pastor André said, waving his arms. "He's here with the truck."

Franz stepped into the headlight. "Thank God." A mumble of relief circulated through the group.

Robert introduced Arthur to his friends and began loading the truck. After everyone found a seat in the back, Pastor André raised his right hand toward his departing guests. "The Lord bless thee, and keep thee. The Lord make his face shine upon thee, and be gracious unto thee. The Lord lift up his countenance upon thee, and give thee peace. Amen."

The group responded, "Amen."

Robert closed the back flap and turned to embrace Pastor André. "Goodbye, my brother. Till we meet again."

"God be with you."

Robert and Arthur jumped in the truck. They drove out of the dark forest onto the road to Marseilles where a safe passage to America awaited his friends.

CHAPTER 79

Safe

Cafe Victoria, Berlin, Germany, 2022

AJ and Brian turned toward the voice behind them.

AJ's phone dinged with an incoming text message.

The intruder climbed through the opening, pointing a gun at them.

Another voice shouted from outside the opening. "Drop it. You're surrounded."

The intruder turned back. Three police officers confronted the intruder with guns steadied on him.

The intruder scowled and relented. "I didn't sign up for this. Here." He surrendered, and the officers cuffed him and led him out.

AJ looked at his last text message. "Safe and secure from all alarms."

A familiar face poked through the opening.

AJ shook his head. "You?"

Lyle Bernstein grinned. "How's that for timing, Brian?"

"Just about perfect," Brian said.

AJ turned to Lyle, then pointed to Brian. "You mean ... He was ... And you didn't ..."

Brian patted AJ on the back. "I'll explain later. Let's take these Picassos out of here and get them back to the hotel."

They repacked the art, exited the cafe through the rear entrance, and loaded their treasure into the rented van. Brian took the driver's seat and Lyle jumped in the passenger side after AJ, already on his cell phone.

"Grace, are you ok? Did anyone hurt you? I'm so sorry." The words jumbled out of his mouth.

"I'm fine, AJ, really. It's a long story. Did you find them?"

"Sure did. Six of them. Had a little extra excitement too. It's a long story."

"Six new Picassos. Whoo-hoo. Bet Brian's excited. Now he can hold that gala he's been planning."

"I love you. I'll check in later."

"Bye, my Benjamin Gates. I love you, too."

"She excited?" Brian said.

"Oh yeah. Now, what's this long story?"

Riding to the hotel, Brian explained everything he had orchestrated for the last two weeks behind AJ's back.

CHAPTER 80

Putting It Together

Albert Becker Art Museum, Irvine, California, 2022

"Hey. That's tight enough." AJ squirmed, face to face with Grace, adjusting his bow tie.

"I want you to look perfect in your Armani tux when you give your acceptance speech," she said, smoothing his lapels.

Grace had convinced AJ to submit his version of the upside-down drawing of Stravinsky from their art date for the gala contest.

"Fat chance that'll happen." His eyebrows flashed up. "Look at you. Where have you been hiding this Vogue creation?"

Grace dressed to impress in her jade-colored, full-length gown, accented with countless rich, opulent hand-beaded sequins. She completed the ensemble with jade earrings matching her life-saving necklace from her grandmother.

The banners hanging over the main entrance to the Albert Becker Art Museum sported a bold version of Picasso's artsy signature superimposed on one of his drawings of Igor Stravinsky. Brian met them at the front entrance wearing a blue tuxedo and a proud smile.

"Can you believe it, guys?" Brian spread his arms. "Our gala is finally happening."

"If everyone knew the story behind getting this exhibit off the ground," AJ said, "it would blow their minds."

"Oh, they'll know when they see the exhibit," Brian said.

After returning from Berlin, AJ and Grace had all the pieces of the puzzle but one. All the craziness revolved around the mysterious mastermind behind everything, from the first system outage at AJ's tech company to the thug who attempted to steal the Picassos in Berlin. The mastermind: Fred Hoffman, history professor at Lines College and Grace's colleague, now arrested and in jail for kidnapping and conspiracy to commit theft. But they still had one puzzle piece missing: the truth about Grandy.

AJ led Grace into the museum. "Turns out, Fred is the grandson of Fritz and Claire Hoffman, who commissioned Picasso for the twelve drawings. But Lyle's grandparents held the soirées displaying them for potential buyers. Fred has a brother, George, but he had no involvement with any of this."

"What are the names of Lyle's grandparents?" Grace said.

"Ready for this?" AJ grinned. "Otto and Emma Bernstein."

"As in the music and the black-and-white photo?"

"The same."

"I knew he was hiding something when I asked him."

The trio continued through the entry. Debussy's *Sunken Cathedral* drifted from the piano in the auditorium. Pictures and articles about 1930s Paris filled the gallery walls, along with portraits of Pablo Picasso and Igor Stravinsky. To top it off, a timeline detailing the history of the Picasso Dozen, complete with the climatic discovery in Berlin.

"What about the six drawings stolen from the Becker?" Grace said.

"Fred blackmailed Lyle in an attempt to steal the drawings, but Lyle outsmarted him," AJ said. "Longer story for later. Lyle confessed to Brian and made a deal."

"Lyle agreed to return the drawings in exchange for immunity from prosecution and the caveat that we gift the twelve drawings to the Picasso estate after the exhibit here," Brian said.

News of the Picasso Dozen had delighted the art world. But another discovery would soon delight the music world.

"When Lyle received the six Picassos, he discovered piano music on the back of each drawing. Stravinsky numbered and signed each page of his composition," Brian said. "Something Lyle kept to himself."

"Interesting thing about the numbering," AJ said. "They are verse numbers from Psalm 84, which has twelve verses. Verse one, page one. And so on."

They reached the entrance to the auditorium.

Brian stopped and turned to the guests behind them. "Ladies and gentlemen, please join me in the auditorium for the unveiling of the Picasso Dozen."

The guests assembled in the auditorium, and Brian stepped up to the podium.

"We are honored to have you here tonight and see for the first time in eighty-five years, twelve portraits of Igor Stravinsky by Pablo Picasso. We've all read stories about art plundered by the Nazis and lost to history. I like to think the story about discovering the Picasso Dozen will go down in the annals of art history as one of the most interesting. If you skipped the display in the hall, I recommend you return and read the historical timeline. The makings of an exciting movie, if you ask me. And now, it is time."

An assistant removed the podium, and Brian stepped to the side.

He pulled a cord, raising the red velvet drapes and revealing the drawings.

"I give you, the Picasso Dozen."

The guests oohed, ahhed, and applauded, giving Brian his special moment of recognition for the historical accomplishment.

He raised his hands, hushing the applause, and smiled. "Thank you so much. Now, it is time to announce the winners of our upside-down Picasso drawing contest."

Grace squeezed AJ's arm. "Got that acceptance speech ready for your prize?"

"I've got my prize right next to me," he said, squeezing back.

"We invited amateur artists to submit their version of the 1920 Stravinsky portrait using the upside-down drawing technique. We were surprised by how many upside-down artists we have in Southern California. Our panel of judges chose one finalist and three honorable mentions. May I have the envelope for third honorable mention?"

A staff member handed Brian an envelope.

"Our third honorable mention goes to ..." He opened the envelope, took the card, and grinned. "Mr. AJ Meyer."

The patrons applauded and turned to AJ, smiling but oblivious to the announcement.

Grace tugged AJ's arm. "AJ. You won."

AJ jerked his head toward Grace. "I did?"

"Yes. Smile!"

AJ quickened a smile and turned to acknowledge the announcement. He whispered to Grace, "Third runner-up. Kind of like third loser, isn't it?"

"Not really. Hundreds of people submitted entries."

Brian finished announcing the winners and presenting the awards.

"When we received the first six Picassos, we didn't know about the amazing gift on the back until our restoration tech, Lyle Bernstein, examined them."

Brian explained the music discovery and the verses on each sheet of music from Psalm 84. He ended his introduction with a reading of the psalm.

"Tonight, it is with immense pleasure that we present the world premiere of *Psalm 84* by Igor Stravinsky."

The crowd applauded the pianist's entrance, a piano performance graduate from Lines College and a walking piece of art in her bold native Kenyan floral kanga. She bowed, took her seat, adjusted the bench, and began. Stravinsky's music styles varied over the years. This piece captured the essence of Debussy's Paris, with its subtle impressionistic style.

AJ closed his eyes and breathed in the music. The black-and-white photo from Grandy's box drifted by, the mysterious sheet music, and finally Grandy's face offering his endearing smile. The piece ended. He blinked and returned to the present. The audience offered a round of applause.

AJ took Grace's hand. "Beautiful."

Brian stepped up. "That concludes our program this evening. But please stay, enjoy the champagne and hors d'oeuvres. The night is young."

The crowd dispersed and strolled through various galleries.

AJ's mother walked up. "Quite a coup, taking third place."

He grinned. "Only because I have the best art teacher in the world."

Evelynn pulled an envelope from her purse. "This came in the mail yesterday. I thought you'd like to read it." She handed AJ the envelope.

He took the envelope and pulled out a letter. His eyes raced back and forth.

"I need to sit down." Grace and Evelynn followed him and sat in a quiet corner. He read the letter a second time, lowered his hand, and turned to Evelynn. "Have you read this?"

Evelynn smiled. "Yes, dear." She caressed AJ's arm. "You have your answer."

"Answer?" Grace said.

AJ wiped his moist eyes. "Here, read this." He clasped his mother's hand and Grace took the letter.

The Holocaust Martyrs' and Heroes' Remembrance Authority
Jerusalem, 5 October 2022
Ref: Robert Meyer

We are pleased to announce the above person was awarded the title of "Righteous Among the Nations," for help rendered to Jewish persons during the period of the Holocaust.

Copies of this letter are being mailed to the honoree, to persons who have submitted testimonies, and other interested parties.

Please see the attached letter from George Hoffman describing the deeds of Robert Meyer with a recommendation for this award.

Yisrael Meir Lau

Chairman of Yad Vashem

Grace lowered the letter and turned to AJ and Evelynn. "George Hoffman? Fred's brother?"

"Read the attachment," AJ said.

Grace flipped to the attachment. "Fred's on the cc list." She read further.

Rescuer: Robert Meyer.

Rescuees: Otto and Emma Bernstein and Fritz and Claire Hoffman.

She set the letter down and tenderly looped AJ's arm, joining his embrace with Evelynn. "Your answer."

"Our answer," AJ said. He reached his arms around Grace and Evelynn, pulling them close. "That's everything we need to know about Grandy."

To you, oh Lord, who works all things together for good.

Scan or tap the QR code to read Fred's blogpost about the Righteous Among the Nations.

ENTER YOUR UPSIDE-DOWN DRAWING OF STRAVINSKY

Try your hand at drawing the famous Picasso drawing and enter it to see it posted on my author website.

The links take you to the complete instructions on how to draw and how to enter.

Scan or tap the QR code to enter your upside-down drawing for posting on my website.

CHAPTER 81

Now For the Rest of the Story

IBM Headquarters, New York, 2022

JAYSON PARRY PULLED OFF the report for the last Nazi tape he'd processed. If it hadn't been for AJ Meyer, he never would have discovered these tapes in the New York IBM archives. But thanks to AJ, Jayson found a goldmine of missing art looted by the Nazis.

It was his for the taking.

Thank You – Please Leave A Review

I HOPE YOU ENJOYED THE BOOK

If you did, kindly take a moment to support this author and post a review.
Scan or tap the QR code to go to leave a review.

ABOUT THE AUTHOR

STEVE NEWCOMB is a passionate storyteller whose multifaceted career mirrors the rich diversity of his new literary work. A follower of Jesus, husband, and self-confessed lover of chocolate, Steve's life journey spans from a choral music teacher in Malibu, CA, to an accomplished musician, computer programmer, and project manager. As a former script writer, composer, and performer of Biblical musicals with His Majesty's Ministries, Steve has toured internationally, co-writing five musicals and engaging audiences across Romania, Brazil, Kosovo, Israel, and the United Kingdom.

Now retired in Asheville, NC, a husband and grandfather, Steve weaves his diverse experiences and deep-rooted faith into his writing, combining his love for art, music, and history with a thrilling narrative that both entertains and enlightens.

Tap or scan the QR code to visit www.stevenewcomb.com

AJ AND GRACE'S NEXT ADVENTURE

What adventure should AJ and Grace pursue next? Should they launch out as investigators for other victims of art heists? Or offer their services to companies such as Christie's auction house?

What's your idea?

Send your ideas to the the author by scanning or tapping the QR code below.

THANK YOU, JOHANNES GUTENBERG

The author operating a reproduction of the Gutenberg press
in Geneva, Switzerland.

The invention of the printing press in the 1400s was a game-changer for publishers and readers alike. Before that, books had to be copied by hand—a slow, expensive process. Then came Johannes Gutenberg's press, and suddenly, books could be made quickly and in large numbers. This meant more people could afford them, and ideas started spreading faster than ever before. It helped kick off big movements like the Renaissance and the Reformation. For publishers, it opened up new ways to share stories and information. Simply put, the printing press made it possible for books to reach the world.